By Harold Coyle

A NOVEL BY

HAROLD
COYLE

UNTIL
THE END

POCKET
BOOKS

LONDON · SYDNEY · NEW YORK · TOKYO · SINGAPORE · TORONTO

First published in Great Britain by Simon & Schuster, 1997
This edition published by Pocket Books 1997
An imprint of Simon & Schuster Ltd
A Viacom Company

Simon & Schuster
West Garden Place
Kendal Street
London W2 2AQ

Simon & Schuster of Australia
Sydney

A CIP catalogue record for this book is available
from the British Library.

0 671 85487 9

This book is dedicated to:
Tommy Dyer, Willie Evans, Marty Wilson,
Rick Britten, "Larry" (Lauren) Burgess, RC
and
the thousands of Civil War reenactors
and living historians dedicated to the preservation
of our national heritage and history.

Contents

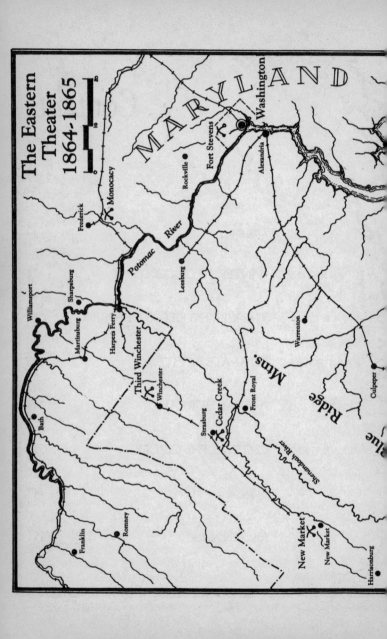

The Eastern Theater 1864-1865

MARYLAND

Washington

Fort Stevens

Rockville

Alexandria

Monocacy

Frederick

Potomac River

Leesburg

Williamsport

Sharpsburg

Warrenton

Martinsburg

Harpers Ferry

Third Winchester

Winchester

Bath

Strasburg

Cedar Creek

Front Royal

Blue Ridge Mtns.

Culpeper

Shenandoah River

Romney

Franklin

New Market

New Market

Harrisonburg

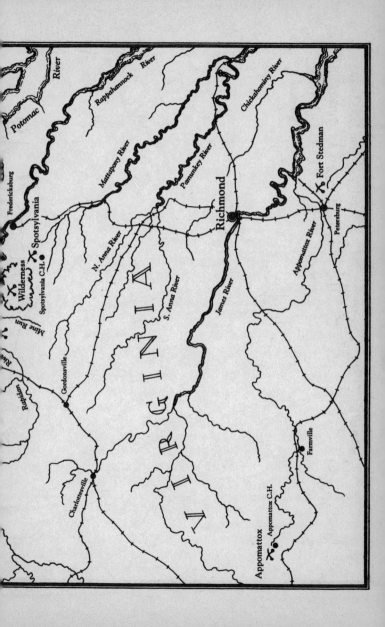

With malice toward none, with charity for all, with firmness in the right as God gives us to see right, let us strive on to finish the work we are in, to bind up the nation's wounds, to care for him who shall have borne the battle and for his widow and orphan, to do all which may achieve and cherish a just and lasting peace among ourselves and with all nations.

Address by Abraham Lincoln to an Indiana Regiment
March 17, 1865

Mississippi, July, 1863

THE RIDE FROM SHERMAN'S headquarters near the Big Black River to Vicksburg didn't take the young Irishman on the chestnut bay long at all. He was good, probably the best courier on Sherman's staff. And, despite an attitude toward officers that could be best described as surly, he was usually given the most important dispatches. "He can be a real burr under your saddle," a staff officer complained of the young immigrant, "but there's no denying that when you want something delivered fast, he's your man."

The dispatch he carried, dictated by Major General Sherman as the young Irishman waited outside Sherman's tent, was for Major General Sam Grant himself, now in Vicksburg after accepting the Confederate surrender the day before. The news from Sherman was almost as welcome as that of Grant's victory. Confederate Lieutenant General Joe Johnston, commander of a Confederate force that had been headed west to relieve the besieged garrison at Vicksburg, had turned back and was retracing his steps to Jackson, Mississippi. "He won't fight now, by God," the excited young staff captain exclaimed as he stuffed the dispatch into an envelope and made an entry into his log of correspondence. "Old Joe waited too long, came too slow, and brought too little. Now with things in Vicksburg over, we're sure to turn on 'em and snap 'em up," he said, snapping his fingers for emphasis, "just like that."

The young Irishman was unimpressed with that sort of enthusiasm and grand claims. He had been in the Army too long, and seen too many grand plans go astray, to allow himself to be caught up by such excitement. The war, it seemed to him, would not be won by the brilliant maneuvers that officers were so fond of discussing. Rather, he imagined, it would end like the campaign they had just concluded. Victory, he reasoned, would come only after the South had been ground down, army by army, regiment by regiment, man by man, until there wasn't an ounce of fight left in the whole Confederacy. Still, he mused as he spurred his mount west, it would be something if this whole mess could somehow be brought to a quick end, once and for all.

When he came across the now abandoned works that surrounded Vicksburg, the sight of this shattered landscape served to abolish even this brief glimmer of hope. Slowing down as he passed from what had been the forwardmost Union positions into the old Rebel positions, the young courier paused briefly to watch a burial detail at work. A gang of barefoot Negroes, wearing cloths that were little more than rags, went about collecting and burying the remains of those poor souls who had died in the final minutes of a long and bitter siege. With great care that surprised the courier, they laid each corpse, blackened by heat and exposure, in the shallow trench that would serve as its eternal home. Carefully, they straightened out each body, when they could, and folded its hands on its chest. As he watched in silence, the Irishman was struck by the coloration and rapid deterioration of the dead Confederates. "Their boys seem to turn bad faster than our lads do," one of the orderly sergeants had explained to him. "Seems it has to do with what they eat." Whatever the cause, the appearance of the line of dead men was both sobering and disquieting.

A Union soldier, standing upwind from the gang of grave diggers and supervising them from afar, noticed the young Irishman's interest in the proceedings. "Strange, isn't it," he said out loud to the courier. "I'd expect the Negroes would just up and throw their former masters into the grave and be done with 'em."

The courier, exiled from his own homeland for activities against the British, pulled his horse's head back as he prepared to continue on. "Maybe they're just taking their time and doing it right," he snapped at the other Union soldier. "After all, I'm sure they're just as eager as we are to see the last of that Rebel scum."

The soldier supervising the Negroes gave the courier a dirty look, but said nothing. With a whistle and a quick dig of his spurs, the courier urged his horse on and into town.

As the young Irishman made his way through the crowded streets of a city the Union Army had held under siege for so long, he was struck by the strange sights that greeted him. Other than shattering every pane of glass in the town of Vicksburg, the incessant cannonading that had pounded the city from land and water seemed to have had little effect. Though there was the stray crater and a shattered building here and there, the town looked none the worse for wear.

Such could not be said for the inhabitants or the town's late defenders. Both civilians and Rebel soldiers wore a sickly, gaunt look that reminded the Irish private of the expression worn by his own parents before they had succumbed to the first potato famine when he had been a mere child. Chilled by this haunting memory, the young man spurred his horse on and continued to make his way through the crowd to the building that now served as the commanding general's headquarters.

Dismounting, he slowly tied his mount to a nearby tree, eyeing a pair of fellow Union soldiers as they chatted with two gaunt Confederates who looked more like scarecrows than warriors. It was amazing, he thought as he pulled his dispatch bag from the saddle and began to make his way to the guarded entrance, how easily the former antagonists seemed to forget that a few scant hours ago they were deadly foes. These Americans, he concluded, were indeed a strange sort, one that would take a great deal of getting used to.

Inside, the young Irishman made his way through the press of staff officers and other couriers to the desk of a large, middle-aged sergeant. Irish, like him, the sergeant showed signs of once having been a big, burly fellow who once had great strength and commanded respect. Age, and a soft job, however, had transformed muscle into pockets of soft flab and changed a hard-etched expression of youthful hostility into one of jolly serenity. Walking up to the sergeant's desk, the young courier flopped his dispatch bag down in front of the older man. "From General Sherman, for the Commanding General himself."

The sergeant, unable to ignore the young man's presence, looked up with an expression of disdain. "Oh, it's you again. Now if you would be so kind as to take your dirty bag off my desk and present your dispatches to me properly, we'll get on with it."

The younger man chuckled. "Oh, touchy today, aren't we?" he responded in an assumed, disdainful voice as he fished Sherman's dispatch from his bag.

The sergeant leaned forward and glared at the private before him. "It has been a very, very busy last two days here. We have no time for your antics."

Unrepentant, the young man drove on, using his best Irish brogue. "Well, have *we* been here, in this fine place of power long enough, *sir*, that *we* are now entitled to use the royal *we* when addressing peasants such as myself?"

Looking out of the corner of his eyes, first to the left, then the right, the sergeant leaned a little farther forward before speaking again. "Listen, you ignorant Irish trash, the commanding general has just been snubbed by that worthless traitor from Pennsylvania, Pemberton, and is not in the best of moods. So I suggest that you finish your tasks here quickly and then take your arrogant little smile and go elsewhere with it. It's not welcome here today."

Intrigued by this bit of news concerning their commanding general, the young courier changed his demeanor and began to press the sergeant for details.

Always eager to display his knowledge of inner secrets of the Army's staff, the sergeant whispered to the now attentive private. "Well, it seems our commanding general went to pay a visit to that scoundrel Pemberton earlier today at Pemberton's headquarters. It seems our general was snubbed as if he were the bastard son come to his own father's wake. Not only did the scum refuse to offer our general a seat, but when General Grant asked for a simple drink of water, one of Pemberton's toadies told the general where he could go to find one. Now, imagine being treated like that, even after dropping the unconditional surrender demand and letting the traitorous Southern scum off with paroles and the right to keep some of their own property."

Stunned, the young courier stepped back and whistled. "Is that the truth?"

The sergeant nodded. "So help me God, it's the very truth itself."

Shaking his head, the private murmured. "Well, I feel sorry for the poor Rebels that'll have to face Old Unconditional Surrender in the future. You can be sure, I'm here to tell you, he won't be so kindly with them when they come begging him for terms."

The sergeant was nodding his agreement when a young staff officer, even younger than the private himself, stepped up to the sergeant's desk. "Well, I don't know about General Grant, but I can tell you two that if you don't cease your chatting and get on with your work, I'll have both your hides," he said.

Angered by the young officer's tone and attitude, the young courier was about to respond with a slurred, "Yes, me lordship," like he used to do with the landowners he worked for in Ireland, but didn't. Such disrespect would, he knew, cost him his position as a courier and mean an immediate return to the ranks of his old regiment. That, with the promise of more hard fighting in the near future, was all but a sentence of death, or worse. Biting his tongue, the private snatched the signed receipt from the sergeant's hand, grabbed his dispatch bag, and beat a hasty retreat out the door. As much as he hated to give in to the bullying of a boy whom he considered no better than him, the young courier knew this war was far from over and would require more sacrifices from the likes of him to bring it to an end. And like many others in the ranks now faced with that awful fact, he had every intention of cheating that fate if he could.

Once away from the crowded city, the private began to look about a countryside that, he imagined, had been beautiful and fruitful before being ravaged by this war of two years. How very sad, he thought, that such magnificent land was owned by such a stiff-necked and foolish people. They would suffer, he knew, for their stubbornness and pride, just as his parents had suffered at the hands of their English lords and masters in the Old World. General Grant and his own General Sherman, the young courier knew with certainty, would make these lordly Southerners pay for their arrogance and high-handedness, much in the same way he hoped to someday make the brash young English lords who had chased him from Ireland pay. All he needed to do, he figured, was to keep his body and soul together and see this thing through until the end. Simple, he thought as he rode off into the late afternoon heat. So absurdly simple. Yet he knew it would be hard, brutally hard, to do so. Too much blood had been spilled by both sides for one or the other to simply give up and walk away from the struggle.

The sight of an old military cemetery reminded him how hard that task would be. Pausing for a moment, he read the names scratched on the ragged collections of boards that marked each man's final resting place. Many of them were badly weathered and already unreadable. Those he could make out bore the names of soldiers from Missouri, some of whom were Union, others Confederate. In one case, two markers, set off to one side, bore the same last name. Only the regiments, and the flags under which they had marched and fought, had been different. The young courier made a face as he patted the neck of his mount. "And they call this a *civil* war."

PART ONE

WINTER OF DISCONTENT

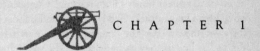

CHAPTER 1

Near the Mine Run in Virginia, November, 1863

AT FIRST, IT WASN'T noticeable. Then, slowly, the darkness that shrouded the bleak and tangled woods gave way to the cold, pale light of early morning. For a moment, the hope that the sun would soon appear to melt away the thick frost that covered everything and warm him cheered Douglas Geddy. It would be nice, he thought, to be warm, really warm and comfortable. He had not been warm, truly warm, since his regiment had entered this forsaken wilderness. Yet that hope, like so many others he had clung to, perished as a brisk gust of cold air slashed through the barren trees like a team of horses driven by a whip. Cutting through the thin, worn blanket that served Geddy as an overcoat, it killed his hope of warmth even before his mind could fully embrace that imagined comfort. Tightening his hand about the clump of blanket held close about his throat, Geddy shook once, stomped his feet, and shook again as a new shiver ran throughout his body.

Anxious to get his mind off his misery, the young man peered through the haze of the diminishing early morning gloom. Here and there, in the thick woods of barren trees, as naked and exposed, he thought, as he was, he could see an officer or a noncommissioned officer moving about the picket line. Colonel William Terry had thrown out a company in advance of the rest of the 4th Virginia the previous evening to protect it, and the brigade to which it was attached, from surprise attack. Screened by this thin line of soldiers, the rest of the regiment busied itself throwing up the breastworks of logs and hard, frozen dirt that Geddy now stood behind in an effort to protect himself from the cold. Confident that there would be no sudden Union attack, Geddy let his mind wander in an effort to forget his own misery. For the longest time, he watched the men along the picket line as they gathered about the small fires they kept burning throughout the night in the shelter of their makeshift earthworks. Taking turns, one or two of them maintained the watch to their front while their comrades gathered about the fire.

Those on the picket line went about morning rituals that were as familiar as cold, hunger, and privation to the soldiers of the Army of Northern Virginia. The men about the fire rummaged through their dirty white cotton haversacks while they chatted with the other men of their small detachment. They were hunting for the coffee, or what the Army passed off as coffee, Geddy thought. Everyone, from Colonel Terry on down, seemed to be obsessed with drinking coffee. Whenever the company stopped, even for the briefest of halts, men would fall out of the ranks and gather up twigs for a small fire. In tin cups, blackened ages ago by repeated use and lack of cleaning, the men of Company J, 4th Virginia, would pour a little water, add half a handful of crushed chicory nut coffee, and set it on, or more correctly, into the pile of burning twigs. Chatting or just watching, the men would wait until their little brew boiled. With hands toughened through years of campaigning and well practiced in the art, they would carefully retrieve their cups. With the same reverence that a gentleman savors a glass of fine wine, the ragged veterans who followed Robert E. Lee would hold their cup before their face, inhale the steam of their coffee, and close their eyes before taking their first sip. In a world that knew no privacy, where individual comforts were pitifully few, the ritualistic drinking of coffee was, for many, an experience that could not be dispensed with.

"You're on sentry duty to guard the company, Private Geddy, not daydream."

The sharp voice of his company commander startled Geddy. Spinning about as fast as he could to face the man, Geddy lost his balance, fell against the log breastworks, and would have toppled over had he not used his rifle as a support to keep him upright. His wild gyrations brought a loud guffaw from Marty Hazard, the company's first sergeant, who stood behind the lieutenant holding two tin cups with steam rising from them. "Gwaud, I've seen elephants more graceful than you, boy." Hazard snorted.

Geddy didn't like the grizzly old veteran. From the day Geddy joined the company as it worked to recover from the beating it had taken at Gettysburg the previous July, Hazard had taken singular delight in harassing him. Had Hazard's torments been restricted to verbal abuse, Geddy figured he could have tolerated it. But the first sergeant was a cruel man, especially when it came to dealing with conscripts such as himself. It seemed to Geddy that it was because he had waited to be drafted and not volunteered to fight for a cause he didn't believe in that Hazard assigned him every loathsome detail given to the company, from filling in old sinks to burying dead cavalry horses.

"Well, Private, do you have anything to report?" the lieutenant snapped when he saw Geddy eyeing Marty Hazard.

Looking back to his company commander, Geddy pondered that question for a second. What was there to report? Nothing had happened. The picket line was still in place and undisturbed. Was the lieutenant, an original member of the regiment like Hazard and a former student at VMI to boot, trying to trick him or was he just harassing him in his own way?

"Well?" the lieutenant demanded.

"No, sir. There's nothing to report. I mean, I have nothing to report."

"Then why didn't you say so in the first place instead of standing here like a bump on a log?"

" 'Cause that's all he is, a big bloody bump. Can't you see it sticking up between his shoulders?" Hazard chimed in.

This caused the lieutenant to laugh. "Marty," he said as he turned to face him, "finish relieving the sentries and roust the company. I need to go and, ah, seek my own relief."

Hazard nodded and chuckled. "Well, you're a braver man than I. I'd think twice about exposing any of my tender parts in this cold."

The lieutenant turned and walked away, calling over his shoulder, gesturing with an exaggerated flair, " 'Tis far better I endure a moment's suffering now than find myself in need at an inopportune time and be thought a coward." Then, as an afterthought, he turned and looked at the slumbering forms lying about under frost-covered blankets. "Have the men prepare whatever rations they have left and be ready to move."

Hazard shot back, "That won't take but a few minutes, seein' hows we haven't been issued anything worth a hoot to eat for days."

Geddy, watching the lieutenant walk away without commenting on the first sergeant's last comment, turned to Hazard for a moment. "Are we moving?"

"Of course we're moving." Hazard snorted. "We're an army, not a fortress. We always move."

Though he didn't much care for the manner in which Hazard ridiculed him every chance he got, Geddy ignored the last comment and persisted. He hadn't asked to be part of this sacred army that its veterans held in such high esteem and had no desire to be part of it, especially given the manner in which he was treated. "No," Geddy persisted, "I mean now. We moving forward into a fight?"

"Forward, backward, sideward, what difference. Regardless what way we move, we're going to find a fight when we get there. Old Bobby Lee wouldn't have it any other way. Now, you just leave plannin' the battles to the general, and our lieutenant, and get on with rousting the company."

Bringing his eyes down to the level where Hazard held the two cups of hot steaming coffee, Geddy wondered if the first sergeant had brought one for him. Not that Hazard was a generous man when it came to the newer members of the company. But he had been on guard, Geddy reasoned, and was quite cold. Maybe the old coot, who in truth was only a few years older than him, was a human being after all.

Seeing Geddy eyeing the two cups and guessing at his thoughts, Marty pulled the two cups in closer to his chest. "Don't go gettin' any silly ideas about this coffee, boy. You just go and do as I told you or you'll be standing guard from now until the cows come home." With sad eyes that reminded Marty of a dog that had just been scolded, Geddy looked away, slinging his rifle over his shoulder and started to go about his latest task. Without another thought, Marty turned away and headed over to the gray U.S. Army blanket that he shared with another one of the original members of the company.

Dropping onto his knees carefully so as not to spill any of his coffee, Marty leaned over the blanket. "Hey, Jimmy, time to get up and get a move on."

Instead of throwing off the blanket, James Bannon stuck his head out from under it like a turtle coming out of his shell. His hat, a brown, broad-brimmed floppy one that had lost its shape long ago, was tied to his head with a wide strip of blanket that served to both keep it on his head and cover his ears. With practiced ease, James brought one hand out, grasped the edge of the blanket that was hung loosely about his neck, and pulled it tight before rolling over to one side and then sitting up. When he was finished, he looked more like a Plains Indian than a member of one of the South's finest fighting units.

Taking the cup that Marty Hazard offered him, James looked around. Here and there men were crawling out from under their blankets and gathering about the small fires that others had already started. Not far from them, a man in another regiment of the Stonewall Brigade was singing "Dixie" and belting out the phrase "*Oh way down south where I was born, early 'pon a frosty morn*" with great gusto every time he came to it.

"Place doesn't look any better by daylight, does it?"

Marty took a sip and looked about also. "I'll take the valley any day of the week, thank you, sir." The valley was, of course, the Shenandoah Valley, home of the men who made up the 4th Virginia and most of the other regiments of the famed Stonewall Brigade. Marty looked down into his cup as he swished the contents about, mumbling as he did so. "Richmond, Fredericksburg, the Peninsular, the Wilderness, Manassas, the Yanks can have it for all I care. Just send me back to my few acres of good bottom land, give me back the team of mules the Army bought from Ma with their worthless paper money, and I'll do fine, thank you."

James looked at Marty. Like most of the men who had been with the regiment since the beginning, Marty was tired. "It's hard to stay all excited and fired up," he confessed to James as they were marching a few days earlier. "This makes it the sixth time they've been down here now by my count, and we've been up there twice. In two and a half years, no one's gained one iota of anything worth being proud of 'cept a whole lot of widows and mothers without sons." Then, looking James square in the eye, Marty shook his head. "Jimmy, I don't know who's dumber, them or us. I mean, they keep comin' even though we trash 'em good every time they do while we stand here clinging to this wasteland like a bunch of brainless scarecrows. I'm tellin' ya, it just don't make any sense anymore."

Marty wasn't the only man who sounded off in this manner. Many men were beginning to tire of the war, now in its thirty-second month. Many a good friend and comrade, including Marty's only brother and James' best friend, had been laid low in their graves during those long months. With the Army of the Potomac on the move again, everyone, James and Marty included, knew many more would join them.

James said nothing as he listened to Marty's ramblings. Judging that the cup Marty had handed him was cool enough to put to his lips, James took a sip. To his surprise, the liquid that he sipped wasn't the bitter chicory blend the Confederate quartermaster passed off as coffee but was, in fact, real coffee. Enjoying it, James took one swallow, then another. Noticing his enjoyment, Marty stopped talking and watched for a moment as a broad grin lit his face. "Nice, isn't it?"

James took the cup away from his lips, held it up as if it were the Holy Grail itself, and whispered in awe. "It's . . ."

"Yeah, I know. I've been saving it," Marty responded with a sly smile and a wink.

James let go of the blanket and held the cup under his nose with both hands, closing his eyes and savoring the aroma. "So, this is why you were so anxious to pull picket duty the other day."

"Well, some fellas from a North Carolina regiment were so anxious to lighten their load when we started, they tossed out all the extra tobacco they couldn't tote. And you know how them Yankee pickets love to trade for real tobacco."

"Any chance of getting any more soon?" James asked before taking another sip.

Marty shook his head. "Naw, least not for several days. The colonel told the lieutenant and me he was expecting some trouble today."

"Some trouble," as Marty put it, meant a pitched battle.

"So, we're finished dancing about with Meade and his boys?"

"Looks that way, Jimmy." Marty sighed as he stood up. "Now you'd best be gettin' a move on and get your share of what this army passes off as rations these days. Hugh's over there at the fire cookin' 'em up now."

"Hey Marty," James murmured as he held his cup up to his friend and first sergeant, "thanks." After taking another sip, he noticed that the new man, Geddy, kept watching them. "Kind of rough on that lad Geddy, aren't you?" he said, motioning toward Geddy with his cup.

"Him? Don't pay him no mind. He'll be gone before you know it."

"You figure," James commented dryly between sips of coffee, "he'll take a hit in our next fight?"

"Well, either that or he'll run and then desert. Ain't none of them conscripts worth the powder to blow 'em to hell."

"You've got to give 'em a chance, Marty. You remember what it was like when we started out, don't you?"

A dark shadow passed over Marty's face. "Yeah, I remember. We was all friends, real chummy. And Matty was alive. So was Will."

Marty's mention of his brother Matthew's name and that of William McPherson, a man who had become to James much more than a friend could ever be, sent a chill down James' spine. The pleasure of the coffee was suddenly wiped away as images of Will's body, twisted and contorted in death, flashed through James' mind.

"Jimmy, I suffered," Marty stated in cold, mournful tones. "I suffered like I couldn't believe possible when Matty died in my arms. To this day I can't think of him without feeling a sharp jab of pain and guilt. Nothing, not my wounds and not all the physical suffering in the world, hurts as bad as the memory of the night I lost poor dear brother Matty." Then, after a brief silence, he added with a bitter resolution, "I decided after that, I wasn't gonna suffer like that again. 'Cept for the passing of Will, I've been able to keep myself from doin' so, too. You might want to make friends with them new boys, but not me. No, sir. I don't want to know who they are, don't want to know nothin' about their mamas or their pas, and don't care what they think." Then the sharpness of his tone suddenly softened to almost a whisper. "There ain't much of me left, Jimmy. Not much at all." Shuffling around like a young boy kicking dirt, Marty felt his sorrow pass. Suddenly, he became adamant. "No, sir," Marty declared, "I'm not about to let some fool boy, 'specially a malcontent like Geddy, get under my skin and tear a piece of my heart away when he up and gets himself killed. Call it hard, call it cold. That's just the way I see things."

James made no effort to rebuke his friend, for what he felt was very near what James himself felt. Used up, was the way some of the other boys in the regiment put it. They were starting to get all used up, inside and out. So instead of pursuing the topic, he gave Marty a faint, weak smile and a nod before going back to enjoying his coffee in silence.

Several feet away, young Douglas Geddy was watching Bannon and Hazard as they sat in silence drinking their coffee. Geddy muttered in a tone of disgust to the corporal next to him. "It ain't right that the first sergeant caters so to that Yankee."

The corporal, surprised at Geddy's comment, looked up and over to where he saw Hazard and Bannon chatting. Then he let out a laugh. "Jimmy Bannon a Yankee? Not lately, *boy*."

Angered by the lightness with which the corporal had dismissed his comment as much as being called *boy*, Geddy shot back. "Well, he was born up North, wasn't he? That damn sure makes him a Yankee in my book."

The corporal, half a head taller than Geddy, turned to face the recruit. With a poke in his chest that hurt Geddy, the corporal leered down at him. "*Boy*, your book means nothin' in this here regiment, 'specially when it comes to Jimmy Bannon. That man might have been born in New Jersey, and I ain't denying it, and his daddy might be a rich Irish businessman, but when it comes to his loyalties, Jimmy is Virginian through and through. And any man, or *boy*, who says otherwise has to deal with me."

Determined not to give in, Geddy stood his ground. "If he's such a good, loyal soldier, then why did he desert last May?"

Geddy's comment caused the corporal's ruddy face to turn brighter red. Realizing he had said the wrong thing, Geddy stepped back, almost stepping on another man who uttered a curse at Geddy as Geddy prepared to receive a punch in the face. Fortunately, the lieutenant came by, causing the corporal to check his anger. When the lieutenant was out of earshot, the corporal closed the distance between himself and Geddy and leaned over him until their noses were almost touching. "James Bannon took the body of his best friend, and the best danged officer this company ever had, home to be buried. It was the Christian thing to do and thank God the regimental adjutant saw it that way. Soon as he was done, he joined up again, marched to Gettysburg with the 40th, and fought his heart out, just like he always has. So you'd better listen and listen good, *boy*." The corporal snarled as he leaned over, forcing Geddy to bend backward. "One more word, just one little word about Jimmy Bannon's loyalty again and I'll butt stroke you up side your fool head myself. Ya hear?"

Geddy, backing away, nodded dumbly. When he was a safe distance from the corporal, he shot a dirty look over toward Bannon, then turned and fled. He didn't much care for this regiment, or the men in it. No one, however, seemed to care what he thought, which made it all the worse.

As the gray, cheerless morning slowly lapsed into afternoon, the soldiers who wore the red St. Andrew's cross of the Army of the Potomac's Sixth Corps' First Division continued to idle away the hours as they waited along the side of a road that was, in truth, little more than a rutted wagon trail. Back and forth mounted staff officers and couriers flew by, spurring their mounts on as they picked their way along the road crowded with wagons, caissons, guns, and troops. All of this was expected by the veterans of the 4th New Jersey. "Maybe one fine morning," Chester Bronawitz mused more to himself than anyone else, "we'll wake up, have a nice leisurely breakfast, and then march straight off into battle without all this muddling about that our dear generals so enjoy."

"Well," Johnny O'Keeth piped up, "if you ask me . . ."

"And I didn't," Bronawitz shot back without looking over to the young Irish corporal.

Bronawitz' comment evoked a chorus of laughter that Johnny ignored. "Well, be that as it may," O'Keeth continued, speaking up so as to be heard over the chuckles of his friends and messmates gathered about, "I think our commanders do a tolerably good job getting the Army into battle."

"Sure they do," Jonah Korffen snorted as he took the pipe from his mouth and looked about the men nearest him. "Now all they need to do is figure out how to win these here battles they be so good at getting us into."

This brought another roar of laughter from all who heard him. "Well, maybe," Johnny snapped back, "if Abe would leave this Army with the same commander for more than a few months, we'd get somewhere."

"Who'd yea be suggesting there, me fine lad?" Amos Flatherly asked. "Not Little Mac again?"

"And why not?" Johnny challenged.

" 'Cause he's a bloody blowhard and pompous ass," Flatherly responded, "that's why. I mean," he said as he got up from lying on his side and settled into a comfortable sitting position, "while we was takin' a beating at Gaines's Mill, he was sittin' way back in the rear worrying about how he'd save all his precious wagons and mules. And when we was marchin' off to Richmond as prisoners, he was sipping fine brandy on some gunboat in the James River. And then," Flatherly added, now excited by his own discourse, "at Antietam he up and lets Bobby Lee slip away after the pounding we'd given that grayback rascal." Grasping his knee, he settled back and shook his head. "No, no thank you, lad. We don't need to see the likes of him again."

Johnny took up the challenge. "Well, Meade's no better. Instead of throwing us at them on the fourth of July, he did nothing and let the whole Confederate Army slip away after Gettysburg, just like McClellan did in Maryland, even though the whole Sixth Corps was barely scratched and ready to fight."

"And how," Korffen countered, "would you know, boy? If ya remember, most of the regiment was way back in the rear, watching to make sure Jeb Stuart didn't steal any of General Meade's precious mules." The subject of being assigned to train guard and provost guard for the better part of a year was a sore one in the 4th New Jersey. Since April, 1863, seven companies had been assigned to guard the Army's train while three others, who considered themselves fortunate, served as provost guards for the Sixth Corps. This onerous duty was made worse by the fact that the regiment, already under a cloud for past performances, missed the two major battles of the year, Chancellorsville in May and Gettysburg in July. Only recently returned to regular duty with the First New Jersey Brigade, it was, perhaps, the driving desire to redeem themselves in the eyes of their fellow Jerseymen that made the men of the 4th New Jersey eager to fight and more annoyed than normal at the delay that kept them from doing so.

"Well," Bronawitz snorted, "with these rutted trails that pass for roads here in Virginia as crowded as they are by the corps up front and ours, it'll be nothing short of a miracle if we get any farther today."

"That'd be just fine by me," Korffen added. "We've been marchin' and countermarchin' ever since July and it's not gotten us any closer to Richmond than we was a year ago."

"At least," Johnny chimed in, "we're in Virginia and we haven't taken another beating."

"And that, my lad," Jonah Korffen pointed out as he thrust the stem of his pipe toward O'Keeth, "is only because Bobby Lee isn't in the mood to fight us, not with Longstreet's whole corps out west."

"Which, by the way," Bronawitz pointed out, "makes us look all the more foolish, seeing how we can't even corner and beat an enemy a full third weaker than he was last year. All in all, I think it would be best if this Army just marched away and found some place nice to camp for the rest of the winter."

There was consensus with what Bronawitz had said and even the ever optimistic O'Keeth found himself agreeing, though he did so grudgingly. "I suppose there would be no harm if we up and went into winter quarters. I mean, the war's been going on for near three years. Another few months, I think, wouldn't matter."

"Well, come hell or high water," Flatherly stated bitterly, "when August of next year comes, I'm for home, no matter what."

"Even if it means that we might lose the war?" O'Keeth asked incredulously.

"Lad, by then, if the Lord sees fit to keep my body and soul together, they'll have had three years of my life and, in my humble opinion, plenty of chances to win this here war. I'll have done my share."

"And who," O'Keeth challenged, "do you think they'll get to finish this if you, and you, and you," he said pointing to the men about him, "up and leave?"

"I agree," Bronawitz added, more to irritate O'Keeth than to support Flatherly. "Let them fine strapping Irish lads who were rioting in Newark and New York this past summer come down here and fight, especially seein' how they've already tasted canister and faced the bayonet."

Taking Bronawitz' last comment as a personal affront, O'Keeth was about to launch into a tirade when one of the men mumbled to the small gathering that the captain was coming. In spite of his anger, O'Keeth eased back onto his haunches and tried to settle down, though his ears still glowed red from his anger and he continued to glare at Bronawitz.

Captain Kevin Bannon, their company commander, bored with sitting about and waiting, was slowly picking his way through the ruts in the road along which his company was waiting. As men turned to look up at him, he'd force a smile, giving each man who acknowledged his presence a slight nod, and continue on. And even though he wasn't in the mood for idle chitchat, when addressed or asked a question by one of the rank and file, he'd provide the man with a suitable answer or response. "It is very different," Kevin had told his fiancée, Harriet Ann Shields, "to be their commander instead of just another officer. They treat me, talk to me, even look at me, differently now."

Harriet, an ever-present and sympathetic ear for Kevin, tried to point out that perhaps it was his achievements at both Chancellorsville and Gettysburg that caused most of the men to hold him in such esteem and awe. Hadn't he, she pointed out, helped stem the terrible rout at the Chancellorsville Inn, earning him a promotion to captain? And hadn't he stood at the wall in the face of Lee's greatest attack at Gettysburg and personally seized an enemy battle flag? "You are a hero," she told him in all sincerity, "and your men admire you."

Kevin knew there was more to it than simple hero worship though, for the men in the 4th New Jersey were hardened veterans, not easily moved by dime novel heroics. "It's power," he told Harriet in a solemn, almost reverent tone. "Before, when I was just their first lieutenant, I had no real power over them. Now, as their company commander, I decide everything, from punishments to reward. I give the orders that will either bring them to safety or send them into the jaws of death. They know that, Harriet, and I think they fear that."

When Harriet tried to counter by arguing that he was taking his position too seriously, Kevin would persist. "I've seen that look before, my dear. I saw the workers in my father's terra-cotta works back in Perth Amboy look at my father in the same manner as he went by. And even though I was his son, and they knew it, they'd talk about him as soon as he'd go by. Just like a company commander, he had power over them and that, my dear, seems to be important, very important." Though Harriet fretted over Kevin's revelations, for she too had seen the same look when people watched her father the judge go by, she declined to pursue the issue. There would be time, she hoped, to save Kevin from falling victim to the all-consuming attraction of power and authority that had so twisted her own father and his.

"Will we be moving on some more today or is this going to be home for the night, Captain?" Bronawitz, a man who feared no man, regardless of rank or stature, called out to Kevin as he walked absentmindedly by.

Halting, Kevin looked at the assembled men but didn't answer. He had been busy thinking over and over again about what Harriet had told him and had completely missed the question. Too embarrassed to ask Bronawitz to repeat it, Kevin stood there and looked at the man for a moment. Only a distant chatter of musketry from way down the road broke the awkward standoff as men sat up and turned their head to listen to the harbinger of battle.

The spattering of rifle fire on their flank caught the men of the Stonewall Brigade off guard, but did not rattle them. Rather, except for those who were in immediate danger, most of the men were curious. "Hey Marty," Big Willie Pool shouted over to Martin Hazard. "I thought we was the last brigade in line?"

Marty, who had stepped out of the ranks to look in the direction of the firing and see if he could determine the seriousness of it, responded without looking at Pool. "We are. We're here to guard the ambulances."

As the firing continued, even picking up in tempo, Joshua Major, who had been marching along next to James, unslung his rifle and brought it up to the ready, glancing down at the lock and hammer. "Well, Jimmy," he said in a determined voice, "looks like we're gonna do some serious guardin' here in a minute."

James, having unslung his rifle and busy checking it, grunted. "Uh-huh. Looks that way, Josh."

Douglas Geddy, who had been marching along, head bowed and eyes glued to the heels of James' shabby shoes, wasn't able to hide his nervousness or confusion. At the first crack of rifle fire, he had stopped dead in his tracks, causing the man behind him to plow right into him. "Jesus, sonny!" his marching companion shouted as he recoiled from the collision. "Ya need to give a fella some warnin' when you're plannin' to stop like that."

Geddy, however, didn't respond to the good-natured reprimand. Instead, he jerked his head high as his eyes darted about looking for the danger he knew was there but could not yet see. Up and down the line, men in the ranks were taking their rifles off their shoulders while officers began to shout orders. "Left into line," he heard repeated by different voices, some of which betrayed anxiety. "Left into line."

Suddenly, without any warning, the men all about Geddy turned and moved away. The jostling by those who wanted to get by or around him only served to confuse Geddy further. "Come on, boys, come on," Lieutenant Hugh Updike called out impatiently. "Settle down and form to the left in line of battle."

With the sputtering of rifle fire drifting down the column, the terrible meaning of the words "Line of battle" hit home to Geddy. They were going into battle! This was it, he suddenly realized, the end. He was going to die.

The idea that he was about to draw his last breath was just dawning on the bewildered young man when, from out of nowhere, a hand reached out, grabbed the sleeve of his uniform, and pulled it, along with him, into the forming line of men. "Over here," James Bannon stated without any hint of emotion or anger. "Right here," he added as soon as he had directed Geddy to the spot next to him in the front line. "Now, come to shoulder arms and listen up."

With his mind all muddled with the confusion of the moment, Geddy responded to James' directions without protest. Without thinking, he brought his long rifle up into his right shoulder, wrapping his fingers about the trigger guard as he looked over at James. With his rifle butt resting on the ground and the long barrel held tight in the crook of his right arm, James was busy draping the scrap of blanket he used as a scarf over his head. Pulling the tattered scrap of wool so that the brim of his floppy slouched hat came down and covered his ears, James began to tie the ends into a good, secure knot under his chin. Glancing over, he looked at Geddy, who was looking back at him, and gave a grin and a wink. "You have nothing to worry about," he said. "Just follow along and you'll be all right."

All right? Geddy thought. They were about to go into battle and get killed and here this man was telling him he had nothing to worry about. That thought was racing through his mind when Lieutenant Updike, marching down the line quickly, thumped him on the chest. "Two," Updike shouted as he went by without stopping, tapping the man to Geddy's left and shouting "one."

"Remember, Douglas, you're a two. Listen up to the orders and remember you're a two," James told him in a rather paternal manner. Then, with a whimsical tone to his voice, he sighed as he looked to his front at the thick woods facing the newly formed line of battle. "Not that it will matter once we go forward."

Geddy was just beginning to feel a little calmer when James said "forward." Looking away from the older soldier to the wall of tangled briars they were facing, Geddy stammered. "Into . . . there? We're going forward, into there?"

"Looks that way," James said without hesitation. "Well, maybe not right away. Not till the skirmishers have a chance to sort out where the Yanks are."

For several moments, Geddy looked at the woods, back to James, and then at the woods again. Farther down the regimental line, he could see that another company had been sent out into the dense thickets, as James said it would, to the front as skirmishers. In seconds, they disappeared. Forgetting the contempt he felt toward James, Geddy looked over to his messmate. "How're we going to be able to sort out our own skirmishers from the Yankees when we go in there?"

James chuckled. "Well, you see, Douglas, that's what's exciting about being a skirmisher. Sometimes your own regiment gets so excited, they start popping off at the enemy before you have time to get yourself out of harm's way."

"Exciting? You consider getting shot at by your own side exciting?"

James shrugged. "Well, I guess it is kind of hard, especially for a new man like you, to imagine that. But in a strange way, it does get to be exciting. You'll see, Douglas."

Geddy didn't think he ever would, but he let the matter drop. Instead, he began to wonder why James, after all these weeks, was finally using his first name, as if they were friends and all. Was the old veteran warming up to him? Or was he just being kind to him, seeing as how he was about to get himself killed? These questions, and many, many more like them, crowded Geddy's confused and troubled mind as he stood there in line of battle, like everyone else in the regiment, listening to the opposing skirmishers pop off at each other and waiting to go forward.

The routine for Harriet Shields and the other members of the First Division's field hospital was always the same as soon as word came that a fight was at hand. They'd pull off the road into the best spot they could find, near a house or barn if possible, and start getting themselves arranged and settled. If there was no structure available, some of the hospital stewards and wagoners would haul out a few of the large hospital tents and set them up so that Dr. White and the other surgeons would have a place to work. Harriet, though not on the official rolls, was now recognized by one and all as much a part of the hospital staff as Dr. White, the chief surgeon. "If that bloody old witch," Dr. White had told Harriet after another failed attempt by Dorothea Dix to have her removed from the field, "sends one more lackey down here to tell me how to run my hospital, I'll personally go to Washington and sew that woman's mouth shut."

Though thankful for Dr. White's vote of confidence and support, Harriet Ann Shields was a woman who could take care of herself, and had proven so on numerous occasions. As the only child of a prominent state judge in New Brunswick, New Jersey, she had been educated beyond what many thought was necessary, or even proper, for a young lady. This education, combined with a strong and independent soul, led Harriet to question and defy first her mother, then her father, and finally the very society that she was being prepared to become a part of. "*What good,*" she wrote in a diary she kept, "*is a mind if one is not expected to think? Or a spirit, if one does not have the freedom to experience life? Though I do not question the need for men and women to marry and have families, I wonder why we must trouble ourselves so with rules of behavior and social etiquette that, in the end, are meaningless and repressive.*" Unable to sit and watch the war from afar, and to the embarrassment of her mother and in defiance of her father, Harriet set out, in December, 1862, on a course that took her, like many of the men marching by, to this nameless patch of woods in Northern Virginia.

When all was set and there was nothing more they could do but wait, Harriet wrapped her torn and mud-splattered cape over the plain, white soldier's blouse and long, stained skirt she wore. Walking out to the side of the road, she stopped, folded her arms across her chest, and waited for the wounded. Finished with his assigned tasks, Albert Merrel, a young lad of fourteen who had joined up as a drummer boy at age eleven but now served as a hospital orderly when he became excess to his regiment, came up next to Harriet and joined her as she watched and waited. "It'll be awhile 'fore any of our boys start comin' down the road. Third Corps was in the lead this morning and the Sixth was in support." To this, Harriet said nothing. Instead, she simply nodded as she continued to watch.

She was waiting, he knew, for Captain Bannon to come down the road. Whenever there was nothing to do like this, that seemed to be all she did. Though Albert loved his mother, as every young boy should, he didn't understand the bonds of affection that drove Harriet to put up with Army life like she did just to be near her fiancé. That she was there, to serve the cause, just as much as he was, never quite sank in. She was, after all, a woman, and women, Albert had always been taught, didn't have the capacity to deal with such matters. Still, Albert humored her, as he had seen other men do, by trying to explain things to her. "I don't expect it'll be much of a fight, least not for our boys today."

Without taking her eyes off the road, still crowded with troops and wagons going forward, Harriet asked why he thought that. "Well," Albert started, taking on an air of authority, "as I was saying, our corps is in support. Given how late it is and how restrictive this terrain is, I doubt if the Third Corps, let alone ours, will have the time to deploy and close up on the Rebels."

Harriet, her mind now diverted from her concerns by Albert's observations, had all she could do to keep from laughing as she listened to Albert speak of tactics and military deployments in a voice that he made as deep as possible in order to sound more manly. Turning her head, she looked down at the earnest young face of her traveling companion. It struck her, as it always did when she listened to him speak of battle, how terrible this war was. Dear boy, she thought to herself, you should be home in school, learning about wonderful far-off places and practicing the skills needed to build our country, not out here studying the cruel art of war. How terrible, she concluded, as she reached out and touched his shoulder, it will be when he finally comes of age and shoulders the musket. Like so many young men before him, Albert would march down the road in search of adventure and manhood only to find pain, suffering, and death. Perhaps, she hoped, the war will end before it gets him.

"Albert," Harriet said suddenly, cutting the boy off in midsentence, "do you suppose Dr. White would let us go forward with the division in the next battle?"

Puzzled as to why she would even think of such a thing, Albert blinked and shook his head. "No way, Miss Harriet. I mean, the doctor likes you well enough and is willing to fight all comers to keep you with us, but I really don't think he'd let you go up to where there's fighting."

Harriet pulled her hand away and folded her arms across her chest. "And why not?"

Again, Albert blinked as he looked at the ground, thought about her question, then looked up at her again. "Well, for one thing, you're a woman."

"Oh, pooh!" Harriet exclaimed. "Annie Etheridge with the Michigan regiments goes into battle right along with her boys in the Third Corps. Well, I'm willing to bet you that she's up there, right now, even closer to the Rebels than our own regiment."

"That's not the point," Albert insisted.

"Oh?"

The look on her face and the tone with which she had uttered "Oh" told Albert that she was getting upset. "Miss Harriet, you've got to understand, a battlefield is no place . . ."

"For a woman?" she exclaimed.

"Yes, exactly!"

"And what do you call Annie Etheridge, and not to mention Private Miller, who's marched into every battle the Fourth New Jersey ever fought?"

Albert sighed. She always brought up Private Larry Miller, who was actually a female in disguise, whenever she discussed this topic. Always. After a slight shake of his head, Albert continued. "You're different than she is. You're . . ."

"I know, Albert. I'm a lady. You always tell me that. Dr. White always tells me that. Even my own dear sweet Kevin tells me that whenever I suggest that I become involved in anything that is remotely useful."

"And dangerous. Please, Miss Harriet, don't you understand? We love you, all of us. From Dr. White all the way down the line. We don't want anything to happen to you."

The pleading look in Albert's face and the sincerity in his voice gave Harriet pause. Letting her guard down, she smiled as she reached out and touched the boy's cheek. "Yes, Albert, I know. Believe me, I know. Still . . ."

The sound of a galloping horse's hooves beating the frozen surface of the road from the direction of the front caught Harriet's attention. As she pulled her hand back to grasp the collar of her cape, she turned to look down the road. Drawing the cape tight about her as a chill ran through her, she watched and listened. In the distance, the cold November wind brought the muffled sound of cannon fire to them and ended their discussion. It wouldn't, she thought, be long now. It never was.

CHAPTER 2

Near the Mine Run in Virginia, November, 1863

JAMES BANNON TRIED TO pay no attention to Douglas Geddy's nervous fidgeting as they lay stretched out on the road, waiting for the word to go forward or move on to somewhere else. The volume of fire that had been stirred up by the advance of the 2nd Virginia's skirmish line told James that the fight would be a heavy one. "That's no cavalry out there," Marty Hazard remarked to Geddy as he sat cross-legged next to James, listening to the rattle of musketry coming out of the dense forest before them. "We'll be goin' against Yank infantry and from the sounds of it, they're in the mood for a fight."

Looking over at the grizzled first sergeant, James could see a gleam in Marty's eye. He was trying to unnerve young Geddy, and from the look on Geddy's face, he was succeeding. As long as James could remember, Marty loved to tease the new men, especially at a time like this. It wasn't that Marty Hazard was mean-spirited. On the contrary, once folks got to know him, you couldn't ask for a better friend, provided, of course, he was of the mind to accept you as one. But to reach that level of familiarity, you had to suffer Marty's badgering until you proved yourself worthy to stand with him as an equal.

James, on the other hand, felt sorry for Geddy, and all new men who came into the regiment. Having been forced to leave his home in New Jersey, and sent south just before the war, James knew what it felt like to be an unwanted stranger in a strange land. Though Geddy was a

Virginian, and he was amongst his own in the 4th Virginia, James saw that he was as lost and alone here, in the midst of his first battle, as James, himself, had been when he had reported to the Virginia Military Institute in 1860.

When he saw Marty look away from Geddy, James whispered, "Don't pay him no heed, Douglas. He's just trying to pass time and ease his own fears by picking on you and getting you all riled up."

Wide eyed, Geddy looked over at James. "You think so?"

With a slight smile and a nod, James responded. "He's always like this before a fight."

There was a hint of disbelief in Geddy's eyes as he looked at James for a moment, turned and looked over to Marty, now chatting with the lieutenant, then back at James. "He doesn't seem frightened to me."

James chuckled. "Well, believe me, in his own way, he is."

"Are you frightened, Bannon?"

James had no need to think about that question. Yes, he was scared, he thought. He was scared beyond belief. Yet his fears were unlike any being felt by the other men in the 4th Virginia. For while most simply feared for their lives or the suffering they would endure if wounded, James was tortured by a very personal image that, to him, was more terrifying than the most dread wound. The memory of seeing his brother, in Union blue, standing inches away from him at Gettysburg, with a look of hatred on his face and a pistol held against James' chest, haunted him nearly every waking moment. That image, together with the thought that the next time he came across his brother Kevin in battle, Kevin might pull the trigger instead of checking his anger, sent shivers down James' spine every time he recalled the incident. Though he had long resigned himself to the fact that he would never make it until the end of this terrible war, the very idea of being killed by his brother was repugnant.

"Fourth Virginia, up, stand up and prepare to advance." The order, echoed by company officers, ended James' solitary nightmare. Pushing himself up off the frozen roadway, he glanced over at Geddy, whose look of anguish was renewed by the prospect of imminent battle. Reaching over, he touched Geddy's sleeve. "Remember, when we go in there, stay close to me. We'll lose formation quick and it'll get confusing as all get out as officers shout and people push and shove you this way and that. But so long as you stay here, next to me, you'll be fine."

Geddy listened and swallowed hard, nodding when James was finished repeating his earlier advice. Before when James had offered it, he had scoffed at the thought. Now, when they were going in for sure, he just listened and nodded. Pride be damned, he thought, he would do exactly what James said.

"Forward at the double, march."

Like a single huge beast, the hundred or so men of the 4th Virginia drew a collective breath, then stepped off, as one, into the thick growth that concealed the enemy from them. Geddy, seeing no clear path into the thickets, hesitated for a second, still wondering if the officers were mistaken about this or didn't realize that it was impossible to advance into such a tangled mass of vegetation.

There was no hesitation, however, on the part of James, or any of the other veterans of the 4th. For them, this was just another fight, like so many countless others. Though the terrain changed, as did the weather, the sights, sounds, and smells all about him were no different than they had been in earlier fights. During the previous summer at Gettysburg, when the unit he was with marched against the Union First Corps, it had been no different. Nor had it been last May, when they went forward, just a few miles farther down the road from where they were now during a fight known as Chancellorsville. It had also been the same in December of '62, when they had advanced against the enemy on a hill just south of Fredericksburg, and again in September '62, in a woods near Sharpsburg. Before that, in August, it had been a railroad cut at Manassas. June had seen them at a place called Gaines's Mill east of Richmond; May, on a hill near Winchester. On and on the list went, James thought, just as the advance and the killing went on and on. The beginning of all this was now just a faint blur and the end, like the enemy, was somewhere up there in the uncertain distance.

Were it not for the fact that his brother, his own flesh and blood, numbered as one in the ranks of those faceless foe, all of this would be nothing more than a mechanical function to him, no different than breathing or eating. But the thought of seeing his brother again put a face on an enemy that had, before then, been little more than a swirling mass to attack or to beat back with shot, bayonet, or rifle butt. The thought that each and every footfall took him closer to another terrible confrontation added to the horrors that this glorious cause generated without hesitation, without stop.

Fighting his way through the brush and thick undergrowth, Geddy managed to catch up to the advancing line, though he tripped once and felt the sharp thorns of some unseen bush rip through the leg of his trousers and cut a gash across his skin. Surprisingly, there was little pain. Whether it was because of the cold or his excited state, Douglas Geddy was able to put that petty concern out of his mind as quickly as it occurred and get back to the one driving thought of catching up to Bannon and the rest of the line. When he did manage to do so, he all but burst out in a smile. Like a schoolboy finding his way into line like he was supposed to, Geddy slid up next to James and slowed his pace, bumping into Bannon's arm as he did so.

If the older veteran felt it, he showed no sign. Instead, he just kept going forward, almost at the double quick now, with his rifle at the ready and his face frozen in a blank, emotionless expression. Some of the men, advancing in small knots since the line was being broken up by the thick vegetation, were starting to yell or scream. Others, like James Bannon, merely kept their mouths shut and their eyes moving from side to side, watching to make sure they stayed with the regiment as best they could and keeping alert for the enemy. Geddy, unable to think clearly and unnerved by the whole experience, leaned over onto Bannon's shoulder, as he had been told, and followed him wherever that took him.

With a suddenness that surprised some of the men, the regiment broke out into a clearing. It was, James saw in an instant, a farmstead. A small one, and a poor one at that. But it had been someone's home, someone's livelihood. Now, it was to be a battlefield, for there, just a few yards' distance, was the enemy, already peppering the ranks of the 4th Virginia with rifle fire. Pausing for the briefest moment, the officers sought to reestablish control and order before the 4th Virginia, sandwiched in between the 27th Virginia on the left and the 5th Virginia on the right, opened up a general fire on the enemy before them.

With the same thoughtless mechanical skill that had carried him through the thickets with the regiment to this spot, James joined in the firing that now erupted along the entire line. Lifting his rifle to his shoulder, he pulled the hammer of his rifle's lock back to the full cocked position, brought his head down to sight along the long steel barrel, found his mark, and fired. Without waiting to see what effect, if any, his shot had, he dropped the rifle butt to the ground, letting the now warm barrel slide through his left hand almost to the end of the muzzle as he reached around to his cartridge box with his right to fish out another round. Without the need for looking, he brought the cartridge up to his mouth, bit the paper end off. As he spat out the bitter morsels of black powder from his mouth that had been caught between his teeth, he poured the powder from the paper cartridge tube down the upturned barrel before stuffing the bullet and remains of the paper, now wadded together, down behind it with his thumb. With skilled and nimble fingers, hardened by rough living and hard campaigning, he withdrew the long steel ramrod from underneath the barrel, twirled it over his left shoulder with a deftness that would have amazed an unskilled bystander, and brought the wide end down into the barrel. Two quick shoves was all it took before James withdrew the ramrod, twirled it again, and returned it to its keepers with one quick motion. Finished loading the round itself, James grasped the rifle with his right hand, repositioned his left hand farther down the barrel, and held the rifle at waist level with that hand while the fingers on his right hand went into the cap box on the front of his belt in search of a small brass cap. Finding one, he grasped it between his fingers and pulled it out. While holding the cap between his thumb and index finger, James pulled the rifle's hammer back to the half-cocked position with the heel of his hand till it was locked. Flipping the old cap off the primer cone, he put the new cap on, took the rifle stock, and brought it up to his shoulder, ready to fire again. All these steps, repeated twice, sometimes three times a minute, were conducted in silence by every man up and down the line as officers behind the firing line looked on, watching their men, waiting for orders, and occasionally surveying the enemy line to determine what effect the regiment's fire was having on them.

Douglas Geddy found himself staring at James Bannon in amazement. In the midst of all this chaos, he, and all the other veterans of the old regiment, simply stood there, loading their rifles and firing them as if they were at a country fair engaging in a marksmanship contest. With everything happening so fast, and the situation changing quicker than his mind could deal with it, Geddy's first thoughts were to slow himself down and sort out what he should do first. That was why he had started watching James. After all, Bannon had told him to stay with him and do as he did. So now he was watching James' every move, even to the point of all but looking down Bannon's rifle barrel to see where he was shooting in an effort to determine if there was some mystical way to know which of the swirling mass of enemy soldiers before them required killing before any of the others.

Bannon was being so calm, so methodical about what he was doing that Geddy all but forgot why he was there and why he was watching this brown-haired, brown-eyed son of an Irish Yankee. Instead, he studied every move, made without any apparent effort or waste of energy as James loaded, aimed, and fired; loaded, aimed, and fired; again, and again, and again. The ease with which he did so, without spilling a single grain of powder or wasting a single motion, soon became as much a marvel to Geddy as James' calm and unflappable demeanor.

He was still standing there, watching James as if that were his assigned duty when Lieutenant Updike came up next to Geddy and shouted in his ear, so as to be heard over the sound of battle. "Fire, damned your hide, sir. Fire!"

Despite the rattle of musketry and the sharp report of a cannon not far off, Geddy jumped when Updike yelled, and twirled in midair so that he faced the officer when he landed. Though angry at the reluctant conscript for failing to fire, the startled look in Geddy's face and his reaction caused Updike to shake his head in disgust. Angry, Geddy spouted back. "Why did you do that? Men are getting killed and you've got nothin' better to do than scare the piss outta me?"

An order from Colonel Terry, the regimental commander, to advance prevented Updike from answering. Looking about, Geddy, excited again by the prospect of something new, saw that the Union line that James Bannon and the others had been banging away at was giving way. In their wake, the Yankees were leaving a carpet of blue figures, some struggling to crawl away, some simply lying as still as the lifeless tree stumps that dotted the field here and there.

"Forward at the double quick. Forward!"

James Bannon, checking his fire in order to save the round he had just loaded for a target that might appear suddenly during the advance, watched Color Sergeant J. H. Lawrence go forward with the new regimental flag that had replaced the one the 4th had lost at Gettysburg. Determined to make sure that this one didn't suffer a similar fate, he followed Lawrence out into the open field.

Like being caught in a great wind that sucks everything along with it, Geddy found himself going forward with Bannon, trying desperately to keep up with the man. But, to his surprise, this wasn't as easy as he thought. Though they were now moving out into an open field, cleared of any natural obstructions, there were new, grisly obstacles to overcome. They were the dead, the dying, and the wounded, enemy and comrade alike, strewn about the ground in a rather haphazard fashion. At first, Geddy tried to avoid these poor souls, taking care to step over or around them. But this required him to keep looking down rather than watching Bannon and struggling to keep his place in rank.

Faced with being a humanitarian in a place where humanity seemed to have no place and staying with the one person who seemed to be his sole guarantee of salvation, Geddy decided to forget about the niceties of life and keep his eyes glued on James. The first time he stepped on what he knew was another man, Geddy cringed. "Lord, forgive me," he whispered out loud. But he kept going, staying up now with Bannon, watching him out of the corner of his eye like a hawk. The second time he stepped on a body, one that quivered under his feet, Geddy didn't even bat an eye. Perhaps, he thought, this is what the old-timers meant by becoming a hardened veteran.

Though he didn't know what had happened, James suddenly sensed, rather than saw, the men to his left stopping. Trusting his instincts without giving it any thought, he stopped too and pivoted his head a half turn in that direction. The line had not only stopped, but after bowing back a little way, it ceased to exist. The Stonewall Brigade had either moved forward unsupported or the units that should have been there were now gone. The reason for this failure became obvious as James watched a sheet of flame and smoke erupt out of a wood line off to their left, causing several men to his immediate left to topple over backward into the men behind them. Without needing to be told, James brought his rifle up, jerked the hammer back to the full-cocked position with his right thumb, and took aim at the dense cloud of smoke that now hung in front of the woods where the Union soldiers were hiding. Not waiting for the cloud to clear, he pointed his rifle at what he thought would be knee height and fired. Then, as before, he fell into the rhythmic motions of reloading and firing that he had mastered so long ago.

Having just overcome his reluctance to step on dead and dying men, Douglas Geddy was ill prepared for the next surprise this battle had in store for him. The sudden stop, in the middle of an open field, and the realization that they were under fire from an enemy force hidden in the woods beyond, was too much for him. Surely, he thought, this was the end! Surely they would all die out there, cut down in the same manner he sickled ripe wheat during the harvest.

As if to confirm this wild assumption, the color sergeant went down onto his knees, struggled for a moment to keep the flag aloft, but was unable to do so. Not even the sight of James Bannon, standing there as resolute as ever, firing away at the unseen enemy as if he didn't have a care in the world, could calm Geddy now. He was just about to step back and turn to run when a man pushed his way forward past him and went over to where the regimental colors and the color sergeant lay. It was, Geddy realized, Ted Barclay of H Company, one of the Liberty Hall boys who had left Washington College to fight in 1861. Ignoring the grueling fire that was now pelting the regiment from both the left and front, Barclay walked over to where the colors lay on the ground, picked them up, advanced a few paces closer to the enemy in sheer defiance, and planted the flag staff firmly in the ground.

He planned to stay, Geddy thought, regardless of what happened. Looking over to Bannon, Geddy saw that he was staying too, firing away without any letup, without any indication that their exposed and dangerous position mattered to him. Though all of this seemed rather insane to him, and Geddy was opposed to doing anything that didn't make sense, he stayed too. It wasn't that he suddenly was swept by a hidden spring of courage. Nor was it out of love for his state or any of the men whom he was standing there with. He stood his ground simply because James Bannon had told him to stay there with him and do as he did and Geddy, his mind locked up with a jumble of thoughts, couldn't think of anything better to do.

It was getting late, James realized. The light was fading and night would soon come. That, of course, didn't mean that the fighting would stop. The time of day or season of the year no longer seemed to matter in this war. The opposing sides were just as content, he figured, to hack away at each other round the clock, day and night, in an effort to add to the already terrible toll that the war had claimed. The idea that it would eventually claim him, didn't much bother James any longer. It was as though that was preordained and it was only a matter of time. The only hope James found he could muster any longer was the hope that somehow, his brother would survive this cruel, brutal insanity called war.

Freed from the need to concentrate solely on the process of loading and firing, James was pondering his fate and that of his brother when out of the blue, he felt his knees buckle and his legs fall out from under him. Without his being able to control it, his fingers flew open, releasing the rifle and ramrod they had held and letting them fall away into the darkness that suddenly surrounded him. He felt his knees smack down onto the ground, heard his breath as it was knocked from his lungs, sensed his stiffened body teetering back and forth for a second, but felt nothing. Only a small voice, calling out quietly from somewhere in the recesses of his mind, could be heard. "James," it proclaimed like a professor in class stating a fact, "you've been shot."

With that, he lost consciousness and toppled over onto his face.

Coming up to his men, scattered about in the woods just off the road, Kevin Bannon called out for First Sergeant Himmel. The old German came up and cleared his throat to announce his presence as he waited for Kevin to speak. "Seems like the ruckus down the road has ended for the night and we'll not be needed. Have the men bed down where they are but be prepared to move on a moment's notice."

From out of the darkness, a voice Kevin recognized as belonging to Johnny O'Keeth called out. "Will we be in reserve again tomorrow or will we be gettin' a chance to fight, sir?"

Kevin turned in the direction that he thought the voice had come from. "Well, now, General Sedgwick hasn't shared that part of the plan with me, Corporal O'Keeth, but as soon as he does, I'll be sure to find you and share the news with you."

Several of the men who were not already asleep, hooted and howled. Amos Flatherly called out from somewhere behind Kevin. "Corporal Johnny, me lad, seems you lost your bet. I'll be around in the morning to collect it, you can be sure."

From a different part of the dark woods, another voice called, "Seems we'll all be around in the morning, thank God." To this, Private Chester Bronawitz added "Amen," with a tinge of sarcasm that highlighted all his speech.

Himmel, after listening in silence, looked about. "You heard the captain. Settle in and get some sleep. And make sure to keep your locks covered and dry. There'll be the devil to pay if I see even a spot of rust on them in the morning."

While there was an anonymous groan or muffled grump here and there, no one dared talk back to Himmel, lest he find himself on the next fatigue detail. Instead, those who hadn't already done so unfolded their ground sheets and blankets, paired off with their bunkmate, and settled in for what was left of the night, leaving Kevin standing in the middle of them.

"Over here, Captain," Himmel called out in a low voice. Following the sound, Kevin came to a nice, flat spot of ground Himmel had cleared for him. "I'll be right over here if you need me, sir," he told Kevin in a hushed voice before turning to tend to his own bedroll.

Left on his own, Kevin threw out his blanket, as he had done on so many occasions, flopped down without bothering to undo his belt or take off his hat, and rolled himself tightly in the blanket. Himmel had already laid out Kevin's ground sheet over a bed of leaves, giving him a comfortable, if somewhat thin, bed to sleep on. Looking up, Kevin could see only patches of sky through the barren branches above.

They hadn't fought today, he thought, even though they were just a few hundred yards from the fighting. What had happened, and who had won, if anyone had, he did not know. All he knew was that one more day of war was over and when he woke in the morning, it would still be there. The war, his company, and the shoulder boards of captain that, at times, weighed so heavy on his shoulders, would all be there, waiting for him. Were it not for Harriet, his dear sweet Harriet, it seemed, at times, as if the weight of all of those oppressive forces over which he had so little control would crush him like he was crushing the leaves beneath him. But she was there. She was always there, waiting for him. Why she did so, he did not know. All that mattered was she did. And for now, that was enough.

As he drifted off to sleep, he gave a fleeting thought to what she was doing. That she was safe and in the rear was sure; still, he wondered if she was as warm and as snug as he was right at that moment. The thought of her, the warm wool blanket, and the freedom from having to make any decisions for a while brought a smile to Kevin's face just before he fell asleep.

Once the wounded started coming back, it was better for Harriet. Though the sight of men and boys, bleeding and shattered by battle, still unnerved her, she was able to push feelings aside and get on with helping as best she could. With Albert at her side, she tended to the less seriously wounded and those waiting to go under the surgeon's knife. A drink of water for this one, a blanket for that one, and instructions to the hospital stewards to remove the one that had passed away before anyone could help him. "Doesn't seem like it was too big a fight," young Albert chirped up while Harriet was wiping the blood out of the eyes of one man with a head wound. "Mostly the Third Corps' fight."

The wounded man shook his head free from Harriet's hands and looked at Albert with wide eyes, now able to see. "Sonny, from where I was, it was plenty big enough." The sharp rebuke, unexpected and delivered with force by a man they had thought at death's door, caused both Albert and Harriet to pull back. Sensing their surprise, the soldier managed a meek smile, looking first at Albert, then at Harriet. "Beg your pardon, ma'am. Sorry for startlin' you so. But I dang near had my head carried away by a shell and I'm just not feelin' like myself right now."

Harriet smiled, a smile that shone like the sun in the warm glow of the lantern light that Albert was holding. "There's no need to apologize. The boy meant no harm. He was just . . ."

"I knows what he was sayin'," the wounded man shot back before facing Albert with a glare in his eyes. "Someday, if 'en you ever get a mind to do a man's work, you might want to go up there and see that there ain't no such thing as a little battle."

Stung by Harriet's reference to him as a boy and the wounded man's attack on his manhood and lack of understanding, Albert stood up, turned, and walked away, forgetting that he had the lantern. Looking back at Harriet, the soldier bowed his head. "Sorry again, ma'am, for gettin' your little helper upset."

Patting the man on his shoulder, she eased him down. "He'll get over it. He's just a little touchy about such things. Now lie here and someone will be along presently to look at your wound."

Without another word, Harriet stood up and followed Albert, taking care not to trip over or step on any of the wounded that lay about in the darkness. Near the entrance of the hospital tent, she caught up to him. "Albert," she said in as soothing a voice as she could manage, "he didn't mean anything by that."

Still smarting, the young man turned to face her. "Oh, yes, he did, Miss Harriet. He meant every word."

Stepping up to him, Harriet put her hands on her hips and began to speak to the boy in a stern tone of voice. "Albert Merrel, you climb off that high horse of yours and remember where you are and what you're supposed to be doing. There'll be time enough, and I'm sure more than enough war, for you to go off and prove your manhood when the time comes. But for now, you belong here and your duty is to help me tend to these men."

Though she knew he wouldn't be happy, for nothing short of joining the ranks would satisfy Albert any longer, her reproach had the desired effect. The boy heaved a great sigh, letting his shoulders slump forward in dejection. "Yes, ma'am," he whispered.

Without thinking, Harriet stepped even closer and wrapped her arms about the young man. "Albert, I've already got one person I dearly love and care about that I must worry about while he prances from battlefield to battlefield risking his life. I don't think I could stand having to do so for another."

Pushing her back, Albert looked at her with a quizzical look. "Miss Harriet, why would you need to worry? I'm not going to go get myself killed or anything. I just want a chance to fight, like all the rest of the men in this Army."

That this lad, Harriet thought, could still think like that after all he had seen was both amazing and appalling. For almost a year she had watched strong young men, most not much older than Albert, go forth into battle, only to see them later come back, transformed into bloodied and shattered shadows of their former selves. That Albert had failed to see what she had seen bewildered her.

"Miss Shields," a hospital steward called out. "Doctor White requests your presence in surgery. He needs help calming some of the men."

Harriet heaved a sigh and shook her head. Though the surgeons often ignored the presence of women in the field hospitals or openly spoke against them, they seemed more than ready to use them when it came time to calm a wild-eyed man about to lose an arm or a leg. Though she respected Dr. White, and he her, grudgingly, in return, Harriet hated being his intermediary in such matters. "Tell that boy," he would say in his gruff manner as he pointed to a wretched form lying on a stretcher outside of surgery, "that if I don't take his leg, he'll die." What he wanted her to do was to calm the patient down and steel him for the horrors of an amputation, often done while the patient was awake. Dr. White used the only female on his staff for this task because he knew a man would try to be brave for a beautiful young woman, even when facing such pain. And though Harriet understood this, and knew it made sense, she hated it, hated it almost as much as she did the war that endangered her Kevin and all she dreamed of.

"Miss Shields?" the steward asked. "Is there something wrong?"

Harriet looked at the man, dropped her head, and shook it. "No," she lied. "There's nothing wrong. I'll be along in a minute."

With him gone, Harriet turned back to Albert. "Albert, I care for you dearly, as dearly as a mother cares for her own son. I just don't want . . ."

Albert smiled. "I know. You don't want to see me hurt. But like I said, I'll be all right. And, Miss Harriet, thanks." With that, he went back to tending to the newly arrived men while leaving her to go off to her irksome task.

At first, James didn't know if the voices he kept hearing were real or imagined, since they kept drifting in and out of his conscious mind for the longest time. Though he tried to focus on them, he couldn't, for his own mind drifted off too, like the soft mournful wind that swept through the branches now stripped of leaves. Everything was a muddle, a terrible muddle in his mind that he could neither make sense of nor organize into a coherent thought. So he stopped trying for a while, and just let himself slip back into the unconsciousness that was as warm and inviting to him as the smile of a pretty girl.

Then, for the briefest instant, the image of a face came to mind, as clear as if she were there, right now, before him. It was Mary Beth McPherson, the sister of his roommate from the Virginia Military Institute, William McPherson. For the first two years of the war, Will had been more than a comrade in arms to James; he had come to mean more to him than his own brother. Will McPherson was dead now, struck down at Chancellorsville just this past May. But Mary Beth, James thought, was still alive. For a moment, he imagined her, as he had last seen her. She had worn a frown that day, a frown that did little to hide the beauty that made her glow like the sun. Will had always told James that she wasn't that good-looking, that she was as ordinary as a summer day. But James loved the summer, and he loved her.

How strange that his wandering mind thought of this bright, clear image of Mary Beth as it faded away into the darkness of his scrambled brain. That I finally found someone that I truly love, he thought, and loves me and I can't find the words to express that love. How strange.

"Yeah," Private William Pool stated in a low voice as he watched for a moment, "he's comin' round, finally." Then, looking across the small fire to Marty Hazard, he shook his head. "I still think we should have taken him to see the surgeon."

Marty made a face and threw the few drops of poor coffee in his cup into the fire, which made a hissing noise. "I wouldn't take a half-dead dog I hated to those butchers. All they're interested in is takin' off your arm or leg, whether it needs it or not. You know why I still got my leg?" he asked as he swung his right leg over into the firelight and patted it. Pool shook his head. "The only reason me and my leg are here together tonight is 'cause the last time I was shot, just down the road from here during the Chancellorsville fight, when they took me to those bloody bastards, I threatened to run through the first man who came within ten feet of me with a saw." He paused as a wicked smile came across his face. "Them fools thought I was kiddin' 'em too, till I took my bayonet out of the scabbard and made a lunge at one of 'em."

Reaching over, he took the battered and blackened coffee pot from the fire, poured himself a fresh cup of coffee, and held the cup as he looked into the fire for a moment. "Well, me and this other fella, who wasn't in a hurry to lose his leg either, took care of each other, just like we're takin' care of Jimmy. Besides," Marty Hazard added after taking a sip of his chicory coffee, "them fellas at the field hospital who claim to be doctors wouldn't have done anything for that gash in Jimmy's head till they ran out of arms and legs to hack off. We did more for him ourselves than they ever would have done. They'd probably have left him out on the cold ground without a blanket or fire. I've seen 'em neglectin' a man who didn't seem hurt bad till the poor devil died for want of a simple bandage."

Pool looked down at his cup, nodded in agreement. Then he looked up again. "What'll we do with Jimmy if the brigade gets into another fight tomorrow?"

Marty scoffed at Pool's question. "*What* brigade? Hell, there ain't enough men left in this here brigade for two decent-sized companies. When the adjutant counted heads tonight, there wasn't more than two dozen souls left who claimed to belong to this regiment."

"Well," Pool countered, "that never stopped 'em before from pushing us into a fight."

Marty thought about this and reluctantly agreed. "They might, I guess, but I don't think so. If they do, well, we'll send young Geddy to the rear with Jimmy first thing. Geddy wasn't worth a damn in today's fight and I don't see no sense in dragging him about with us tomorrow if there's fightin' to be done. No sense at all."

Finishing his coffee, Pool stood up and stretched his arms out over the dying fire. "It's bed for me. Even if we don't fight tomorrow, someone will figure out some place new to march us to. They always do."

Marty yawned. "We'll march, all right. I just hope . . ." Then, without finishing his sentence, he let his thought go. Hope, these past few months, had been at a premium. And if that day's brutal, yet inconclusive fight was a harbinger of things to come, then hope would be an even more precious commodity tomorrow. Without another word, Marty stood up, gave Pool a nod, and went off to wrap himself in his blankets next to James Bannon, the last man in the world he really gave a damn about.

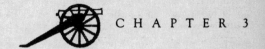 CHAPTER 3

Winchester, Virginia, January, 1864

WITH TWO SHAWLS DRAPED over her stooped shoulders, Mary Beth McPherson held her arms across her chest with hands balled up and tucked away for warmth as she moved about the kitchen preparing a meal of bread and watery soup for herself and her mother. It was cold in the house, bitter cold. Despite her best efforts, there seemed to be nothing she could do to get herself, or the house, warm. She thought about the cold as she sliced the dry, almost tasteless bread they now depended on. It was as if the war, not content with draining away the life that had once animated this house, was now sucking away the very warmth that gave life to the earth itself. With the fighting and suffering having gone well beyond any measure of reason or logic, Mary Beth wondered if the people in both Washington and Richmond would continue until every creature in Virginia, large and small, was as cold, stone dead as the headstone on her brother's grave.

That thought caused her to stop and glance out the window toward the small family cemetery plot. All the McPhersons, when their time came, were buried there. Two whole generations were there, she thought, and now we're starting on the third. One small marker stood at the head of her sister's grave, a child she had hardly known who had died shortly after birth when Mary Beth was only eight. Her mother had greeted that event with great courage and determination. "It was God's will" was all she said as she turned away from the grave of her last-born child and got on with living.

She was not, however, as understanding when she learned of the passing of her oldest child, William Keith McPherson, struck down at the age of twenty-two during the Battle of Chancellorsville just that past spring. "Why?" she had wailed when she had heard the news. "Why have they taken my baby? Why?" But there was no one to give her an answer. Her husband of twenty-five years had gone to Richmond, exiled from his own home by Union occupation forces for aiding and abetting the enemy, an "enemy" that included her son. There he had died in an accident at the Tredegar Ironworks, where he had labored ten hours a day, six days a week for a wage that barely brought him enough to live on. The minister of their congregation wasn't there either to provide Elizabeth McPherson any solace and comfort, for he had gone off with the local militia to provide them with spiritual guidance during their time of trial. This self-appointed task had been cut short the previous winter outside of Fredericksburg by a bout of dysentery that proved to have no regard for a man's vocation or close association with God.

None of those who were with Elizabeth when they lay William's body to rest with his forefathers could provide her with an answer. Daniel McPherson, her fourteen-year-old son, seemed impervious to the suffering of the family. Instead of dwelling on sorrow and loss, Daniel's mind was alive with the images of a glorious and noble cause and how he could best escape the narrow confines of life at home to join in the defense of that cause. James Bannon, who had deserted the ranks of the 4th Virginia to fulfill a pledge William McPherson had extracted from him, to see that he was buried on his own land, was too filled with images of his own ghosts. He could offer no solace or comfort, not even for himself. And Mary Beth, a girl of indomitable spirit and a will of iron, was herself foundering under the weight of the same questions that so tormented her mother.

The night after they had interred William, the want of hope and the despair of a future that promised only more despair and loss came crashing down upon her like a weight. While sitting with James Bannon alone in a kitchen that had once been filled with the chatter of a whole family, Mary Beth was struck by the horrible changes that war had brought to their family. "It is," she told James as tears welled up in her eyes, and held his hand as if she were clinging to it for life itself, "as if there were only darkness and sorrow ahead."

James, his humanity exhausted by two years of grim war, had no brave words to cheer her, or hope to share. His heart, she finally realized, was as dead as her brother.

"Beth, you're too concerned with what's out there and not what's still in here."

Her aunt's sharp admonishment, intruding into her dark, private thoughts from nowhere, caused Mary Beth to jump. With a jerk of her head, she turned toward the kitchen door where her aunt stood, cape and bonnet still on, waiting to be welcomed in. "Oh, dear Auntie, I didn't hear you come in the front. Forgive me, please come in. I was just . . ."

"I know what you were doing, young lady," her aunt snapped. "You were forgetting your duties with the here and now."

Slowly, Mary Beth bowed her head as she turned her face back to the window to take one more fugitive peek at the cold, snow-covered family plot. If, she thought, the truth be known, her real concerns were not with those who were already there, but those who would follow, in particular the one person who made all this suffering bearable, James Bannon. In the silence that followed a tender and unrepentant kiss, James had asked Mary Beth if, when his time came, she would see to it that he was buried next to his friend, her brother, if at all possible. "I have no place of my own that I can call home, Mary Beth, no place to spend eternity. And except for you and Will, I have no one. So I'd be much obliged if, when the time came . . ."

Though she was appalled that James was so shorn of hope that he was unable to stop the thoughts of impending doom at a time when they should have been celebrating the joys of life, Mary Beth kissed his warm forehead, gave him the best smile that she could muster, and promised that she would see to it.

"How's your poor dear mother?" her aunt demanded in an effort to keep her niece's mind on her duties.

Reluctantly abandoning her troubled thoughts, Mary Beth turned away from the window and walked over to the table set for only one. "She was feeling much better this morning. I think she may even get out of bed for a while today."

"Oh, poor dear Lizzy," her aunt moaned as she removed her cape and draped it over a vacant chair at the table. "She always took family tragedies to heart so. I can remember when our own dear mother passed away, God rest her soul. Lizzy wouldn't eat for a week."

"Well," Mary Beth chimed in, "she has been eating."

"What?" her aunt shot back. "Colored water that you pass off as soup and bread sliced so thin you can see through it? A church mouse couldn't live on that."

The sharpness of her aunt's remarks stung Mary Beth. "It's all we have, Auntie. I'm doing the best I can."

Unruffled by the young woman's defense, the older woman continued her hounding. "If you'd listened to me instead of that Yankee trash you're so fond of and kept your brother Daniel here instead of sending him off to VMI, you'd be in a lot better shape."

"James felt Daniel would be much safer at VMI than here, Auntie, and I agree. Had we not sent him there when we did, he'd have either run away with the Army when they were here in August or be riding with Mosby's gang. I know it."

"Oh," her aunt moaned. "Dear foolish girl, why do you insist on defending the men who have turned their backs on you and your poor wretched mother in your time of need? First your brother, God rest his poor soul, leaves school to run off to war like a starry-eyed child. Then your father manages to get himself sent through the lines by the Yankees and goes to Richmond where misery and an untimely death are his reward. And finally, the shiftless scoundrel who professes to love you convinces you to send your brother away before he marches off to rejoin Lee and his army of scarecrows. Can't you see that if you don't start putting your foot down and insisting that either your brother or that Irish scum you've become so fond of live up to their responsibilities to you, they never will?"

Biting her lip, Mary Beth said nothing. What did she know about men? Mary Beth thought. With a face frozen in a perpetual frown and a figure like a plum, her aunt had never been seriously courted by any man. The one who finally did tie the knot with her was half her size in girth and always well on his way to being drunk. Her brother Will always used to comment that any man lashed to a woman such as their aunt needed all the courage he could muster to face her. There was no use, however, in arguing with her aunt. She was, Mary Beth knew, a good person at heart and, in her own way, trying to help. Unfortunately, her aunt hadn't been blessed with a temperate tongue or amiable character. In an effort to end her aunt's current tirade, Mary Beth went to the table and lifted the bowl of soup and a spoon. "Auntie, could you be a dear and take this in to Mother while I tend to the tea?"

Though she hadn't quite finished her haranguing about the McPherson men and James Bannon, the older woman agreed. "Might as well see what I can do for my poor wretched sister," she snarled as she walked over and took the bowl of soup and spoon from Mary Beth's hands. "Lord knows, if she waits for her own children to do what they should, she'll die for want of attention."

Though the anger welled up in Mary Beth, she managed a forced smile and a weak "Thank you." When her aunt had left the room, Mary Beth turned back to the window.

How awful, she thought, it must have been for James to grow up in a family that was as cold and loveless as the one he had described to her when he had seen her last. Though he continued to profess a genuine affection for his brother, whom he had briefly seen at Gettysburg, Mary Beth suspected that his feelings for him now seemed to fall just short of love.

Heaving a great, deep breath, Mary Beth slowly let it out. Then she muttered as if she were talking to James instead of her own reflection in the cold, frosted window glass. "At least I've been blessed with the warm love that only a family can give a soul and, by the grace of God, will know it again. Now be safe, my love, and hurry home to the one who loves you, now, always, and until the end."

Perth Amboy, New Jersey

SLOWLY, AND THEN ONLY after taking a quick, fugitive glance to either side, Kevin slid the dark, double oak doors of his father's study aside. When they were just wide enough to admit him, he entered the room quickly and closed the doors, after looking to see if anyone had seen him. Pausing, he leaned backward against the doors, looked up at the ceiling, and took a deep gulp. God, he thought, I am acting like a child.

But then, lowering his eyes, he looked about the room and allowed the memories, long suppressed, to flood back. He had good reason to fear this room, he thought, as his mind conjured up image after image of his father's face and paraded them before his mind's eye. More often than not, those images were twisted in anger. This was the room, Kevin thought, more than any other, that represented the oppressive sadness that high-lighted his childhood.

Slowly he looked about the room, studying all its furnishings and fixtures, all the while feeling as uncomfortable at being in there as he felt in his suit of fine, tailored civilian clothing (so unaccustomed to him after the coarse texture of his uniform). In one corner, between two windows, the massive desk sat like a forbidding castle keep. Seated safely behind it, his father would survey all before him with narrow, piercing eyes before issuing his edicts and judgments. How many times, Kevin wondered, had he and his brother James been brought to task for some transgression or another before that imposing desk. Too many times, he concluded, too many.

Subconsciously, his eyes were drawn to the corner of the desk where his father had always kept his pistol. This conjured up another shadow, a darker one, that began to creep out of the recesses of his memory. The images of the past, unblurred by five years, passed through his mind with a terrible slowness that was maddening. There was the girl, standing on a dock on that cold December night, watching, in horror, as two brothers argued over their shared affections for her. Then, the gun, taken by him, from the very drawer he was staring at, for God knows what reason. He had never feared his brother. James had spent his entire life, up until that night, shielding him from an abusive father as well as the taunts and fists of the workers' boys who always seemed to be spoiling for a fight. Why, Kevin thought now, as he had so many times before, had he felt the need to take his father's gun? Why?

There could never be, he knew, a good answer to that question. Not then, and not now. There was only the bitter memory of his standing there, holding a gun at arm's length at his very own brother. And the shot that rang out as loudly in his mind now as it had in his ear that night. In all the battles he had survived during the last two and a half years, no sound was ever as terrifying as the sound of that shot that night.

That shot, and the horrible realization that his anger had killed the first person he ever truly loved, weighed as heavily upon him now as it had four years before.

"Kevin?"

The sound of Harriet's voice behind him caused Kevin to jump. Spinning about, he yelled, before he had time to think. "Dear *God*, woman, don't sneak up on me like that!"

Caught off guard by his response, Harriet let go of the knobs of the double doors and drew back. "I . . . I didn't mean to . . . I was just . . ."

Though still shaking from the memories that had been racing through his mind and Harriet's sudden appearance, Kevin managed to calm himself. "I'm sorry, dear Harriet, I was just . . ."

"I'll come back later," she responded as she looked down and began to withdraw farther into the hall.

"Oh, please, don't go," he pleaded as he stepped out and caught her by the arm. "Please, come in and, well, talk, if you'd like."

Though still leery, Harriet allowed Kevin to guide her into a room that she had never been in. "This room, it's my father's study," Kevin blurted as he swept his free arm about the room. "It has, ah, always been a very, very imposing room to me and . . ."

For a moment, there was silence as the nervous smile left Kevin's face and a cloud of darkness gathered about his brow. That he was very troubled by something was painfully clear to Harriet. It was more than just being there, again, in a house he was clearly not comfortable in. There was something more sinister lurking about in the corners of his mind that she had yet to see. From his demeanor, Harriet could tell that Kevin was still unable to come to terms with whatever it was, let alone tell her. Taking a step closer to him, she placed a hand on Kevin's forehead and wiped away some of the sweat that had beaded up on it. When her hand came to rest on his cheek, Kevin reached up and cupped her hand in his, pressing it against his cheek and smiling as he did so. "Dear Harriet, forgive me. I shouldn't have barked at you so."

Satisfied that the crisis had passed, Harriet returned his smile.

Though troubled that this man she so dearly loved didn't trust her enough to share his deepest, darkest thoughts with her yet, she let it pass. In time, she thought as she gently stroked his cheek with her thumb, perhaps he would see fit to unburden himself and open his soul to me as he had opened his heart. "I am sorry," she finally whispered. "I shouldn't have come in here without knocking."

Pulling back, Kevin took her hands in his and looked about the room. Harriet did likewise. It was a man's room, she concluded, dark and imposing to the point of being gloomy and oppressive. Heavy draperies all but blocked even the slightest ray of sunlight from the rows of thick books that lined the bookshelves, which ran from floor to ceiling. What few decorations there were in the room were dark and massive and lacked any hint of grace or elegance. "As boys," Kevin mused as he continued to look about, "my brother and I would sneak in here, just as I did, and look around."

"What were you looking for?" Harriet inquired.

Kevin laughed and shook his head. "I don't know. I suppose we were looking for the secret."

Harriet stared at him. "What secret?"

Kevin looked down at her, then turned his face toward the massive portrait of his father hanging over the mantel. "I think we were trying hard to find the secret of why he treated us like he did." Again, Kevin laughed before he looked back at Harriet. "I suppose it was foolish of us to think that we would find the answer in here. Still, we had to start somewhere, I guess." Slowly, the smile left his face as he looked down at the floor.

Stepping closer to him, Harriet bent down slightly and imposed her face on Kevin's field of vision. "That's nothing to be embarrassed about, my dear Kevin. Why, when I was a child, I used to crawl along the floor behind my mother and slowly lift her skirt to see if she really had legs under all those hoops and slips she wore."

This revelation caused Kevin to throw his head back and laugh. "Ah! I can remember my brother and I would sit on the steps of this house just after we moved in here from our old place near the terra-cotta works, watching the women go by and speculating whether they were walking or riding on some kind of wheeled cart."

"You can't be serious?" Harriet responded.

"But I am. I mean, if you think about it, it sort of makes sense. They all went along the sidewalk, so smoothly and gracefully, without any of the jerking and bobbing that the boys or workers we were so familiar with do when they walked. James concluded that since no one could walk naturally without doing so, the fine ladies who passed up and down this street had to have some type of mechanical assistance. So we concluded that they used some sort of cart, like the ones the workers used to move bricks about the terra-cotta works."

Harriet started to laugh uncontrollably, bringing a hand up to cover her face. "Oh, dear Lord, I can't believe that. Did you ever try to, I mean, did you ever . . ."

"Look?" Kevin asked. "Well, what do you think?"

"Oh, Kevin, I'm shocked."

Half seriously, Kevin added, "Not nearly as shocked as your father is going to be when he finds out you're staying here instead of with a friend."

The mention of her father's name brought a chill to Harriet's voice. "I'm afraid that when it comes to me, my father is beyond being shocked. He as much as told me so when I came home last week."

Though he was sorry that he had brought the subject up, Kevin felt that this was as good a time as any to discuss a matter he had been contemplating for some time. "Harriet," he began stiffly, "as you know, when my furlough is up at the end of the month and the regiment reforms in Virginia, I must go, but . . ."

Anticipating his next statement, Harriet looked him square in the eye and shook her head. "Kevin Bannon, I am not going to stay here in New Jersey while you go off to war. And don't even think of trying to talk me into doing so."

Patiently, he drew her closer and took her hands into his. "You have done more than anyone could ever ask of a woman. More, in fact, than many men in this state have done. But I think it's time you let someone else do the grim work that is so, well . . ."

"Unladylike?" Harriet's eyes narrowed. "Kevin, you're starting to sound like my mother and those worthless cronies of hers whom she calls friends. I sat with them, knitting and sewing sock after sock while listening to them gossip about this one or that one. Besides," she added, "who will the surgeons get to tell some poor boy that he has to lose his leg? Who will they find who is willing to sit and write a letter for a dying man, telling his wife that he won't be coming home and imploring her and his children to be as brave as he had been? Who will go about the tents each night, bidding men in pain good night and closing the eyes of those who never will see another? Who . . ."

With tears welling up in her eyes and her voice choked with emotion, Harriet found it impossible to go on. Kevin, barely able to hold back his own tears, drew her into his chest and wrapped his arms about her. As he swayed from side to side, he patted her back. "I don't want you to see that anymore, dear Harriet. I don't want you to go."

With her head resting against his chest, Harriet caught her sobbing for a moment as she struggled to catch her breath. Finally, when she was calm, she spoke in tones barely above a whisper. "Believe me, dear Kevin, I don't want to go either. But I must. Like you, I have no life here any longer. To come back here, to surrender to my parents' demands, would be like dying of suffocation." Pulling away, she held Kevin's arms and looked up at his face. "Whatever future I may have is bound to yours. For better or for worse, Kevin Bannon."

In an effort to lighten the terrible mood, Kevin added, "For richer or for poorer?"

Harriet, not to be put off by his remark, concluded, "Till death us do part."

Unable to respond, Kevin pulled Harriet back against him. This time, Harriet returned the embrace. "There is," she said with a tone of lightness and hope in her voice, "so much for us to share."

Kevin, looking beyond her, at the corner of his father's desk, swallowed hard as he thought, And so much that we will never be able to.

Trenton, New Jersey

WITH A WAVE OF his hand, Judge Melvin Shields beckoned for one of the white-gloved servants. With great deftness, the young man weaved his way through the brightly lit room crowded with men in formal attire smoking thick, rich cigars. With a slight bow, the servant offered his silver tray of crystal champagne glasses to the judge, who took one and turned away from the servant without so much as a nod or wink of thanks.

"Gentlemen," he announced with the commanding voice that had earned him a reputation in New Brunswick's county courthouse, "a toast." Lifting his glass, he looked about the room until he saw that all present had a glass of the fine French wine he had ordered special for this occasion. Then, with a smile, he turned to face the guest of honor. "Gentlemen," the judge said with great flourish when he felt the time was right, "I give you the next president of the United States, our very own George B. McClellan."

After an enthusiastic chorus of "Hear, hear," the men all lifted their glasses of shimmering French wine toward the diminutive general and Judge Shields. The general, sent to his home in Trenton to await orders after being replaced as the commander of the Army of the Potomac in November, 1863, was pleased with the attention and adoration. He bowed deeply and lifted his own glass in a salute. "Thank you, gentlemen, for your trust and confidence, both when I served this great nation in the field and now, as I accept the great challenge that you have thrust upon me." This brought another round of enthusiastic "Hear, hear"'s that filled the room and brought a sly smile to the general's face.

From across the room, Edward Bannon noticed that Judge Shields was sporting a broad, unabashed smile. It reminded Edward of the look that a cat wore after a particularly satisfying meal. "It seems," a gentleman behind him whispered into Bannon's ear, "our esteemed judge has a larger appetite than our humble state can satisfy." This caused Edward to chuckle as he lifted his glass and took a sip. "Yes," he said with a grin, as he eyed the others in the room, lining up to shake the general's hand. "And he seems to have plenty of company."

"Aren't you going to sally forth and join the multitudes?" the gentleman behind Edward sneered.

"I have no need to grovel at our diminutive guest's feet in search of recognition or favor. In time, when he needs to fill his political war chest with my gold, he will find *his* way to me."

"Yes," the gentleman said with a sigh as he looked down and swirled the expensive French champagne in his glass. "That seems to be the way of things, these days."

Edward Bannon turned to face the gentleman behind him, fixing his eyes with a hard, uncompromising gaze. "That, sir, has always been the way of it. Only fools and idealists believe otherwise."

Not wishing to push the matter, the gentleman nodded, muttered a few words, and backed away, leaving Edward in command of the field.

Puffing out his chest, Edward placed the thick cigar in his mouth and turned to leave the room when Judge Shields, after introducing all those men of note to the general that he cared to, caught Edward's attention. At first, Edward pretended not to notice the judge, choosing instead to concentrate on the fine cigar he was enjoying. Not to be put off, Judge Shields left the general's side and strolled across the room, smiling and nodding at those who were worthy of his attention as he did so.

When he was near enough to speak so as to be heard without shouting above the clink of glasses and the babble of conversations filling the room, Judge Shields called out to Edward. "My dear Mr. Bannon, I would appreciate a moment of your time." Though the judge's tone had the ring of an order rather than a request, a habit of the judge's that annoyed Edward, Edward Bannon cocked his head and smiled. "Why, sir. I would be a cur if I were to deny our gracious host such a humble request."

Embarrassed by Edward's loud response given so that everyone about him could hear, the judge closed the distance until he was close enough to whisper his next request. "What I need to discuss with you is, for me, a rather delicate matter. Could we do so in private?"

With a wide smile, Edward leaned back slightly and threw out his arms in an exaggerated motion, again responding louder than necessary. "Why, of course, my dear judge, as you wish." Then, with a motion of his hand, he pointed to the door. "Please, lead on."

Despite his best efforts, as Judge Shields made his way through the crowd, his embarrassment was showing as he apologized every now and then to an important guest for having to leave him for a moment. Once in the hall, the judge led Edward to a private study where a servant, not much younger than Edward, appeared as if by magic, bearing into the room upon a silver platter a bottle of fine brandy and two elegant snifters. The judge told the servant to leave the tray after he had served Edward. When the servant was gone, and before the judge had time to speak, Edward lifted his brandy snifter toward the door being closed by the servant. "You know, my dear judge, as I dined on the marvelous fare you provided for us tonight and listened to General McClellan's fine speech, I could not help but think that twenty years ago, the only way I could have gotten into that room was if I had been carrying a tray of food." Then he stopped and looked down at his hands and shook his head before looking up at Judge Shields. "Even then, I doubt if these hands, the hands of a common day laborer, would have been suitable to serve the likes of such a fine man as our dear general."

Preoccupied with other thoughts, Judge Shields missed Edward's bitter sarcasm. Instead, he just nodded absentmindedly and muttered, "Yes, yes. Times are changing indeed."

Surprised that he had not solicited a more passionate response, Edward decided to cease his goading and turn to the matter at hand. "What is it you want of me?"

The judge paused at first, which was very unusual. In the past, Judge Shields had displayed no such hesitation when he was soliciting contributions for political candidates whose election would benefit both of them. Edward, an Irish immigrant who had amassed great wealth and power in numerous businesses throughout the state, had always given freely in an effort to achieve entrance into the elite circles that his humble birth and ruthless business practices would, ordinarily, have kept him out of. Judge Melvin Shields, a member of one of the state's most noted families, had political ambitions that neither he nor his family could afford. Since Edward had the money but not the background that could ever pose a threat to him, Shields had seen an opportunity to establish an alliance that would provide for both their needs without undue cost to either.

"As you realize," Shields began slowly, "when General McClellan becomes president, a whole new world of opportunity will open for those who support him. He is a man who prizes personal loyalty and will, I am sure, reward it handsomely."

Swirling the fine old brandy about in the snifter he held, Edward mused out loud. "You speak as if our little Napoleon were all but elected."

Shields scoffed at Edward's inference. "Surely you don't think that abomination of a man who sullies the proud office of the presidency with his antics stands a chance to be reelected? Why there is even serious discussions within his own party about dumping him in favor of a more moderate, more accommodating candidate."

"Accommodating to whom?" Edward challenged. "The northern Democrats or . . ."

Edward didn't need to finish his statement. The judge understood what he was driving at. "This war has gone on too long and it has been far too expensive, not only in terms of the wealth and lives that we have squandered but also in the personal liberties that Lincoln and his gang of black Republicans have so easily tossed aside whenever it suited their purposes. Responsible men, such as you and I, and those in the other room, all realize that it is time to recognize the obvious and put an end to the fighting now, while we still have something left of this world of ours that we have worked so valiantly to preserve."

Edward didn't respond at first. Instead, he took a sip of his brandy and wondered what Shields knew of work. He wondered if, by chance, the two men had been born side by side they would still be standing here, now, in this room, engaging in this conversation. No, Edward concluded as he looked over at the judge. Though he admired the judge's political astuteness in most matters, the man had no backbone. "You didn't ask me in here to discuss the war and our Little Napoleon's political future, did you?"

Shields, stirred to argue the case for political accommodation with the South, heaved a sigh as he prepared to change subjects. "No, no, I didn't. I asked you in here, Edward, to ask a favor of you."

With the wave of his hand holding the brandy snifter, Edward gestured for the judge to continue. "I would be much in your debt if you could use your influence over your son, Kevin, to encourage my daughter to remain in New Jersey when he returns to Virginia."

Fighting the urge to smile, Edward looked down into his brandy. "Well, Judge Shields, I am honored that you credit me with such power over my strong-willed son, but . . ."

"There can be no buts, sir," Shields interrupted with a desperateness that surprised even Edward, a man seldom surprised. "My daughter's continued presence with the Army of the Potomac has been, and continues to be, an embarrassment to me and my wife."

Seeing the opportunity to toy with a man who prided himself on being able to control everyone within his sphere, Edward walked about, gesturing as he did. "Well, this is news to me. I mean, my son, who just recently began to come to terms with me after years of estrangement, seems to think that your daughter's presence with the 4th New Jersey is, in his words, a source of great pride and honor to the men of the regiment. They are, he states repeatedly in his letters, the envy of the brigade." The annoyed look on the judge's face encouraged Edward to continue with vigor. "Why, just last week, before your daughter came to visit, Kevin stated that every officer and man in the regiment considers himself to be blessed with the presence and noble services of the daughter from one of the most respected families in our state. And to tell you the truth," Edward

Bannon added, "after finally having the opportunity to spend a little time with her, I can appreciate their sentiments. She is a very, very charming creature."

From the corner of his eye, Edward could see that his statements were irritating Shields to the point of physical discomfort. "Be that as it may, sir," Shields countered as calmly as he could manage, "both my wife and I, as well as several people of note, differ in our view of that sad situation. The idea that any lady, or girl, of virtue can maintain that virtue as well as her standing in society while traveling with an army like a camp follower is ludicrous."

"Why, my dear Judge," Edward responded with feigned confusion, "I would have expected just the opposite would be the case. I mean, after all, I have been given to believe that this nation prided itself on the sacrifice of those women who braved the odds years ago, who endured untold adversity and hardships to build this nation out of a frontier wilderness. I would think that any father would be proud to see his daughter doing everything in her power to stand by the man of her heart in his greatest . . ."

Edward's reference to the courtship between their children angered Shields. "A daughter's place is in the home of her parents until such time as she is properly given away, married, and has a home of her own."

Stopping, Edward thought about Shields' outburst. "Given away," he muttered out loud. Then he looked up at Judge Shields. "You mean the way a slave owner trades one of his slaves off for profit?"

Angered and no longer able to control himself, Shields slammed his snifter on the table, causing the brandy to splash about. "No! That is not what I mean, and you damned well know it."

Rather than become angry himself and deal with Shields directly, Edward smiled as he walked about the finely appointed study. "Over the years, in my drive to amass power and wealth, I managed to forget how and why I had started that dirty and cruel climb." He stopped and looked over at the judge, who stood in the middle of the room, staring at him red faced and angry. "It wasn't until your daughter—and she is a grand, lovely creature, Judge Shields—came to me asking for my help to get her and her gifts to the Army in Virginia that I began to remember my own dear wife."

With a suddenness that brought a soft, warm smile to the old Irishman's face, Edward Bannon saw before him the image of the green-eyed, red-haired girl who had stolen his heart so many years before in Ireland. When he spoke again, it was her image, her smile, that guided him about the room. "We were poor, Judge Shields, dirt poor. When we started, it seemed we never had a shilling or a scrap of food left over from one day to the next. But we were happy. So long as we had each other, we were happy. Had she not come along, I would have spent my life stumbling down to the pub every night to drink my fill with the rest of the lads until I had passed out drunk or was thrown out for fighting like so many of my long-departed friends. She changed me, Judge Shields, gave me something more than ambition, more than direction. She gave me something that I had never had before, or since."

Stopping, the old man looked down at his brandy snifter and half-heartedly fought to hold back the tears. "That woman loved me," he concluded after a moment. Then, eyes now cleared and shoulders thrown back, he looked over to Judge Shields. "She loved me with the same power and abandon that your daughter loves my son. And though I've never been much of a father to Kevin, I'll be damned, sir, if I will do anything to deny him that love. Not now, not ever."

The tone of Edward's voice and the look in his eyes told Judge Shields that there was no power on earth that would shake that man's determination to leave matters as they stood. Realizing that further efforts would only provoke anger, Judge Shields decided it was time to drop this matter and get on with other, equally important issues. Swallowing, Judge Shields lifted his chin as he struggled to regain his composure. "I trust you understand that I had to try, since Harriet is my only daughter and as a father . . ."

"You have no need to explain," Edward responded. "I understand," he added. "I understand perfectly."

"Then I trust we can drop this matter and continue with our mutually beneficial friendship?" Shields asked haltingly.

With a sly smile, Edward nodded. "Why, of course, my dear judge, of course. Now, you have guests, I am sure, who are jealous for your attention."

Regaining his composure, Judge Shields smiled. "Yes, I do. Please, sir, if you would accompany me back to the ballroom, we can get on with the business of the night."

Edward put up a hand. "In a minute, if you don't mind. I'd like to admire this room and its fine paintings."

Eager to escape Edward's presence, Judge Shields nodded and was gone, leaving Edward alone. When he heard the door shut, Edward walked over to the fire and looked into the burning embers for a moment. "My dear sweet Mary, God rest your soul. Will you ever forgive me for what I have become and the way I treated your babies?"

At that moment, a log burned through and broke in two, dropping into the embers and causing the fire to flare up. Rather than step back, Edward let the warmth of that sudden blaze sweep over him, remembering as he stood there the warm embrace of his dear Mary. Smiling, he let a tear well up in his eye and fall away down his cheek. "Thank you, my love. Thank you."

CHAPTER 4

South of the Rapidan, Virginia, February, 1864

WITH A CHAR-TIPPED STICK, James Bannon carefully maneuvered the ends of two burning logs back into the center of the fire and close to the blackened pan that contained their dinner. It wasn't much of a dinner, especially since the contents of that pan had to feed the four men who shared the rough little log hut. In that pan, some chunks of bacon—which were in truth more gristle than meat—mixed with hard bread that had been soaked in water and then crumbled and thrown in were frying up nicely. Off to one side of the fire and surrounded by bright embers was a covered pot, containing eight small doggers, round biscuits made from cornmeal and water, that Marty Hazard had found in an abandoned farmhouse. Together with the weak coffee that boiled in the pot hanging from a discarded bayonet hammered into the side of the wooden fireplace, this would be dinner.

Pulling away from the fire, James blinked his watering eyes and coughed from the smoke that spilled out of the crude wood and mud fireplace and into the hut. Though a far cry from a proper fireplace that drew all the smoke up and out, it was much superior, not to mention safer, to many of those used by other members of the regiment. Though it was hard and time consuming, James was glad they had taken the time to line their chimney with the thick layer of mud. The boys next door, who had built their chimney using nothing but old pork barrels with the ends staved out, had lost most of their hut, as well as two blankets and a rubber poncho when that chimney had caught fire two days prior. "I'm sorry," young Douglas Geddy had kept yelling to Marty as he joined other men in throwing dirt and water onto the blaze, "for complainin' when we were fixin' our hut. I'll never say anything about your orders again." That promise, James recalled with a smile, had lasted less than an hour when Marty handed Geddy his rifle and pointed to the door. "Your turn for guard, now get."

A rush of cold air chilled James as the crude door, made out of the pilfered floor boards of an abandoned farmhouse, was flung open. Several men clattered in from the cold. James didn't stir from his seat or say a word. After a quick glance, he just turned back to face the fire and tend to his cooking.

"Lordy!" Marty Hazard proclaimed as he moved behind James, placing a hand on his back to keep his balance and let James know he was there, "I can't see how it can keep getting colder and colder. There's got to be a limit, there's just got to be." Moving to the other side of James so the other two men could come in, Marty began to take off his accoutrements, shaking his head as he did so. "No wonder all them Yankees north of the river are in such a hurry to push south. They just wanna find a place where it's warm."

Joshua Major, the next man in the door, let out a laugh. "Well, now, if they come on down here, we'll send 'em straight to hell with all those other fellas we've sent, won't we, Jimmy?"

James managed a weak smile and nodded. "I suppose so."

The final man in the door, Douglas Geddy, didn't stop to put his rifle up on the crude wooden pegs hammered into the wall between the logs for that purpose but headed straight for the fire. From behind James, Marty shouted out. "Hey, boy! You raised in a barn or somethin'? Close the door."

Tucking his head between his shoulders like a puppy that had been admonished, Geddy turned and shoved the door into place. Since it wasn't on real hinges, this took some doing. Still, when done right, it proved to be a snug fit, just like everything else in the little hut. Finished, he turned and looked back at the other three men. "Sorry."

While the other two men went about stripping off their tattered overcoats and blankets James gave Geddy a wink and a smile. "Don't fret any. Old Marty wouldn't be Marty unless he was bullying someone smaller."

Pausing as he unwound a scarf that was twice as long as it needed to be, Marty looked over at Geddy, then James. "Now that's a dang lie, Jimmy Bannon, and you know it. Why I'm the friendliest, most loved man in this here camp. Ain't that so, Josh?"

"*Ha!*" Joshua Major roared. "Maybe there's a polecat or two here abouts that's taken a likin' to ya, but no man alive will ever fess up to callin' you a kindly, warm-hearted soul."

"Why I'm just bowled over. Jimmy, did you hear what Private Major just said? He said I wasn't liked."

At first, James ignored Marty and concentrated on stirring the mix of grease, bacon, and lumpy hard bread in the pan before him.

"Jimmy, aren't you gonna say anything on my behalf?"

James gave Geddy another wink. "Well, now, Marty, ordinarily I would. But . . ."

"But what?" Marty challenged, going along with the joke.

"Well," James whined, "it's Sunday, Marty, and you wouldn't want me telling no lies on Sunday, would you?"

Josh Major let out another loud hoot that filled the room. "Why, if it wasn't for that cracked head of yours," Marty responded, "I'd whomp you up the side of it." Then, after the laughter died down some, Marty added, "How is your head doing?"

James lifted his hand to his head, as if to check it. "Better, much better. I think I'll be able to join you on picket duty tomorrow down at the river."

Finished stripping off his outer garments, Marty pulled up a stool and sat down at the fire next to James. He reached across him, lifted the lid from the pot with the corn doggers in it, and pulled one out. As he pulled back and sat upright, he waved the dogger in front of James' face. "Now don't you go rushing anything. That Yankee bullet rattled your head and all that book learnin' of yours real good."

"Not to mention giving you a permanent part that's straighter than any my mama could ever manage," Josh Major added as he pulled up an empty cracker box on the other side of James and sat on it. Like Marty, he grabbed for a corn dogger that he dipped in the thick hot gravy that James had made in the pan. "Head wounds are funny things, though," he added thoughtfully. "You need to listen to Marty. I had a cousin who was kicked in the head by a mule once while he was out plowing in his pa's field. Well, his ma told him to lie still and rest, but my cousin was more stubborn than the mule. Said no mule was going to keep him from finishing his plowing."

Taking a bite out of the dogger, Josh kept talking as he chewed. "Well, he finished all right. He no sooner got the last furrow cut and what do you know, wham," Josh shouted as he slapped his knee, "he up and keels over, deader than a doornail."

James gave Josh a look, but said nothing. Instead, he turned his face back toward the fire and pulled the pan with the bacon and hard bread bits in it away from the fire. Marty, looking first at James, then over to Josh, shook his head and laughed. "Well, Josh," Marty chuckled, "as always, your words of comfort are, well, priceless."

Missing the point of Marty's verbal jab, Josh flashed a broad smile and slapped James on the knee. "Why, thanks. I'm always glad to be of help."

As Marty roared with laughter and Josh wondered why he was doing so, Geddy came up behind James. Without a word, Geddy began to pass tin plates to him. James, taking each plate, carefully dished out the mix he had in the pan before passing it on to one of the other men gathered about him. Everyone, except Geddy, who couldn't reach them, helped themselves to the corn doggers. James, fishing two of them out, plopped them on Geddy's plate for him. With no place near the fire, Geddy retreated to the lower bunk and sat there, eating his meal as he watched and listened to the other three men who shared stories about home, family, and friends, both those still living and those who were gone. Most of the talking was done by Marty and Josh. James, though he would smile every now and then, nod in agreement, or add an occasional word or two, didn't say much. Instead, he stared intently into the fire as he slowly ate his meal, thinking, Geddy thought, more than listening.

After a while, Marty began to notice James' quiet, withdrawn mood. Even Josh, never mindful of what was going on around him when it came to others' thoughts or feelings, began to lapse into silence. Finally, by the time the four men had finished their coffee, no one was speaking. Like four monks, they sat there in their tiny hut, their faces lit only by the soft orange glow of the dying fire as they stared at its glowing embers and mounds of white ash or down at their empty plates while each man retreated into his private thoughts.

It was Marty who broke the solemn mood. Looking down into his empty cup, he sighed. "If we're to have warm food for breakfast, we need some more wood."

Josh grunted. "You mean we're gonna have somethin' for breakfast?"

James answered in a matter-of-fact manner without looking away from the fire. "I managed to save some bacon, rice, and cornmeal, expecting we'd have a few lean days without any rations issued."

At first Josh was angry, upset that James had been holding food back while he was all but starving to death. But then, after a sharp glare from Marty, he checked himself and reconsidered his reaction. "Well," he finally managed in a low voice, "I guess you done right by doin' that. It's just that . . ."

James looked up at Josh and gave him a sad smile. "I know. I should have told you what I was doing. Sorry."

With the crisis averted, Marty stood up. "Josh, take young Geddy here and go find us some wood for the morning."

"Now? In the dark?" Josh protested. "Looks to me as if we have more than enough."

For the briefest of moments, Marty stared at Josh Major. Finally, understanding that Marty wanted to have a word in private with James, he nodded his head. "All right, Marty, I'm goin', I'm goin'."

Grumbling to himself, Josh stood up, gathered his ragged coat and tattered scarf, and started wrapping himself carefully in them. Geddy, without a murmur, did likewise. When the two were gone, Marty took his seat next to James, poured himself a fresh cup of coffee, and studied his friend's intense expression for a moment. "Jimmy, you want to tell me about it?"

James didn't answer at first. He didn't even acknowledge the question. Instead, he continued to stare at the fire. Finally, just when Marty was about to ask again, James spoke, still without looking at Marty. "I saw him, Marty. Saw him plain as day." He looked over at Marty. "He was as close to me as you are now."

For a moment, Marty panicked and pulled back, believing that James was talking about his long dead friend Will McPherson. Seeing the look on Marty's face, James smiled and reached out with his left hand to touch Marty's knee. "No, Marty, there's no need to worry. I'm not talking about Will." Pulling his hand back, James looked at the fire again as his face settled back into its sad, thoughtful expression. "He's gone from us, Marty. Gone forever and no power on earth will ever bring him back."

After a moment's silence, curiosity finally got the better of Marty. "Well, if it wasn't Will, then who was it that you saw that's botherin' you so much?"

"My brother, Marty. I saw my little brother, Kevin."

Marty Hazard leaned back for a moment and studied his comrade's face. Though relieved that James' head wound wasn't making his last surviving friend unbalanced, Marty wondered what had triggered this unexpected bout of melancholy. In almost three years of knowing him, Marty couldn't recall a single instance when James had ever mentioned his family, whom everyone assumed was still alive and living comfortably somewhere back in the North. When Geddy had asked Marty about that, Marty had rebuffed him. "His family and who he talks to about it is his affair. Though I often wondered myself 'bout it, I never thought it was worth botherin' Jimmy over. As far as I'm concerned, there isn't a man in this brigade who can equal him in a fight, outlast him on the march, or stretch our pitiful rations as far as he can. What he thinks and who he chooses to share those thoughts with are none of my concern. And they best not become yours, either, or I'll slap you up the side of your fool head myself."

Though he still believed what he had told Geddy, Marty figured this was no time to drop a subject that was bothering his friend so much. "When'd ya see him, Jimmy? And where, for heaven's sake?"

"Gettysburg," James answered in a low, even voice. "This past July at Gettysburg, on the third day."

"Was he, I mean . . ." Unable to ask if he was dead or not, Marty dropped his question and allowed James to continue at his own pace, when he was ready.

James didn't react to Marty's unfinished question. Instead, he cocked his head up, staring past their crude fireplace and the sparks that rose from the failing embers and peered at an imaginary figure only he could see. "He was standing there, Marty. My very own brother, in the uniform of a Union captain, staring me straight in the eyes. Yet he wasn't my brother, at least not the brother I knew. There was determination, real determination, that burned in the eyes of my little brother like I had never seen before." James looked at the embers. "His face was contorted with anger and hate, Marty. He was looking at me, with a pistol against my chest, and he hated me."

As James spoke, Marty watched as his friend's expression clouded over. "Even when he saw me for who I was, even through the astonishment that transformed his face in an instant, I could still see the hate in his eyes, burning through his words." James paused as he brought his knees together, wrapped his arms about them, and lowered his chin till it rested on his forearm. "Even when he pointed my father's gun at me on the night we shot poor Martha Anderson, the mayor's daughter, by accident I wasn't afraid of him. Not until that moment, at the wall there at Gettysburg, did I ever imagine that I would be afraid of my brother."

Marty waited a minute, confused by James' mingling of two events that he had never spoken of before. Finally, when it became clear that James had no intention of telling him more about either, Marty broke the silence. "But he didn't shoot, James, did he?"

When he responded, James didn't look at Marty. Rather, he kept his eyes riveted on the fire before him. "No, he didn't shoot, not this time." Then, with the snap of his head, James turned and looked at Marty. "But what about the next time? What happens when he and I meet each other again?"

For the first time in months, Marty understood James' quiet withdrawal from the circle of comrades he had once enjoyed. He had always thought it was Will's death that had caused him to change so. "Jimmy, there's always the chance you may never see him again."

"And there's also the chance," James snapped back, "that I will. What then? Do I shoot him before he shoots me? My God, Marty, what do I do?"

"I know it's not the same," Marty started slowly, "but you know I lost my brother, a brother that I loved just as dearly . . ."

"But *you* didn't do it," James countered with a force that caused Marty to draw back. "Someone else, some faceless foe took Matthew from us, just like he took Will. This is different. This is . . ."

Unable to finish, or find the right words, James turned away from Marty and buried his face in his arms. After a moment, Marty heard the sounds of soft muffled sobbing. Slowly, carefully, he raised his right hand and brought it to rest on James' heaving shoulder. "I know me and the Lord have had our differences, and there have been a few times when I wanted to curse him for what he's done to my brother, and Will, and all those other good fellas we've known. But, Jimmy, we've got to trust that he'll see us through all this and somehow, he'll make it right. It's all we got, the belief that he'll see us through this mess, somehow, someday."

James, his eyes red, looked up at Marty. "And if he doesn't?"

Marty had no answer. There was, he knew, none worth giving. Instead, he looked away from James and stared at the fire. James, understanding his friend's silence, looked back to the fire also. Together, the two men sat quietly, each alone, each lost in his own thoughts.

North of the Rapidan, Near Brany Station, Virginia

WALKING SMARTLY PAST THE well-turned-out guards posted at the entrance of the ballroom built by the Second Corps especially for this ball, Kevin Bannon led Harriet to the edge of the brightly lit dance floor and paused. Dressed in a gown she had to send to Washington for, Harriet held tight to the sleeve of Kevin's new dress uniform as she looked about the room in sheer joy. All along the walls of the massive sixty- by ninety-foot ballroom hung red, white, and blue bunting, studded with the state and regimental flags of the corps. On either side of the dance floor were pine tables, crowded with punch bowls and trays of every imaginable delicacy. At the far end of the room a military band, hand picked and well rehearsed by the sound of their music, played a waltz to which dozens of animated couples, dressed in radiant ball gowns and smart dress uniforms, glided effortlessly about the dance floor. The bright lights playing on the gay decorations, the sound of music filling the room, the smell of fine food, expensive perfumes, and wool uniforms mingling together, even the feel of Kevin next to her, excited Harriet in a way she hadn't felt in a long, long time.

Fearful that she might feel uneasy about coming to an event such as this where she didn't know anyone, Kevin looked at her when he felt her draw nearer to him. Harriet's eyes were alive and darting all about the room as if she were looking for someone. "Is everything all right, dear?"

With a shake of her head that caused her long curls to wiggle and a blinking of those big, expressive eyes that Kevin so loved, she shook herself out of her trance and looked up at Kevin. Flashing a broad smile, she gave his arm a squeeze. "Lovely, dear Kevin. Everything is so lovely."

Relieved that this had not been a mistake, Kevin drew in a deep breath and smiled. "Well, then, let us advance and be recognized."

That didn't take long. From across the room, several officers of the 12th New Jersey Volunteer Infantry caught sight of Kevin and motioned to him to join them by raising their glasses. As they made their way toward them through the crowd, Kevin tried to point out to Harriet the officers whom they were approaching. "The lieutenant colonel there is Thomas

H. Davis of Camden, New Jersey. He commands the regiment. The major next to him is John T. Hill. He was acting commander of the Twelfth at Gettysburg when I fought with them on the third day."

Then, without warning, the scene before Kevin's eyes was transformed. Instead of smiling faces in natty blue dress uniforms, all Kevin could see was the image of his brother, James, face contorted by anger and blackened with powder and dirt, wearing a torn and tattered gray jacket. Only Harriet's tug on his uniform sleeve pulled him back from that momentary lapse. "Is there something wrong?"

Flashing a broad smile, he looked over to Harriet. "No, nothing at all." Though she knew better, she said nothing. Instead, she stayed by his side while he went about the gathering of officers from the 12th and introduced them to her. Carefully trained by her mother in all the social amenities and graces, Harriet endeavored to charm each and every officer, smiling as she cocked her head slightly, dipping into a graceful curtsy when in the presence of a particularly important man, and using a soft and delightful tone when she spoke. Even officers who were accompanied by their wives, and there were many there for this occasion, went out of their way to meet Harriet and chat with her, if only for a moment.

Kevin, never having been properly schooled in ballroom etiquette, was quite happy to let Harriet take the lead here. The fact was, he, and not Harriet, was uncomfortable being there, even though every officer of the 12th New Jersey as well as the staff of Smyth's Second Brigade of the Third Division welcomed him warmly. "You should have stayed with us after Gettysburg," one major admonished Kevin. "General Smyth was quite serious about seeing that you be given a brevet to major."

With the shy, disarming smile that he had become noted for, Kevin shook his head. "I am quite content in the Fourth New Jersey."

The major gave Kevin an odd look, for he knew that the 4th was not held in very high regard, even by their own brigade commander. Stepping closer, the major whispered, "The offer, my friend, still stands. Fact is, I believe you could even secure yourself a position in the Twelfth as Major Hall's replacement."

Pulling back, Kevin looked over at Hall, then back at the major. "Is Major Hall to be promoted?"

"No," the brigade staff officer responded. "He's resigning his commission. It seems his rheumatism has gotten the best of him. I hear that he's planning on doing so in the next few days." Then, pointing a finger at

Kevin, the major mused. "Why, with your connections, and those of that lovely young girl of yours, I'm confident you could have both his rank and his position."

It irked Kevin that the major had made no mention of his abilities or his performance at Gettysburg, or elsewhere. Must it always be, he thought, that who you are and what sort of connections you have matter most? And his reference to Harriet as a girl also irritated him. He looked over at her as she spoke to a general and a pair of colonels. Noticing his stare, she looked over the shoulder of one of the colonels and broadened her smile for an instant in acknowledgment without ever losing her place in the conversation she was holding. It had been a long time since he had thought of Harriet as a girl. Even back in New Jersey, she always seemed to be older, or more correctly, more mature than he was despite the fact that he was older than she by almost a year.

Turning back to face the major, Kevin looked down at the cup of punch he was holding and smiled. "I thank you, sir, for the kind offer. I am flattered. But this would not be a good time to leave the regiment."

"Ah, yes," the major responded. "Kilpatrick's hare-brained plan to raid Richmond and free the prisoners on Belle Island. I've heard of it. I wish you better luck south of the Rapidan than we had earlier this month. The Twelfth alone suffered eleven wounded for nothing."

Kevin was shocked that information about General Judson Kilpatrick's plan for a cavalry raid south was so well known, and his face showed it.

"Why so surprised? Members of his own staff have been bragging that they'll push Stuart's boys aside and be in Richmond before Bobby Lee knows they're there."

"Well," Kevin responded glumly as he stared at the makings of another failure, "I just hope Stuart's staff doesn't get wind of it. I dread the thought of another wasted march through the Virginia countryside."

The major shook his head. "As we all have." Then he added as he glanced to one side and lowered his voice. "Marching about looking for an opening to nip at Lee is a damned sight better than bashing our heads against Confederate breastworks, don't you think?"

Kevin nodded. "Either way, sir, we don't seem to be making much progress."

"Well," the major mused as he prepared to leave Kevin, "I expect something will turn up in the spring. This is an election year, after all, and Old Abe needs to show results if he expects to get four more years, doesn't he?"

Yes, politics, Kevin thought, the other part of the equation. Connections, a good family name, and politics. With a nod and a slight bow, Kevin excused himself and headed for the punch bowl. A group of women, wives of some of the officers, were gathered near the table when Kevin approached. Though he didn't mean to, he could not help but overhear their conversation as he filled his cup. "Yes," an older woman said in a voice that was a bit too loud. "That's the one, in the light green gown trimmed in lace." Turning, Kevin looked at the women, and then over to where they were looking. The woman they were describing was Harriet.

"Imagine," a short, round woman said, "the nerve of her coming to our affair."

"Well," added another, "I understand her escort and fiancé is quite a hero. Captured a Rebel flag single-handedly at Gettysburg."

"Humph," the older woman responded. "He might be brave, but he certainly shows no judgment when it comes to selecting a proper wife. No self-respecting gentleman, at least not one from Massachusetts, would ever allow his name to be associated with that of a common camp follower."

Such talk wasn't new to Kevin. The wives of some of the officers in his own brigade spoke of Harriet in much the same way. In the name of domestic tranquillity, their husbands never seemed to defend Harriet, even though they themselves praised her efforts when their wives weren't in camp. Though he didn't like hearing such talk, Kevin didn't become upset. Instead, he slowly advanced toward the circle of women. Standing erect, he took a drink, then pointed toward Harriet with his cup. "I hear she's considered quite an angel by the men of the First New Jersey Brigade. A tireless worker, an invaluable aide to the surgeons, and a kind and tender heart who'll listen to the stories of lonely soldiers far from home."

The older woman turned and looked at Kevin, raising her nose slightly after looking him up and down. "You can't expect men who are far from home to be able to differentiate between a real lady and a common trollop."

"Oh," Kevin disagreed with a smile, "I hear she is anything but common. She has, I am well informed, a very good education in the classics."

"Which probably explains," the short, round woman pointed out, "why she's behaving like she is. I always knew that an education confused girls and led them to turn their backs on their proper duties and responsibilities."

Having fun, Kevin cocked his head at the short, round woman. "You don't consider nursing our wounded and tending to the needs of our soldiers proper for a lady?"

"Of course not," the older woman shot back. "If *only* you knew what kind of woman does *that* sort of thing, you'd understand."

Stepping back, Kevin held the cup across his chest and lifted his other hand to his chin. "Well, yes, I suppose you are correct, dear lady."

"Of course, I am right, young man." Turning, she looked at Harriet. "Why if I was her mother . . ."

"Oh," Kevin moaned, "thank God you're not."

Confused by his statement, all the women in the tight little group turned to look at Kevin. With a broad smile, he returned their stares. "Now, my dear *ladies*," he announced with much flourish and a deep bow, "if you would excuse me, my fiancée awaits my presence."

After handing his cup to the older woman, who stood dumbfounded and took it without speaking, Kevin marched across the dance floor, walked up to Harriet, took her arm, excused them from the general she was speaking to, and led her onto the dance floor. When the band struck up a lively waltz, Kevin stepped off with a purpose and twirled about through the crowd, taking special care to come close to the older woman and her cronies as often as possible.

As he danced with Harriet, he felt himself become lost in the gaze of her smiling green eyes. With Harriet in his arms, all concerns and worries, even the troubling image of his estranged brother, faded into oblivion. In their place, a woman of strength and character, unlike any he had ever known before, filled his thoughts. I will, he promised himself as they held each other as tightly as they could, see this war through until the end and make this woman my wife, no matter what it costs.

PART TWO

THE
KILLING
FIELDS OF
SPRING

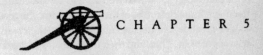

CHAPTER 5

On the Rapidan, Virginia, May, 1864

SLOWLY, PONDEROUSLY, THE LONG columns of the Sixth Corps wound through the fields and forests north of the river and made their way to the Rapidan, again.

They had been up since midnight, packing away whatever last-minute items the men still thought they needed and starting small fires to burn useless items accumulated during the winter. By dawn, they had been in ranks and ready to move. But they didn't move, not right away. Instead, they waited, as they waited now, patiently for their turn to take their place in the seemingly endless blue columns headed south, again.

From where Kevin Bannon stood, watching the columns snake down to the twin pontoon bridges at Germannia Ford, everything seemed to be as it should have been. There was nothing new to this day, the Army's seventh "On to Richmond" drive. It was, Kevin thought, as he watched regiment after regiment march by, a far cry from the first march he had made under McDowell in the summer of '61. There had been a gay, almost carnival atmosphere in the ranks that moved along the road that led to the First Bull Run. Even the uniforms worn by those early regiments reflected that gaiety and were, by today's standards, comical. Now, with the exception of the big, heavy artillery regiments, finally freed up from years of garrison duty in the forts that surrounded Washington, the cohorts that paraded by Kevin had the look of lean, hardened veterans, somber in both dress and demeanor.

You could always tell a veteran unit, Kevin mused. They were the ones that didn't seem to have two hats in the entire unit that matched. Even when the hats were of the same pattern, the owners of them seemed to take great delight in customizing them to their own particular taste and manner of wear. That, and their unit's small size, marked them as an outfit that had seen many a hard fight. That they would soon be smaller still was a given, for the advance that had, until now, gone like clockwork, would eventually invoke a reaction from their nemesis, just as it always had.

Kevin was still deep in thought, watching the regiments go by when Samuel Gaul came up and joined him. " 'Once more unto the breach, dear friends,' " he stated as he held his arms out as if to embrace the masses going by.

Kevin turned, folded his arms, and shrugged. "Go on, Sam, finish the quote."

Dropping his arms, Gaul looked at Kevin, then at the soldiers going by. "Yes," he muttered before looking up at the sky, " 'Or close the wall up with our English dead.' "

"Were it but Englishmen, and not ours, who would be doing so, I'd be far more merry," Kevin sneered. "But seeing as our British cousins, had they chosen to join this affair of states, would be on the other side, I suppose it's better we have no English dead to contend with. Yes," Kevin said, "it's best between us and those of us that remain."

Smiling, Gaul came up next to Kevin and slapped him on the back. "Remain? You say 'remain' as if we were down to our last handful. My God, man, with Burnside's Ninth Corps, we number close to one hundred and twenty thousand men in the ranks, or so I've been told. Even with Long-street back, Lee can't have more than seventy thousand men to stop us."

"Sam, since when have numbers mattered to that man," Kevin countered as he pointed across the river. "And what makes you think he wants to stop us?"

Gaul looked at his friend with a sour expression. "Surely you haven't fallen under the sway of all the 'Bobby Lee the Invincible' stories, have you?"

"No, I haven't. But," Kevin stated as he turned to face Gaul, "if I were a gambling man, and I'm not, mind you, I'd have to hedge my bets since, to date, we've not done well down here, especially in this place." He waved a hand at the trees about them that characterized the wide strip of forest known as the Wilderness.

"This *place*, as you call it, my dear Captain Bannon, will not play a part in this campaign. We'll be through it by tomorrow and out in open country, where our numbers and our guns will settle all old scores."

Kevin snorted. "You are, sir, the eternal optimist."

"And you," Gaul countered, "the quintessential pessimist."

"Well, Sam, I hope you're the one who's right. We need to bring this thing to an end."

Eager to change subjects, Gaul smiled. "Speaking of bringing things to an end, my dear sir," he asked haltingly, "did you, ah, speak with your fair maiden about, ah . . ."

Kevin shook his head and smiled. "No, I didn't." Then he looked up at Gaul. "But I was going to. I swear to God had we stayed in camp another day, I was going to . . ."

"Ha," Gaul bellowed. "How many times have I heard that one? Last fall, just before the Mine Run affair, all you kept telling me was, next week, next week. Then it was to be a Christmas surprise. When that didn't come to be, you claimed you were going to marry Harriet while you were home on furlough. Since then, it has become, well, a joke."

"A joke?" Kevin shot back.

"Yes, my dear Captain Bannon, a joke. Every morning, as the adjutant reports to the colonel, the colonel will simply ask, 'Well, has he?' to which the adjutant, half-smiling will respond, 'No, sir. But maybe next week.' "

Part out of embarrassment, part out of anger, Kevin's cheeks began to turn bright red. "Well, I am glad you are all having a good laugh amongst yourselves at my expense."

Though he tried not to, Gaul laughed as he attempted to calm his friend. "Oh, please, Kevin, don't be angry. We're just, well, curious. I mean, it's obvious that the two of you will be married. I knew that from the first time I saw the two of you together. It's just that we can't understand why you haven't just up and done it."

Kevin looked over toward the river and the unending line of men crossing or waiting to cross, as he let his anger pass. Finally, he looked back at Gaul. "I haven't, Sam, because I love her too much to make her a widow."

Kevin's sober response wiped away Gaul's smile. Sheepishly, he looked down at the ground for a moment, then back up at Kevin's eyes from under the brim of his cap. "In our hearts, Kevin, I think we all know that. There are times I wish I didn't have to carry that burden about with me."

In the silence that followed, the two men looked down at the river. Finally, after watching for several minutes a plain-dressed general astride a big chestnut mare down by the river, Kevin spoke. "Do you really think his coming east is going to make a difference?"

Gaul, now subdued, shook his head as he studied General U. S. Grant. "Lord, I hope so. With all my heart, I hope so. Otherwise . . ."

There was no need to finish his statement, for both men knew that if the Union suffered another humbling defeat at the hands of the Confederacy, Lincoln would fail in his bid for reelection. And with him would go their dream of one, united country. That all depended on what they did in the next few weeks weighed heavily on those of the Army who cared to give the matter much thought. That, together with the realization that achieving success was going to be costly, no matter who led the Army, made the beginning of this campaign more sober and solemn than any Kevin could remember.

When word finally came that they were moving, Kevin and Sam Gaul rejoined their commands and took their place in the long column of blue headed into battle, again.

South of the Rapidan, Along Orange Plank Road

THOUGH THE PACE OF the 4th Virginia was brisk, their officers repeatedly called out to the men up and down the line of march to close up. On the side of the road, wherever there was a break in the dense woods big enough, stern-faced general officers and their staffs sat upon horses that pranced about in nervous anticipation. These, and other telltale signs, left no doubt that this was the opening move of their fourth summer of bloody campaigns.

In the ranks, every man faced the prospects of battle in his own way. From two ranks behind him, James Bannon could hear Josh Major voicing his opinion of the whole affair. "Well, Virg," he called over to Virgil Hallett, "I can say I really don't mind leaving that camp. It wasn't too bad in the winter when everything was frozen and all, but I'll tell ya, it sure was starting to get ripe."

"You know, Josh," William Pool shouted to him, "I was beginning to think the same thing. Only now, after marching next to you all mornin', I've come to the conclusion that it wasn't the camp that smelled so bad."

Several of the men about Major and Pool began to laugh. Confused, Josh Major looked about him. "What's that suppose ta mean?"

"Josh," Lieutenant Updike called from the side of the column, "do me a favor and don't go and hurt your brain trying to figure it out. Just concentrate on keeping it closed up, okay?"

Josh Major was a good man who was, in Marty Hazard's words, "Just this side of bein' simpleminded." James, though he liked Josh, had to agree with Marty, which was why he and Marty were always on guard to make sure no one took advantage of him or did anything mean-spirited to him. That didn't mean that James or Marty fought all his fights. In cases like this where it was simple kidding, James didn't say a word. He just sort of let things follow their natural course and kept to himself, as he usually did during a march.

At that moment, his mind was wandering about from one subject to another in no particular order. Like most of the men in the ranks, arranged four abreast in normal march order and in columns that stretched on and on for miles, James was bent forward with his head bowed slightly. At this angle, his eyes fell upon the heels of the man in front of him. The shoes this man wore were not much different than those worn by any other man belonging to the Army of Northern Virginia who was lucky enough to have them. They were the rough brown lace-ups with wooden heels, known as brogans. Whatever mud had gathered on them had been knocked off by this morning's march, except for a few traces still caked about between the sole and uppers. No one much worried about the condition of shoes anymore, at least not as far as polish and cleanliness were concerned. Just having a pair that was serviceable was all that mattered anymore to the men in the ranks.

As they marched and James watched, he could see that the man in front of him would soon join the ranks of the shoeless. Both heels were well worn, with signs of a slight crack showing on the left heel. On the right shoe, James could see a small gap developing between the sole and the upper leather. They wouldn't last more than a couple of weeks of hard marching, James figured. But then, it wouldn't matter much. The man's feet would be toughened up and the weather would be hot. Boots during summer campaigns were considered a hindrance by some. It wouldn't be until the fall that he'd miss them.

Suddenly, James felt a wave of sadness sweep over him. Looking up and to his left, he studied the trees along their line of march. Alive with the lush greenness of a new spring, they looked the same, he thought, as they had when he and Will McPherson had set out for Harpers Ferry together three years prior. The season and the men he marched with, like the leaves on the trees, were young and so full of life, just as they had been in the spring of '62 and '63. But the heat of the summer, like the many battles of the 4th Virginia, always followed, toughening leaf and men, until both were sinewy and mature enough to endure the heat of battle, the harshness of summer. Yet no matter how tough a leaf became, James thought, in due course nature would take it, just like this war without end was slowly taking them all, one by one. They were, he concluded, all destined to fall away like the dried dead leaves of the fall despite all the promises of life that each spring brought forth.

Slowly, James let his head drop and turned his face, once more, to the front. The gap in the man's right shoe looked bigger now. No, James thought, those shoes won't last long. But perhaps, he concluded, with another big battle in the making, they might last just long enough for the man wearing them. With that grim thought stuck in his mind, James trudged on, one man lost in his thoughts amongst thousands, moving forward at a brisk pace into the forest and wilderness of Virginia.

One Mile South of the Rapidan, near Germannia Ford

WHEN DARKNESS CLOSED DOWN about them at the end of the first day of this new campaign, the soldiers of the 4th New Jersey drew in closer to the small cook fires each little clutch of men had started. As Kevin Bannon made his way from one group to another, he couldn't help but notice that the men were quiet. Even the talkers in his company of just under forty men seemed to be subdued by a mood that Sam Gaul described as reflective melancholy. "Perhaps," Captain Charles Paul commented that night to a group of officers gathered about a fire that served as regimental headquarters, "the gloom of these forests is affecting the men. It is said that the Germans are a sad and dour race due to their ancestors' close association with such places as the Black Forest."

Kevin listened, but said nothing as this theory was batted back and forth by his fellow officers until it was discarded and another substituted in its place. Like his men, Kevin felt the same dark foreboding, a feeling more than a thought, which the Wilderness they were passing through brought forth from the depth of each man's soul. The 4th New Jersey hadn't fought in these woods the year before, as he had. They didn't carry with them the memory of the rout and panic that had marked the second night of that battle. Their minds weren't deeply etched with the vicious and confused fighting around the Chancellorsville Inn, as his was. For his fellow officers, men who had not participated in a major engagement since December, 1862, this campaign was a chance to prove, once and for all, that the 4th New Jersey was as good, if not better, than any regiment in the brigade, if not the whole Sixth Corps. For Kevin, the pending battle that hung before them was real, as real as if it had already happened. Yet it hadn't. Instead, it hung out there, somewhere close by, like a vicious predator stalking them in the dense and tangled Wilderness just beyond the light of their cook fires.

Looking up from the fire, Kevin's eyes darted about, almost as if he were looking for the imagined beast he knew to be waiting. "You certainly are the quiet one tonight, Mr. Bannon," a fellow company commander called out. Kevin, having lost himself in his own thoughts, hadn't been keeping up with the conversation that had been going on back and forth across the fire. Blinking, he looked at all the faces, lit with the eerie, shimmering, yellow glow of firelight, as they stared at him.

For several seconds, no one said anything. Finally, Sam Gaul, seeing that Kevin had been deep in thought and was at a loss as to what to say, broke the silence by stretching his arms and yawning. "Well, gentlemen, I for one intend to make one more round of my company and then it's bed for me. This getting up at midnight and marching about all day is hard on body and soul and, if I understand the lay of things correctly, we'll have another day of it tomorrow."

"Well," a young lieutenant on his first campaign piped up, "if you ask me, I'll gladly roll out of bed every day at midnight and march till dusk if that marching takes us closer to Richmond."

"I suppose you noticed," Sam Gaul stated to the young officer, "that not only did no one ask you, but I believe no one much cares what your druthers are." As the other officers broke out in laughter, Gaul moved behind Kevin and tapped him on his shoulder. "Care to go along with me?"

Without hesitation, or saying a thing to the others, Kevin turned to leave with Gaul. Then, as if called back by an inner voice, he stopped, faced about, and looked at each of the men still standing about the fire. They were all very much alive, he thought as he watched them laughing over Gaul's comment or chatting with a companion next to them. Still, Kevin could not let go of the idea that some of those young, smiling faces would soon join others that were now nothing more than memories. Looking away, toward the dark forest to the west, Kevin peered into the blackness in search of the beast that was, he knew, closing in on them for the kill.

On the Orange Plank Road

NOT PAYING ANY ATTENTION to what was going on around him, James Bannon plowed into the back of the man in front of him when the column was halted just short of the intersection with the Germannia Plank Road. Used to such occurrences, the man, the same one whose shoes James had been studying so intently the day before, said nothing. Instead, he was standing on his tiptoes, looking about in an effort to see why they had stopped so suddenly. Also looking around, James couldn't see much to the front or rear on the crowded road. Above, through a break in the trees, he could see the sun beating down on them from a clear, blue sky. That put the time about noon, but that was all he could be sure of. The sounds of gunfire, mostly the spattering of rifle fire here and there, was muffled by the dense woods that separated James from the distant combatants.

Coming up next to James, Marty Hazard took his long rifle off his shoulder, set the butt of the stock in the dirt on the road, and grasped the muzzle end of it with both hands. Just then the sound of a ragged volley from somewhere up ahead drifted back to them. "Well, now," Marty said perking up a bit, "sounds like someone just bumped into a heap of trouble."

James, looking at the thickets that enclosed them, chuckled. "That's the only way, I guess, anyone's going to find anyone else if we fight here. I can't imagine why Grant would want to fight us in such a godawful place as this. They'll never be able to use their artillery, let alone his great huge force they're supposed to have."

Marty, leaning over his rifle, spat onto the roadway. "Seems to me it makes no difference where we fight, just so long as we get on with it."

Douglas Geddy, who had been marching along next to James in silence most of the morning, shook his head. "Does this regiment always fight in the woods? I mean, last fall, our only fight was in the woods not far from here. And some of the boys who had fought at Gettysburg said you were in the woods when the regiment did most of its fighting on the third day."

Marty looked over to Geddy and smiled. "Well, I guess we're just lucky, ain't we?"

An echo of orders to leave the road and make their way to the right came rippling back through the ranks from front to rear and ended their brief conversation. Looking over to that side of the road, the north side, both James and Marty shook their heads. Marty whistled. "I'll bet General Walker spent all morning looking for the worst part of these here Wilderness forests before he found the thickest, ugliest patch of woods to march us into."

James, rearranging his equipment to make sure that it would be behind him and out of the way as much as possible, laughed. "Ah, Marty, quit your complaining. Least you won't have to worry about running into Union cavalry while we're in there."

"Since when," Marty shot back, "has anyone had to worry about that? In three years, I've yet to see my first dead cavalryman."

Lieutenant Updike's order to come to attention and file to the right, by column, into the woods, cut the lighthearted conversation short. Making their way through dense switches and scrub oak that was even more difficult to pass through than pine trees, on occasion the 4th Virginia came across a man belonging to General Stuart's mixed brigade of North Carolinians and Virginians. One young man, his face bleeding from a cut inflicted by a branch that had smacked him in the face, grabbed James' arm as he went by. "Hey, have you seen where the Twenty-third Virginia went to?"

Anxious to keep up with the men in front of him, who had already been swallowed by the dense growth, James pulled away from the youth, doing nothing more than pointing to his right. "Keep going that way and you'll find them."

From behind James, Josh Major shouted out, "Either that, boy, or you'll find the Yanks."

This comment brought a hail of laughter for a moment until everyone got back to the business of keeping up with the man in front while avoiding, as best they could, swinging branches that came flying back from the man in front, sharp thorns that ripped away bits of clothing and flesh, and vines that wrapped themselves about ankles and feet. After a while, the only voice James heard was Updike's as he continued to shout back, "Keep it closed up, men. Keep it closed up."

In due time, the order to halt, followed by the command to face right, brought their ordeal to an end. "All right, men," Updike shouted when everyone had managed to push and shove their way into position as best the vegetation would permit. "Okay, men. We're to start building breastworks facing to the east."

Marty looked about. "Say, Lieutenant, sir?"

"Yes, First Sergeant?" Updike responded patiently.

"Which way is east?"

In the Wilderness

WHEN THE NEW JERSEY Brigade went forward, it did so in fits and starts. Regiments and companies moved forward, speeding up to a double-quick one moment, then slowing down, or even halting, the next moment in order to conform to the movement of the unit on its immediate left or right. The reason for that was quite obvious and, given the nature of the dense woods, unavoidable. From his position on the 4th New Jersey's far left, Kevin found it impossible to keep his eye on the regimental commander. Only the forward motion of the company to his right alerted him that he needed to give the order for his company to advance. How the regimental commander, let alone the brigade commander, would be able to control anything once serious fighting started was beyond him.

Concerned with his own company, Kevin looked to the right, down its staggered line as it moved forward. None of the neat precision that he had been able to instill in them on the drill field during the winter and early spring was evident here. Instead, men went along, mostly in clusters, as best they could. When faced with a tree trunk or a particularly nasty patch of briars, they would move around them as individuals, crowding the men in formation next to them one way or another. Once clear of the obstacle, the man avoiding it would find himself behind the man whom he had been next to, or even in front of, a moment before. Shifting back into his own position as quickly as the ground littered with fallen tree trunks and vines permitted, the man would soon find himself either faced with a new impediment or being pushed aside by someone else avoiding his own obstructions. Kevin himself was not immune from such concerns as he divided his time, as best he could, between keeping in alignment with the company to the right, listening for commands from the regimental commander, watching his own company, and picking his way forward through the tangled forest.

It should have come as no surprise, then, when a thin line of Confederate riflemen sprang up without warning from the ground and fired into the advancing ranks of the 4th New Jersey at a range of forty yards.

For a moment, the line of Jerseymen wavered, as some men tromped on stoically while others brought their weapons to their shoulders to fire, and still others sought safety behind the very trees that they had been trying to avoid a moment before. Kevin himself was at a momentary loss as to whether to press the advance and close with the enemy or stand and fire. Looking to his right, he tried to make out what the regimental commander was saying. This effort, however, was quickly defeated by the deafening roar and billows of smoke produced by a ragged volley delivered by the company to his right. Turning his attention back to his own command, he took one step out to the front and ordered the company to halt and prepare to fire. His efforts were for naught, for the men, collectively, had already decided on their own to do so, opening a lively fire in the direction which the enemy had disappeared into.

Not sure of his own senses in the confusion, Kevin turned to his first sergeant. "Sergeant Himmel, can you see anything?"

Taking a step forward, Himmel squinted his eyes and scanned the front where everyone was shooting. Then he shook his head. "I can see nothing. No enemy. But I could be mistaken, sir."

Kevin knew better and proceeded to yell for his company to cease fire and reform their ranks. This was no easy task as many of the men simply could not hear Kevin and some of those who could decided that they knew better than he did and continued to fire until a sergeant or corporal grabbed their shoulder or shouted in their ear to hold their fire. For several minutes, the men shuffled about in the thick smoke produced by gunfire as they settled back into the ranks. Kevin, pulling out a handkerchief, wiped his brow, looked to where the regimental commander stood, and waited for the order to advance. As he did so, he noticed that the smell of burning leaves and woods was now mixing with the stench of burned powder. "There'll be hell to pay, First Sergeant," he commented dryly. "The woods are on fire."

Himmel, busy loading his rifle, looked up, catching a glimpse here and there of a small fire in the undergrowth. "Ya, it will be a hot fight. It would be best we keep moving, I think. Maybe we'll come out of these cursed forests."

When the word echoed down from company to company, finally reaching him, Kevin gave his company the order to advance and watched as it lurched forward, into the smoke, to continue the advance.

The firing to their left came as no surprise to the men of the 4th Virginia. After having built up the best breastworks that time and tools on hand permitted, the men had settled down to wait for the enemy or a new order to move. The lighthearted humor and lively talk of the morning had been replaced by a quiet, solemn mood as men took out small pocket Bibles and read them or simply mumbled silent prayers.

The sounds of battle, followed by the familiar odor of burned powder, drifted over their positions from the south. Marty Hazard, sitting with his back to a tree as he slowly rubbed the barrel of his rifle with a dry rag, looked off into the dense forest in that direction. "The boys back on the road are either catching hell or givin' it to the Yanks."

James looked in the same direction, chuckled, and then turned to Marty. "I suppose it's a little of both. Usually is in a fight like this."

Geddy, looking in the same direction as the two veterans, then back at them, wondered what they were looking at. "Do you think that fight will make it up this far?"

Marty laughed. "Well, boy, it will either find its way to us or we'll go lookin' for it as both sides feel for the other's flank. Either, or . . ."

"Or," James interrupted, "we'll find our own little fight right here as another Union unit tries to cut their way around to the rear."

"Either way, boy," Marty concluded, "we'll be in it for sure by sunset."

Unnerved by the inability to do anything about such a catastrophe that seemed so near at hand, Geddy began to squirm, looking one way, then the other as he tried to figure out which way the unseen danger would come from. When the firing to their left rear broke out, he all but jumped out of his skin. "What's that about?" he shouted in dismay.

James Bannon and Marty Hazard, looking in the general direction of the firing, listened intently as the spattering of individual rifle shots was followed by a series of solid volleys. "Well, Jimmy boy," Marty mused, "seems like you win the prize for guessin' right this time."

Geddy, unnerved and confused by Marty's response, looked, listened, but still did not understand. "What's he mean, James? What's going on?"

The appearance of several men, Confederates, coming from their left and running for all they were worth toward them and away from the gunfire, delayed James' response. Instead, James brought himself up on one knee, pulled the hammer on his rifle back to the half-cocked position to make sure a cap was firmly in place, and looked off in the direction that everyone was now watching.

"Damn it, Bannon! What's going on?"

With a face that betrayed no emotion, James looked back at Geddy. "We've been flanked, Douglas."

It wasn't an easy advance, nor was it steady. The regimental line would advance, or more correctly, lurch forward several yards, stop, fire a ragged, disjointed volley or two, and then move forward again in an uneven wave rather than a precise, straight line. Kevin, now far more attentive to what was going on in front than before, seldom saw anything that justified the volumes of fire that the regiment, and probably the entire brigade, was throwing into the woods before them. That there was someone out there was made obvious by the zing of scores of miniés flying through the air nearby and, every now and then, the moan of a man in the ranks as he was hit and went down. Strange, Kevin thought as he divided his time between watching his own unit, listening for orders from his commander, and keeping an eye open for an enemy attack, that despite all the noise and chaos going on all about him, he could still pick out the peculiar thud that the large .58 caliber miniés made when they hit a man square on. He wondered whether it was just his imagination or if, in fact, he really was hearing the sickening noise that served as death notice to a man in his own ranks.

The sudden appearance of dead and wounded Rebels underfoot alerted Kevin that their firing had not been for naught. They were closing with the enemy and, from judging the angle of their now abandoned earthworks, the First New Jersey Brigade had hit the enemy in the flank. Encouraged and feeling confident for the first time that day, Kevin waved his pistol over his head and shouted down the line of troops. "Keep pushing them, men, we've got them. Keep pushing."

Like rabbits that had sensed danger, the men of the 4th Virginia, with and without their officers' having to tell them to do so, began to leave the breastworks they had worked on and turned to face the new threat coming down upon their flank. Colonel William Terry, commander of the two hundred or so who made up the 4th Virginia, had fallen back to a position that was at a sharp angle to the regiment's original position. There, with the aid of his staff and company commanders, he was forming a firing line with which to meet the enemy and protect the flank and rear of the next regiment down the line. This wasn't an easy task. Not only did the woods and undergrowth make anything resembling a line near impossible, but the flight of frightened and confused men from the 5th and 27th Virginia through the new line also added to the chaos. General James Walker, commander of the Stonewall Brigade, was in the midst of the confusion, helping Terry build a line while trying to rally the panicked elements of the two regiments that had born the brunt of the Union flank attack.

For his part, Lieutenant Updike, catching a glimpse of the regimental colors and the colonel standing with them, turned, yelled for his men to follow, and made straight for the colors. Marty and James, side by side, followed Updike. Everyone else, including Douglas Geddy, followed them. Already some of the companies that had been nearer were forming to the right of the colors. Updike, knowing his position was on the regiment's far left, ran behind those companies, trailing a line of men. Once past the colors, he began to judge how much space he needed to leave for those companies that needed to form between him and the colors. When he got to where he judged he needed to be, Updike stopped and faced about. Stretching his right arm out and pointing to where he wanted the company line formed behind him, he shouted at the gaggle of men coming up with James now in the lead, "Company J, Fourth Virginia, here. Form here."

With an ease born of experience, the veterans fell in place directing or physically manhandling the newer men into their proper places. "Form and settle down," Updike shouted as he trooped the front of his company line with an occasional glance over his shoulder. "Make sure you're loaded and primed."

Though he was sure that he had done so, James brought his rifle up to the ready, put his thumb on the hammer, and checked to make sure that the little copper percussion cap hadn't fallen off during their sprint through the woods. Satisfied as soon as he saw it, he looked over to Geddy. "Your piece primed and ready to fire?"

Geddy, who was clearly shaken by the experience, didn't respond. Instead, he watched as the last survivors of the 5th and 27th Virginia flew past their thin line. With wide eyes and a wild expression, Geddy turned to face James. "Does the colonel intend to stand here and fight?"

In a voice that was so calm that it was unnerving, James asked, "You got any better ideas, Douglas?"

Before answering, Geddy took one quick glance to the rear, at the backs of men now out of the fight, and then to the front, where smoke from small fires and burned powder hung close to the ground. Though he longed to turn and join those who had already fled, he was too paralyzed by fear to move. Besides, his troubled mind reasoned, if he fled, he'd be headed into a great unknown, going away from the only people who now mattered and whom he could rely on to pull him through this. Though there was now no doubt that he would be in the midst of a real battle within minutes, maybe seconds, the dangers of the unknown, to be faced alone if he ran, seemed more daunting to him at that moment. With a jerky shake of his head, Geddy finally responded. "No, guess not."

"Hey Jimmy," Marty Hazard called out from behind. "Make way and let me in." Without taking his eyes from the front, James shouldered his way to the left to make way in the front rank for Marty Hazard. "Getting slow in your old age, Marty?"

"My leg, boy. It's that darn blamed leg the Yanks seem to have taken a fancy to. Two bullet holes in three years in the same leg would be enough to slow down a saint the way I see it," Marty replied.

"Dear Lord," Josh Major hollered from somewhere off to the left. "The end must be near. Marty Hazard is comparing himself to the saints now."

"Settle down, men. Cut the chatter and settle down." That command, coming from Colonel Terry, brought all conversation in the ranks to an end. In silence, the men stood waiting, listening to the sounds of battle, now to both their front, left, and rear. Mixed together, the cries of wounded, the crackling of wood burning, and the shouts of orders, some near, some far, were the only sounds the men heard as they watched.

"Heeere they come," Marty stated in a slow, soft tone.

Peering through the smoke, James could make out the fleeting images of men, looking more like shadows, as they emerged from the dense woods and undergrowth choked with smoke. "Fourth Virginia!" Colonel Terry commanded. "Ready! Aim!" He paused, looked once more to confirm that the people coming at him were wearing Union blue, then shouted, "FIRE!"

The impact of the sudden volley was staggering. Before Kevin Bannon knew they were in trouble, the second sergeant belonging to the company to his right lurched forward, doubled up, and fell to the ground at Kevin's feet. Leaping up and over the stricken man at the last minute to avoid tripping over him, Kevin landed on one foot and fought to gain his balance. He lost, falling backward against the ranks of his own company.

As he scrambled on the ground in an effort to get up, someone from down the line—the colonel he thought—gave the command, "Ready, aim, fire!" in quick, jerky shouts. His company, he saw, responded in a haphazard fashion as some men less shaken by the sudden volley delivered at close range responded faster than others. Seeing no sense in slowing down their rate of fire in order to deliver a massed volley, Kevin shouted from where he lay, "Independent fire, fire at will."

First Sergeant Himmel, standing before Kevin and believing that Kevin had been hit and was issuing his dying command, gave Kevin a sorrowful look, then turned his attention to the company, repeating Kevin's command to ensure that it had been heard. "Fire at will, men. Fire at will."

When he saw that his company was holding its ground and returning fire, Kevin turned over and began to rise, just as the Confederates delivered another, more ragged volley. A sharp pain, like a man hitting him in the small of the back, forced Kevin back down on the ground. Stunned this time, Kevin lay sprawled, facedown on the ground for a moment while he fought to catch his breath. Around him, he could hear his company and the rest of the regiment firing for all they were worth while the air was filled with the zing of return fire. Bits and pieces of leaves and twigs, shot off by bullets fired too high, fell down all about him like rain.

He was, Kevin decided, in hell. Screams of men just hit and the moans or animallike shrieks of men already wounded combined with the continual clatter of rifle fire, adding to Kevin's impression of unbridled carnage and death. It is safe down here, he thought as he struggled to regain his senses. If he stayed there a little while longer, he would be safe from all the horrors and dangers that were filling the air just a few feet above him. But with his next thought, he reminded himself that he was an officer, a company commander. He was expected to lead his men, regardless of the danger, regardless of the cost. He had, by his own hand, accepted the commission that had been offered him. He had, by his signature, pledged himself to perform all duties expected of an officer, a pledge he had renewed just a few scant months before. And besides, as he began to think in practical terms, the body that lay across his back was heavy and making breathing difficult.

With some effort, Kevin managed to twist himself about till the body on him lay across his stomach. With a shove against the corpse with one hand, and push up off the ground with the other, Kevin managed to sit up.

The man who had fallen upon him and knocked him onto the ground now lay across his legs, lifeless. For a moment, Kevin looked at the body out of nothing more than simple curiosity as to who it was. Then when he recognized the shape and form of the body, for there was no longer a face to speak of to assist him in recognition, Kevin felt his stomach turn. Laying his hand upon the still chest of his dead first sergeant, Kevin let out a groan. "My dear Frederick," he whispered in words that were lost to all except himself, "good-bye."

The frantic rate of fire that the 4th Virginia had initially greeted the horde of Union troops creeping about their flank had slowed to a steady pop-pop-pop as each man began to take his time with reloading and firing. Though he had been with the regiment for nine months and had listened to the stories of James Bannon and Marty Hazard, Douglas Geddy, in his second battle, was beginning to wonder about the sanity of his messmates. In the beginning of their fight, Geddy had fancied that he had seen targets when he went to take aim and fire. At least, he thought, he had seen something.

Now, however, he saw nothing. The woods, thick and impenetrable before the fighting started, were now filled with great clouds of smoke from rifle fire and burning woods. The white, acrid smoke stung and burned his eyes, causing them to water, further obscuring his already limited vision. Between shots, as he brought his rifle down to reload, Geddy would wipe the sleeve of his wool shell jacket across his face in an effort to clear the sweat and tears from his eyes. The sensation reminded him of being downwind of a particularly smoky campfire. Unlike a campfire, however, where one could easily shift to one side or another to escape the bothersome smoke, there was no place, from what he could see, where there was a patch of woods free from the thick, choking haze.

Besides, even if there was someplace nearby where he could find a breath of fresh air, he wouldn't be able to go over to it. To one side stood James Bannon, his face frozen in a stonelike expression that betrayed no emotion as he mechanically loaded his rifle, brought it up to his shoulder, aimed, fired, and brought it down again to reload. To the other side was Marty Hazard. Unlike James, he was exhilarated. It seemed to Geddy that the chaos, confusion, and smoke that so annoyed him animated Marty to extremes of excitement and agitation that Geddy had never witnessed before in any man, living or dead. Where Bannon stood silent and stoic, Hazard shouted, and even gestured at the enemy, who were, for the most part, masked by the smoke that their firing only seemed to add to. "Try this one on for size, you filthy Yankee," he'd yell as he shouldered his rifle, took aim at God knew what, and fired. Or as he loaded, he'd lean forward, jutting his jaw as far as he could, and shout above the din of battle, "Come on, damn ya. What are ya waiting for, you lily-livered trash. Come on and fight." Not even the necessity of having to step around the body of Lieutenant Updike, lying facedown at their feet, with white knuckled fingers clawing their way into the layers of dried leaves and dirt, seemed to moderate the extremes of either men. They were, Geddy reasoned, possessed, perhaps mad. Yet as bad as that was, he thought, he was there with them, standing between them, firing blindly, wildly, at an enemy who only made its presence felt by felling another man in the thinning firing line. Thank God, Geddy thought as he went about ramming another round home, the smoke worked both ways. Otherwise, he reasoned, things would be far worse.

No one seemed to be in much of a hurry to continue the slow advance that had taken the 4th New Jersey this far. Rather, everyone, from the men on the firing line to those few senior officers Kevin caught an occasional glimpse of, was quite content to stand where he was, firing away at the shadowy enemy line that had stopped them in their tracks. Perhaps this was where they were supposed to be. Perhaps they were holding the enemy's attention while another brigade or division was swinging about the enemy's open flank beyond. Kevin hoped that was the case, for he had no great desire to continue the advance or charge into the steady and murderous enemy fire that poured through the smoke-filled woods like invisible fingers of death. No, Kevin thought as he watched his men stand and return the Confederate fire, he was quite content to hold his ground here. Let another brigade go blundering about through the woods in search of the enemy's flank and glory, provided, of course, that someone at division or corps had the mind to order that.

Walking slowly along the rear of his ranks, stepping carefully over the bodies of those who had already been stricken, Kevin watched his men as they went through the slow, tedious drill of reloading and firing, something that became more and more difficult as their rifles fouled from hard, continual use. That they hadn't made any difference to the situation for the past hour didn't seem to bother his men or his superiors. All was in order, Kevin decided, and was as it should be.

As he approached Johnny O'Keeth, the young Irish sergeant stepped out of ranks. He was now the second ranking noncommissioned officer in the company by virtue of survival. "Begging the captain's pardon, sir, but we're beginning to run low on ammunition."

This sent a chill down Kevin's spine. Once before, during the Battle of Gaines's Mill, the regiment had stood on the firing line, much as it was doing now, and had expended all of its ammunition. Though it had been relieved by a fresh Pennsylvania unit, the 4th New Jersey, with empty cartridge boxes, had been compelled to surrender when it had run smack into a Confederate unit in their rear. Suddenly, the image of a Confederate unit finding their flank, instead of vice versa, began to haunt Kevin. Placing his hand on O'Keeth's shoulder, he leaned forward. "Okay, Sergeant. Go down the line and find the regimental commander, the adjutant, or a field grade and tell them we're down to our last few rounds. I'll spread the word here to slow the rate of fire and take better aim."

"Sir," O'Keeth responded in surprise, "there's not a bloody whole lot we can take aim at. The boys and I have been banging away in whatever direction the rifle barrel was pointed at. We can't see the blasted enemy, no more than I imagine they can see us."

Kevin closed his eyes, smiled, and shook his head. "Yes, yes, I know. Still," he added as he opened his eyes and looked through the firing line in the direction where the enemy fire was coming from, "we must be doing some good, otherwise they wouldn't have kept us here firing all this time."

O'Keeth, having grown suspicious of the military wisdom of his superiors, looked in the same direction that Kevin was staring at. "Well, I suppose you're right, sir."

Though he was just as suspicious as O'Keeth, Kevin didn't show it. Instead, he looked at Johnny, smiled, and patted his shoulder. "Of course I'm right. Now get on with your task and make it quick. I don't want to be left standing here with nothing but an empty cartridge box and a smile to greet a Rebel charge."

"Oh," O'Keeth beamed back with a broad smile. "No need to worry about that, Captain. First Sergeant made sure each of the boys had an extra ten rounds in their pockets before stepping off yesterday. We'll do okay."

The mention of Himmel caused Kevin to look down to the front of his tunic. Himmel's blood, now dried to a dark stain, served as a bitter reminder that this fight, regardless of whether it turned out to be a foolish blunder or brilliant stroke, had cost him dearly. Turning, Kevin began to walk away, calling to O'Keeth as he did so, "Go on, Sergeant. Get on with it. And be quick about it."

At first, there was little to indicate that the enemy fire had slackened. Then, as if by instinct, the men, one at a time, fired their last round, brought their rifles down, reloaded them, but did not return them to their shoulder to fire. James Bannon, with his head cocked to one side, listened for a moment. Marty Hazard did likewise. "What do ya think, Jimmy boy? Yanks have enough for the time being?"

James shook his head. "They're rotating units. Bringing up a fresh regiment, maybe even a brigade."

Without having to be told, Marty lay his rifle down, its barrel literally smoking from firing, and began to pull at a log behind him. "Well, if they gonna keep it up, we'd best improve our positions while we got the chance." Marty looked up at Geddy. "Come on, boy, give me a hand with this."

Without anyone having given the order, most of the men scrambled about the small area where they stood and foraged for anything that looked like it would be useful in stopping a bullet. Geddy and Marty worked together. James stood alone, behind a tree, and watched and listened. While they were still building their hasty breastworks up a little higher, James moved away from his tree and crouched behind it. "Best take up your rifles, boys. Here they come again."

Geddy, already exhausted by his efforts, choking from the fumes of burning wood and gunpowder, and sickened by the sight of dead and wounded scattered about the thin firing line, moaned. "Oh, God, no. How much longer do they expect us to continue like this?"

James looked over to Geddy. "God has nothing to do with this," he snapped. Though he felt for the boy, he had no words of comfort for him. It seemed, James thought, as if he had used them all up, a long time ago. Now, as he checked the cap on his rifle to make sure it was snugly fit to the cone, he whispered, more to himself than to Geddy, "Until the end, my friend. Until the end."

What sort of end that would be, James did not know. Nor did he have time to ponder that question as a new unit, having replaced the 4th New Jersey and the rest of the First New Jersey Brigade, opened a vicious, if poorly aimed volley fire on their line.

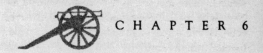

CHAPTER 6

In the Wilderness, Virginia, May, 1864

FOR HARRIET, THE SOUND of gunfire, followed in short order by an unending stream of wounded, was the end of a dream, a fantasy. The gallant and boastful officers, who had stood so proud, so resplendent in their dashing uniforms during the winter balls and formal dress parades, were now being carried back to the field hospitals by the cartloads. As they were taken off and laid out on the barren ground, she could see that the youthful kiss of life that had colored their cheeks was gone, drained till only a sickly, pale white remained. Eyes that had glimmered and glistened in the soft, warm candlelight of quiet dinners and gaily lit dance floors now sank into dark hollow sockets, lifeless pools of blackness, or jumped into frenzied twitching as they bore the suffering that included both their own and that which they had just recently witnessed. The spring, a time of great promise, natural beauty, and reassuring rebirth, Harriet knew, was over. In its place, the renewal of war brought back the killing season.

With well-practiced hands and a calmness that belied the horror and revulsion she felt inside, Harriet went about assisting the hospital stewards and surgeons as wave after wave of mangled and maimed men were sorted according to their wounds and needs, and prepared for further treatment. Over here, those who did not appear to be too badly wounded were set down and, when time permitted, given some attention. There, nearer to the surgical tents, the men whose wounds demanded immediate attention were taken and prepared by doctors and medical orderlies for the rigors of surgery. And off to one side, near the growing line of dead poorly concealed from the still living, were those men for whom there was no hope. Harriet, for her part, tried to spend as much time with these lost poor souls as she could.

On days like this, when she was in the midst of so much suffering, so much human wreckage, Harriet would pause and wonder, sometimes out loud, whether what she was doing really mattered. She often debated this issue with herself in her diary. "*Is my presence here,*" she asked in different ways many, many times, "*in this terrible place of carnage, suffering, and death, worth the horrors I find myself exposed to almost daily when the killing season is upon us? Are the sacrifices, both of my own personal comfort, not to mention ostracism by family and the social class which, I am told, I should be joining, commensurate with the good I am doing? I find myself asking these questions almost nightly in the quiet of my own little tent after the last note of taps fades into the darkness and before I pass off to sleep. And yet, when the sounds of battle drift back toward the field hospital, even before the first wounded man makes his way to us, all such concerns disappear.*

"*I do not pretend to regard myself as highly as our esteemed Doctor White or the other surgeons whose skilled hands work tirelessly in their efforts to save lives. Yet, somehow, I know that my contributions here are important. Perhaps not to the nation or our cause, but rather to the men who march in the defense of both and whom fate has chosen to suffer for them. I have poured a few drops of water over too many a parched lip, washed away the grime of burned powder, dried mud, and caked-on blood from too many faces, or simply held the hand of boys, for a mere moment, as they prepared themselves to pass into the great unknown of death to doubt that I am needed here, now. A soothing word, a friendly smile, a warm, gentle hand, I believe, is, at times, as important to these men in their hour of greatest need as the surgeon's saw or splint. So I stay, endure, and serve. And of course, I pray. Each and every night, I pray that this will all end, that the horrors that are paraded before my eyes, both when I am awake and when I sleep, will come to an end. But they continue. Dear Lord, they continue. And so long as they do, so must I.*"

Harriet wasn't sure if the sentiments she harbored were shared by the handful of women who worked in the hospitals so near the front. For they, like the shattered men they sought to comfort, put on a brave and noble front. That was, after all, expected of her. Despite all her education, despite her own doubts, and in spite of her apparent rejection of social convention, Harriet carried on in a manner befitting a lady.

Working quickly and quietly, Harriet went from soldier to soldier, a rag in one hand, a cup in the other, and half a dozen or so canteens taken from those who would never again need them over her shoulder. When she could, she would smile as she approached each man who was conscious, kneeling at his side so she could wipe the cool rag across his hot forehead. Those who could, even when they were in pain, would return her smile, even if it was twisted and contorted with pain. As she worked quickly, a wipe across the brow that turned and ran down one side of the face and then up the other, Harriet would offer them a drink. Most accepted. When they could, they would prop themselves up on an elbow and take as much as she offered. Those who couldn't sit up would be helped by Harriet. Placing her hand behind their head, she would lift it slightly, watching the soldier's expression for any sign that she was causing them pain.

Often, the men would grasp her hand as she brought the cup to their lips. In part, this was to steady the cup as well as control the amount they took in. But there was also a need on their part to touch Harriet, to feel a hand that was, compared to theirs, small, soft, and soothing. A year and a half ago, such familiarity by a stranger would have been greeted by shock and immediate withdrawal of her hand. But much had changed in that time. Like the common soldiers whom she now tended, Harriet came to view the cold aloofness that was a hallmark of proper Victorian society as something to be scorned.

Every now and then, Harriet would come across a man so badly disfigured by his wound that she had all she could do to control her revulsion. Face wounds were common, she was told, when men were fighting from behind breastworks and for her were the most difficult to deal with. A wound to an arm or leg, even in the chest or abdomen could be ignored simply by locking eyes with the soldier she was tending to. In those cases where a man would ask her to look at his wounds and tell him if she thought they were bad, Harriet would respond with a warm smile. "I'm sorry," she would respond. "I'm not a trained surgeon and I really wouldn't be able to judge its severity," even if she knew better. But a face wound, that was different. There was no way of averting her eyes when she was with a man so injured. And though she tried hard not to show it, often her feelings showed through. One man, his lower jaw all but shot away and hanging by a few stray strands of torn flesh and muscle, started to cry as Harriet stared at him. Though she often thought about avoiding men wounded in this manner by simply bypassing them, Harriet's sense of dedication drove her to endure the horror, time, and time, and time again.

Almost as difficult for her were those who asked her, in their agony, to write their wives, mothers, sisters, or whomever. Harriet would listen patiently as she cleaned the man up and gave him water, knowing full well that she would, by the time she reached the next man, forget the poor boy's name and the person she was to contact. Only at night, sometimes months after the fact, when all was quiet and the wind blew outside her tent, did these names come back to her like ghosts returning from the beyond to haunt her. When they did, she would rise from her cot, regardless of the hour, and write down as many of the names as she could remember. This legacy of all the horrors she was witness to was the most unsettling to Harriet. Even the sights, sounds, and smells of the surgical tent paled, in Harriet's mind, when compared to the idea that she had, through her own human frailties, failed to honor a dying soldier's request.

In the course of making her way up and down the unending line of soldiers to which more wounded were added faster than she and the surgeons could manage, Harriet would come across faces that had become, to her, more familiar than those of her own family. In many ways, the 4th New Jersey and the First New Jersey Brigade were her family, which only served to make seeing them deposited here, at the field hospital, all the more tragic. The number of times she came across a face she was familiar with was a good indication of which units were in battle and how it was flowing. Today, for the first time in a long time, many of those faces she knew so well belonged to the 4th.

Although practically every soldier who was not unconscious or totally consumed by pain was happy to look at Harriet and spend a few seconds with her, the men of the 4th New Jersey were especially animated. Oftentimes, while she was leaving one man and making her way to the next, her mind busy trying to push the image of the last poor soul she had been with into some dark recess, a soldier who recognized her would call out her name. "Miss Harriet! Miss Harriet!" Sometimes she would know who it was without having to look. Unfortunately, too many times, the voice and appearance of a member of the 4th New Jersey was so altered by suffering that even when she did look, she did not immediately make the association. Though few of them realized this, and most of the time it was truly unavoidable, Harriet chided herself every time it happened.

On this day, there was a goodly number of men from the 4th mixed in amongst the wounded. "We were right in there with 'em," Samuel Rhuddy of B Company told Harriet between sips of water. "We were goin' through the woods, lost I thought, and then they just jumped right up in front of us, like frightened jackrabbits."

Though she tried not to encourage the men to talk about what was happening, for fear that they, in their excited state, would speak of the death of a member of the regiment she was fond of, Harriet was also anxious to hear if Kevin was safe. Jonah Korffen, shot in two places because he refused to leave the firing line after his first wound, told Harriet of Himmel's death. "He was standing there, Himmel was, blazing away like the rest of us, for there was no need for him to direct us, when the captain went down at his feet."

As he spoke, Harriet's eyes grew large as saucers and her heart skipped a beat.

"Old Frederick looked down and thought the captain was through. We all did, Miss Harriet. But then he started to rise, pushing 'imself up onto his hands and knees shakin' his head like a dog does."

While part of Harriet wanted Korffen to skip the details and simply tell her of Kevin's fate, she had no desire to hear more, not even the end. Yet she said nothing as she slowly wrung, tighter and tighter and tighter, the dirty, bloodstained rag she used to wash faces. "Well, Frederick, the poor dear fellow, suddenly jerks, grabs at his face, and keels over right on top of the captain, who's still on his hands and knees. Bang," Korffen stated with emphasis, "they both go down."

Holding the twisted rag tautly between her white knuckles Harriet finally could hold back no more. "Kevin? Was he . . ."

Korffen, confused for a moment, for he had thought that he had made it clear that Kevin was all right, looked at Harriet's face and realized the distress his babbling was causing her. "Oh, no, Miss Harriet. Your young captain, he's just fine. Had the wind knocked out of him and all. But when I left, he was still there, with the rest of the company, banging away for all they were worth at the Rebs."

Finally able to breathe, Harriet heaved a great sigh, laid her hand on Korffen's chest, and tried to thank him. No words, however, came out. Instead, she began to cry, hiding her face in the rag she had used on so many soldiers before and would, before the day was finished, use on so many more.

Behind the hasty breastworks that they had thrown up after being relieved from the firing line, the soldiers of the 4th New Jersey kept a wary eye to their front while trying, as best they could, to get some sleep. The night, however, would bring them little rest. As they curled up, ever mindful to keep their rifle well within arm's reach, the men did their best to block out the sounds of a battle that had not yet run its course. Though they were familiar, these sounds were nonetheless the stuff that nightmares were made of. The cries and moans of wounded men, left stranded between lines where they had fallen, were even more pitiful and desperate due to the fires that had been started by the incessant fighting that had consumed the entire day. Here and there a man would call out for someone to come and pull him away from the approaching flames. Though many men wanted to help, few dared to do so. The woods were filled with sharpshooters and skirmishers just waiting to pick off the brave soul who was foolish enough to respond to the cries of a stricken comrade.

Kevin, sitting with his back to a tree just behind the stretch of line held by his diminished company, didn't even try to sleep. Instead, he sat there in silence and listened to the anguish of the night while his eyes stared vacantly over the top edge of the breastworks before him and his mind wandered from one random thought to the next. It had not been, he concluded, a particularly exhausting day. Though any day of battle was tough on a man, those that included fatiguing forced marches and endless shuffling from one place to another through woods or broken terrain were far more exhausting. Yet their losses—both his company's and the regiment's—told a different story.

Slowly, Kevin ticked off the names of those who hadn't answered the company roll call and worked to link each name to the image of a face in his mind. Some of those names, though they were his men, meant little to him. Like checking entries in a ledger, he would quickly make a mental notation and move on to the next one. Others, such as Frederick Himmel, caused him to pause and reflect. They had been together a long time, almost three years. They had weathered many a battle and faced a multitude of crises in their efforts to make their company an effective fighting force and keep it together as the Army marched from one defeat to another. That Frederick Himmel was no longer with him, no longer alive, was hard for Kevin to acccept. Three years of being a soldier, seeing men fall by the score on a single day, did little to soften this blow. Even worse was the idea that his body, mutilated by gunfire and contorted by the throes of death, lay somewhere, out there, waiting to be consumed by a fire that made no distinction between Union and Confederate. Kevin yearned to see Himmel alive again, just as many times before he had yearned to see the young girl he had once loved and for whose murder he felt responsible. He almost expected to see the old German step out of the woods to their front, standing tall and alive, and come over to the very spot along the company's line of works that he was watching.

That imagined vision was still racing through Kevin's mind when Sergeant Johnny O'Keeth came up to the tree where Kevin sat. Kneeling down and leaning on his rifle for support, O'Keeth looked to make sure Kevin was awake before he started talking. "Mules are coming up with a resupply of cartridges, Captain Bannon. I'm going to take a detail of men over to where they are."

O'Keeth's words, spoken with authority, were a pronouncement, not a request. Since the loss of Himmel, he had stepped forward without being told and assumed many of the old German's duties. Kevin, for his part, said nothing. There was nothing that needed to be said. Losses amongst the noncommissioned officers of the company had been particularly high. O'Keeth, though he was a very junior sergeant, was the only one Kevin had left at the moment. With a wave of his hand and a very slight nod, Kevin acknowledged O'Keeth. "You've done well today, Johnny," Kevin finally stated in a matter-of-fact manner, using O'Keeth's first name, as was his habit. "I just wish we could have brought Frederick's body back with us."

O'Keeth looked over the top of the breastworks, out into the no-man's land where small fires cast an eerie glow on the tangled branches that hid the stars from view. A shrill scream, sounding more like a pig's squeal than a human's cry of pain, pierced the night. The fire had reached another wounded man. Except for O'Keeth's quick, almost instinctive crossing of himself, neither man moved, and neither man spoke a word for several minutes as they waited for the poor soul to finish his death throes. Finally, when a degree of quiet returned, O'Keeth lifted himself off the ground but did not stand upright. To have done so would have been to invite a sharpshooter's bullet. "I'll be on my way now, Captain. Is there anything you'll be needing while I'm gone?"

Kevin couldn't think of anything that O'Keeth could do or bring that would make this night pass any quicker or more peacefully. "No, nothing at all," he responded with a tone that betrayed his exhaustion.

"Do you think we'll have at 'em again in the morning?"

Kevin took a deep breath and let it go before answering O'Keeth. "If it isn't us, Johnny, it will be someone else with us in support. And if it isn't us, it will be them coming for us. Either way, it will be a long day."

Though the answer wasn't what he had hoped for, and left O'Keeth wondering about his captain's state of mind, he didn't press the issue. Without a word, he turned and went about his duties, leaving Kevin to continue his sleepless vigil.

It was the Confederates of Ewell's corps who struck first in the morning, fifteen minutes before Sedgwick's Sixth Union Corps was to go forward. Cannon, laboriously moved into positions during the night, added their voices to the gunfire that opened as soon as it was light enough to see. Young Geddy, still puzzled over what had happened the day before, was just as confused now. After spending a sleepless night listening to the moans and groans of wounded men, occasionally punctuated by the shrieks of a helpless man being consumed by fire, Geddy was on the verge of a nervous breakdown.

Unable to bring himself to peer over the top of the breastworks they had worked much of the night to construct, Geddy slouched down, until he was almost lying on his back, and looked up at the men to his left and right. On one side, James Bannon had already passed into the same trancelike state that had possessed him throughout the entire fight yesterday. Dropping back behind the cover of their breastworks, James would settle on one knee as he mechanically went through the steps of reloading his rifle. All the time he was doing so, he kept his eyes fixed on the top edge of the breastworks, as if he were watching to make sure that no one came over the top. The thought that perhaps the enemy was attacking suddenly sent a shiver through Geddy. Convinced that he would be unable to do anything to prevent it, and even worse, defend himself, Geddy shut his eyes and began to mumble a prayer.

"Hey, you." Marty Hazard's voice, and a quick kick in the side, caused Geddy to open his eyes. "What in the hell do you think you're doin' down there?"

Geddy opened his mouth to respond, but nothing came out. As he looked up at the angry sergeant, whose eyes were glowing with a wild frenzy that was accentuated by his wiry beard, he couldn't think of anything to say. He was scared, frightened beyond belief. Nothing had prepared him for this, nothing. The wildly romantic stories printed in the newspapers that spoke of standup battles fought on nice, clear rolling fields had never described what a man with his stomach laid open by a minié ball looked like. Even the stories that the old soldiers had swapped during the long winter months, livened up with their peculiar brand of black humor, failed to come close to capturing the grim realities of war. If anyone should have been asking what someone was doing, Geddy reasoned, it should have been him asking the others.

Unable to solicit a response, Marty stood up as high as he dared and again gave Geddy a sharp kick in his side. "God damn you, boy! Get off your worthless ass and get up here and shoot or I'll shoot you myself right where you lay."

Marty's words caught James' attention. Without bothering to pause his reloading, James looked over, first at Marty, whose face was now contorted in a most unnatural way by anger, then down at Geddy, whose eyes and mouth were agape. Though he didn't think Marty would actually shoot Geddy, James knew enough not to take that chance. Pausing in his routine, James rocked back on his heels and reached behind him with his free hand, grabbing Marty's arm and giving it a shake.

With a quick snap, Marty turned to face James. "What?" he spat out angrily.

"Leave him be, Marty. He's scared out of his wits."

"He's a coward," Marty screamed as he returned his gaze to Geddy. "He's nothing but a dad-burn coward and if he doesn't start fightin' I'm gonna personally splatter those wits of his all over the ground."

James tightened his grip on Marty's arm and gave it a jerk. "No, Marty. Leave the boy alone."

Now just as angry at James for interfering, Marty pulled his arm away, almost forgetting about the withering fire that was passing over their heads without end. "Don't you tell me what to do," Marty shouted back. "Just who in the hell do you think you are?"

"Your friend," James shouted above the din of rifle fire. "And I'll be damned if I'm going to let you do something you'll regret the rest of your life."

Ready for just about anything except this, Marty's face lost its angry expression as he pulled away a step. He wasn't about to give in just yet. "He's a coward, Jimmy. A coward. And you know I hate cowards."

"He's not a coward, Marty. He's shaken and confused. We've all been like that and you know it. Now leave him alone and he'll be fine soon."

Though Geddy was thankful for James' intervention, he wondered how, in all the confusion, made worse by the suffocating smoke of burned powder that drifted all about, he was supposed to recover his nerve.

Seeing that Marty still wasn't quite ready to give in, James turned to Geddy and grabbed his arm. "Slide on back a few feet, Douglas, and start loading that pile of rifles we gathered up last night. When you have one loaded, pass it up to me and I'll pass my empty ones back to you. Okay?"

Grabbing at the chance to get off the firing line and away from Marty Hazard, Geddy nodded and scrambled past Marty to where James had sent him. When he was over next to the rifles, he started to do exactly what James had said. Satisfied, James looked back to Marty. "He'll do us more good back there than up here firing into the air."

Though he knew James was right, Marty refused to give in completely. "Damn you, Bannon. You're too blamed soft-hearted for your own good. Did you know that?"

James smiled. "Yeah, I guess so. Otherwise, I wouldn't waste my time trying to help a wild old coot like you from doing something stupid."

Marty shook his head. "You smart-ass VMI cadets are all alike." Then, with a grin on his face, he settled down next to James, brought his rifle up and rested it on the top of the breastworks. After cocking back the hammer, he took careful aim, squeezed the trigger, and watched for a moment. "Ha! Take that, you yellow-bellied Yankee," he shouted with glee. Then he turned to face James. With a sly grin on his face, he winked before going about the task of reloading.

The firing was almost continuous and, though most of the bullets passed over the heads of Kevin Bannon's company, more than enough found their mark. For their part, his men returned the fire, though Kevin suspected most of it was unaimed and just as wild as the Confederate fire that kept them pinned. With no orders to advance, and no room for any initiative, Kevin found himself with little to do but hang back, behind the firing line, and watch his men. Some of them, he noted, kept up a fairly steady fire, popping off a round every minute or so and taking their time in reloading. Others, like Private Miller, lay low for the longest time, barely peering over the edge of the breastworks, watching for a target. When one did appear that seemed worthwhile, Miller would slowly, methodically bring his rifle up like a hunter does when bringing his weapon to bear on prey. Just as carefully, Miller would pull the hammer back to the full-cocked position, take careful aim, and, when all was right and he was ready, finally fire. Though Miller and those who operated like him put out far fewer rounds, Kevin realized that they, and not the others, were the real killers that day.

Word about what was going on around them, past their own little cluster of men, was rare. Major Vickers, on one of his rounds up and down the regimental line, told Kevin of the early morning attack on the division's right. "It was heavy fighting," he said as the two knelt several feet behind Kevin's company line. "They came in just as we were getting ready to go over to them ourselves."

Kevin, thankful that they hadn't attacked at 5:00 A.M. as had been planned, simply nodded.

"Looks like no one is going to be able to budge the other fellow from these two lines," Vickers concluded. "At least not against fire like this. We hope Burnsides will be able to find their flank south of the turnpike and shake them loose."

"And if he doesn't?" Kevin asked.

Major Vickers gave Kevin a dark stare. "If that happens, well, we'll find out what old Unconditional Surrender Grant is made of."

The animosity that many Easterners, men of the Army of the Potomac, felt for the Westerners was very evident in Vickers' voice. John Pope had come from the west in the summer of '62, full of boasts and promises, only to be thrashed as thoroughly as any Union commander had been by Lee. And though Grant had made no promises and done little in the way of bragging about his record, the newspapers and some of Grant's own staff officers let it be known that things would be different now that he was in command. Looking about, reflecting on their plight, and listening to Major Vickers, Kevin saw little to indicate that they were doing any better now, in the opening stages of this campaign, than they had in past campaigns. "Well," Kevin finally concluded, "if someone is going to shake this deadlock loose, I hope they do it soon. I can't see us keeping this up for very long."

"Neither can I," Vickers responded as he looked up and down the line. "This is not my idea of how to fight a proper battle."

Though Kevin wondered if there was a "proper" way to fight a battle, he said nothing. Instead, he exchanged a few more comments with Vickers before that officer started to make his way back up the line. With nothing to do, Kevin settled back behind the firing line to watch his men as they went about sweeping the ground between them and their enemy with a deadly fire that no mortal could endure, while they waited for something to happen to get things moving again.

That something finally came late in the day, but not where they had expected it and from the wrong quarter. At about 6:00 P.M., the skirmishers who had been in front of the brigade came scampering back with the news that the enemy was attacking in force. Assuming that they were headed for his part of the line, Kevin, like all the other company commanders in the 4th New Jersey, quickly passed up and down the rear of their firing line, making sure the men were up and alert, for the day had lulled many into a rather sluggish and dull state of inattention.

Word of an enemy attack, however, was more than sufficient to knock them out of it. The men were up, crouching behind their breastworks, and readying their rifles as Kevin went up the line. "Make sure you mark your targets," he warned his men, "and aim low." In these close quarters, Kevin realized, they would be able to get two, maybe three shots off before a foe, if he was determined and didn't stop in the open to fire, was upon them.

The forest, so recently quiet except for an occasional rifle shot or the boom of a distant cannon, came alive with the high-pitched screech of the "Yip-yip-yip" known as the Confederate yell. Johnny O'Keeth, up on the right of the company line, where Frederick Himmel used to post himself, called out when he saw the enemy. "They're going in over to the right."

Pushing his way to the breastworks between two of his men, Kevin carefully lifted his own head above the top of the breastworks just in time to see the massed enemy formations coming out of their own works and running, moving forward as rapidly as they could, toward the far right of the Union line. "They're going into Seymour's brigade," he shouted to no one in particular. This caused Kevin some concern. That brigade, composed of men from Ohio, Pennsylvania, and Maryland, had launched a massive attack earlier in the day that had been shredded by concentrated Confederate small arms and artillery fire.

Amos Flatherly, who had witnessed that bloody failure, watched now as the surging wave of Confederates took a volley of fire without any appreciable effect. Slowly he looked up and down the regimental line, then behind them for some evidence of a supporting unit. When he saw none, and heard no response from Union artillery, Flatherly shook his head as he turned to Kevin. "I sure hope those boys over in Third Division have enough fight left in 'em to hold. I'd surely hate to have them come rolling down on top of us, especially in the dark."

Denny Cummins, standing on the other side of Kevin, leaned back and shouted at Flatherly behind Kevin's back. "What's the matter, Mick, afraid of being in the woods in the dark?"

Flatherly leaned back to respond. "You bet I am. And if the Rebs get behind us, you will be too."

Knowing of the Confederate habit of attacking in echelon, Kevin turned away from the mighty host that continued to stream forward against their far right flank unchecked. "Look sharp, boys," he shouted to his anxious command. There'll be more coming at us in a minute or two." After watching the reaction of his men, Kevin looked to his front, slowly scanning the line of enemy works across from his to see if the enemy opposite them was, in fact, preparing to step off and widen the attack. Caught up in the excitement of the moment, Kevin hadn't noticed that the volume of enemy fire from across the way was beginning to pick up again. Ducking a bit, he looked carefully for any sign of a brave but foolish officer standing up or a standard being thrust aloft to initiate a charge against his works. When he saw none, he turned his attention back to the right.

The Rebel yell continued to echo through the dense woods without pause, without any sign of diminishing. At times, it even drowned out the screams of pain of young men from both sides going down with mortal wounds. Added to the roar of rifle fire that had now become continuous, that yell created an eerie warbling note in the cacophony that was slowly starting to make its way down the line toward where Kevin stood. With no commands to give, and nothing to do, Kevin stood with his company, a helpless captive of a strange and deadly contest that promised to engulf them all.

It didn't take long before the telltale signs of a disaster in the making began to appear. As the deafening roar of gunfire, the screams of men engaged in close combat, and the shriek of cannonballs passing overhead drew near, new sounds were added. To their rear, the scampering feet running through the woods for all they were worth began to become more and more evident. Kevin, like many of his men, looked to the rear and watched for a moment as blue-clad figures, some with their arms flailing, made their way to what they hoped would be safety. Having participated in too many military disasters themselves, the men of the 4th New Jersey said nothing. With tight lips and stern expressions, they gripped their rifles, pulled their cartridge boxes around to the front, or with their thumb nervously toyed with the hammer of their piece, causing a clicking noise as they pulled it back slightly, then let it go. Dear Lord, Kevin prayed silently to himself as he watched more and more refugees from the fight to their right flee in terror into the growing darkness, give me the strength to hold this company together and do our duty.

Finally orders came down. The regimental commander, making his way from one company commander to the next, warned them that the First New Jersey Brigade's line was being bent back and to the rear. The 4th, he said, would continue to hold where they were but in case the 1st New Jersey Volunteers and the other regiments in the brigade broke, the 4th would leave their works and wheel back at a ninety degree angle to form a new line. "We have to stop them," he repeated as he went by, "if no one else does."

Darkness began to fall across the woods, causing Kevin to wonder if he should be pleased to see it or concerned. Visions of a similar fight a year ago, not far from the Chancellorsville Inn, began to come back to him. "They're doing it again," he muttered. "Damn it, we're letting them do it again." Both Flatherly and Cummins, surprised somewhat that Kevin had uttered a curse, didn't move or respond as they continued to wait, watch, and listen.

Not even the flow of fresh troops from their left headed into the fight did anything to diminish their apprehensions. "You know, Captain," Flatherly quietly told Kevin as they watched a New York regiment move to the north across their rear, "I think it's harder standing here, waiting with nothing to do, than it is to be fighting."

"It's having to depend on someone else," Cummins added, "that I don't like. I'd rather be with them fellas," he said pointing to the trail elements of the New Yorkers, "going up there to do something than standing here."

Kevin nodded. "So would I. But this is where we were told to stay and stay we will. Right?"

The two men, understanding the meaning of Kevin's statement, nodded their assent with his pronouncement. "Yes, sir. We'll stand," Flatherly announced with great determination. "We'll stand here with you till hell freezes over if they let us."

"That," Kevin added, "is what we need to win this war. We need to stand, no matter what."

And stand they did, though they were never called on that night to fight. The Confederate attack, delivered too late with too little, ran its course, like so many other attacks that day, and slowly receded, leaving both sides locked together for another night in a nightmare that would forever be known as the Wilderness.

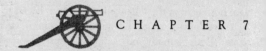

CHAPTER 7

In the Wilderness, Virginia, May, 1864

EXCEPT FOR THE EVER-PRESENT layer of thin, white smoke that filled the woods all about them, the third day of battle dawned clear and quiet. The last great effort of the previous day, led by General Gordon's brigade of Georgians, had done nothing to break the stalemate, or so it had seemed to the men of the 4th Virginia as they stirred at dawn. "At least they let us have some peace and quiet," Marty Hazard dryly commented as he checked his rifle and prepared for another day's hot work.

Except for a few minutes of fitful rest, Douglas Geddy had been unable to sleep for a second night in a row. The constant moaning and groaning of countless wounded lying between the lines, and an inescapable fear that at any moment the Yankees would suddenly swoop down on them out of the darkness, had robbed him of the rest that seemed to come so easily to Marty. He felt like telling the grizzled veteran that he was crazy, but didn't. No need, he figured, to antagonize a man who thought that he was a coward.

When the skirmishers, sent forward after dawn, returned with the news that the Union entrenchments were vacant, a cheer rose from one end of the line to the other. To a man, the 4th Virginia came to its feet and advanced into what hours before had been a deadly, fire-swept no-man's land. Stopping here and there whenever they found an inviting haversack or cast-off knapsack, they swept over the abandoned Union works in search of food, coffee, blankets, shoes, and whatever else they lacked that the retreating Union soldiers had thoughtlessly abandoned. With his mouth stuffed with food and one hand hungrily searching for more in a bloodstained haversack he held, Marty Hazard looked up to James Bannon and smiled. "See there, Jimmy boy," he said with great glee as bits of unchewed food fell from his mouth. "I told ya they'd go slinking off in the night, just like they always do."

Josh Major, sitting on a log as he tried on a pair of shoes he had taken from one of the many Union dead that had not been consumed by the fires that still burned here and there, shouted back. "You're lyin', Marty Hazard. You said nothin' of the kind."

Turning to face Josh Major, Marty pointed a bony finger from a fist holding a half-eaten biscuit. "If I wasn't in such a good mood, I'd come over there and whup your butt."

Josh laughed. "Hazard, you're a blowhard. You ain't never beat me in a fair fight and never will." Then, spying a corpse wearing what appeared to be a better-looking pair of shoes than the ones he was trying on, Josh threw the boot he had in his hand over his shoulder and ran to the new corpse to retrieve the better shoes before someone else did.

James, who had gone about gathering up haversacks, had just settled down on the ground with his legs spread apart when Marty and Josh had begun arguing. He looked over to Marty and Josh for a moment. Seeing that there was still a smile on Marty's face and that there was no danger of their coming to blows, James said nothing and went back to what he was doing.

Carefully he poured the contents of one haversack after another out onto the ground between his legs, a huge pile of food, personal items, and extra ammunition. Once he had the contents of four haversacks and two knapsacks mixed together, he began to pick through his trove of treasures. Those items that he saw no use for were thrown over his shoulder. This included such things as a straight razor, a couple of combs, a Bible, and a tin of shoe polish. Anything that looked like food was piled carefully over to one side while ammunition was piled to the other. When he came upon a small parcel that was carefully wrapped in brown paper, he ripped it open. Inside were lemon candies, the kind he used to buy as a child with pennies he stole from his father's desk.

Pausing, he held up the delicate candy between two dirty fingers and studied it as a jeweler would study a rare gem. He could remember how frightened he and his brother Kevin were whenever they entered his

father's den on such a raid. Kevin, more often than not too skittish to be of
any other use, always stayed in the hall as a lookout. James, with great
deftness, would dash in, quickly but carefully pull out the desk drawer, and
fish out a few of the coins his father always seemed to leave there. James
made sure that he never disturbed anything else, for his father was a
meticulous man who always noticed the slightest disturbance of his things.
James was also careful to make sure that he didn't let his greed get the
better of him and take too many coins. Just enough for their immediate
needs were all he ever took. Just enough. James thought about that
concept as he raised the small lemon candy to his mouth. Such a wonderful idea. Just enough.

As he sat there, silently enjoying his surprise treat, young Geddy
came up next to him and sank to his knees. "You suppose," the young man
asked half haltingly, "they've really gone? That we've beaten 'em and
they've retreated back north?"

Images of his brother, his home in New Jersey, and the past disappeared as James' eyes once more embraced the scene of carnage that
surrounded him. As his tongue lovingly wrapped itself about the sweet,
tasty candy, slowly drawing off its flavor, James looked over to Geddy.
"What difference does it make?" he asked with words that were slurred by
his efforts to enjoy his treat and talk at the same time.

Geddy looked at James with a questioning stare. "What do you mean,
what difference does it make? It makes every difference."

Knowing what Geddy was really interested in, James smiled as he
continued to enjoy the lemon drop. "Listen, Douglas. Maybe they have
gone back north, and maybe they haven't. Wherever they are, you can be
sure that either they'll be back or we'll go after them. Always turns out
that way, you know. And until one of our armies beats the other so bad
that it can't get up again, it will keep on going like that."

Geddy looked at James, blinked a couple of times, but said nothing.
James didn't know if the boy believed him or not. He sort of wished
himself that it wasn't true. But he had been on too many campaigns to
think otherwise. "Look, Douglas," James finally said in a fatherly way after
he had swallowed the last of the lemon candy, "why don't you forget about
such things and go find yourself a haversack or two filled with food? You
could use a good meal, and believe me," he concluded as he waved his
hand over his own cache of prizes, "there's more than enough out there for

everyone." Then looking about as he heard some of the officers shouting for men to fall in, James added, "Best get going before they ruin the party."

Standing up, Geddy looked around, watching the other men as they ignored the shouts of their officers and continued to go about their scavenging. For a brief second Geddy thought about taking James' advice and joining in. But then his eyes fell upon the twisted body of a dead Yankee. The sickly gray face of this man was contorted by the anguish he had felt in his last moments of life. His mouth, frozen open as it had been when he uttered his last shriek, was now home to dozens of flies that lazily crawled in and out of it. The thought of going near this man, let alone touching him, caused Geddy's stomach to suddenly churn. Turning his face away, Geddy took a couple of steps, bent forward at the waist, and began to throw up.

Marty Hazard, finished gathering all he could carry, came up to James who was busily packing away those items of food he cared to keep. "What's with him?" Marty asked, pointing over to Geddy.

"Nothing, really," James said without having to look up. "Just the usual, nervous stomach. He'll be fine as soon as we get away from here and he has had some time to sort all this out."

Marty thought about that for a moment, then nodded. "Yeah, I guess so. Well, the colonel's callin' us, Jimmy boy. Guess we're gonna be moving soon. How 'bout you lookin' after him while I gather the other boys."

James replied with a nod as he continued to stuff his haversack. Finished with that, he grabbed two packs of cartridges, shoved them in the pocket of his trousers, and got up. After a quick scan of the area, he sighed. "We'll all feel a lot better," he whispered, "once we're out of these god-forsaken woods. A whole lot better."

After a short march that had started at midnight, the 4th New Jersey, along with the rest of the First New Jersey Brigade, settled into new positions in another part of the Wilderness. The opportunity to eat something and get a few hours' sleep before the new dawn did little to dispel the gloom that had settled over Kevin's small command. "We've been whipped again, boys," Amos Flatherly announced as they went about improving their new line of breastworks. "Old Bobby Lee's done taken on another one of our West Point generals and sent him packing." Even Johnny O'Keeth, by far the most optimistic man in the company and always ready to point out that things weren't really as bad as they seemed, could find nothing to say.

Standing off to one side, watching his men go about their work in glum silence, Kevin wondered if there was anything he could do to cheer his men up or dispel their pessimism. Slowly he searched his tired mind for words or phrases that would cheer his men, but found that he could not come up with anything positive about the past few days' efforts. Other than the fact that some of them were still alive, for now the campaign appeared to be a failure. Any efforts to evoke their passions with slogans or appeals to their patriotism would be greeted with scorn. No, Kevin thought, it was best to let them be for now. After almost three years of war, they knew what the score was as well as he did and what it meant to them. A failed campaign not only delayed their return home, but it also offered the Confederates another opportunity to kill more of them.

When work on the breastworks was finished, the men settled down to tend to personal chores. While some immediately started cleaning their rifles, badly fouled after two days of heavy use, others pulled out pencil and paper and scribbled down a quick letter to loved ones back home. Knowing that news of a big battle would cause their families concern, these soldiers were anxious to reassure them that they had survived. Like his men, Kevin was eager to do likewise. For a moment, as he watched Johnny O'Keeth struggling with his letter, carefully scratching every wavering stroke of every letter he wrote, Kevin wondered if there would be time to go back and visit the First Division's field hospital to see Harriet. He had done this before, at Gettysburg and again during the Mine Run Affair. And though she was always busy when he found her, his appearance on both of those occasions had been greeted with great enthusiasm and obvious relief.

Looking over to where his regimental commander stood with several other officers, Kevin was about to go over and ask permission when he stopped himself and looked about at the forest that surrounded him like prison bars. He suddenly realized that he had no idea where he was. Somehow, no one had seen the necessity of informing the company commanders where, exactly, they were. Though he was sure that he could find out that bit of information, as well as where the division's field hospital was, Kevin wondered if he would be able to find his way back. The last time he had been here, in the spring of '63, he had managed to become lost twice. It wouldn't do, he thought, to get lost this time, not while the enemy was so close at hand and liable to strike at them from any direction.

Besides, he reasoned as he slowly stretched his sore arms out before him, he was tired, dead tired. They would be retreating back north across the Rapidan soon, he concluded, probably after dark. He'd need his rest if he was going to keep up with his company during the long, painful night march they'd be making. No, he concluded. It would be best if he stayed here and got some sleep. There'll be plenty of time, he figured, to see Harriet as the Army waited for the president to appoint a new commander. It would take time, maybe months, before a new grand strategy for taking Richmond was formulated, debated, and prepared. There always seemed to be plenty of time.

Shortly after darkness, the Stonewall Brigade was formed up in columns and headed south. Buoyed by what they believed had been another success, the men around James talked loudly about one thing or another, laughing frequently, and, in general, enjoying their good fortunes. Only Douglas Geddy, still groggy from a few hours of fitful sleep, seemed unaffected by the jubilant spirit. Marching next to James in silence, he let his head drop low between his shoulders, bobbing this way and that as he followed the press of men through the darkness. James worried about the young man, a reluctant warrior who seemed incapable of adapting to army life. From the first day Geddy had joined the unit, Marty predicted that he would desert once he had the chance.

Yet Geddy had not deserted, at least not yet. James, after seeing better men do so for more trivial reasons, found himself wondering what was keeping a man who would never be able to deal with all that being a soldier entailed in the ranks. Though Geddy, like every other member of the regiment, had been paraded to watch the execution of deserters who had been caught, James knew the odds of being caught, tried, and given the death penalty were slim. Far too many a man, he knew, had deserted and gotten away with it. No, he thought, it wasn't the fear of execution or punishment that kept men like Geddy from deserting.

Pushing his way forward into the next rank, James came up to Marty, who was loudly humming a tune that James did not recognize. "Marty," James interrupted without preamble, "why don't more men like Geddy desert?"

James' question caught Marty by surprise. Turning to face him in the darkness that hid all features of James' face, Marty craned his neck back, then shook his head. "What in tarnations brought that up, Jimmy?"

"Oh, I was just thinking."

"Jimmy," Marty responded with a slap on James' shoulder, "in my opinion, you do too much thinkin'. You'd be a lot better off, and a sight more happy, if you just took things as they were and didn't bother yourself with trying to figure everything out."

James chuckled. "Well, to tell you the truth, Marty, there have been many a time that I wish I could. But you see, that just isn't my nature. Now, back to my question."

"You just don't give up, do ya?" Marty asked in jest.

"Marty, I'm serious. What keeps Geddy, and lots of other men, in the ranks when common sense tells them they shouldn't be here?"

Marty leaned over and tapped Josh Major, who was on the other side of James. "Hey Josh. Why do you think we don't have more desertions?"

Josh, who had been engaged in a lively conversation with Denny Cummins, looked over to Marty, and shrugged. "I don't know. Maybe," he added after thinking a moment, "the fellas don't want to miss the fun."

"Fun?" James asked in puzzlement.

"Ya, Jimmy, fun," Josh came back without hesitation. "I mean, look around. Everyone's had somethin' to eat. We're all together. We're sharing stories and all. What more could you ask for?"

"What about the killing, and the loss of friends?" James asked sharply. "Do you think that's fun?"

Josh hesitated for a moment as he thought on that. When he did, his voice was a little softer. "Jimmy, life ain't easy anywhere. Back on the farm, it's hard work, day in, day out. Ya get up in the mornin', go out in the fields alone. Out there ya work all day under the blistering sun doin' the same thing you did the day before, the year before, as long as ya can remember. The same thing. At night, ya come back so tired you don't have any strength left to do much of anything except eat and go to bed. Day in, day out, it's the same thing. Slop the hogs, mend this or fix that. Ya see the same folks, walk the same fields, come home to the same tired old two-room house. Hear the same stories. I watched my old man get old before his time and die without ever having done anythin' other than plow the same tired dirt year after year after year. Livin' ain't easy, Jimmy, not here in the Army, not back home on the farm. At least here we have friends, lots of friends. And we go places, see things, and enjoy each other's company." There was a pause, and then, with his face turned up toward the sky, partially hidden by the branches that covered the roadway, Josh added, "Ya know, Jimmy. When this is all over, I'm gonna miss this. I really am."

Though Josh's answer was far more than James or Marty had expected, it didn't satisfy James' curiosity about Geddy. "Well, I guess I can understand that, Josh," James stated slowly, although in truth, he found Josh's reasoning hard to accept. "But what about Geddy back there? He's not having fun. He's been miserable since the day he got here and hasn't changed since."

Josh chuckled as he glanced back at the stooped figure behind him. "Oh, him? Well, he's afraid."

"I know that, Josh. I'm pretty sure we're all afraid of dying," James shot back.

"It's not dyin' that's got that boy by the tail. It's shame."

"Shame? How so?"

"Oh, that's easy," Marty chimed in. "Ifen Geddy does desert, where does he go?"

James shook his head. "Why, he goes home, of course."

"Maybe not, Jimmy. Maybe everyone back home is in favor of this war. Maybe when it came his time, everyone that mattered to him told him it was his duty to go, just like his brothers and cousins and friends already had."

"So you're telling me," James interrupted, "that Geddy's here for no other reason than because it's expected of him?"

"That's right. And odds are, that'll keep him here. 'Cause if he shows up back home, all in one piece before the war's over, he'll never be able to look another honest soul in the eye."

James stared at Marty for the longest time. "So you're telling me he'd rather face this than live with shame?"

Though Marty knew the answer, he asked James anyway. "Why are you, the son of a New Jersey businessman, here marching along the road with Virginians?"

James recoiled as if he had been slapped. He hesitated, thought about not answering at first, then, slowly, responded. "I joined because Will McPherson joined."

"And you stayed with Will, no matter what. You even risked desertion to take him home and bury him."

James listened to Marty's statements without uttering a word. Then, after he finished, James slowly added, "And I came back because . . ."

"Because we were all you had. We're more your family now than your own family," Marty finished.

For the longest while, James said nothing. There was really nothing to say. His own brother, a captain in the Union Army the last time he saw him, was a stranger now, a person who had changed over the long years of separation. He had to have changed. The boy he left behind in 1859 could never have stood where he saw Kevin standing, flashing an expression of anger that had distorted his brother's face almost beyond recognition. Marty had hit it right on the head. These men around him, joking and talking loudly as they marched along to God knew where, were more of a family now than the one that he had been raised with. And except for Mary Beth McPherson, a girl he thought he was in love with, he had no one else. No one.

Marty finally broke the silence. "Jimmy, there's a lot of foolishness about this whole thing. I don't pretend to understand it, 'cause I figure there is no way to understandin' what we're really doin' all this for. All I know is that we're here, we're doin' what we're told to do. And for some reason, a reason each man only knows for himself, we feel we need to keep doin' it."

"Even if it means dying?" James asked sharply.

Marty laughed. "Hell, Jimmy boy! We're all gonna die. The Good Book says that, plain as day."

Their conversation, twisting and turning one way and the next, was cut short by whispered orders from the officers. "Quiet in the ranks. The Yankees are marching parallel to us."

Ignoring the order, Marty looked over to the side of the road, then to James. "We've been marchin' to the southeast, ain't we?"

James thought about it. They had gone forward from their works when the march had started, which meant they had started to the east. Though the woods could turn one's sense of direction around, especially at night, James knew they had not gone north, for they would have crossed the Rapidan a long time ago. Marty was right.

"Well," Josh finally offered. "I guess the Yankees haven't been whooped enough."

"Guess not," Marty added. Any further comments were cut short as a brigade officer rode up next to the three comrades and told them to be quiet. For the rest of the night, and well into the morning, the long columns continued to march in silence until the sounds of gunfire, up ahead, announced the beginning of a new battle.

West of Spotsylvania Court House

THE APPEARANCE OF THE Fifth Corps commander, agitated by the growing battle that his command was already engaged in, at the head of the New Jersey Brigade signaled the end of the long night's march. Kevin watched as Major General G. K. Warren reined in his horse and shouted to the first officer of the brigade he saw. "Whose brigade is this?"

The officer, Lieutenant Charles R. Paul of the 15th New Jersey who was serving on the brigade staff, responded that it was Colonel Brown's.

"And where is Colonel Brown?" Warren demanded.

Lieutenant Paul gestured toward the rear of the column, where Colonel Brown was. Warren, however, ignored Paul. Without further ado, Warren took command of the brigade himself and led the Jerseymen, tired from almost twelve hours of nonstop marching, forward at the double to plug a gap in the line he was developing. Deploying in a woodlot, the brigade took up positions, as best they could, and awaited further orders as Confederate artillery lobbed a shell or two at them every now and then.

Shortly after noon, Kevin was called away from his company and informed that there would be a massive attack by both the Fifth and Sixth

Corps at 1:00 P.M. Hurrying back to his company, Kevin passed down the line of his command, still lying on the ground at the edge of the woodlot looking out across a small marsh toward a hill where the Rebels were dug in. "We'll be going forward soon," he repeated as he moved down his line, bent double with an eye toward the enemy lines. "Keep closed up on the right and don't stop to fire until we're in the Confederate works."

Automatically, the men began to stir, checking their rifles, rearranging the haversacks that they had been pulling food from as they waited, and unsnapping the flap of their cartridge boxes. Since their rifles were still unloaded, here and there a man slipped a percussion cap on the cone of his rifle, cocked the hammer back full, and pulled the trigger. One sharp snap after another followed up and down the line as those who hadn't done so capped their pieces off to dry out any moisture that might have accumulated in the barrel during the long night's march. Those who were extra cautious, or concerned, did so twice.

"Do you suppose these are the same fellas we faced back in the Wilderness?" Johnny O'Keeth asked when Kevin returned to his place on the company's right after making his rounds.

Kevin looked over to where the regimental commander waited before responding. "If they are, they either somehow got the drop on us and started moving before we did or they flew. Those earthworks up there are fresh and took some time to prepare."

Johnny looked up the hill they expected to be storming soon and studied the enemy positions for a moment. Then, with a nod, he accepted Kevin's judgment. "Yep," Johnny finally concluded. "The Rebs beat us here and by the looks of it, they're dug in deeper than a groundhog. Boys," he mumbled as he looked about, "we've been humbugged again."

Tensed and ready, Kevin waited. He thought about giving his company the order to load, but decided not to. No other company commanders, as best he could determine, had done so yet. So he waited. As the minutes passed, he pulled out his pistol, looked down at the cylinder, and gave it a quick twirl. It was loaded and ready. Holding it across his knee as he knelt behind a decent-sized tree, he first looked down his line again, then over to where his regimental commander, like him, waited for the word to spring up from ranks and advance.

But the minutes passed and Lieutenant Colonel Ewell didn't move. No one, as far as Kevin could see, was moving. There was, he thought, a delay. Someone wasn't ready. Someone wasn't quite satisfied with their dispositions. So they waited. Keyed up and ready, they waited. Ten minutes past the hour, then thirty minutes past the hour. The heat of the day, made more unbearable by the strain of holding himself ready to pounce on a moment's notice, was beginning to wear on Kevin. Shifting his weight from one knee to the next, he groaned as the stiff muscles in his legs sent a spasm of pain up his back. "Well?" Amos Flatherly asked impatiently. "Are we goin' or not?"

Though the question was directed to no one, for Amos was staring straight forward toward the enemy works when he asked, Kevin knew it had been meant for him. Taking off his cap, Kevin wiped his forehead with the sleeve of his jacket. "Let's not get excited. We'll go, I'm sure, when they're ready."

Turning to face Kevin, Flatherly directed his next question straight at Kevin. "When who's ready, Captain? Our slow-witted generals or the Rebs?"

At another time, under different circumstances, Flatherly's insubordination would have angered Kevin. But here, and now, it didn't. From where he sat, he could see no reason for delaying the attack, an attack he knew they would eventually have to make. The delay, he and the rest of his company could see, only gave the enemy infantry across the marsh and up the hill from them more time to dig a little deeper while their cannons lobbed a few more shells at the Union line. Kevin, replacing his cap, shifted himself about so that his back was now against the tree, and eased himself down into a comfortable position. Stretching his arms carefully so that they went over his head and behind the cover of the tree, he faked a yawn. "Sergeant O'Keeth," he announced in a loud voice.

"Yes, sir," Johnny snapped back eagerly.

"Please wake me when the colonel expresses his desire for this company to advance."

Confused by his commander's request, Johnny watched in silence as Kevin pulled the brim of his cap low over his eyes, crossed his arms over his chest, and appeared to go to sleep. Amos, disarmed by his commander's response, laughed. "Now there you are, lads," he roared. "That's the first sensible thing I've seen all day." After joining Flatherly's laughter for a moment with their own nervous chuckles, the rest of the men in Kevin's company eased themselves into comfortable positions, careful to keep their rifles off the ground, and tried to catch as much rest as the situation and time permitted.

The two-hour halt that the 4th Virginia and the rest of the Stonewall Brigade was given shortly after dawn did little to prepare them for the grueling march that followed. It did not take long for the accelerated pace, heat of the day, lack of sleep, and scarcity of water to take its toll on James Bannon, Marty Hazard, Josh Majors, Douglas Geddy, and the rest of the mass of men making up Edward "Allegheny" Johnson's division.

Keeping his place next to Marty Hazard, James Bannon trudged along. Bent over to better support the load of his rifle, blanket, and cartridge box, James stared vacantly at the dusty roadway immediately in front of him. Whatever thoughts he had lingered for only a few moments before breaking free from the weak bonds of a mind numbed by exhaustion and the tediousness of the march. Not even the sounds of a new battle, growing louder with every passing hour, could shake James from his trancelike state.

James was so withdrawn from all that was going on about him that he didn't notice when Josh bolted out of the ranks, staggered over to the side of the road, and threw up what little breakfast he had managed to choke down before falling asleep during their two-hour break. Only when Josh returned to the column and shoved his way back into the ranks did James take note. And then he did so only because Josh bumped him, by accident, on the arm as he reeled for a moment. "Anyone have any water left?" Josh called out, knowing that James Bannon, no matter how hot the day, always seemed to have some in his canteen.

Without a word, without taking his eyes off the road in front of him, James' hand searched along his side until it found his canteen. Groping, the searching hand finally secured a firm hold on it and pulled it up and over James' head. Josh reached up, took it from James, and finished freeing the canteen's straps that clung to James' other equipment. "Thanks, Jimmy," Josh mumbled as he jerked the cork free from the canteen's neck and took a sip. He didn't drink the first mouthful. Instead, he swished it about his mouth, then, bending forward at the waist, spat it onto the ground. With the taste of vomit gone, Josh was able to enjoy the second sip. Replacing the cork, he wiped his mouth with his sleeve, shook his head, and handed the canteen back to James. "God, that tasted good."

Again, James said nothing as he took the canteen, slung it over his head, and used his hand to put it somewhere amongst his other gear where it didn't bang against his leg or get in the way of his marching.

"How far do ya think we've gone, Marty?" Josh asked now that he was feeling reinvigorated.

"Doesn't make a difference how far we've been," Marty snapped back. "It's how far we got ta go that counts."

"Okay," Josh responded. "How far do ya think we got to go before we stop?" Josh asked.

"How the hell do I know?" Marty growled. "Do I look like an officer?"

For the first time, James moved his head. Looking over at Marty, the faint trace of a smile fell across his face. "Rest assured, Marty, nobody would ever make that mistake."

Surprised that James had said something, let alone what he said, caused Marty to jerk his head back. "Now who invited you into this con-ver-sation, boy?"

"Free country, isn't it?" James replied.

"Free? Like hell!" Marty shot back. "Only thin' we're free ta do is march our legs off from one end of this state to the next."

"Well, Marty, then we are free. Isn't that right, Douglas?" James asked.

Douglas Geddy, marching behind James, didn't respond. Looking back, Marty doubted whether the boy had heard the question. Bent over so far that his head almost rested on James' back, Geddy's jaw dropped down, leaving his mouth half open as he breathed through his mouth in order to take in enough air to keep up at the blistering pace they continued to move at. Marty turned back to James. "He's with us, Jimmy boy, but he ain't with us, if ya know what I mean."

James nodded, then looked down at Marty's right leg, which was moving along as fast as the other but with a decided limp. "You gonna be able to keep up?"

Seeing where James was looking, Marty straightened himself up as best he could and threw out his chest. "James Bannon, I'll march you and any man into the ground any day of the week, and twice on Sunday."

"Well," Josh Major responded, "if we keep this pace up for much longer, you just might get the chance to do that. Where do ya think we're headed?"

James looked up at the sky, then straight ahead before answering. "Southeast. We're still going southeast."

Colonel Terry, the regimental commander, leading his horse, came up next to Josh who asked him, in a rather nonchalant manner as he pointed in the direction they were marching, "Colonel, what's down that a'way?"

Colonel Terry, as tired as any of his men, lifted his head, looked down the road for a moment, then turned to Josh. "A place called Spotsylvania Court House," he responded.

"We gonna get a chance to rest awhile when we get there?" Josh asked hopefully.

Colonel Terry looked down the road, just as James had done, and listened to the distant boom of cannon fire. He shook his head before looking at Josh to answer him. "I don't know, Josh. We'll just have to wait and see."

The attack that had been scheduled for 1:00 P.M. never materialized. Instead, the 4th New Jersey, along with the rest of the brigade and the whole First Division, continued to lie where they had been stopped earlier in the day and waited for more orders. Sometime around five-thirty, those orders came, personally delivered by General Warren, not far from where Kevin sat, his back still resting against the tree he had snuggled up to earlier in the day. Kevin watched as General Warren rode up behind the brigade shouting, "Where is the commander of this brigade? I ordered it into action an hour ago."

Without waiting for an answer, Warren spurred his horse and rode over to where the 15th New Jersey Volunteers lay waiting. "Who is the commander of this regiment?" Warren now demanded in a rage. Colonel Penrose, commander of the 15th, stepped forward. "I am."

Looking down from the saddle at the colonel, Warren shouted his orders. "I ordered this brigade into action an hour ago. Colonel, form your brigade and charge. I want to develop that hill."

Perplexed, Penrose looked over to the hill that they had been facing all day and that General Warren was now pointing at. Not knowing what else to do, the colonel of the 15th New Jersey saluted, and then went about organizing the advance as quickly as possible.

Having heard and witnessed the confrontation between the regimental commander of the 15th and the Fifth Corps commander, the soldiers of Kevin's company didn't need to be told by Kevin what they were about to do. They had had all afternoon to contemplate the long-delayed attack and now, it seemed, they finally had orders to execute it.

Yet when Penrose finally began to carry out the attack he had been so unceremoniously ordered to make, he did so with only his own regiment and the 3rd New Jersey. As the 3rd went forward as skirmishers and the 15th stepped off in line of battle, Kevin looked down his own regimental command for any sign that they were about to form up and follow. Not seeing any movement on the part of the regimental commander or any of the other companies, and with Colonel Penrose absorbed with commanding his own regiment, Kevin shrugged, looked at Johnny O'Keeth, and shook his head. "Damned if I know what's going on."

O'Keeth didn't respond. Instead, he propped himself up on his elbows and watched the 3rd and 15th go forward. With nothing better to do himself, Kevin did likewise.

The attack, Kevin saw, went well. Confederate skirmishers, firing as they went, gave ground as the two New Jersey regiments left the cover of the woodlot and advanced into the marsh that lay at the foot of the hill the attack was headed for. Wading through the marsh, the ranks of the 15th New Jersey passed through the thin skirmish line of the 3rd New Jersey and started up the hill toward the enemy entrenchments, now alive with activity.

Amos Flatherly, watching from his position, shook his head. "The Rebs are holding their fire till the Fifteenth gets close." Together with the rest of his command, Kevin watched and waited for the inevitable volley that would, no doubt, shatter the 15th. The enemy, South Carolinians and Mississippians, didn't unleash it until Colonel Penrose and his men were within fifty yards. When they did, it came with a deafening crash. One, then another volley of fire staggered the 15th, but didn't stop them. Johnny O'Keeth, excited by the display, got up on his knees and started rooting. "They're gonna make it! By God, they're gonna take the hill." Several other men, caught up in the moment, also got up and waved their hats, hooting and hollering as if they were watching a footrace at a county fair.

When the lead elements of the 15th disappeared over the rim of the Confederate works, Kevin looked down the line again to where his regimental commander was, knowing full well that any minute he would stand up, wave his sword over his head, and give the order to advance.

But the order never came. Kevin watched and waited, but never saw any indication that his regiment, or any of the other regiments in the brigade, were going to move forward in support of the 15th. Looking back up at the hill where clouds of smoke engulfed the spot where the 15th had gone in, Kevin could see little at first. Then, after several minutes of the ceaseless rattle of musketry, men in blue began to pop up, here and there, out of the entrenchments and start streaming down the hill. In groups or alone, the soldiers of the 15th retraced their steps, some walking with a deliberate casualness while others ran for all they were worth. Wounded men staggered or crawled as best they could to keep up with those who weren't.

Saddened by the sudden reversal of the 15th's fortune, Johnny O'Keeth turned to Kevin. "What happened? Why didn't we go with them and support them, like the general ordered us?"

Kevin sighed, looking first out across the marsh where the survivors continued to retreat under fire from the enemy, then over to where his own colonel waited. The reasons, Kevin knew, were many. There always seemed to be lots of reasons why this Army never seemed to be able to get the upper hand for long when it was fighting Lee's Army of Northern Virginia. He had heard them all around the campfires at night and during receptions and balls that livened up every winter camp. They all seemed good and very valid, especially when explained by one of the West Pointers who never seemed to be at a loss when it came to explaining such things.

But out here, in the heat of battle, with the remnants of a shattered regiment staggering back from a botched attack, none of those excuses made any sense or seemed to matter. Glancing back to the front, Kevin's eyes swept across the hillside, now dotted with blue, lifeless figures. Slowly, he shook his head as he surveyed the scene before him. When he finally did look back at Johnny, there was a tear in his eye, one lone tear for the 101 men of the 15th New Jersey lost in a hopeless charge that lasted less than twenty minutes. "Damned if I know, Johnny," Kevin whispered. "Damned if I know."

CHAPTER 8

Spotsylvania, Virginia, May, 1864

IT TOOK MARTY HAZARD several minutes to rouse James Bannon. Exhausted by their march from the Wilderness and a hurried effort to throw up earthworks in the darkness, it was well past midnight before James was able to wrap himself in his blanket and throw himself on the muddy ground as a drenching rain pelted him. Even then he wasn't afforded an uninterrupted night's rest, for he was awakened once for a short stint of sentry duty that passed without incident. As with all of his companions, the effects of six days of ceaseless effort were beginning to take their toll on James' body as well as his state of mind.

Sitting upright, he leaned against the mounds of freshly turned earth. With his blanket still draped over his shoulders, James looked around, blinking his eyes as he tried to focus them. "You best wake up there, Jimmy," Marty chided him as he held a cup of coffee under James' nose. "We've got a whole mess of work to do."

James looked around at the other men of the regiment. In the predawn gloom, he watched for a moment as some of the men, already up and fully awake, worked on their defenses or brewed coffee over small fires while others, like himself, were just being roused. After taking a sip of the rich Union coffee Marty always seemed to have plenty of, James shook his head, blinked his eyes again, and yawned. "I thought we finished the works last night."

Marty shook his head. "Well, the colonel doesn't seem to think so.

And after looking at where they plopped us down last night, I had ta agree. And I garuntee you, Jimmy," Marty stated as he waggled his bony finger at him, "I'm here to tell you, as soon as you're woke up and get a look at where we are, you'll get a hustle on and start diggin' and choppin' like everyone else."

The look of concern on Marty's face, an expression that he seldom sported, was enough for James. After taking another sip, James threw his blanket off his shoulders, carefully so as not to spill any of his coffee, and started to stand. Marty, however, grabbed James by the arm and kept him from rising too high. " 'Less you want to add another hole somewhere to that head of yours," Marty cautioned, "you'd best keep it down."

For the first time, James took note of an occasional gunshot, some quite close. Dear Lord, he thought as he shook his head, had fighting become so commonplace for him that he no longer noticed it and was able to block out the sounds of danger and potential death so easily from his mind? Or was he just getting too tired to care? Either way, James was thankful that he had someone like Marty to look out for him.

"We're stuck out here," Marty continued as he pointed to some of the dirt and log works about them, "in sort of a horseshoe. The whole division's here. Dole's Georgians are over there, on the left, and Hay's Louisianans are to the right. Beyond them, somewhere over there are the other Virginia and North Carolina regiments."

More alert now and able to focus on things, James looked around more carefully in the growing morning light. All about them in a large semicircle, men were moving. Like the men in the 4th Virginia, most of the other units were hard at work digging or carrying logs here and there to shore up the earthen works. Every so often, James caught sight of a man, bent low at the edge of the works, with a big heavy rifle equipped with a long sight over the barrel at the ready, peering out over the top. James pointed to one. "I see some of our sharpshooters keeping the Yanks occupied."

Marty smiled. "Well, one good turn deserves another. I was thinking of taking a crack at the Yanks myself a bit later on."

"You know, Marty, it only serves to rile the other folks up."

"Jimmy," Marty said, "you must be gettin' soft in your old age. I mean, sleepin' late, worryin' about disturbin' the enemy. Why, hell, after what they've put us through the last few days, they deserve to be riled up."

With a single gulp, James finished the last of the coffee. "They've become pretty persistent lately, haven't they? Seems it's going to take more than one whupping to send Grant packing back north."

This comment caused Marty's face to drop slightly. "Yeah, seems that way. This fella sure ain't no McClellan. He's a fighter. But that's fine by me," Marty added quickly, a smile returning to his face. "Some of the fellas say that this Grant is the best they got. The way I see it, if our Bobby Lee can beat him, maybe, just maybe, this fall, when Black Abe goes to his people for reelection, they'll be so tired of all this foolishness that they'll elect someone more disposed to making peace and leaving us alone."

Though Marty was trying to put the best light on the grim situation that they found themselves in that morning, the thought of another long summer and fall of fighting, especially if it meant fighting like this, horrified James. It wasn't that he didn't think he could do it. After all, he had done so for three years, often surprising himself by how much he could endure. It wasn't the suffering or want of proper food, clothing, and shelter that bothered him the most. It was the odds. As James saw it, the simple truth was that more fighting meant that there would be more of a chance of dying. With only six men left in the company, James realized that his odds of making it through another six months of war, especially if it continued at this pace, were slim, very, very slim.

Eager to change the subject, James turned his cup upside down, letting the few drops that remained in it fall into a dirty pool of muddy water at his feet. "Any rations this morning?"

Marty frowned. "Unless you got somethin' left over from the other day, no."

It was James' turn to cheer up his friend. "Well, Marty, I guess you're in luck."

"I knew I could count on ya, Jimmy." Marty beamed. "I don't know how you do it, boy, but you always manage to come up with somethin'. Even when everyone else is fresh out of everythin', you always have a bit of food squirreled away somewhere nice and safe. You're like a camel with your water and a pack rat with your food."

"Everything but coffee. I leave that in your capable hands." Then looking about again, James asked where Geddy, Josh Major, and Will Pool were.

"Sent 'em out on a wood cuttin' detail. The colonel plans to keep us workin' on the breastworks till they're this high," Marty said, raising his hand up to his neck. "After that, we need to dig somethin' he called a traverse to protect us from Yankee cannon over there," he stated, pointing to one side of the semicircle of works, "and another to protect us from more Yankee guns over there," he added pointing in the opposite direction. "Ta tell ya the truth, Jimmy, when the boys saw where we was and where the Yanks was, there wasn't a single complaint about workin', not even from Geddy."

James nodded. "Guess we oughtta join them, huh?"

"Well," Marty stated, taking on a haughty tone, "as the commander of this here company of ours, and one of the two oldest members of it, I believe we deserve a short break for some breakfast before we start our labors." Then, with a note of concern, he added, "that is, provided you have enough for both of us."

"I'll always have enough for you, Marty. You know that."

With a smile, Marty slapped James on the back. "Jimmy, I count on it."

Kevin slowly made his way back to where the regimental commander had gathered the other company commanders. Most of the other commanders were already there, waiting for Kevin and another lieutenant. When he saw their glum faces, far more grim than their current situation warranted, Kevin sat down next to where Sam Gaul had settled. "What's up?"

Gaul, poking absentmindedly at the ground with a stick, didn't look at Kevin. Nor did he answer right away. "Oh, please," Kevin pleaded as a sick feeling came over him. "Don't tell me Grant's been relieved."

"No, not that bad. Though I'm sure the beating we took back there in the Wilderness isn't going to sit well with folks back home. I think Lincoln is pretty well committed to Grant. Besides," Gaul sighed, "who else is there if Grant goes? Not McClellan again."

Kevin nodded. Then anxious to return to where they had left off, Kevin asked Gaul what other news he had.

"Our own Colonel Brown's gone," Gaul went on in the same tired, monotone voice he had announced the other changes with.

"Killed?"

"No," he responded, slowly shaking his head as he took his stick and jabbed its point again and again into the ground with something akin to a vengeance. "Relieved. Seems General Warren didn't much care for what some say was a poor showing yesterday during the attack we were supposed to make with Fifth Corps."

"Who's got the brigade now?"

"Can you believe it? Penrose Rose of the Fifteenth," Gaul responded with obvious disdain.

Kevin thought about that for a moment. "He seems to be a good man."

"I don't think so," Gaul shot back. "You saw how he took less than half the brigade forward yesterday when Warren told him to attack. He left the First, Second, Fourth, and Tenth in the woods where we couldn't support him while he took his own regiment up the hill, alone, and got it shot up. I'll tell you," Gaul stated as he turned to face Kevin, shaking the dirty end of his stick at him, "I don't like the idea of an officer with that kind of poor judgment taking over the brigade. Things are bad enough without our own commanders making silly mistakes like that."

There was no sense arguing, for Gaul, Kevin knew, had a point. He was about to say that had General Sedgwick been there, the 15th wouldn't have gone forward like that, alone, but the thought of their dead corps commander only served to compound the depression he felt. After holding the ground overlooking the marsh and hill where the 15th had left so many of their own all night, listening to the suffering of wounded men and enduring a soaking rain, the New Jersey Brigade had been relieved and pulled back to a reserve position. Sitting less than a half a mile from the enemy lines, Kevin and his men watched as the enemy busied themselves improving positions that already looked quite formidable.

Earlier in the day, while some of the men were talking about this amongst themselves, General Sedgwick and some of his staff appeared. His uniform, as torn and as muddy as any other in his corps, marked him as the kind of leader Kevin, and the rest of the men in his corps, could look up to and admire. He was their general, loved by all in the Sixth Corps and respected by those that mattered throughout the rest of the Army. It therefore came as a shock when Kevin saw the general, standing with several men of an artillery battery, suddenly stiffen, and then fall over.

"General Sedgwick had just finished inspecting our positions," one of Kevin's friends in the 14th New Jersey later told him before Kevin left for the meeting of the 4th's company commanders, "when he went over to a battery that the enemy was sniping at. He reprimanded the gunners for ducking every time they heard a rifle shot. 'Why they couldn't hit an elephant at this distance,' he told them." His friend, not wanting to continue, paused. After a moment or two, he finished his story. "They were standing there, the general standing there, like he always does, tall and commanding, and then, bang, just like that, a Reb sharpshooter got lucky and shot him, right in the head."

Saddened by the loss of a man they had all grown to respect and love, Kevin looked away as his friend continued his account of Sedgwick's death. "The commander of the battery was so angry, he trained one of his guns on the spot where everyone had seen the puff of smoke the Reb sharpshooter's rifle made and fired a shell at it. Seems the shell burst right over the Reb."

"Well," Kevin added, unmoved by this last bit of news, "we got the worst end of that trade." Everyone in the brigade, and corps, agreed. And though their own division commander, Brigadier General Horatio G. Wright, moved up to replace Sedgwick at corps and Brigadier David A. Russell of the Third Brigade was given the division, Kevin knew that Sedgwick's loss would be felt. The costly campaign that they had embarked on, it seemed to him, was no respecter of rank or merit.

When their commander, Lieutenant Colonel Charles Ewing was ready, he cleared his throat and began to address his assembled commanders. The brigade, he stated, would be moving shortly, over to the corps' left. Exactly what they were to do when they got there wasn't made clear by Ewing. Gaul, listening in silence, continued to jam his stick in the soft, muddy ground. "You suppose," he asked Kevin after Ewing dismissed them, "someone is thinking about attacking those works over there?"

Though he never thought of himself as a pessimist, Kevin knew the truth. "Yes," he replied glumly. "I suppose if we can't get around them, Grant will order Meade to go through them. He's a fighter, they say."

"Yes," Gaul nodded in agreement. "So they say."

The confidence the soldiers had in what Marty Hazard claimed was an impregnable position was badly shaken on the second day of their defense of what was being called the Mule Shoe. In the late afternoon, as Marty, Josh Major, and James were working to shore up the log wall designed to hold back the mounds of dirt that separated them from any potential attackers, a great flurry of firing broke out to the left. Pausing, Marty and James both looked up and over the edge of the earthen works. After watching for a moment, Marty pulled his head down, lest he become the next victim of a Union sharpshooter. "Hey Jimmy," he called to James, who continued to watch the well-disciplined ranks of Union troops quickly cross the open field that separated the two lines. "Them boys look serious. Go find Geddy and Will and tell them to fall in, here, under arms."

Convinced that this was more than a simple probe, James dropped to the ground and took off on the double back to where the other two men were starting a fire to cook their pitiful rations. "Douglas, Will," James shouted as he headed straight for his own rifle, belt, and cartridge box. "Get your gear and hightail it back to the wall, on the double."

Will Pool, who had been listening to the growing commotion over where the Georgians were, needed no one to tell him something bad was happening. Geddy, less attuned to the telltale signs of danger, looked at James with disgust. "Ah, gees, Jimmy," he protested as he held a blackened frying pan in one hand. "I just got this bacon out and . . ."

With no time for an argument, James simply turned to him and snapped. "Shut your mouth, boy, and get a move on." Then, looking beyond where Geddy squatted before his small cook fire, James caught sight of a wave of blue-clad figures as they came over the earthworks to their left and started to overwhelm the dumbstruck Georgians before them.

The expression of concern, bordering on fear that he saw on James' face caused Geddy to look over his shoulder. The image of so many Union soldiers, right there, in the midst of their works, panicked Geddy. Dropping his frying pan into the fire without a second thought, Geddy jumped up and sprinted for the pile of gear his rifle was resting on. He grabbed his rifle and cartridge box without bothering to take the time to throw his cartridge box over his shoulder and followed James, who had already run past him with Will Pool, back to where Marty and the other members of the 4th Virginia were forming.

Colonel Terry, recognizing the danger to his flank, was preparing to swing his regiment to face the left, when men of the 2nd and 33rd Virginia, two other units belonging to the Stonewall Brigade, came streaming through and past them. Surprised like everyone else, they had been afforded little opportunity to form up before the sudden rush of Union troops, swerving both left and right as soon as they had entered the Confederate works, was upon them. A near rout, caused by this collision between the various regiments of the brigade, was stopped by the brigade commander himself. Coming up behind, General Walker, with sword drawn and eyes flashing, shouted and threatened any man who tried to go back to the rear past him while directing the regimental commanders of the 4th, 5th, and 27th Virginia to form a line of battle facing the onslaught of Union troops.

James, quickly followed by Geddy, pushed his way into the firing line being formed just in time to hear the order to come to the ready and aim. Geddy, with his rifle in one hand and his cartridge box and belt in the other, was in no condition to respond. Dumbly, he stood there for a moment, rooted to the ground, as he looked over James' shoulder at the mass of blue headed at them. Colonel Terry's command to fire momentarily wiped that image away, as the regiment's gunfire threw up a thick, white cloud of smoke.

"Why the hell are you just standing there? Shoot, damn it, shoot!" an officer behind him shouted into Geddy's ear. Before Geddy could turn his head to face the man, he was gone, headed off down the line to yell at someone else.

Looking back to the front, Geddy could see the Union troops had stopped and were in the process of trying to return the 4th Virginia's fire. Loss of their forward momentum, as well as the devastating fire that the men around Geddy were pouring into them, was causing confusion in their ranks. Strange, Geddy thought, as he managed to get his cartridge box over his head and into place. A moment ago, he had been deathly afraid of them. Now, with the two ranks standing as close as they were, he could clearly see that there were men in the enemy ranks as fearful of him and his comrades as he had been of them.

As quickly as this thought came, Geddy pushed it out of his head. With his belt in place, he was ready. Fishing a round out of his cartridge box, he started to load his rifle, all the while glancing back, over his shoulder, on the lookout for the officer that had yelled at him.

As he had two days before, Kevin watched the dying gasps of a gallant effort to break the formidable Confederate lines. Though the numbers involved in this attempt were considerably larger, and the overall assault had been far better managed, the end results were the same. Staggering back, alone or in small groups, the men of Colonel Upton's Second Brigade came back under punishing enemy fire that was more brutal than that which they had faced when they had gone forward. Artillery firing canisters, and victorious Confederate troops that had been rallied at the last moment to counterattack into the gap created by their initial thrust, pelted Upton's men every step of the way.

Sam Gaul, coming up from his post on the picket line being held by the 4th New Jersey, went down on one knee next to Kevin. "What happened?" he asked as he watched in disbelief. "A few minutes ago, they were going strong, rolling up the Confederate lines. What broke them?"

Kevin turned his face away from the sorry spectacle. "Same old story," Kevin responded bitterly. "Just like it happened to us two years ago at Gaines's Mill, and again that December at Fredericksburg. No support." Taking his hat off, Kevin wiped the sweat from his forehead before looking back as the last survivors of Upton's attack regained their own lines. "Someone over there," he continued angrily, "maybe our very own brigade commander with one whole day's experience, decided he couldn't do what he was supposed to do or just didn't understand his orders."

Then, putting his cap back on and pulling it down low over his eyes, Kevin looked back at Gaul. "Not that it much matters." Slowly Kevin scanned the Confederate works, only yards from where the forward line of his company, spread thinly in small groups, manned the picket line. "I don't know how they do it, but somehow they always manage to get us to go forward, to make one more try, one more attack against positions like those even when common sense tells us that we shouldn't." Kevin turned to Sam. "You'd think after three years of this either we'd be smarter or they'd have come up with something better than head-on attacks."

Gaul didn't respond to his friend's comments, not at first. Like Kevin, he was becoming concerned with their Army's inability to overcome an enemy they knew to be smaller in number, underfed, and poorly equipped. Most of the officers in the regiment, at least those who hadn't been killed or wounded already this spring, were beginning to show the strain of one frustrating failure after another. In the seven days since leaving their winter camps north of the Rapidan, neither their brigade nor any other brigade in the Army that Gaul knew of had once managed to catch the Confederates at a disadvantage. Everywhere they turned, the Confederates were there, waiting, dug in, ready. Every attack they had been in or witnessed had been a failure. Though the Confederates had suffered, their losses and failures didn't seem to bother them. Nothing seemed to keep them from stealing a march on the Army of the Potomac and frustrating the most carefully prepared maneuver or gallantly led attack. Nothing.

"I'm telling you, Sam," Kevin continued, "if someone doesn't start making some progress toward bringing this war to an end, we're going to lose it. Everything we've worked for, everything we've suffered will be for nothing. *Nothing*," Kevin repeated with anger as he pounded his fist on his bent knee.

For a moment, Sam Gaul didn't respond. It had been bad enough when he heard the men in the ranks talk like this. To hear officers of Kevin's caliber utter such sentiments alarmed him. Yet deep down in his heart, Gaul knew Kevin was right. Back home in New Jersey, a state that had always been lukewarm in its support of Lincoln's war aims, efforts were already under way to replace Lincoln with a president that would be willing to recognize the South's right to leave the Union and end the war in defeat. And though every man in the regiment was against this, a fact borne out by the number who chose to reenlist for another three years or the duration rather than give up on the cause like many of the men in the 1st, 2nd, and 3rd New Jersey had, the Army's inability to defeat the Rebel Army in the field frustrated even the most noble sentiment. Victory, as Kevin so clearly pointed out, would depend on their success, which seemed to be as elusive today as it had been two years before when they had been turned away from the very gates of Richmond.

Placing his hand on Kevin's shoulder, Gaul gave him a shake. "We have to keep trying, Kevin. If you really believe in what we're doing, like I know you do, we have to keep trying."

Kevin reached up and placed his hand on Gaul's. Then he looked down and nodded. "I know, Sam. I know," he whispered. "And I'll go on, damn it. I'll do what I . . . what we set out to do." Then he removed his hand, turned, and looked back at his friend. "But it angers me that so many good men are being thrown away like that."

"And it does me too," Gaul reassured him. "But what are we to do?"

Gaul didn't expect an answer, and Kevin didn't give him one. Instead, the two men sat together in the failing evening light and listened to the all too familiar sounds of the battlefield.

Peering over the top of their protective works, James Bannon watched and listened. The men of the 33rd Virginia, who had volunteered to go out in front of the brigade's line and set up abatis so that a Union attack didn't surprise them as it had Dole's Georgians, were already out there working in the dark. James listened, trying to pick up any reaction from the Union line. So far, as best he could tell, there had been none.

Marty Hazard, standing next to James, listened too. "You sure you wanna do this?" Marty whispered.

James, his head cocked, continued to listen for a moment. Then he looked at Marty's face, its features hidden by the darkness. "We don't have much of a choice, do we? If I don't go out there soon, those boys in the Thirty-third will pick those Yankee bodies clean and we'll go hungry tomorrow."

While Marty nodded in silent agreement, Douglas Geddy looked on in horror. It was one thing for him to go about an abandoned battlefield and pick through the personal items of a dead man in relative safety. But to go out, between two opposing lines, in the dark, was an entirely different matter. "What happens if you get lost, Jimmy?" Geddy asked nervously.

James laughed. "Not likely. We're uphill, out in the open, and they're downhill in the woods."

"But, I mean," Geddy explained quickly, "what if you can't find your way back to our part of the line? Do you think another regiment's going to believe you and let you back in?"

James didn't look back as he continued to scan to the front. "Well," he replied slowly, "if that happens, I guess I'll just have to do some fast talking." Then he looked back at Geddy and winked. "Won't I?"

Geddy didn't respond. He was mad, he thought. They were all mad. Living like this, in the mud, under almost continuous fire from two sides, without proper rations and no relief in sight, was madness. That any sane man would endure this, of his own free will, was not possible. That he would do so, and then willingly risk his life like James was about to do, in the hope of finding a couple of handfuls of food on a dead body somewhere out in the darkness was utter madness.

"Remember, Jimmy," Josh Major stated from behind Marty, "if you need us, we'll be here waiting."

"Well," James said as he made one more sweep of the area, "if I'm going to go, I guess I best be going." Then, as he had before, he turned and winked at both Marty and Josh. "I'll be awhile, so you boys don't need to wait up for me."

Marty patted James' shoulder. "I'll be here, Jimmy. Now don't go gettin' yourself killed, ya hear?"

"Is that an order?" James snapped back.

Concerned, in his own way, Marty shook his head. "No. It's a request from a friend."

James smiled. "Well, since you put it like that, I guess I'll have to do my best." Then, after planting both hands on the top log of their works, James gave himself a boost up and started to crawl out into the dead space between the lines. Marty, stepping up to where James had been, watched James go until he couldn't see him any longer. Even when he was out of sight, Marty waited, watching and listening for his comrade and friend.

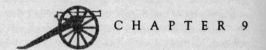

CHAPTER 9

Spotsylvania, Virginia, May, 1864

RELIEF FROM DUTY ON the picket line by the First New Jersey during the day, and movement to the rear, was welcomed by Kevin Bannon and his company. So was the rain that started falling. At least in the beginning it was. By late afternoon, as it continued to fall with only an occasional break, it turned from blessing to curse. Even a resupply of fresh rations in the early evening did nothing to relieve the cold dampness that chilled man and beast to the bone. The continual struggle required to keep their cook fires going took away whatever small comfort and enjoyment those rations ordinarily would have brought. "First we're marched to death," complained Amos Flatherly as he gnawed on a half-cooked chunk of bacon, "then we're left sitting in front of the whole Reb Army in this godforsaken country without a chance to strike at them. Given half a chance, we'd beat 'em, boys. I know it."

"What makes you so sure, Flatherly?" Johnny O'Keeth challenged from his spot near the fire.

" 'Cause we're mad," Flatherly shot back. "Madder than hell at being led about like a bunch of sheep to the slaughter."

Kenneth Miller shook his head. "Ya know, Amos, I don't think I like the idea of being called a sheep."

"And no one's led us into the slaughter," Denny Cummins threw in, then, looking skyward, he crossed himself and added, "by the grace of God and the Holy Mother."

Though he could see that he wasn't able to whip up any support for his position, Amos nevertheless persisted. "Well, say what you like. It's only a matter of time before it's our turn. Ain't that right, Captain?"

From across the dying fire, Kevin Bannon looked up from where he'd sat with his head down between his shoulders as he dozed off to sleep. Stirring, he looked around at the faces now staring at him. In the darkness of the woods, the flickering fire only partially illuminated each man's face, leaving large areas that were shaded by their rough features. This gave each man a strange, almost supernatural appearance. Kevin yawned before answering. "If I was you, Amos, I'd be careful about what I hoped for. I always believed that if you expect the worst, the worst is sure to happen."

"If you ask me," Flatherly said bluntly, "what could be worse than this?"

Leaning forward, Kevin took his hands from his pockets and looked into the fire for several seconds before answering. What, indeed, he thought, could be worse? Then, without any prompting, the list of things that preyed on his mind day in and day out unraveled like a ball of yarn rolling across the floor. Murdering the girl you loved started that count. The exiling of your only brother by a father who measured the value of every human he came into contact with in the same cold, detached manner with which he measured his fortune came next. Falling in love with a girl who was so far beyond his own social class that it frightened him was not far behind. And finally, but by no means last, there was the nagging fear that somewhere, out there on the other side of the works in the enemy camp, your only brother was waiting, waiting to avenge the death of a girl he had loved and lost to Kevin.

Looking up, Kevin glanced at each of the attentive faces that were looking at him as they waited for an answer. "What could be worse?" Kevin started. "I'll tell you what could be worse." Then he hesitated as a chill ran down his back that wasn't caused by the cold. Instead, it came from the same feeling he had felt when he looked into the faces of his fellow officers during their first night in the Wilderness before the fighting had begun. As the familiar feeling of dread grabbed him, Kevin felt his breathing become more difficult, more constricted. Though he tried not to believe in the ghosts and premonitions that the old Irish workers he and his brother used to listen to spoke of when they spun their ancient Celtic stories for them, Kevin never fully discounted their validity. The fact was, he realized as he looked at the silent men whose faces were lit by the most unnatural light of the dying fire, that at times like this, one could almost believe that you could see imminent death in the faces of the living.

"What could be worse?" Kevin repeated as he slowly stood up. Looking down at his men, Kevin spoke slowly, distinctly. "The thought of losing more of you. The idea that sometime, very soon, I may have to lead you forward, again, into a useless charge that will do nothing but kill more of you. That," Kevin snapped, "is my worst nightmare. Can anyone think of something worse?"

Stunned into silence, not even Amos responded. Only the sound of raindrops softly falling through the trees, hissing whenever one fell into the fire, broke the silence. The strange, trancelike standoff was shattered suddenly by the sound of hundreds of tramping feet, accompanied by half-hearted whispered orders of officers calling to their men to close it up and the creak and grind of caisson wheels off to their left. Turning, Kevin peered into the darkness for a moment. "Second Corps' coming up on our left," he stated to no one in particular as he continued to look into the woods beyond the tiny circle of light his fire provided.

Then Kevin turned back to face the men sitting about the fire who were also looking into the blackness where the sound was coming from. "It could be a long day tomorrow, men," he finally stated almost absentmindedly. "Best get whatever rest you can."

When they did respond, the men who had been around the campfire did so slowly. Even then, they glanced over to the woods to their left, alive with the sounds of many men in motion, wondering all the time if their captain knew something that they didn't.

Unable to sleep, in part because of the rain and in part because of an uneasiness he felt, James Bannon threw off the gum blanket covering him and got up. He was wet, head to toe, more from his own sweat from sleeping under the rubber gum blanket he had wrapped himself in the rain. Sitting up amongst the sleeping men, James looked about, blinking as drops of rain ran down his forehead, mixed with the sweat that had beaded up, and ran into his eyes, stinging them.

Outside the small circle of his comrades and friends, sleeping fitfully in the mud like he had tried to do, James could see other small knots of men, just like his, by the light of small watch fires. It was, he thought, as he looked up and let the raindrops fall into his open mouth, a thoroughly miserable night.

Lowering his head, he swallowed the drops he collected, and continued to look around. It was then he noticed that the battery of artillery that had been set up next to where they had made their little camp was gone. Was the Army getting ready to move again? he wondered. Stirred by this thought, he stood up, wrapped his waterlogged blanket about his shoulders, and picked his way between the sleeping men over to where Will Pool was standing guard. "Is there something going on?" James asked innocently.

Pool, who had been paying no attention to anything behind him, was startled by James. Spinning about in the mud, he drew away from James before catching himself. "Jesus, Jimmy! What'd ya mean sneaking up on a fella like that for?"

Taken aback by Pool's wild reaction, James cocked his head. "I didn't mean to frighten you or anything. I just saw the cannon was gone and was wondering . . ." James stopped when he noticed that Pool wasn't paying any attention to him. Instead, Pool had gone back to looking to the front, out over the top edge of the works he had been standing guard at.

"Hear 'em?" Pool asked quietly.

Turning his head so that his good ear was oriented toward the Union lines that Pool was facing, James listened for a moment. Faintly, he could hear orders being passed in voices that their owners thought were hushed. Mixed in was the creaking of heavy wheels, artillery or caissons, James thought, and the snapping of branches. "Was a lot louder earlier," Pool finally said quietly. "You could almost feel the tromping of a lot of feet coming from over there."

At first, James didn't answer. He listened for a moment more, then turned to face their own rear, toward the narrow neck of open space that connected their horseshoe-shaped defensive works with the rest of the Army. Made barely visible by the light of watch fires were a number of guns, limbered to their own caissons with horses still in harness, lined up and pointing to the rear. Pool, noticing James staring at the guns, looked back. "They started pulling out a while ago."

"Anyone else move? Any of the infantry units?" James asked.

Pool shook his head. "Not that I saw. Some officers were wandering about. One of them, I think General Johnson, seemed pretty upset with one of the artillery officers. But that's all."

Looking back out into the darkness made more ominous by a thick fog that was settling in, James stood next to Pool for several minutes and listened to the distant orders for enemy soldiers to close it up repeated time and time again. When a shiver ran down his back, James glanced once more at the guns behind them, then over to Pool. "I sure hope those guns are back in place or we're out of here before the Yankees come at us in the morning."

Shaken by the calm, matter-of-fact manner in which James made his statement, Pool was about to challenge James' assumption that the enemy was preparing to deliver a major attack, but then hesitated. James had been with the regiment for three years, Pool reasoned, almost a whole year longer than he had been. That, along with being a former VMI cadet, all but made James' views on tactics like gospel. Looking back into the darkness to their front, Pool swallowed hard. "I guess I do too, Jimmy."

Despite his best efforts, Kevin was unable to find any escape through sleep from the misery of the cold and rain. At intervals, he stood up and walked away from the small fire a few sentinels kept going before returning to the log he had been sitting on all night. The closest he came to sleep was an occasional period when he would doze off for a few moments. The bobbing of his head, however, ended that, rousing him back to full consciousness and the desire to stand up again and walk about in shoes that were as waterlogged as every other part of his uniform.

It was near dawn, when the darkness of the forest was beginning to give way to a dirty gray light, that a sudden shout from thousands of voices off to his left startled Kevin just as he had started to drift off again. Jumping to his feet, he turned to face that direction as the deep, throaty cry of "Hurrah" echoed through the woods. Almost immediately, a number of cannon cut loose with a thunderous roar made more spectacular by the dense fog that still enshrouded them. A sentinel who had been sitting next to Kevin came up next to him. "The Second Corps is going in, ain't it?" the sentinel asked excitedly.

Kevin listened as more shouts of "Hurrah" rose from the foggy woods, first drowning out the sound of rifle and cannon fire, then in turn being drowned out by it. Kevin nodded. "Yes, Second Corps is having a go at them." Turning toward his own command, Kevin surveyed the expressions of his men, who had been roused from their fitful sleep by the Second Corps' attack. Without knowing how he knew it for fact, for no mention of an attack had been made the night before, Kevin whispered, more to himself than to the sentinel next to him, "And we're going to be following them, soon."

At first, they didn't see them. The fog that hung before the 4th Virginia's positions was too thick to see much of anything past a couple of dozen feet. "Jesus, Marty, where are they? I can't see them!" Will Pool shouted as he danced about on the firing step nervously.

Leaning on his rifle, Marty Hazard, with James Bannon at his side, peered into the fog as if he could actually see something. "Just slow down, Will," Marty said with a cool, slow deliberateness. "They'll be along presently."

"Well," Pool stammered in response, "it's not like I want them to come, ya know. I was just . . ."

"And why in blazes don't you want 'em to come?" Josh Major shouted. "We're ready for 'em. We're ready to beat 'em senseless like we've always beat 'em. Ain't that right, Jimmy?"

James Bannon didn't respond to Josh's foolish boast. He was keyed up by the sudden call to arms, the wild and excited state of the skirmishers who had fled before the horde of advancing Yankees, and unnerved by the uneasy feeling that he had been struggling with all night. Instead of joining in the nervous chatter his messmates threw back and forth, James simply continued to peer into the thick morning fog. "You know," he finally admitted to Marty quietly, "when I was a kid, waiting outside my father's study to be punished, I used to stare at the doors of that room, hoping that they would never open."

"I take it," Marty stated dryly, "they always did."

"Yes, Marty, they opened. Always."

Then, with a suddenness that was startling, the fog lifted. Geddy, standing at James' shoulder, stepped backward and gasped, "Oh, my God!"

Before them, not more than a third of the distance between their works and the woods that had concealed the Union for so long, a moving wall of blue was revealed. Marty looked to the left, then to the right at the dense ranks of Union soldiers that appeared to go on forever.

"Must be a whole corps!" Josh Major exclaimed.

Close enough now to see their faces in the steady, fine rain, James lifted his rifle when he heard one of the officers behind him shout the order to aim. He found little comfort in the reluctance or trepidation that many of their faces betrayed as the Yankees, collectively, eyed the formidable Confederate works before them and tried to halt. Though he had confidence that they would throw this attack back, like so many others before, James also knew that battles were wild affairs where luck and fortune ruled and favored no one side. Settling for a big man with a determined look on his face, James took careful aim at the Yankee's midsection and waited for the order to fire. When it came, James, and everyone around him, instinctively squeezed the trigger till it released the hammer.

With a snap, the hammer of hundreds of rifles crashed down onto the metal caps set upon the small, tapered cones that opened into the rifle's chamber where the black powder of the loaded cartridge lay. And that was all that happened. Just a snap. There was no loud discharge, no massed volley. James felt no kick from his rifle or saw any puff of white smoke lingering about the muzzle of his rifle. His rifle had misfired. The spark from the cap setting on the cone wasn't strong enough to ignite black powder that had grown damp during the wet night. Worse, as James slowly became aware of his plight, he also realized that almost no one else had fired. Like himself, the men to his left and right were pulling their heads back, looking down at their rifles, and slowly accepting the horrible fact that they had not fired.

Glancing up, James saw a sudden transformation sweep the silent blue ranks before him. The horde of enemy soldiers, who moments before wore expressions as grim as a death mask, came to life. They too realized what had just happened. While they didn't know that it was lax discipline on the part of many a Confederate officer, rather than fate, that had saved them from a massed volley that would have devastated their ranks, it didn't matter. What did matter was that they had just been given an opportunity to close with their hated antagonist who, for the moment, was all but defenseless.

As a cheer rose in the Union ranks and they lunged forward in one final rush, the men all about James became animated. Some, like Marty, refused to believe that they were in trouble. Instead, they calmly brought their pieces down to the ready, pulled the hammer of their rifles back, flicked off the used cap, and replaced it with a new one with which to try again. Will Pool, still wearing a stunned expression on his face, had stepped backward one pace, all the while fishing in the pocket of his cartridge box for the ball screw that he intended to use to draw out the failed cartridge. Josh Major, believing there was precious little time for any such foolishness, had also stepped back, but was reaching for his bayonet instead. And Douglas Geddy, not sure what to do, stood there with wide eyes that darted all about wildly.

Then, before James, Marty, or anyone else had much of an opportunity to do anything of value, the Yankees were through the obstacles in front of Jones' brigade to their right, and flooding into the works. Confederate defensive lines and Union tactical formations lost all cohesion as the wave of blue rushed forward. Here and there small knots of men in gray and butternut came together to form pockets and broke the wave like rocks on a shore. But like the rocks, they were submerged by an angry, raging sea that surged around, and eventually, over them.

In an effort to stem this tide, officers ran about, shouting, yelling, cursing, and shoving. General Walker, their brigade commander, rode amongst his men, half-dressed and excited as he alternated between shouting encouragement to his men and hurling defiance at the enemy. Their division commander, armed with nothing more than his hickory walking stick and blazing eyes, flailed at the assailants that flooded his works until James saw him overwhelmed and hauled into the blue mass by his enemies.

It was their own regimental commander, Colonel William Terry, who brought some semblance of order to the confused melee that was sweeping the muddy horseshoe-shaped positions. With the same clarity of mind that had allowed him to react quickly and effectively on the first day of the Wilderness fight, Terry saw what needed to be done, rallied his regiment, and fought to salvage the situation. With Jones' brigade of Virginians gone and the overwhelmed remnants of Hays' Louisianans in their death throes, Terry ordered his regiment to fall back and form a new line in the mud perpendicular to the formidable breastworks now rendered useless by the collapse of sister units. Pushing and shoving, officers with swords in one hand and pistols in the other, quickly forced the 170 odd men of the 4th Virginia into two lines of battle.

The men, once settled into the ranks, worked frantically to put their rifles into firing order. Marty, frustrated and angered by his failure, had thrown his fouled rifle down into the mud and rushed at a Union soldier who had run out before his comrades. Grabbing the muzzle of the Yankee's gun just behind the bayonet, Marty gave the rifle a quick jerk and twist. The Union soldier, shocked as much by the wild appearance of Marty, made more fearsome by the fire that shone in his eyes, let go of his rifle and ran back into the safety of the milling mass of blue soldiers still working to subdue the last of Jones' men. Armed now with a clean and serviceable piece, Marty returned to his customary place next to James and began the familiar task of loading and firing.

For James, the task of returning his rifle to a state of readiness was somewhat easy. As was the custom of many who loaded their weapons while on guard duty, James had not wadded and shoved the empty paper of the cartridge down the barrel of his rifle after pouring the powder and miníe ball into it. This left the loose-fitting bullet and powder free to fall out if the rifle was turned upside down, which was exactly what James needed to happen right now. Walking backward, with his face turned to the enemy, James flipped his piece upside down, shook it several times, then turned it back upright. Just to be sure that there wasn't any wet powder left in the chamber, James brought the rifle up to the ready, jerked back the hammer, slipped a fresh cap on the cone, and pulled the trigger. After he heard the cap snap, he automatically went about reloading while an officer grabbed the sleeve of his jacket and dragged him into line.

Geddy, psychologically overwhelmed, found himself powerless to do anything. It was only the press of his comrades about him and the physical prodding of a regimental officer that kept him with the colors. Seeing Geddy standing in the front rank, dazed and ineffectual, James reached out, grabbed a handful of cloth, and jerked him back. "Get behind me, Douglas," James yelled in Geddy's ear when it was close enough to his mouth, "and stay there." Unable to do anything but comply, Geddy gave way to James' manhandling and heeded his advice. For the next several minutes, he did nothing but stand there, rifle clasped between two hands whose knuckles were turning white from the death grip he held it with, staring at a jagged rip just below the collar of James' jacket.

While Union soldiers of the first wave went about subduing the few remaining pockets of resistance that still stood before them and rushed to seize the cannons that stood idle and limbered near the open mouth of the horseshoe, fresh Union regiments poured through the gaping hole ripped in the Confederate defenses and began to roll up units that still stood their ground. Formed into a rough semblance of a line, the men of the 4th Virginia were able to meet this new threat on something of an even footing for several minutes. Firing quickly and at will, James, Marty, Josh, and Will Pool settled into the drill of firing, loading, and firing again that had become second nature to them. For James, this routine served to calm him and create the momentary illusion that their plight was not without hope.

Marty, however, with a better view of the mass of Union soldiers surging around their open right flank and rear, knew better. "I don't think we can stand here like this and hold 'em much longer, boys," he yelled above the roar of battle made more deafening by the shouts of victorious Yankees, the hurrahs of fresh Union reinforcements who continued to flow into the horseshoe, and the screams of men dying or facing certain death. In the midst of this, General Walker went down, off his horse and into the mud, with a bullet in his elbow. Their very own Colonel Terry, who had rallied them and was ceaselessly moving up and down the firing line, also went down with a wound. Taking all this in, Marty began to sense impending doom. "If we don't leave soon," Marty shouted in James' ear as they both reloaded, "we'll be sitting the rest of this war out as prisoners."

Too busy at first to pay Marty any heed, James continued to fire and reload, fire and reload. It was only when a group of Yankees, propelled forward by a reckless abandon that defied all logic, smashed into the 4th Virginia's line near James that he suddenly comprehended the hopelessness of their situation. "*Run!*" someone yelled. "Run for your lives!"

For Josh Major, that warning came a second too late. Concentrating on fishing out another round from his cartridge box, he didn't notice the mad charge of a Yankee every bit as big as he was till the last second. When he did, he had no time to react, no time to dodge left or right. Hitting him at a dead run, the Union soldier thrust the full length of his eighteen-inch bayonet into Josh's midsection, knocking him over and pinning him to the muddy ground. With a sweep of his rifle butt that was more reaction than conscious thought, James caught the big Union soldier under the chin, smashing Josh's assailant's jaw in a shower of blood, bone, and teeth. Letting go of his rifle, the Yankee fell over backward into a clutch of his comrades who had been following him.

Stepping backward, James knocked Geddy over onto his buttocks as James turned to grab for the rifle that the Yankee had left standing upright stuck in the ground and Josh. James' arm, however, was pulled away by Marty. Looking over to him, James was shocked to see the color literally drain from Marty's face, now only inches from his own. With eyes bulging and an expression that could only be caused by excruciating pain, Marty opened his mouth, but failed to utter a word or sound. Instead, like a statue that had toppled from its base, Marty Hazard fell over sideways, twisting James' arm in a death grip that brought tears to James' eyes.

Even before he was able to respond, before the words were able to make their way from his horrified mind to his mouth, James felt a pair of hands pushing him away from Marty. "Run, damn you, sir. Run, or die where you stand."

Caught off guard, James had only enough time to reach over and grab the sleeve of Geddy's coat before being swept away by the shattered refuse of the 4th Virginia. Like a drug, the word *run* animated James' legs to carry him away from the carnage even as his head turned to the rear to search for Marty. In the awful swirl of blue and gray and mud, it was impossible to see anything resembling a clear image of what lay behind him. Only a brief glimpse of the quivering stock of the upright Union rifle that continued to pin Josh Major to the ground marked where James had been a moment before.

Now galvanized into an action that he understood, Geddy took the lead away from James. "Let go of me, you son of a bitch!" he yelled. "Let go of me or I'll kill you."

Geddy's words and his wild flailing tore James' attention away from what was behind them. Angered as much by Geddy's cowardly self-concern as by the knowledge that he could do nothing to help those who had meant so much to him, James lunged after Geddy. Seeing the response he had provoked, Geddy took off with all his might for the rear. Through the gap and into the woods the two men ran, ignoring the dead and wounded, both blue and gray, they stepped on and leaped over.

Only when they came to a solid wall of Confederate soldiers, forming up to advance in line of battle, did James finally manage to catch Geddy, who was now more fearful of his comrade than he was of the Yankees. With Geddy finally within reach, James brought his rifle up and prepared to bring it smashing down on the cowering young man. And he would have too. Both James and Geddy knew it. Had it not been for the intervention of two officers, James Bannon would have murdered in a fit of passion a man whom he had labored so long to protect.

The first officer was a stranger. Seizing James' rifle at the last moment, the major jerked it away from him. With his free hand, he shoved James into the ranks. "Save that for the Yankees," the major yelled with a thick Virginia accent. Then, turning his attention to Geddy, he pushed the bewildered boy between two of his own men. "And you! Get your sorry ass in those ranks and stay there, or I'll shoot you myself." Guessing that the Virginia major had witnessed his shameless flight, Geddy said nothing as the bearded corporal to his right glared down at him.

James was in the process of catching his breath and collecting his thoughts when the second officer, a tall mounted figure riding a dappled gray horse, appeared inches before his face. Looking up, he immediately recognized the figure of his Army commander, Robert E. Lee. In all his time with the Army of Northern Virginia, in all his campaigns, James had never been this close, had never been so near the man he had followed month after month, year after year. As Lee continued to ride by, James was tempted to reach out and touch the tall leather riding boot that he could actually smell.

Around him, the men of Pegram's brigade looked up in awed silence as their beloved commander rode by and stopped before another figure that was familiar to them all. Upon seeing Lee, General John B. Gordon paused in his preparations for counterattack and saluted his commander. "What do you want me to do, General?" Gordon asked.

With a calmness that belied the anxiety he felt, Lee turned to Gordon and ordered him to proceed with his attack. Saluting, Gordon started to head away and continue his preparation but stopped when he saw that the commanding general rode to the center of his line and turned his horse to the front. Knowing what Lee intended to do and having no desire to see him do so, Gordon rode over to where Lee sat waiting to advance. In a voice loud enough for his men to hear above the din of the battle that continued to rage just beyond the trees, Gordon admonished his commander. "General Lee, this is no place for you. Go back, General. We will drive them back."

In the silence that followed as Lee continued to look to the front, the men around James broke ranks and surged forward, surrounding the two general officers. James, his fighting blood up and eager to charge forward to rescue his fallen comrades, went along with the throng.

"These men," Gordon continued when Lee made no move to leave his self-appointed post, "are Virginians and Georgians. They have never failed. They never will. Will you boys?" he asked as he turned his stern gaze down upon the soldiers who now pressed them.

Possessed as he had never been possessed before, James joined the chorus of men as they screamed "No, no," over and over.

Lee, however, was not moved. With his eyes fixed to the front, the tall gray commander stood his ground and waited. As his men began to break into a chant of "Go back, go back," Gordon dug spurs into the flank of his horse and forced his way through his men until he was in front of Lee and between him and the enemy. In desperation, he leaned over and reached for Traveler's bridle. He caught it, but then dropped it. Before Gordon had the chance to try again, a tall sergeant who had been standing near James stepped through the crowd and grabbed the bridle of the commanding general's horse. Amidst the cheers of his fellow Virginians and Georgians, the sergeant led a subdued Lee to the rear.

Relieved that he would not have the death of his beloved commander to worry over, Gordon took his place and turned to his troops, now returning to their ranks and dressing the line of battle. With the sound of the Union advance growing near, Gordon cried out above it and issued the only order he needed to. "Forward! Guide right!" As one, the men stepped off and crashed into the woods before them, determined to live up to the pledge that they had given their commanding general.

Geddy, held captive by the men to his right, left, and rear, could not believe that he was going back into the hell on earth that he had barely escaped from. Didn't these men know, his outraged mind screamed as they moved forward, what was happening up there? Didn't these men realize that they were about to die? Jerking his head this way, then that, Geddy saw nothing to indicate that they might give way to reason, that they might come to their senses. With eyes fixed straight ahead and jaw set in the peculiar manner that he had seen James, Marty, and Josh use when going into battle, Geddy realized that there would be no redemption. There would be no last-minute reprieve. They were going back to fight an enemy who was as determined and mad as they were.

When it came time for them to go forward, Kevin Bannon had made his peace with himself and God. It was shortly after they had pushed their way through a thin line of scrubs and trees and were reforming in preparation for the advance that Kevin looked up into the gray, cheerless sky. "I am," he whispered as the raindrops splattered on his face, "in your hands." Then, when he looked down and his eyes fell upon the chaotic scene before him, Kevin added, "thy will be done."

Finally ordered forward, the 4th New Jersey did so with the 1st New Jersey on their left, nearer to the horrendous fighting that continued to go on unabated in the apex of the contested Confederate works. To the right, the 15th New Jersey rubbed shoulders with the 4th, forming the extreme right flank of the Union forces so far committed to this fight. The order by Colonel Penrose, the brigade commander, to hold their fire until after they had penetrated the enemy works played on Kevin's mind. He intended to fight close in, hand to hand, if the Confederates chose to stand and receive them. With nothing more to say, either to his men or his maker, Kevin looked down the ranks of his company one more time, straightened himself up, and then turned his gaze toward the enemy works.

The works that were the immediate object of their advance, however, were already occupied by Union forces. For several minutes, the New Jersey regiments stood in the open area between the wood line where they had come from and the earthworks that they had advanced on. Finally, the brigade commander gave the order to right face, quickly followed by the command to advance at the double quick. Tucking his right, sword arm tight against his side to keep that worthless weapon from swinging about wildly as they moved over the broken ground, Kevin tucked his head down and followed the second sergeant of the company in front of him.

At first, a belt of young pine trees and cedars that had been left in the killing ground between the lines gave the brigade, running across the enemy's front, some cover. Slowly, however, the density of this line of trees thinned, exposing the long column of Jerseymen to an ever-increasing volume of Reb fire. With his head down and the tip of his sword now just below the lobe of his right ear, Kevin felt the urge to yell something. Trying to find something appropriate to yell, he intently watched the cartridge box of the sergeant in front of him bob and bounce about. His first thought was to scream at the top of his lungs, over at his regimental commander about the stupidity of running across the enemy's front like this. But he quickly decided against this. Though he knew in his heart that this was true, this was neither the time nor place for such open and potentially corrosive criticism. The idea of turning and shouting encouragements to his men was also quickly discarded. While such sentiments had been popular early in the war, his men now viewed any appeals for patriotism and valor as demeaning and useless. Panting now from his exertions, and forced to pay close attention to where he put his feet lest he trip over the body of a Jerseyman from a unit up ahead who had been shot dead or was too badly wounded to crawl out of the way, Kevin gave up all thoughts of yelling anything.

Just about the time when the thin line of trees disappeared, the order to march by the left flank ended their headlong trot down the line of enemy works and redirected it into a charge against a stout section held by a determined foe. The frustration Kevin's men felt about their inability to lash out at their enemy for so long turned into anger and rage. Tearing away the abatis and other obstacles that the Confederates had planted before their works to slow the Union advance, the First New Jersey Brigade rushed madly into their assailants.

The Confederates, a brigade of Mississippians, met the Jerseymen without flinching, without yielding. Equally keyed up to a fevered pitch by days of sniping and skirmishing, they held their ground, firing and fighting from one side of the stout earthen and log breastworks while the soldiers of the First New Jersey Brigade pulled up along the opposite side. Without any hesitation, without the slightest concern over the insanity of the situation that was developing, the hardened veterans of both sides settled down, on their respective sides of the same earthworks, and went about the grim task of pouring as much fire into their enemy as the cumbersome loading and reloading process permitted.

Once he was satisfied that as many of his men as were going to make it to the works were there and fighting, Kevin went about adding his contribution to the carnage and chaos that exploded all about him. With a thrust, he jabbed the tip of his sword, an item he had always considered useless as a weapon, into the slippery mud next to his chosen position. Switching his pistol from his left hand to the right, he popped up, stretched his arm out, and tried to take aim at the first thing that came into his field of view. A shower of splinters and the whine of bullets whizzing past his head discouraged this, forcing Kevin to throw himself, face first, down into the mud.

For a second, he lay there, listening to the terrible sound of continual rifle and cannon fire that came so fast that individual shots could no longer be distinguished. He could almost imagine, he thought as he lay there and collected himself, that he could see the stream of Rebel bullets as they flew over the works, inches above him. Wondering how best to return effective fire without getting himself killed, Kevin craned his head over to one side in an effort to see if there was a gap in the logs he could shoot through. Seeing a promising spot, he began to claw away at a patch of mud that had been crammed between two logs in the same manner poor folks filled in chinks in log cabins. When his hands proved to be insufficient, he reached over and took the rifle of the second sergeant he had been following in their mad rush to this spot. Since the sergeant was gut shot and rolling about on the ground beside him in terrible pain, Kevin figured he wouldn't be needing his bayonet. With a twist, he freed the eighteen-inch triangular blade and went back to picking away at the tough patch of mud between the logs as the overwhelming drive for self-preservation and action pushed aside any lament Kevin might have felt for the stricken sergeant's fate.

That did the trick. After several quick jabs and a bit of prying, Kevin managed to break up the packed mud and create a gap he judged to be large enough for his purposes. With a heave he threw the bayonet over the logs in front of him, point first, and turned his attention to his pistol. A quick check to make sure it was free of mud, a twirl of the cylinders to make sure all the caps were still in place, and he was ready.

What he was not ready for, however, was the sudden and unexpected appearance of the muzzle end of a Confederate rifle that appeared right before his eyes through the gap in the logs he had made. Pulling back at the last second, Kevin, without thinking, reached out and grabbed the rifle barrel just as the unseen owner of the weapon pulled the trigger.

Stung by the heat caused by the firing of the rifle, Kevin let go, allowing the Confederate rifleman to retract his weapon through the hole. Instinctively, Kevin pulled away from the gap and rolled over onto his back. Ignoring the shower of wood chips and splinters kicked up by enemy bullets that smacked into the logs inches above his head, Kevin carefully inspected the palm of his hand. Because of the dirt and mud, it was difficult to tell if it was burned. Anxious to find out, he wiped his palm across the breast of his coat and started to hold it up when, out of the corner of his eye, he saw the rifle muzzle come popping through the gap a second time. With a quick, downward sweep of his right arm, Kevin managed to knock the protruding barrel down just as its owner fired, sending a bullet along Kevin's side that clipped the toe of his shoe.

Giving up on trying to see if his hand was burned by the first run-in with the hidden Confederate rifleman, Kevin lay his pistol on his chest. Pulling a pair of thick leather gauntlets from his belt, he quickly worked one over his left hand. Ready, he took his pistol in his right hand, rolled over on his side so that he could see the gap between the logs, and waited.

For a third time, the muzzle appeared out of the gap. With a lunge, Kevin reached out, grabbed the rifle barrel with his gloved hand, and held it firm until he felt it fire. Then, holding it firm as the owner of the rifle struggled to pull it back, Kevin flopped over onto it, thrust the barrel of his pistol through the gap, and fired. A sudden end of the struggle to retract the rifle told Kevin his ball had found its mark.

Triumphantly, Kevin gave the rifle barrel a heave, forcing it back through the gap without a hint of resistance. Easing himself back over onto his right side, Kevin looked down the line of works where his men, as he had just been, were engaged in their own separate little duels, often with an enemy they never saw despite the fact that they were sometimes only inches away. How long, Kevin wondered, as he pondered how best he could exert his limited influence over this chaotic and deadly impasse, could this continue? Though his instincts told him that there was a limit to what even battle-hardened veterans could endure, he had seen too much and knew better. They were in a killing frenzy, he realized, all of them. And nothing, not even the normal limits of physical endurance, would keep them from satisfying that primeval urge. Nothing.

The idea, the hope, that James Bannon held on to of rushing back into the horseshoe-shaped circle of works and saving Marty Hazard disappeared as soon as the counterattack led by Gordon came crashing out of the woods and into the arms of the Union advance. There was, for the longest time, a great deal of milling about and confusion, on both sides, as some Union troops gave way and others, determined to hold on to every inch of ground they had thus far gained, stood, fought, and died without yielding. Into this swirling mass, follow-on Union regiments and brigades, meant to support and exploit the earlier success, crowded into the already packed horseshoe, hindering the efforts of Union commanders to reorganize and meet Gordon's new threat.

Unable to even recognize where he was, let alone where the 4th Virginia had made its last stand, James Bannon settled into a traverse that he judged to be a suitable position to fight from. Together with four or five other men, they crowded into a space that under ordinary circumstances would have been large enough for only three. And on top of that, there already was a lone Confederate rifleman, cradling a discarded Union knapsack in one arm while he went about the task of reloading his rifle and firing.

Looking up at James and the new arrivals, the Confederate with the knapsack greeted them with a smile. "Glad to see you boys," he said with a cheeriness that was completely out of place in the swirling confusion and horror that surrounded them. "Was wonderin'," he continued as he watched James and the other new arrivals settle into the steady routine of loading and firing, "when you boys would be along." Then, as if he didn't have a care left in the world now that help had arrived, he carefully lay his rifle off to one side and started to open the knapsack.

"What in blue thunder," asked a skinny, wiry sergeant who had taken up a position next to James, "do you think you're doin'?"

Pausing for a moment, the lone Confederate with the knapsack looked up at the sergeant with a face as serene as a child's. "I need a change of underwear real bad like. I was kind of anxious to see if there was any fresh things in this here knapsack." Then without further ado, the lone

Confederate went back to sorting through the personal items that had once belonged to a man now lying dead somewhere out there in the muddled, fire-swept horseshoe.

Though he kept to his duty, James watched in utter amazement as the man selected those items of clothing that he wanted from the knapsack. Carefully, he laid them out so as to keep them out of the mud. When he had all that he wanted, the lone Confederate then proceeded to undress himself, down to his bare skin as if he were in the privacy of his own home. Unable to ignore this strange spectacle, the sergeant that had accompanied James watched as the lone Confederate put on the fresh, clean underwear, socks, shirt, and trousers that he had so valiantly defended for so long. When he had finished putting his old jacket back on, then his accoutrements, the lone soldier, with a wisp of a smile on his face, took up his rifle, resumed his position among his fellow soldiers, and went back to the task of loading and firing.

Turning to James, the wiry sergeant shook his head. "I don't believe it! Of all the . . ." Pausing, he looked back at the lone soldier, lying there amongst the sergeant's own men, happy as a clam as he continued to fight the Yankees with a steady, well-measured pace. With a shake of his head, the sergeant dropped the matter and turned his full attention to the enemy, now grudgingly giving ground in the face of murderous Confederate fire. Only when they reached the earthworks they had so recently swept over did the Union soldiers stop. Then, like James and his new comrades in arms, they took whatever cover they could find and continued to return, shot for shot, the fire that was being directed at them.

Once more, James thought about Marty. Once more, he considered going out into the open bay of the horseshoe to find his friend. And, once more, after looking over the dismal landscape where the dead and dying of both sides merged into a grotesque pattern of mud and blood that reminded James of a poorly made quilt, he realized any efforts to find Marty out there would be suicidal. With his passions cooled by the harsh realities of the ceaseless, bloody grinding away that the two armies were engaged in, James let his mind go. Already numbed by the spectacle of a battle that had become little more than massed murder, James blocked out the smells and sounds that pounded him with as much impact as the enemy's fire. Instead, he turned his full attention to the mechanical process of loading and firing, loading and firing, loading and firing. As the minutes stretched on into hours, and the hours dragged by, James didn't allow any thoughts, concerns, or feelings to interfere with the cold, deadly execution that he had become so good at.

Not more than ten feet away from where James lay fighting his own little war was Douglas Geddy. A prisoner of circumstances that he never seemed able to master, Geddy had been swept along with Gordon's attack. The sergeant who had taken on the task of keeping him in the ranks squirmed and clawed at the mud before him, offering Geddy a modicum of cover from the awful fire Union soldiers, not more than twenty yards away, were directing at him. Twice, Geddy knew, the big sergeant had been hit in addition to the one shot that had knocked him down to start with. Twice he had watched the man's already tortured body jerk, rear up, and then quiver in a new spasm of agony as another bullet smacked into the side exposed to enemy fire with a thud that was as pronounced as it was sickening.

Dear Lord, Geddy thought as he looked to one side, then the other, in an effort to find escape, when will this stop? When, he repeated over and over, will this horror stop? Another thud, inches from his head, caused Geddy to turn his face to the front. As he did so, the tall sergeant, hit for the fourth time, thrust his face, covered with mud and streams of blood, right at Geddy's. Pulling back in fright, Geddy watched and listened as the sergeant, eyes bulging from their sockets and jaws agape, let out one long moan, then died. Death, much to Geddy's distress, did not soften the sergeant's final expression of pain and suffering. If anything, Geddy imagined that the slow transformation of colors, from pale white to ashen gray, made the sergeant's death mask more ghastly.

This was insane, he thought as he stared at the sergeant's face, smelled the odor of blood, loose bowels, and urine as it mixed together with the mud they both lay in. There was no escape, he realized. There was no escape from the constant pounding in his ears of rifle and cannon fire that was so continual that it all merged into a single, steady roar. Even in death, Geddy realized, as he watched the sergeant's body shudder again from the impact of another bullet, there was no escape.

"This is madness!" he yelled. "*Madness!*" The sergeant inches away had been mad. James Bannon was mad. Everyone all about him, Geddy saw, was mad. And now, as he screamed and howled like a wild animal until his lungs ached, Douglas Geddy realized that he was going mad. Throwing his rifle away, Geddy scurried forward as close as he could to the body of the dead sergeant, drew his legs up into his chest, covered his ears, and began to scream over and over again, adding his cries of anguish to those of so many others.

Even the appearance of a section of guns belonging to the Fifth U.S. Artillery did little to sway the battle for the 1st New Jersey Brigade. As had happened with every gallant, superhuman effort made that day, the appalling mathematics of a constant, murderous fire canceled any advantage gained and extracted a terrible price. For the gunners of the section, it was the loss of almost every one of their horses and the death or wounding of most of their fellow artillerymen.

Kevin, making his way slowly along his diminished line of men, glanced back every now and then to where the surviving gunners continued to stand to their duties despite the brutal beating they were taking. As he passed Amos Flatherly, the outspoken private from the workers' slums of Newark thrust his dirty finger past Kevin's face and pointed at the battered gunners, now unable to keep up their rate of fire. "We're finished, Captain," Flatherly yelled. "All you dandies who run this Army and play at being officers have done us in. Rich little boys like you have murdered us all for your precious glory and honor. I'll not stand here and take it any longer. I'll be damned if I'll follow you or any other dandy one more minute."

As frustrated as Flatherly, perhaps even more so because of the nagging feeling of responsibility he had for the men he had led into this slaughter, Kevin drew back and stared at Flatherly for a second. Perhaps he was right, Kevin thought. No, he corrected himself, he knew he was right. Just yesterday, Kevin remembered, he had uttered almost the same sentiment that Flatherly was now spouting. Still . . .

Then, when Flatherly turned to get up, Kevin snapped. Rearing up on his knees, despite the fact that this action now exposed him to enemy fire, Kevin reached out, grabbed Flatherly by the collar, and jerked his body up until Flatherly's face was inches from his. "I'm tired of your incessant mouthing off. *Tired!*" Stunned, Flatherly reached up, grabbed Kevin's hands, and hung on to them lest Kevin's grasp twist Flatherly's sack coat tightly about his neck and choke him. "You think you're so special, so smart," Kevin continued as he shook the startled man. "You're not, you know. Not by a damned sight. You're nothing but trash. Yellow, slovenly white Irish trash. You've always been trash and if I let you go, you'll die trash."

Then, to everyone's shock and surprise, Kevin stood upright, dragging Flatherly along with him toward the nearest cannon. Stunned, and overpowered by Kevin's strength, multiplied by his raging anger, Flatherly could do little but follow along. Once at the gun, Kevin let go of his tormentor. As he continued to eye Flatherly, Kevin reached over and seized the ramrod from the hands of a wounded artilleryman, who had been using the long staff more for support than for driving home shot and shell. Ignoring the fact that the gunner, relieved of his support, fell to the ground as soon as Kevin took it from him, Kevin thrust the ramrod into Flatherly's hand. When the private took it, Kevin let go of the frightened man's collar. "We're going to stand here, Flatherly," Kevin yelled above the din, "you and me. If you're man enough to stand here with me, as an equal, the two of us are going to do something important. If not," Kevin added, pointing to the wood line to their rear and safety, "drag your miserable body out of my sight and be gone."

Anger replaced fear and confusion. Grasping the ramrod in both hands, Flatherly's first instinct was to strike down this mad man who stood screaming insults at him. Then, with the ramrod held across his chest, Flatherly leaned forward and yelled into Kevin's face. "All right, Mister Bannon. If you find me a shell, I'll show you and anyone who cares to watch what a true son of Ireland can do."

Pivoting on his heel, Kevin walked slowly, deliberately around the artillery piece to where an astonished artillery private stood, fuse in hand. "Where are the shells?"

The private, sweat rolling from his brow and cutting glistening white streaks down his dirt- and powder-blackened face, pointed to the caisson. "Canister," he stammered. "We're using double canister. It's the round with . . ."

Kevin cut him short. "I know what it looks like." Stalking off, past the body of an assistant gunner who had been cut down running back to the caisson for more ammo, Kevin found the limber chest, reached inside the open box, and fished out two heavy rounds of ammunition. With the same deliberateness with which he had walked to the rear, Kevin returned to where Flatherly still stood, holding his ramrod firm and with an expression of anger and defiance that told Kevin that this man was going to hold true to his word.

When he reached the muzzle of the gun, Kevin held one of the canister rounds under his arm while he hoisted the other up to the muzzle and carefully fitted it into the bore of the gun. Once it was in and started on its way down the bore, he took the second round and brought it up. Not being trained gunners, neither Kevin nor Flatherly realized that when firing double canister, the propellant charge affixed to the second canister round needed to be knocked off before loading. To load the second round with the charge still attached could cause the barrel of the gun to burst. Though the artillery private at the rear of the gun saw what Kevin had done, he said nothing. This was no time, he figured, to draw out the second round and do it right. It would be easier, and faster, if they just fired the two rounds as they were and prayed the gun tube stood the pressure.

When Kevin stepped away, Flatherly stepped forward, looking away from Kevin only long enough to bring his ramming staff up and into the bore. With the fury of all the anger felt for Kevin at that moment, Flatherly rammed the two rounds down with quick, violent thrusts. Finished, he withdrew the ramrod, stepped back, and yelled to the gunner. "Fire the bloody thing, man."

With a deftness brought about by many hours of drill and actual practice of his trade in battle, the gunner shoved a thick wire into the fuse hole to puncture the cloth powder bag of the first round. Withdrawing the wire, he inserted the fuse, grabbed the attached lanyard, and stepped away. Looking over at Kevin and Flatherly, he motioned for them to step away from the muzzle farther with a single, quick sweep of his arm, closed his eyes, and gave the lanyard a firm pull. With a flash and a boom, the cannon discharged the two rounds of canister with a kick and buck that sent the gun up into the air and a foot or two back.

Enshrouded in smoke, Flatherly looked across to where Kevin stood, watching to see what effect their work had had. "Well, Captain, sir," Flatherly shouted out defiantly, "are you going to stand there like the statue of a dead saint or go fetch me another round?"

Looking over at Flatherly, Kevin let a small grin curl his lips. "So long as you're here, *Mister* Flatherly, I'll bring you rounds to ram home." Then, as before, Kevin pivoted and headed back to the rear for two more rounds.

Together the three men continued to fire the artillery piece despite the hail of gunfire, most of which was wild and inaccurate, that was hurled at them. On his fourth trip back to the caisson, Kevin took a glancing blow to the side of his head that sent him sprawling. Though stunned, he quickly got up, shook his head, waved to the others that he was fine, and staggered forward the rest of the way. By the time he returned to where Flatherly waited, Kevin had managed to recover most of his senses and push aside the terrible throbbing that wracked his head.

Looking over at his captain, Flatherly's features softened for the first time when he saw the rivulets of blood running down Kevin's cheek. "Are ya hit bad?" the Irish private asked.

Only after loading the last of the canister rounds did Kevin raise his hand and shake his head, indicating as best he could that he was fine. Not waiting for Flatherly to finish ramming the rounds home, Kevin started back to the caisson, fearful that if he stopped moving, he'd pass out.

He did have to pause on this next trip, however, to inform the gunner that they had gone through all their canister. Accompanying Kevin to the caisson, the gunner patiently showed the stunned captain of infantry which rounds to use next. Selecting an exploding shell, he explained how to set the fuse of the shell for a one-second delay. That, the gunner figured, was all it would take for the round to clear their own men and reach the Confederates. When Kevin nodded that he understood what he needed to do, the gunner returned to his post and Kevin made his way back to where Flatherly patiently waited.

Caught up in their own little worlds, absorbed in the execution of their strange, yet dangerous duties, Kevin and Flatherly ignored the rain that continued to fall and the cascades of gunfire directed at them. Still, no matter how poorly aimed it was, the sheer volume of fire took its toll again. For a second time, Kevin felt the sting of a bullet as it burned its way into his right thigh, gouging away a chunk of muscle and skin a good three inches long. Though not as devastating as the hit in the head, the burning sensation began to spread up his side and curl its way around his back, causing Kevin to wonder how much longer he could continue.

It was the third hit, another glancing blow that cut an ugly furrow along the side of his chest and broke a rib, that finally knocked Kevin down for good. With a round in one hand and his face in the mud, Kevin lay where he had fallen, trying hard to organize his thoughts, to focus on something, anything, as he gasped for breath. His mind, however, was too exhausted, too wracked with pain to permit him to do so.

So he just lay there, unable to move any longer, and listened hazily to the continuing fury that tore the air apart above him. He felt the pounding of horses' hooves and heard the jingling of harnesses as a fresh gun battery came forward to relieve the decimated gun section that Kevin and Flatherly had kept alive. The crisp orders barked by artillerymen with hoarse voices mingled with the ceaseless whining and groans of a battle that no one controlled. Moans of wounded men, perhaps, Kevin thought, his own moans, joined the terrible, chaotic cacophony of noise that assaulted his brain, which swirled with pain from three wounds. The only thoughts Kevin could hold on to for more than a few fleeting seconds was the feeling of relief that he was now out of it, and a deep, crippling sorrow that he would never again see Harriet, a woman he now knew he loved more than life itself. Even when Amos Flatherly, finished with helping the gunner hitch his piece to a limber, came back and picked Kevin up in his arms to carry him back to the division field hospital, Kevin could do little more than look Flatherly in the eyes for a moment, then lay his head on the big Irishman's chest.

The brutal contest dragged on even as the leaden gray sky gave way to darkness and the rain continued to pelt the combatants, Northerner and Southerner, with the same relentlessness with which they assaulted each other. In mud that covered every stitch of his clothing, James struggled on, side by side with strangers whom he had never before laid eyes on, in an effort to kill other men who had become nothing more than fleeting images that occasionally filled the sights of his rifle.

Had anyone taken the time to lay his weapon aside and spend a moment or two pondering what they were doing in the tiny plot of Virginia, he would have immediately been appalled by the unquestionable insanity of his fellow men. Cursed by nature, hidden from the eyes of a God believed to be merciful and by a cloak of hatred that was as thick as the smoke that clung to the ground, the combatants stubbornly clung to positions that were, in themselves, worthless. Hour after hour, from dawn until well past midnight, they kept to their grim, brutal task of killing. Logic and sanity, the objective observer would note, were as foreign and out of place here as God himself.

But there was no man in this place this day who could lay his duty and his passions aside. Driven on blindly by a fanaticism never before seen in the course of a war already noted for its brutality, James Bannon, his new comrades, and every man still alive in that hellish place lay into his opponent with abandon, without a second thought, and without a single regret. In the process of defending mud holes and barren ground strewn with corpses, any last vestiges of honor or glory that might have survived till then died. In the killing frenzy of that day, the American way of war ceased to be an art and gave up all pretenses of being a science. Instead, it became nothing more than an exercise in annihilation. Slowly, and with grim mathematical certainty, the two armies ground away at each other. Endurance and numbers, rather than courage and skill, were all that mattered now. The war that had begun in the airy spring of 1861 between two armies attired in colorful and gaudy uniforms, and driven on by verbose and high-minded rhetoric, now promised to eradicate the flower of its youth until one side or the other could bear the cost no longer. The dream of independence for the South and the noble defense of the Union for the North were now nothing more than a nightmare of killing, suffering, and brutality.

Shortly after midnight, a hand from behind shook James' leg. "We're pulling back," a strange voice whispered. Blinking, James looked around. The man he had come forward with to this position earlier that day was lying on his back, face up and stone cold dead. When he had been shot, and how many times, James had no idea. All he knew was that at some point during the long day and brutal night, his companion had stopped returning fire. There had been no scream, no moans, no final words. Nothing but the cessation of activity to mark his passing.

Drained of all energy, and numbed beyond belief by the horror of the entire day's experience, James gave no further thought to his friend Marty Hazard or his other companions who had been cut down so early in the day. He didn't even pay any attention to Douglas Geddy as he fell in behind James once they were in the woods behind the firing line and headed to new earthworks erected for them to defend. With the same mindless mechanical motion that had kept him firing round after round for hours on end, James let his feet carry his limp frame along until the man in front of him flopped down, into the mud, at their new position. In a daze, James looked about in the darkness for a moment in a vain effort to orient himself. Only after realizing that it would be impossible to do so, he allowed his legs to give out, causing his whole body to collapse to the ground and into a heap of torn, muddy uniform and worn flesh. Even as his rifle, fouled beyond use by continual firing, fell across his lap, James was sound asleep. He would remain asleep, jerking fitfully every now and then, until well into the next morning despite rain that pelted him and his comrades. They had survived a nightmare, though only for a moment. In time, James, and many others who had survived the battle waged for control of the horseshoe-shaped entrenchments, came to realize that only death offered them release from the nightmare that they now found themselves immersed in. And death, they knew, was very much in season.

PART THREE

SEPARATE BATTLES

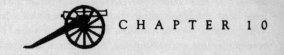 CHAPTER 10

Winchester, Virginia, May, 1864

THE BEAUTY OF THE lushness of the forest that burst forth from every tree, every bush, and every plant was lost on Mary Beth as she slowly walked along the well-worn trail. In years past, the flowering of spring had always held the promise of life renewed and served to dispel the cold gloominess of the recent winter. But this year was different. Even the sweet, fresh smell of flowers that filled every breath she took failed to rouse Mary Beth from the keen depression she wore like a dark cloak. With her head bowed low between her shoulders and her vacant stare fixed on the muddy forest trail before her, Mary Beth was unable to break away from the problems she found herself confronting. Not even the company of her horse, Bucky, walking along with her to the secluded pasture where she turned him out to graze, did anything to lighten her invisible burden.

"It's spring, Bucky," she mumbled to the horse as if to remind herself of that fact. "There's so much to do if the crops in the field are going to amount to anything by harvest time." Though she had lived through the cycle of tilling, planting, and nurturing crops since she was tall enough to follow her mother into the fields, there were many things that she did not understand. "I wish Father were here, Bucky." She sighed. Then, stopping, she turned and faced her horse, who looked into her eyes as if he were understanding every word she spoke. "I wish everyone was back here where they belonged. But I especially need Father. He'd know what to do and when. He always did."

Mary Beth's father had been a good man, a kindly man, who had always been an excellent provider and farmer. Yet he had been, like every male head of a household in their small farm community just outside of Winchester, a man of tradition. To Mary Beth, raised in the close-knit community that was her universe, all the men who had families seemed to be stamped out of the same mold. Whenever she could, Mary Beth would sneak away from the kitchen or the gathering of women during social gatherings and creep to where the men were gathered to listen in on their conversations. All of them, it seemed to her, spoke of the same things, in an almost identical manner. And they all did the same thing, at the same time, when it came to farm work. In the springtime, Mary Beth could visit any of her friends' homes and find the same scene being played out by the same people at each of them. The men, and those sons old enough to handle a team, were plowing the fields, breaking up the earth for the new season's crop. Behind them came the young women, girls, and boys too young to plow, seeding or planting in the freshly turned soil. Back home the mother, also caring for any child too young to be of use in the fields, was busily preparing meals for all hands. When the crop was in, other chores, assigned in a similar manner, were performed. And at harvest time, the cycle was completed, as that which they had sewn and tended was gathered.

"It's the timing," Mary Beth confided to Bucky. "That, and the techniques of how you handle the plow, and the problems of keeping the furrows straight have me baffled." Bucky, responding at the right moment, nodded his head. With loving gentleness, Mary Beth stroked the flank of his well-groomed neck as she laid her forehead upon the horse's. "Oh, Bucky, I do wish James were here. I know he's not a farmer, and probably wouldn't do any better than I can, but . . ."

Without warning, the horse pulled back from Mary Beth and snorted. Surprised, Mary Beth stepped back. "What's the matter, boy?" she asked as she tried to regain her composure and stepped forward again to calm the only friend she seemed to have left in the world. "I know I should be wishing to have Father back, for he's always been the one who knew what to do. But he's dead, boy." She paused, rubbed her horse's neck as her eyes began to moisten, and took several deep breaths to compose herself. "He was thrown out of the lines and died in a terrible accident in Richmond and there's nothing we can do about that. And Will . . ."

The memory of her older brother's death a year ago this month still brought tears to her eyes as she gave way to feelings she had struggled so hard to hold in check. Clutching the horse's bridle, Mary Beth pulled herself closer to the horse and laid her face against the warm, shiny fur of his neck. When she was finally able to compose herself, she stepped back, wiped a tear away with her sleeve, and continued. "At least Daniel's safe down at VMI. You remember when James and I spoke about that when he was here last summer after Gettysburg. So long as Daniel is there, he'll be safe from being drafted into the Army or running away and joining Mosby like he said he was going to. And Mother, well, you know she hasn't been the same since she heard that Father had passed on and we had to bury Will. Even if her mind was all of a sudden back here with us, she knows less about tending crops than I do. So you see, don't think badly about my wishing to have James back. He's our only hope, Bucky. Maybe this time, if he leaves the Army again, he'll stay and . . ."

"We'd have to shoot him as a deserter, little lady," a strong, sharp voice boomed out from behind Mary Beth. Jumping from fright, she spun about, clutching Bucky's bridle to keep from toppling over, and turned to find the source of the voice. On the narrow trail, not more than twenty feet away, a big man, mounted on a flea-bitten gray horse, sat looking down at her. "Unless, of course," the man continued as he sported a big, broad grin, "that's the Yankee major you're pining over. Then we'd be obliged to shoot him."

Frightened, Mary Beth stepped back until she was standing next to Bucky. The big man's torn and dirty clothing that was a motley collection of uniform parts and civilian attire, the scraggly beard that covered his face, and the carbine resting across his saddle left no doubt in Mary Beth's mind that he was one of Mosby's men. It had been his sneaking up, and not Mary Beth's conversation, that had spooked Bucky. That knowledge, however, was of little consequence or consolation to Mary Beth at the moment. Not knowing what else to say, she demanded, "What are you doing here?"

The man laughed. "Why, little lady, I'm here to save you, since your poor sweet Jimmy boy has gone off and left you."

Fright now gave way to fear as she looked into the man's leering eyes. "I don't need any protection from the likes of you, thank you very much. Now if you don't mind, I have to get on back to my farm and start plowing."

"You know," he stated slowly as he ignored her request, "it's a crying shame to use a good, strong saddle horse like that for plow work. Such a healthy, noble animal belongs in the cavalry."

The sudden realization of what this man was after sent a chill down Mary Beth's spine. Tightening her grasp on Bucky's bridle, Mary Beth began to slowly back up. "You can't take my horse from me. He's all I've got. Without him, well, I wouldn't be able to plow and if I don't plow . . ."

Mary Beth and Bucky's rearward progress was suddenly brought to a jarring halt as Bucky reared up. Turning away from the big man on the flea-bitten gray, Mary Beth struggled to bring Bucky under control. During her efforts to do so, she noticed that another gray-clad rider, astride a lean chestnut, stood blocking their retreat. With Bucky under control, Mary Beth's eyes darted left and right in an effort to find an open escape route. "You have no right," she stammered as she continued her search. "You have no right to take my property like this."

The big man threw his head back and laughed. "Little girl, we're at war. We have every right, by order of the government in Richmond, to procure whatever resources we need to defend you from the Yankees." Then getting serious, he leaned over his carbine. "Don't worry. You'll be paid well for what the horse is worth."

This hollow promise angered Mary Beth. Though she knew she shouldn't, she gave up her search for an escape route and stepped forward out of Bucky's shadow. "What are you going to pay me with, your worthless Confederate money?"

Stung by her rebuke, the big man sat upright in his saddle. "If you're a loyal Virginian, that money is your money too."

The big man's icy response was a warning that came too late. Quickly, she tried to appeal to her tormentor's emotions. "My father's gone, thrown out of the lines for helping you back in '62. He was killed during an explosion in the munitions factory he was working at in Richmond just last summer. My older brother died at Chancellorsville with the Fourth Virginia. My younger brother is at VMI. My mother isn't at all well in the head anymore and needs constant watching. And my fiancé is still with Lee. I've got nothing else but this horse and a farm that will die if you take him."

Mary Beth's appeals had no effect. The big man remained unmoved. "You forgot to mention that Yankee major on Millroy's staff that you used to see. Seems to me that you're placing bets on both sides."

The mention of James Sutton was, Mary Beth realized, a death knell.

They were local men riding with Mosby, or at least men who had been around long enough to know all the local gossip. And like most of Mosby's rangers, they considered themselves something special, apart and above the norms that governed the conduct of other men. These men, she knew, had no intention of leaving without Bucky. Still, she could not give in without a struggle. "That Yankee major is the same one who wrote the order to send my father away. How can you even . . ."

Tiring of Mary Beth's arguing and anxious to get back to his company, the big man stood up in the saddle to stretch, looking around as he did so. Mary Beth thought he was doing so just to make himself look bigger. "I'm not here to argue with you, girl. And I damn well am not going to take no for an answer. Now, let the horse go and get yourself home. We have to be on our way."

She was about to pull Bucky into the woods in an effort to escape when a hand reached under the horse's neck, grabbed the bridle, and jerked the horse's head away from her. Surprised by the unexpected appearance of a third partisan, Mary Beth lost control of the horse's bridle before she realized what was going on. Recovering, she ducked under Bucky's neck as the horse began to rear and pull away from a third soldier she hadn't seen and kicked him in the shin. "You let go of him right now or I'll give you something you'll never forget."

Angered by Mary Beth's attack as much as he was by the horse's rearing, the soldier shoved Mary Beth back with his free hand, causing her to stagger and trip over a log behind her. Stunned, but only for a moment, Mary Beth scrambled to her feet and rushed at the big man on the flea-bitten gray. "Is this how you defend us?" she screamed as she beat on the mounted partisan with her balled fists. "Is this how you're going to win this cursed war, by stealing from your own kind?"

In an effort to avoid her punches, the big man jerked his horse's neck sharply to one side and away from Mary Beth. Freed from her beating, the big man started to ride off. Unable to do anything else, Mary Beth screamed insults at him. "I hope you pay," she screamed as tears streamed down her checks. "I hope you and all you *brave* men burn in hell for this." Unmoved by her anger, the big man and his companions turned their backs on Mary Beth and rode on down the trail, pulling a reluctant and unruly Bucky behind them.

Stunned, exhausted, and bewildered by this latest attack on her and her family, Mary Beth sank onto her knees, doubled over, and began to beat the ground and cry with abandon. How could God, she wondered as she wailed, or any people who called themselves civilized, allow their own kind to suffer so? How? she wondered, without any hope of finding an answer.

South of New Market, Virginia

"THEY'LL NEVER LET US fight," Cadet Sergeant Chandler stated matter-of-factly as he crouched before the small smoky fire that struggled to stay burning. "You know it as well as I do. They'll never let us fight."

"If that's so," another cadet sitting next to Daniel McPherson challenged, "then why did they have us march all night, in the pouring rain, to get here? Answer me that."

"This isn't the first time they've sent us on a wild goose chase, you know," Chandler replied. "Look at last December. Remember how they called us out to chase Averell's cavalry only to be told after trudging through the freezing rain that we weren't needed?" He looked up at the leaden gray morning sky that showed no sign of clearing. "Except maybe for the fact that it isn't as cold," he concluded as he looked back at the small circle of cadets trying to cook their breakfast, "this is no different."

Daniel, who listened intently to the argument between Chandler and the others gathered about the fire while they cooked their morning meals, said nothing. He wasn't sure how he felt about this whole affair and didn't know whom to believe. At sixteen, he was one of the younger cadets, though the honor of being the youngest went to Cadet Lewis S. Davis, who had just turned fifteen. On one hand Daniel, like all the other cadets at the Virginia Military Institute, had been elated when word came that they were to march north to join Major General John C. Breckinridge's small army defending the valley against a new incursion by the German-born Union General Franz Sigel. When the 254 cadets, led by 7 faculty officers serving as staff and field officers, had marched out on May 11, Daniel was excited. Like the rest of his classmates, he had pounded his feet on the wooden bridge over Woods Creek, north of the institute, just to make it shake and sway. He swapped stories with his friends, bragging about what they would do when they finally got to fight, and whenever the fifer whistled up a tune, he sang with more enthusiasm than skill. For he was finally on the adventure of his life, an adventure that had been denied him for three years because of his age. And though some of the older cadets sneered at the idea that they would actually do something useful, Daniel and his friends intended to enjoy themselves, come what may.

Over the course of the next three days, however, his enthusiasm waned as hard marching, rain, and ceaseless taunting from veterans who made fun of everything from their youth to the neatness of their uniforms took most of the excitement out of this adventure. Any illusions that Daniel or his fellow cadets still held that this was just another wild goose chase were finally dispelled when they were awakened shortly after midnight on the morning of May 15 and ordered north at a fast pace. In darkness that was almost absolute, the Corps of Cadets, almost lost in the long columns of Breckinridge's army, marched north in silence through the mud toward the red glow of campfires lighting the sky to their front. This vision was made more ominous by the fact that this May 15, a Sunday, was also the first anniversary of the burial of the institute's and the South's greatest military hero, Stonewall Jackson. Jackson, a devoted Christian, never fought on Sunday if it could be avoided. When he had violated this self-imposed restriction at Kernstown in March 1862, he had suffered his only battlefield failure. Such thoughts and sights that night, together with their own personal reservations, weighed heavily on each cadet as they marched north, wondering as they went whose campfires lit the sky so.

Chewing on a piece of half-cooked bacon that was more gristle than meat, Daniel continued to listen to the banter of the older cadets as the debate swayed to and fro. The crack of rifle fire drifting down from the north caused Daniel to pause in what he was doing and turn his face to that direction. Other cadets who had also done so stared into the distance as they attempted to gauge the importance of the firing. "Imboden's cavalry," one of the older cadets stated blandly. "They must be skirmishing with Yankee troopers somewhere up the pike." Turning, Daniel studied the cadet who had made the last statement in an effort to determine if he was speaking with some degree of knowledge or merely guessing, like the rest of them. By the look on his face, Daniel came to the conclusion that he was guessing.

After several minutes, the cadets, one by one, returned to their previous thoughts and activities as the sound of fighting grew more general. There was less chatter now as each cadet made more of a concentrated effort to hide his own fears and apprehensions. This brief moment of nervous silence did not last long as the sound of hooves beating the ground, followed by cheering, liberated Daniel from his dark foreboding. Standing this time, he looked down the line of campfires in the direction that the cheering was coming from to learn what was causing the excitement.

Unlike the rifle fire that was still somewhat of a mystery, the inspiration of the cheering was immediately obvious. General Breckinridge, mounted on a magnificent black horse and followed by his staff, was trooping his line as he headed north to the sound of the gunfire. When he began to pass where the Corps of Cadets had been waiting, Cadet C. C. Randolph cried out, "Boys! Three cheers for General Breckinridge!" All of the cadets, now on their feet like Daniel, roared out the mightiest *hurrah* they could manage. In response, General Breckinridge reined in his mount and raised his hand in acknowledgment. "I compliment you on your spirit," he announced to the pleasure of the cadets, but then cautioned them to be as quiet as possible, since they were now so near their enemy. "We have more serious work to do," he added before continuing his ride down the line of troops waiting to go into battle. Like the rain that continued to fall on and off, Breckinridge's words dampened the cadets' momentary burst of enthusiasm.

When he was gone from sight, Cadet Chandler sighed. "He'll not use us," he pronounced. Still undecided, Daniel was torn between wishing that Breckinridge would allow them to fight and hoping that he didn't. After all, Daniel's troubled mind reasoned, though this was as good a time as any to find out if he was as brave as his brother, the urge to delay that final test seemed to grow stronger as the time for it grew nearer. As other cadets about him returned to their former activities, Daniel remained behind, still wrestling with his thoughts. Looking up at the dark sky, Daniel wished that he could speak to his brother, if only for a moment. "Stay with me, Will," Daniel whispered in prayer, "and help me to do what is right."

Though two other cadets heard Daniel's words, they said nothing. Like Daniel, they too were turning inward in an effort to prepare themselves for what was to come. And come, it did.

If truth be known, John C. Breckinridge, a forty-three-year-old Kentuckian who had served as vice president of the United States under James Buchanan, indeed, had no intention of using the cadets in battle. Before assuming command of the Valley Department in February, 1864, he had fought in some of the most vicious western battles of the war, from Shiloh, Corinth, Vicksburg, and Stones River to Chickamauga and Chattanooga. From personal experience, he understood as well as any man the horrors of war and was determined to spare the young Corps of Cadets that experience if at all possible.

Yet every step he took that spring to defend the vital Shenandoah Valley from the Union brought the Corps of Cadets, and young Daniel McPherson, closer to battle. The situation the former vice president faced left him no choice. The advance of two Federal columns, one under Brigadier General George Crook out of West Virginia with the mission of severing the Virginia & Tennessee Railroad, and the other, under Franz Sigel himself, advancing from the north left him few choices, none of which were very promising. To stop this combined force of more than sixteen thousand men, Breckinridge had fewer than half the Union number, which included every militia man not already serving in the Army and, of course, the cadets of the Virginia Military Institute.

Breckinridge's plans for that Sunday called for the cadets to remain in reserve during what he called "the bloodiest part of the fighting." Yet he candidly admitted to a staff officer that, should the occasion require it, he would use them freely. When, by late morning, Breckinridge's scheme for enticing the numerically superior Union forces to attack him failed, he decided to attack them. At 10:00 A.M., after studying the enemy dispositions and the terrain, Breckinridge announced to his staff, "Well, I have offered him battle and he declines to advance on us. I shall advance on him." Then, as his enthusiasm for this enterprise began to rise, he turned to the commander of his cavalry, Brigadier John D. Imboden, and announced, "We can attack and whip them here, and I'll do it."

This attack began shortly after 11:00 A.M. with skirmishers leading the advance of Breckinridge's two brigades of infantry. The cadets, held in reserve on Shirleys Hill, prepared for action by stripping off their overcoats, dropping packs and haversacks, and sending off several first-year cadets to fill canteens. During this brief lull, Breckinridge came up to the assembled cadets as he had earlier that morning and addressed the cadets again. "Young gentlemen," he shouted over the rumbles of a battle already building in intensity, "I hope there will be no occasion to use you, but if there is, I trust you will do your duty."

"You can bet it'll be a cold day down below before they send us in," Cadet Chandler mumbled as Breckinridge turned to ride on to another part of the field. A cadet officer, standing behind Daniel, heard Chandler's comment. "Quiet in the ranks," he snapped in the same manner that Daniel had heard many, many times before on the institute's parade ground. This wasn't the parade ground, though, Daniel thought as he nervously gripped his rifle and looked about out of the corners of his eyes. This was a farm field, not much different from those his family owned one hundred or so miles to the north. The mud from the incessant rain and the furrows cut for planting would make the advancing difficult, he figured, just as it had been when he was a boy following his father about as he plowed land that the McPhersons had owned for nearly a century.

The sudden vision of his father, shoes caked with mud from working in the family's fields, flew through Daniel's mind. For the first time in weeks he wondered how his sister was making out with the spring planting. It would be hard for her, he realized as he stood there waiting to advance through the mud, with all the men gone. Mother would be of little help, he reasoned, and their aunt would be more of a nuisance even if she did bother to make the offer to help. It would be up to Mary Beth, Daniel concluded, to keep the farm going.

From out in front of the corps, Colonel Scott Ship's booming voice shattered Daniel's image of his father and his thoughts of home, jerking his full attention back to the reality of the here and now. "Listen to your officers," he cautioned the cadets in his charge, "and obey their orders."

Then, after a pause to swallow a breath of air, Colonel Ship shouted, "Battalion, forward."

Without thought, Daniel and the other cadets in ranks stepped off and began to move toward the growing battle. As Cadet Color Sergeant Oliver Evens shook the water out of the institute's soaked colors and hoisted them aloft, the fifers and drummers struck up a tune meant to help the cadets stay in step. The mud, however, as well as the sloping hill, made this difficult, just as Daniel had anticipated.

Still, when they crested the hill and began to march down into the valley behind the advancing infantry of Wharton's veteran regiments, the corps did so in perfect order. For a moment, everyone on this part of the field who was not engaged in battle turned to watch the cadets as they advanced. Even some of the townspeople watched from their shelters. One small girl, struck by the neatness of their uniforms and the strange flag they followed, excitedly yelled, "The French have come! The French have come!"

Not all attention that was drawn to them was admiring or welcome. With the main Confederate line of battle momentarily obscured by masking terrain, the cadets following in their footsteps provided a new target to Union gunners deployed on high ground north of New Market. Daniel was struggling to keep his place in ranks and stay in step when the first enemy shell exploded near Cadet Color Sergeant Evens. Startled by his first close-up experience of war, Daniel all but jumped as his head jerked sharply to see what had happened. Evens, just as startled, hesitated for a moment as if in a daze. Then, seeing that he was all right, continued on.

That this first round fired directly at them had no effect gave the cadets who witnessed it a momentary, though false, sense of security. For Daniel, the sight of several men lying on the ground before them put an end to that illusion. They belonged to Wharton's brigade, cut down by the same Federal artillery that was now ranging on the cadets. Daniel was wondering what his odds were of joining those unfortunates on the ground when a shell exploded just down the line from him. Unlike the first round that had merely shaken some of the cadets, this one found its mark and caused the line to waver for the first time. Some of those near the point of impact began to stop and turn to help those on the ground or staggering about. Colonel Scott Ship, seeing this, called out sharply, "Close up, battalion." For a few moments more, a couple of the cadets, reluctant to leave their stricken comrades behind, hesitated. But then, prodded by cadet officers and sergeants, even these last few obeyed.

After that, there was no more need for Ship or anyone else to give the order to close up. Like those around him, Daniel just leaned forward, as if he were marching into a strong wind, and kept going. He ignored the dead and wounded men under his feet, just as he ignored the screams of a fellow cadet as a Union shot ripped a great gap in the ranks next to him. Without looking back, Daniel inclined toward the center of the cadet battalion until his shoulder touched that of the next cadet over and continued to advance.

Once under the lee of the hill where Wharton's brigade had deployed, the cadets paused. All about them they watched as guns that had been behind them were run up to new positions to support the main Confederate attack. Daniel, wiping his forehead, looked over to where Cadet Chandler stood looking back over the ground they had just advanced across. He wanted to go over to Chandler and ask him if he still believed that Breckinridge wasn't serious about using them, but didn't. What was the point, Daniel concluded, in doing so? The look of bewilderment on Chandler's face told him that he was just as shaken by this experience as everyone else.

For the better part of a half hour Daniel and his fellow cadets waited in the shallow valley as the sound of cannonading and gunfire ebbed, then grew in intensity once more. When Wharton's brigade went forward again, Daniel felt his stomach knot up in anticipation of the order to follow. When it came, the cadets obeyed, as before, and stepped off in fine style, though there were fewer following the colors now than had done so before.

If their numbers were fewer, the signs of battle weren't. One stricken Confederate, seeing the boys come on, propped himself up on an elbow and began to cheer the cadets on. For his trouble, he was riddled with several bullets that tore at flesh and clothing with horrible effect as Daniel watched. Again he felt the knot in his stomach tighten. For a moment, as he came up to, then was obliged to step over, the tattered corpse that had a few moments before been a living man, Daniel felt bile rising in his throat. Gripping his rifle tightly, he closed his eyes, swallowed hard, and moved on without looking at the dead man again.

When the corps came up parallel to the town of New Market, it paused again. Up ahead, on the crest of Manor's Hill, Wharton's units were deployed and engaging the Union forces that were before them but out of sight from the cadets. "You suppose," Cadet George Marymen asked Daniel, "this is as far as we'll go?"

Daniel looked about. "We're in it, George," he finally stated. "And I don't think we've seen the worst of it yet." As if to emphasize the last point, Daniel watched as a gun battery, which included the cadet battery, went careening up the pike toward a new position. One of the cadets riding a caisson, seeing Daniel, let go with one hand and waved wildly at him. "We're going to give them . . ." the cadet shouted. And though the chatter of hooves and screech of wheels of the next gun and caisson drowned out the last of the cadet's words, his broad smile told Daniel that he was excited and anxious. Dropping the arm he had raised to wave back, Daniel felt the knot in his stomach twist again. How in the Lord's name, he wondered, had his brother Will survived so many fights if this was what it felt like to go into battle.

As before, the line to their front went forward, and the corps followed. Cresting Manor's Hill, Daniel was able to see the scope of the battle for the first time. Wharton's line of battle, to their front, was descending the northern slope of the hill they were on and heading into a wheatfield near a small white farmhouse on the next rise of ground. To the front left was another line of troops, Echol's brigade, moving forward on the other side of the valley pike. And out in front of them all, at a greater distance, were masses of blue infantry, some in line of battle, some in clusters and clumps, all giving ground before the gray host that extended across the valley. "Oh, Lordy!" George Marymen declared. "Will you look at that?"

A cadet officer behind Daniel, equally awestruck, whispered in a hoarse voice, "Well, there they are, boys. There they are."

"Quiet in the ranks," the order came from the officers leading the cadets. "Close up and keep your alignment."

This was becoming more and more difficult, Daniel noticed. The freshly planted fields were strewn with the refuse of both armies now, not to mention dead and wounded left behind. A Union soldier, who looked to be all but unscathed, stared quizzically at Daniel and his comrades as they marched by. Another Yankee, less shy but more severely wounded, propped himself up as the corps approached. "Who in tarnations," he shouted, "are you fellas?"

"Virginia Military Institute, Yank," a cadet sergeant responded.

The wounded Yankee laughed. "Children! They're sending children after us. Lord help the Union now," he mocked.

Just short of the white farmhouse, the corps came to a halt along a rail fence. Taking up positions behind it, the cadets worked to improve their cover as they watched the line of infantry before them. What the cadets had thought was heavy fire before now proved to be little more than a preliminary as Union guns and volleys of rifle fire ripped at the ranks of Wharton's brigade. An occasional shot that missed the front ranks whistled overhead accompanied by the whiz of an odd stray bullet. "Damn," George Marymen muttered as he watched. "It must be terrible up there."

Daniel said nothing as he bit his lip and watched. "You suppose," another cadet asked sheepishly, "General Breckinridge is going to continue his attack?"

To this, no one answered. All the amateur tacticians and cadets who had freely given their opinions on everything were just as silent as Daniel as they watched the wreckage of the forward units start to come back toward them. Though they suspected that this was not good, none of them knew for sure what it meant.

Over on the valley pike, where General Breckinridge sat astride his horse, he knew exactly what it meant. Parts of the 51st Virginia and the 62nd Virginia of Wharton's brigade, deployed in full view of the enemy guns, had been badly mauled and were starting to give way. Though the retreat wasn't general, it left a gap in the center of his line that Breckinridge could not ignore. At first, he stated his desire to contract his line, drawing units on either side of the gap closer together to close it. A staff officer, however, advised otherwise. "General," Major Charles Semple coolly recommended, "why don't you put the cadets in line? They will fight as well as our men."

Without hesitation, Breckinridge responded. "No, Charley, this will not do. They are only children and I cannot expose them to such fire as our center will receive."

Semple didn't agree. "General, it is too late. The Federals are right on us. If the cadets are ordered up, we can close the gap in our center."

This time, Breckinridge paused before he responded. Looking over across the fields toward the white farmhouse where the gap was, he studied the ground for a moment. Then he looked back at Semple. "Will the boys stand?" he asked with great deliberateness.

"Yes," Semple responded without hesitation. "They are of the best Virginia blood, and they will."

For a moment, no one spoke as Breckinridge looked across the valley again where the gap still yawed open. In his mind, one thought after another came to the forefront, was considered, and then passed on as he weighed his options. His staff, used to the deliberate manner in which general officers made such decisions, sat and watched in silence. Finally, with tears forming in his eyes, he looked over to Semple. "Put the boys in," he said with great sorrow. Then he added, "And may God forgive me for this order."

The gap the cadets were to fill was almost directly to their front. At the direction of Major Semple, the corps went forward into a hail of cannon fire that made their previous experience seem trivial. One of the first shots found its mark not far from Daniel. Ripping through the ranks of Company D, it killed cadets Charles Crockett and Henry Jones instantly. Cadet William Cabell, the company first sergeant, went down, his chest ripped open. As Daniel went by him, he could see Cabell tearing at the muddy earth in his agony. With great effort, Daniel tore his eyes away from his fellow cadet and fixed his gaze on the white farmhouse they were advancing on. As his company passed to the west of it, Daniel heard the steady, unbroken thump of enemy bullets hitting the clapboards. The noise reminded Daniel of hailstones. That the fire was so intense frightened him but did not cause him to stop.

With the rest of his company, he continued on, past the house, through an orchard, and on to the fence. More cadets went down as they passed through the green orchard. A cadet, hit in the stomach, stumbled and fell before Daniel. Pausing so as not to trip over the stricken cadet, he dropped to his knee to see if he could help his stricken comrade. The other boy, looking up and seeing Daniel, pointed toward the fence and shouted. "That is the place for you. You can do me no good."

Pulling back, half in obedience to the fallen cadet and half in horror as he watched blood gush from his comrade's wound, Daniel stood upright. At first, he looked over to the fence where the other cadets were already forming. Then, for the briefest of moments, Daniel looked back to the rear. There would be safety back there, he suddenly thought. No shooting, no dying. To go forward would be . . .

As these thoughts raced through his mind, he looked down at the ground they had just covered. Cadets—dead, wounded, and dying— littered the route. These were no longer the odd strangers that he had encountered on their journey up to this point. These were fellow cadets, friends. He knew them by name and much, much more. To go back, over their bodies without having accomplished anything, Daniel realized, would be to betray them. And though the knot in his stomach was now so tight that it seemed ready to burst, Daniel turned his mind away from any further thoughts of flight and hurried forward to join the other cadets at the fence.

When he made it all the way forward and rejoined his company, Daniel found that he had difficulty finding a place along the rail fence. "Look at 'em come, Daniel," Marymen shouted when he saw Daniel drop to his knee and point his rifle.

After checking to make sure the cap was still snugly on his piece's cone, Daniel looked up. Three sets of colors, marking the center of three Union regiments, were moving toward them in a rather disjointed fashion. The regiment to their front was in the lead, having stepped off first. The regiment to the left of that one was coming up, but slowly. Though he thought he should wait until an order to fire had been given, for everything that day had been done, so far, according to precise orders, Daniel gave up waiting when he saw the cadets to his left and right hoist their rifles and fire. Without thinking, he did likewise.

It was only then that it struck him what he was about to do. It didn't matter much that the enemy bearing down on them had fired indiscriminately at them as he and his fellow cadets had advanced. The images of fallen soldiers that had been burned in his memory didn't change anything either. And none of the slogans he had heard bandied about concerning fighting for freedom and states' rights seemed to matter one iota. What counted, Daniel suddenly realized as he looked down the long barrel of his rifle, was that he was, by his own hand, about to take a life.

Now the knot that had been so persistent all day finally made one more twist, sending a pain throughout his body that was almost numbing. For a moment, he felt faint. The scene before him grew hazy as everything in a circle about his vision began to dim, then grow black. Still, though it was wobbling badly, Daniel kept his rifle held aloft. "Dear God, Will," Daniel called out in desperation, "help me."

Then, when he was sure he was about to lose all his sense, Daniel took a deep breath, pulled the stock of his rifle deeper into his shoulder, took one last look through his sights, and squeezed the trigger. If he had in fact fired at anything, which he would never know, it didn't matter. What mattered was that the kick of the rifle knocked him back into full aware- ness with the same shocking suddenness that being doused with a bucket of cold water does. Now there was no longer any need for thought. He had done it. He had fired on the enemy. And for better or worse, he was committed. Dropping his rifle from his shoulder, he began to reload his piece as quickly as his shaking hands would let him.

To Daniel's front, the 1st West Virginia Infantry Regiment, the unit that had stepped off into the attack first, was the first to falter. After less than one hundred yards, the men in its ranks decided that they had had enough of the galling fire that racked them and began to draw back. Their sudden and unexpected absence left the two regiments on either flank isolated. When Daniel was finished ramming down his fifth or sixth round, he saw there was no point in firing at the retreating regiment. Instead, he shifted his fire to the left against the Union unit over there that continued to come on despite the efforts of its own officers to stop it. "Good Lord," Marymen shouted above the din of battle, as he did likewise, "look at 'em drop."

Now used to reloading, Daniel was able to look up and scan the terrible scene before him while his hands worked frantically to return the ramrod to its stored position. The unit on the left was indeed suffering terribly, so much so that it was finally forced to yield, as the center regiment had. This maneuver, though necessary, left a battery of Union guns deployed on the slope of a hilltop unsupported in the field. They would have to leave soon, Daniel concluded with a feeling of relief, because they had been delivering a most devastating fire against his portion of the line.

The Union battery commander, a German immigrant named Albert Von Kleiser, also saw this sad state of affairs. With two Confederate banners coming toward him and no formed infantry unit in support, he had no choice. He ordered the gun crews to bring up their horses and limber the guns. It was time for them to go back.

Then, like a great curtain being raised on the final act, the skies opened and poured all the rain they held upon the fields below. To the accompaniment of thunder and lightning that streaked across the sky, the Confederate line began to advance, first on the left where the 51st Virginia Regiment and the 26th Virginia Battalion had held the line, then the Corps of Cadets. And though they were not the first to go forward, for that honor belonged to the color sergeant of the 26th Battalion, it was the advance of the Corps of Cadets that captured the attention of both friend and foe.

Caught up in the excitement, and no longer troubled by the knot that had earlier been so crippling, Daniel placed one hand on the top rail of the fence he had moments ago used for cover and hopped over it in a single bound. Once on the other side, and back in ranks, he went forward with his comrades. Together, with heads bowed and shoulders hunched, they advanced. Fighting a terrible enemy fire directed at them from rifle and cannon, sheets of rain that fell from the sky without letup, and the unyielding mud that literally sucked one shoe, then the other off his feet, Daniel advanced. Though some officers shouted orders, he could no longer differentiate them from the screams and howls of the wounded and dying and the deafening roar of battle that seemed to grow in intensity with every step he took.

Now Daniel's world became nothing but a jumble of images. Cadet Charles Randolph, marching upright, shouted to his comrades, "There's no use in dodging, boys. If a ball's going to hit you, it'll hit you anyway." Then, as if he had prophesied his own demise, Randolph was hit and fell from sight. Cadet John Upshur, leaning heavily on his rifle, struggled to stay up with fellow cadets who called back to him to close up despite the fact that his knee had been smashed by an enemy ball. Fifteen-year-old Cadet Samuel B. Adams, losing a shoe, stopped, turned around, and sat on the ground as he retrieved the precious lost shoe and put it back on. All of this, and more, Daniel somehow took in as he went on toward the Union battery where he could see Yankee gunners scrambling to limber their guns and pull them away before the cadets reached them.

Only once, when they were just yards from the guns and the shredded remains of the West Virginia regiment, did the Corps of Cadets pause and waver for a moment, as if to catch its breath. Then, anxious to finish the thing, they went forward as a body, unbowed and unstoppable. Unwilling to meet their foes in hand-to-hand combat, the Union infantry melted away, followed quickly by the remnants of the Federal battery, leaving the field, one cannon, and their center in the hands of the cadets.

Though flush with a victory that was as much a surprise to them as it was their enemy, the cadets held their ranks and responded to the situation presented to them. With a smart wheeling movement to the left that took them over and around dead artillery horses and Union gunners, the two lefthand companies turned to face the flank of a Union regiment that was still attempting to reform after its aborted attack. Elated, Daniel fired his rifle into them without any hint of the trepidation he had felt when he had first taken aim at another man. Like his fellow cadets, he poured round after round into the flank of the Union regiment before them as the 51st and 26th Virginia did the same along their entire front.

It was only when the last of the Federal units finally turned to quit the field that the corps finally lost the parade ground formation that had held it together all day. With all thoughts of the dead and dying forgotten for the moment, Daniel joined his fellow cadets as they raced forward after the fleeing Yankees. Behind them they left a field littered with the wreckage of two armies as well as a legend that would outlive them all.

CHAPTER 11

Washington, D.C., June, 1864

THE UNENDURABLE THROBBING PAIN that racked his head finally became so overwhelming that Kevin Bannon began to moan. It started as a soft, almost breathless grunt. This first sound was quickly followed by another, stronger gasp as he twisted his head first to the right, then jerked it back to the left when it became obvious that the first move had only made the pain worse. The third moan was the first to actually sound like a word, though anyone other than Kevin would have been hard pressed to tell what that word was. It wasn't until he repeated it twice, and shifted his legs, an action that sent a shaft of pain throughout his body, that the words "Oh, God," actually became distinguishable.

Looking up from the book she had been reading, Harriet watched as Kevin's body twisted and quivered. She was used to this by now, having spent the past two weeks at his side, day and night. The first time that he had convulsed like this had both excited and worried her. Her response of great joy and relief was soon frustrated by the realization that Kevin's actions were more spasms than deliberate acts. "His brain's afire with pain and fever," an elderly major whose bed sat next to Kevin's remarked when he saw Harriet's disappointment when Kevin failed to respond to her touch and voice. "With as many holes as he's collected," he continued glibly, "it'll be awhile before he's back with us here." The major had thought about adding, if he ever did make it back, but didn't. A devoted husband and father of three himself, he saw the passionate concern in

Harriet's eyes whenever she tended to Kevin's wounds or responded to his needs. There was no need, he figured, to add to her anguish.

In truth, he was right. From the moment that Private Flatherly had come stumbling into the First Division's field hospital until well after she had managed to settle Kevin into a decent field hospital in Washington, D.C., Harriet had been tormented by the fear that she would lose the only person she had ever loved. "*It is strange,*" she scribbled quickly in her diary one night in the close confines of the small room where they stored linen and had set up a bed for her, "*to have used the word love for so many years, yet never understood its meaning. How freely we have all used the word without ever realizing that love is, in truth, an emotion, a passion that comes of its own accord without warning, without thought. It is only now, at a time when I am faced with its loss, that I am so keenly aware of my need to share it with the one person who has opened my eyes to its sweet, all-consuming power. Day after day, I sit in lonely vigilance, watching Kevin as he struggles from within to hold on to a life that is as dear to me as it is to him. Often, I find myself praying that the fates that brought us together, and punished him so severely for doing his duty, will allow us to share, if only a moment, the love I now feel for him.*"

Putting her book aside, Harriet stood up, turned, and leaned over Kevin in an effort to listen closely to the words he tried to utter. As she was doing so, his body shuddered. Pulling her head back, she lay one hand gently upon his hot, sweat-soaked brow. With her other, she gave his hand a gentle squeeze.

The sudden sensation of a soft, cool hand upon his forehead, the first pleasant sensation that Kevin was conscious of, caused his eyes to fly open. And though the image was blurry and distorted, in an instant he recognized the source of his solace. Blinking, he attempted to clear his vision before taking Harriet's hand in his and uttering her name.

In all her life, Harriet had never felt such elation, such joy. Though she had never been a deeply religious person, the sudden realization that her prayers had been answered was too overwhelming for her to take. Sitting down quickly before her knees gave out, Harriet threw her arms across Kevin's body and began to weep without shame.

"I must admit," Harriet spoke softly as she lifted another spoon of soup up to Kevin's waiting mouth, "I wasn't much help when they brought you in." Though he was interested in what she was saying, the small sips of soup that she carefully doled out to him required all of Kevin's attention. Yet even though he did his best to capture every drop of the warm liquid, much of it ran out of his mouth, which failed to respond properly, and dribbled down his chin.

"If it were not for little Albert Merrel and Doctor White," Harriet continued as she withdrew the spoon and pulled it back to refill it, "I'd have been a total wreck."

For a moment, Kevin's eyes shot from watching the progress of the spoon to Harriet's calm, attentive eyes. Albert Merrel, a former drummer boy who had been sent back to the field hospital when the diminished size of his unit made his services unnecessary, was no longer little. The fact was, just before the May campaign had begun, Albert had come up to Kevin and all but demanded that he be allowed to join the 4th New Jersey as a rifleman. Already short of men and always eager to take one good willing volunteer rather than wait for a handful of reluctant bountymen and conscripts, Kevin had just about made up his mind to send for him when he had been wounded. Perhaps it was better, Kevin thought, as he watched Harriet lift a full spoon from the bowl and guide it carefully to his waiting mouth, that he had been wounded. It spared, it seems, young Merrel from the horrors of Cold Harbor.

Noticing his stare, Harriet took her eyes from the spoon of soup she had been balancing once she saw Kevin's mouth clamp tightly about the handle. "What are you thinking?" she asked innocently.

Not wanting to share his dark thoughts with her and disturb her anymore than he already had, Kevin's mind, still badly rattled and slow in responding, fumbled about for something to say. "I was just thinking how lucky I am to have a woman as lovely and as caring as you at my side."

Caught off guard, Harriet's eyes dropped as she blushed.

Though it caused him pain, a pain that shot through his body and caused him to wince, Kevin reached up with his good hand and took

Harriet's two hands, which were momentarily suspended over his chest. "I mean it, my dear, sweet Harriet. And though I wish I could say that I thought of nothing but you while I was sleeping these past two weeks, since the moment I saw you standing there, holding my hand yesterday, I've been . . . well . . ."

Harriet looked into his eyes. A smile slowly began to light her face as she freed one hand from his grasp and laid it over his.

"Well," a voice from the foot of the bed rang out, "I am certainly glad to see the two of you have managed to meet in the here and now."

Harriet's immediate reaction was to pull her hand away as her entire face turned a deep shade of crimson. Looking down to the foot of his bed, Kevin was surprised to see a stately woman of color, in a dress that was as neat, trim, and delicate as she was, looking down at them with a bemused smile and a twinkle in her eyes.

"Kevin," Harriet announced haltingly as she recovered from her momentary embarrassment, "this is Anna Belle Johnson. She has helped me a great deal since we've been here. She's even lent me some of her dresses."

Taking one hand off her hip, Anna Belle waved it in protest. "Captain, this woman of yours needs as much help as the Corps of Engineers needs to build a bridge."

Kevin, still holding Harriet's hand, gave it a squeeze as he looked over to Harriet and smiled. The neat, trim dress she wore, a far cry from the plain white blouse and coarse blue skirt she wore in the field during campaigns, was as appropriate for her as any he had ever seen her in back in New Jersey. "Oh, yes," he said with a smile. "That goes without saying."

"Well, seeing as you were rather indisposed these past two weeks," Anna Belle continued, "I thought I'd mention it to you, though I sort of figured that you already knew that. The true nature of a fine, intelligent woman like your Harriet can't stay hidden under slips and lace forever."

Though he was enjoying watching Harriet, who had now turned her face back to him, Kevin wanted to study the crisp, articulate Negro woman who was speaking so highly of Harriet. "Are you assigned to this hospital?" he asked innocently in an effort to find out more about Anna Belle.

This question brought a sly smile and a sideways glance from Anna Belle. "Well, my dear Captain Bannon, it is obvious that you've not met our esteemed chief surgeon."

Though he wanted to pursue this last point, Harriet, now recovered from her momentary bout with speechlessness, jumped in. "Anna Belle is a volunteer here. She's a teacher here in Washington as well as a lobbyist in Congress working for the freed slaves."

This last statement, as surprising as Anna Belle's speech and appearance, must have showed on Kevin's face. "Surely you don't think," Anna Belle stated quietly, "that we are all ignorant fieldhands."

"Well, I, a . . ."

"My father was a free man, and my mother a free woman," Anna Belle began to explain patiently. "I attended school in Boston where I taught before the war broke out. At the invitation of a member of Congress who knew my father, I came down here to do what I could in helping with the slaves newly freed by the Army of the Potomac. And even though I do so enjoy bringing light to the minds of so many young children that had only known darkness and ignorance, I felt, like your Harriet, the need to do more. So I come here, as often as I can, and help those who have done so much to help my people."

"Help?" the major in the bed next to Kevin's protested. "If I could, I'd have that woman tried as a Southern sympathizer."

Taken aback by the sharp words, Kevin rolled his head over and stared at the major for a moment. Only after seeing that there was a broad smile on his face, and that Anna Belle responded to his taunts with her own, did Kevin realize that it was all in jest. "You're lucky you've been unconscious for so long," the major continued after he gave Kevin a sly wink. "The severity of your wounds have spared you that woman's dictatorship."

"I'll have you know, my good Major Crawford," Anna Belle retorted, "that if I had left you on your own, you'd still be lolling about in the same ill-fitting and filthy shirt you were wearing when they brought you in here two months ago."

Kevin, having assumed the major was a recent casualty like him, looked over to Harriet with a quizzical look on his face. "The major is a cavalryman who was wounded in a skirmish with some of Stuart's horsemen in March."

"Yes," Crawford growled. "And thanks to our dear Miss Anna Belle, I've been doomed to suffer for that bit of ill luck ever since."

Harriet leaned over and whispered in Kevin's ear. "Don't mind them. They carry on like this all the time. They really like each other."

"I heard that," Anna Belle snapped, causing Harriet to sit upright and look down at the sheets on Kevin's bed sheepishly.

The good-natured, if sharp, exchange between Major Crawford and Anna Belle, who had moved over to his bedside and was messing with his pillow and sheets, came to an abrupt end when an Army surgeon in a long white coat entered the room. As if on cue, Anna Belle and Harriet both left the room through a door opposite the one the surgeon was standing in. After watching them disappear, Kevin looked at the surgeon, who now entered the room without a word, and then over to Crawford. "What's that all about?" Kevin asked.

In a hushed voice, Crawford explained. "Our noble healer is of the opinion that women have no place in the world of medicine. 'Too scatter-brained to understand the science,' he claims, 'and too squeamish to stand the sight of blood.' So he keeps them out of his ward when he can."

Though it caused him pain to do so, Kevin moved closer to Crawford to continue the hushed conversation while the surgeon examined a man across the room. "What about Harriet and Anna Belle?"

Crawford let out a muffled chuckle. "I don't think the man's been born who can deny Anna Belle. That woman is going places. And your fiancée, well. When the good doctor was informed that she was the daughter of an important judge in New Jersey who would make his life miserable if he denied her, well."

Kevin looked at Crawford quizzically. "Judge Shields? Intervene on his daughter's behalf for my sake?"

With a wink and a smile, Crawford acknowledged Kevin's confusion. "Your sweetheart explained it all to Anna Belle and, in turn, she shared Harriet's unhappy story with me. Fortunately for your Harriet, the doctor doesn't have enough of a backbone to stand up to a good fight and wasn't bright enough to check Harriet's story out."

"But the idea of Harriet using her father's name," Kevin protested, "doesn't sound like her. She's every bit as proud and stubborn as the judge."

"Believe me when I tell you, young man, a woman in love," Crawford explained, "will do whatever she has to in order to be with and care for the one she loves."

Easing back onto his pillow slowly, Kevin thought about Crawford's last comment as the surgeon made his way from bed to bed. When he reached Crawford's he stopped, looked down at the major, and gave him a cold, contrived smile. "Well," the surgeon announced without even bothering to turn the sheets down and examine Crawford, "seems your big day will be here soon. Your artificial leg will be ready for final fitting and a try by the end of the week."

Kevin watched as Crawford responded to this news without a word or change of expression. "If it all works out," the surgeon continued, ignoring Crawford's failure to be cheered by his news, "you'll be up, out of here, and on your way home before you know it."

Then, without another word, the surgeon turned, walked over to Kevin's bed, and began to examine Kevin's wounds. As he handled Kevin's leg, then arm with all the grace of an ironworker, he never said a word to Kevin. Only when he was finished did he say anything. "Lucky man you are," he stated with an insincerity that was evident to all. "Any one of these wounds could have killed you, and one should have left you a cripple." Then, standing up, he looked down into Kevin's eyes. "The surgeon who took the time to work on you, more time than he should have, managed to save your leg, given all the skin and muscle that were laid open."

Not knowing what to make of the surgeon's statement or how to respond, Kevin watched as the surgeon turned, again without another word, and moved down the row of beds. "He's a real charmer," Crawford announced quietly. "A real prince among men."

Over the next few days, Kevin's fever broke and he began to feel more comfortable, though he was never entirely without pain. One afternoon while Harriet was reading to an adoring and attentive Kevin, Anna Belle came breezing into the room, snatched the book out of Harriet's hands, and announced that it was time for Kevin to stop lounging about so much and get out of bed. "You have no more need for your fiancée to dote on you so than I have any need for another head. It's time you got up on your own two feet and started doing for yourself, Kevin Bannon."

And though he protested loudly to both Harriet and Anna Belle, neither woman paid him any attention. "Anna Belle's right," Harriet finally concluded as she turned down the sheets on one side of the bed and prepared to help Anna Belle swing his legs over the side. "The sooner you get up and about, the better you'll be."

"But shouldn't we wait till the surgeon's here or says something?" Kevin protested between spasms of pain as the women worked to get his legs over the side and him off his back.

Anna Belle made a face. "Oh, pooh. If you waited for that man to get you out, you'd have roots in this bed that reached down to the floor. Just ask Major Crawford."

In an effort to find some sympathy during this sudden and excruciating ordeal, Kevin looked over at Crawford. If the cavalry major felt any sympathy for the suffering of his fellow soldier, he didn't show it. Instead, he shrugged. Then with a chuckle, he added, "Best cooperate, young Bannon. They've got you outnumbered."

Unable to resist their persistence, Kevin gave in and started to work with the women. After getting him in an upright position with his feet dangling off the edge of the tall bed, the two women paused while Kevin recovered from the pain and got over a sudden bout of dizziness. "Do either one of you dear ladies," Kevin asked as they supported him for a moment, "know what you're doing?"

"Oh, hush up, Kevin," Harriet chided. "You're starting to sound like a spoiled child."

"Or," Anna Belle added as she glanced over to Crawford, "an old mule of a cavalry major."

"Ah, excuse me, ladies," Crawford protested. "I've said nothing. I'm keeping my own counsel as you torture my poor, unfortunate friend over there."

"Good," Anna Belle responded as she looked over at Crawford with a smile. "And if you know what's good for you, you'll let us deal with one cripple at a time."

Kevin, recovered from the bout of dizziness, looked over at Anna Belle and protested. "Dear lady, I am not a cripple."

With a broad smile Anna Belle nodded. "Well, I'm glad to hear that. In that case, you'll be able to join Harriet and me for a little stroll."

Before he had time to regret his statement or even to think, the two women had Kevin on his feet. "There now," Anna Belle declared with great satisfaction. "That's not so bad, is it?"

It was fortunate that Kevin was unable to answer, for if he had, the only words that he would have choked up would have been oaths and curses. The feeling of his bare feet on the wooden floor never reached his conscious mind, because the stabs of pain from his wounds in his shoulder, arm, and upper leg all slammed into him with terrible effect at the same instant. And though he fought it, Kevin's eyes rolled back into his head for a moment as what little color he had in his face drained away and he started to swoon.

Anna Belle, used to this sort of thing, leaned back against the side of the bed for support, dragging Kevin along with her. Harriet, sensing this, conformed as quickly as she could. "Now, now, Captain Bannon," Anna Belle whispered in soft, soothing tones, "stay with us and all will be well."

The momentary rest against the side of the bed, and the support of the two women allowed Kevin the opportunity to catch the breath that the sudden and intense pain had knocked from his body, and rally to fight the pain. The placid expression that had fallen across his face when he had been on the verge of fainting was now replaced by a contorted, twisted one as he struggled to master the pain.

Anxious to get him away from the soft comforts of the bed he was leaning on lest he give way to the natural desire to escape the pain of this exertion by falling over backward into bed, Anna Belle looked over to Harriet and motioned with her head that they were going to stand up again and go forward. "All right, Captain Bannon, you've had your rest. It's time to move on."

Before he could protest, the two women had him back on his feet again and away from the bed. And though the bed was behind him and it would have been the easiest thing in the world for him just to lurch backward, away from his tormentors and into the safe, warm clutches of his bed, Kevin was unable to force even this simplest of plans through the waves of pain that wracked his body.

Working in tandem, part supporting and part dragging, the two women moved Kevin out into the aisle between the rows of beds and down toward the door at the far end. Kevin, unable to protest as he needed all his strength to keep from screaming in pain, only managed an occasional glimpse of the room about him. To him, the images that made their way through the excruciating pain were disjointed. The view of a bearded soldier, sitting upright in bed and dressed in a white hospital gown, flashed before his eyes and then disappeared as a new wave of pain swept over him. Then, as the agony subsided, the long corridor between the beds leading to the door came into view. He was just beginning to wonder if the two women intended to force him all the way down to that doorway when that thought was crushed by spasms of agony.

Even the words and sounds that broke through into his unconsciousness were strangely disembodied and unreal to Kevin. On one side, and he couldn't even determine which one it was, he heard smidgens of Anna Belle's words to Harriet. "Though it gives the doctors fits," she was telling Harriet as they moved ponderously forward, "I've always been told it's best to get them out of bed as soon as you can." If Harriet responded to this, Kevin couldn't tell. Everything about him was totally disjointed, distorted, and jumbled about like the contents of a poorly packed haversack.

Sometime during this brutal ordeal, Kevin realized that the trio had managed to turn around and head back for his bed. "All right, Captain Bannon," Anna Belle advised Kevin, "you're back at your bed." Those words, coming through his suffering like an answer from above to a prayer all but brought tears of joy and relief to his face. Any relief that Kevin did feel, however, was quickly eradicated as Anna Belle, leaning over him as she and Harriet tucked him in, added, "We'll get him up and on his feet again this afternoon after the surgeon makes his rounds and again this evening after dinner."

And though he wanted to protest this sentence, the sensation of being back in his own bed, safe from the worst ravages of the brutal agony he had just endured, was just too enjoyable to spoil with protestations. Instead, Kevin allowed himself to succumb to the blissful embrace of sleep that promised to take him away from this place of suffering and pain. Sleep, Kevin mused as he felt himself slipping away, had to be what heaven was.

By the time the nine o'clock bell rang and the gas for the lights along the walls was turned down, Kevin was usually asleep. Though his first fever had broken, he was exhausted by the desperate struggle he had waged to survive his wounds during his long delirium. Kevin's retreat into a sound slumber, however, did not end Harriet's nursing and cares. Often soldiers who were near enough to hear whatever book Harriet had been reading when Kevin had passed from consciousness would implore her to continue. "Till the end of the chapter, please," one would ask, or "You can't leave us to wonder all night about what happened to that great white whale," another would insist. So Harriet would move her seat out into the aisle between the beds, and read on. In the process, she would lose track of where she had left off with Kevin. Not that he ever noticed or minded. Just having her attention was more than enough to satisfy him.

The formal call for quiet and sleep did not necessarily mean that sleep was possible. On the contrary, Harriet observed. The sights and sounds of day were replaced with an entirely different collection, each as unique as the man who originated it. From her little cubbyhole of a room where her bed was, Harriet could hear the slow, steady gait of the night watch as he moved ponderously from floor to floor, and along the halls both upstairs and outside her door. On nights when the wind from the outside caused the old hotel that housed the hospital to creak, Harriet would imagine that she was on a sailing ship. As the wind outside whipped the building with great, steady gusts, and the reassuring *tromp, tromp, tromp* of the watchman's steps transformed themselves into the beat of crewmen above deck tending the ship, Harriet allowed herself to picture Kevin and her aboard a boat that was taking them from this place of suffering away to a place where there was no war, no hatred.

But it was only a dream, and other noises in the night often served to remind her of that. At intervals that were all too frequent, the watchman's sedate cadence would be replaced with hurried footfalls that scurried this way at first, and then back in the company of new feet. Sometimes it would be upstairs, sometimes it would be outside her own door. Regardless of its source or time, Harriet would spring from her bed, quickly dress herself with whatever clothing would fly into her hands first, and rush forth to Kevin's side to make sure that the flurry of activities was not on his behalf. Even when she was greeted in the halls by the sight of a stretcher bearing the remains of a soldier who had lost his final fight being taken away in solemn procession from one of the upper floors or another room, Harriet would not, could not, turn back from her investigation.

Such events happened often enough that the watchman for the ward where Kevin was did nothing more than acknowledge Harriet's appearance with a slight nod and a weak smile. A kindly old man with an arm that had been ravaged by grapeshot earlier in the war, the ward watchman never spoke to Harriet, or interfered with her comings and goings, though he always made sure that there was a chair near Kevin's bed for her.

Each time she came in the room, Harriet would do the same thing. Carefully, so as not to disturb Kevin's fitful sleep, she would lean over him and feel his brow. Then she would move her hand down, placing it gently upon his chest to check his breathing, just as Doctor White had taught her. Only when she was satisfied that all was well would she settle into that chair and compose herself by gazing at Kevin's sleeping form and whispering a silent prayer of thanks.

Though these alarms, sometimes two or three times a night, were taking a toll on her, she didn't complain. "It is better that I respond and satisfy myself that he is well," Harriet responded to Anna Belle's frequent protests that she needed to stop rushing to Kevin's side all hours of the night, "than remain in my own little bed, torturing myself with doubt and fear." And though she continued to pester Harriet daily about this, Anna Belle did nothing to stop her. Anna Belle understood Harriet's feelings on this matter too well. For she had lost her only son, a brilliant young man of eighteen with a promising future, to a Rebel bullet in July, 1863. As headstrong as his mother, he had rushed to war with Lewis Douglass, the son of Frederick Douglass, in April of that year. And though he had made his mark on history at Battery Wagner with the 54th Massachusetts, his death had left a gash in his mother's heart that no solace would ever heal.

As she struggled to compose herself after seeing that all was well, Harriet would listen to the sounds Kevin made as he slept, and watch his face. Kevin's face was like a mirror that reflected the thoughts that tumbled through his mind. When reviewing a battle from the past, his expressions became stern. As his brow creased with stark, stern lines of concern, he would twist his head this way and that, often mumbling commands or warnings that Harriet seldom was able to understand. If the engagement that ravaged his sleep that night had been particularly vicious or cruel, Kevin's whole body would twitch and jerk, almost as if he were trying to physically respond to his own mumbled orders. At first, Harriet would try to calm him. But her best efforts were frustrated. "It's best, miss," a soldier in another bed nearby advised her one day after he had watched her the night before, "to let him deal with his ghosts and demons as best he can on his own. The sooner he's freed them from wherever he's hidden them, the happier he'll be."

That there was some truth to this was borne out by watching Kevin. Even on his worst nights, Kevin would reach some sort of conclusion, some point in his nightmare where the pain and suffering and horrors of war came to an end. Sometimes this conclusion would be sudden, almost startling, like an orchestra's feverish beat just before the ringing down of a curtain on a particularly rousing performance. At other times, the transition from agitation to serenity was slow, almost imperceptible, like the ebbing of a tide. Regardless of its ending, each nightmare was accompanied by a final accounting, whispered like a first sergeant calling the roll, of those who perished. Some of the names were familiar to Harriet, evoking images and memories in her mind. Others were not. And every now and then, a name, often repeated and strangely out of place amongst all the male names listed before, would be repeated. Harriet did not dwell on this, for whatever had gone on before was somehow intertwined with who and what Kevin was now. Besides, for Harriet, all that mattered was that after he had finished his final accounting of his past, Kevin's troubled expression would soften.

It was this final transition that would free Harriet from her concern and worry. In a way, it even pleased her. Liberated from the harsh realities of war, Kevin's true nature shone through the agony and suffering that had marked his passage into manhood. The lines were smoothed out and the furrows in his brow disappeared, leaving in their wake a very pleasing portrait of youth. For a moment, Harriet would be free to recall the long walks she and Kevin had so often enjoyed back in New Brunswick when their love had been fresh and unfettered by the concerns of politics or the world. Slowly the dark stuffiness of the room she and Kevin were confined to melted away and was replaced with the open crispness of a park in winter. That they would one day again walk through those parks together was more than Harriet's fondest hope; the dream was her only salvation.

So Harriet would watch and listen to Kevin, waiting until she was satisfied that all was well before leaving his side or slipping away into her own thoughts and dreams. On more than one occasion she would suddenly be awakened by the harsh rays of the morning sun streaming through the windows of the room only to find that she had laid her head down on the bed next to Kevin and fallen asleep sometime during her lonely vigil. Waking with a start, she would look around, jump up, and as she had before, place her hand upon Kevin's forehead to ensure that all was well. Only after she was sure that it was would she conclude her vigil with a silent prayer that it always would be.

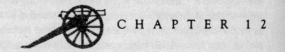

CHAPTER 12

Richmond, Virginia, June, 1864

WALKING SLOWLY DOWN MAIN Street, James Bannon took great delight in looking in the shop windows. It had been a long time since he had been free to wander about the streets of a big city, a terribly long time. And despite his instructions to hurry on to the Richmond and Petersburg Depot at the corner of Main and Eighth Street, he intended to enjoy every moment he could. His only regret was that he had been afforded so little time to clean himself up before he left with the provost guard to escort prisoners to Bell Island. Still, James quickly learned that his sadly disreputable appearance and overpowering smell were a blessing of sorts. A month's worth of dirt, grime, and sweat, not to mention a uniform that would be a disgrace to a scarecrow, kept the citizens of the Confederate capital more than an arm's length from him as he wandered from shop window to shop window. It was, he mused, as if he were walking about in his own little bubble, safe from the hustling and jostling of others.

Stopping in front of a millinery shop, James paused to study a pair of fine hats sitting in an otherwise empty window. Gaily decorated with bright ribbons and bows, they stood out in sharp contrast to the weathered and dingy appearance of the shop, sadly in need of repainting. He didn't pay much attention to the small sign written in an elegant, flowing script that proudly announced that these hats represented the latest in women's fashions directly from Paris. Even if he had, he wouldn't have troubled himself with the fact that the blockade runner who brought them into this country did so at the expense of other items more critical to the survival of the Confederacy. Instead, he stood there, attempting to picture Mary Beth wearing one of those delicate creations. Yet as hard as he tried, and as clear as he could picture every fine feature of her face, he could not marry the two images. Instead, his mind could see only her face framed by her long hair, loosely bound up in a bun from which dozens of stray hairs fell away. Her bonnet, even when she bothered with one, hung flopped over one shoulder on her back, its large checkered bow pulled tight against her throat.

Looking up from the fine woman's hat, James' vision of Mary Beth was suddenly replaced with that of a figure he hardly recognized being reflected back to him from the store's window. His first reaction was one of disbelief. "My God," he murmured, "is that me?" A gentleman passing behind James slowed, thinking James was addressing the question to him. When he saw that the ragged stick figure was only mumbling to himself, the man blushed in embarrassment, then quickly picked up his pace as he hurried on down the street.

For the longest time James stood there gazing at his own faint image, trying hard to make sense of what he had become and what it all meant. While the tattered shreds of clothing that served as his uniform were understandable and quite easily forgiven, the face that stared back at him was difficult to accept. Deep furrows that emanated about the mouth and eyes etched their way toward hollow cheeks that looked like craters. About his eyes, streaked with red and lacking even the slightest hint of luster, were dark, deep circles that would have, under any other circumstances, been comical. Even the color of his skin, despite ceaseless exposure to the blistering Virginia sun, was a matter of great concern, for it reminded him of the hue taken on by men freshly killed in battle.

Yet as bad as all of this was, it was the eyes that struck James the hardest. Though never a jolly and easygoing sort of fellow, James' eyes had always been clear, bright, and expressive. Now, as James carefully studied his image, the only expression he imagined that he could see reflected from his eyes was sorrow and sadness. His eyes had seen much, he realized, in the past three years. They had watched men come into his life as strangers and grow into friends who had become dearer to him than his own family. Those same eyes had seen most of those men disappear, one by one, over the years. Sometimes the parting had been quick, violent, and bloody. Others had gone from his sight quietly, almost peacefully. Still,

James realized as he stared at his own eyes, in the end, they were gone, all of them, too many of them.

Despite the heat of the June day, a sudden chill caused James to shake all over. Filled with a deep feeling of melancholy, James almost began to whimper. Since the savage fighting at Spotsylvania and the loss of Marty Hazard, James had been in a stupor caused by physical and mental exhaustion. Without Marty, lost somewhere in the swirling blur that the hell of Spotsylvania left burned in James' mind, James had no one whom he could care for. He didn't have a friend, of flesh and blood, that he could touch and who, in his own need, could touch back. And though there was always Mary Beth, she was nothing more than an image, a reflection as cold and untouchable as the one that stared at him from the window he stood before. As had happened so many times before, James was on his own again, lost in a strange world over which he had no control, and in which he had no clear role.

"There ya are, Jimmy," Dale Wint shouted while he was still half a block away. Gladly turning away from the store window, James watched as Wint limped up toward him. He had not seen Wint since March, 1862, the day James and Will McPherson had dragged Dale off the field at Kernstown, shot through both legs. That the South's plight was so bad that cripples like Wint were being reassigned to front line units should have bothered James, but it didn't. After the Wilderness and the nightmare of Spotsylvania, nothing seemed to surprise James. "While you've been off enjoying the sights of this fine town, Jimmy," Wint beamed as he came close enough to James so that his foul breath overpowered James' own stench, "me and the other boys have been searchin' high and low for ya."

Instinctively, James looked up at the sun, still high in the sky, then back at Wint, ignoring the odor that reeked from every stitch of clothing Dale Wint wore. "As I recall, we don't need to be at the Virginia Central Station till dusk. Did someone decide the war couldn't go on without us?"

Wint ignored James' sarcastic remark. Barely missing a government clerk as he swung his rifle off his shoulder and slammed the butt end down on the pavement, Wint leaned forward and stared at James. "Oh, that? No, they ain't changed that, least not yet. Last I heard we still meet at dusk. It's just that the colonel wants to see you, right away."

"Couper?" James asked as his face twisted about as if he were sucking on a lemon.

"The one and only. Like me, he's been called back from his duties here in Richmond to fill out the ranks of the regiment." Then noticing James' sour expression Wint chuckled. "You and old Abner never did see eye to eye. Somethin' come between you at VMI?"

James looked down the street, past Wint. Subconsciously, he shifted his haversack and cartridge box, items that seemed strangely out of place in this city, about his waist. "You could say that," James slowly replied.

" 'Cause you're a Yankee?"

Wint's question caught the attention of two women who were passing by and gave them a start. Swinging wider into the street to avoid the unsavory pair, they continued to watch James as they walked down the street, putting their heads together to chatter once they were far enough away not to be heard. "Can't say that I won't be happy to be away from this place." He snorted as he nodded at the women. "They're all either high society types or whores." Then leaning closer to James, he winked. "Though, to tell you the truth, I don't think there's much difference anymore, not in this town."

James looked at Wint skeptically. He suspected that there were still many virtuous women in Richmond, despite its wartime reputation, but didn't much feel like arguing the point. Wint had always been as crude as he had been tough when it came to soldiering. And since James now judged all men by the latter, he could live with the former.

"What's the matter with you?" Wint shot back. "Iffen you'd been with the provost guard in this town as long as I've been and seen all the stuff that goes on hereabouts, you'd agree. I'm really lookin' forward to gettin' back to the regiment and the camp."

James was about to tell Wint that there was no more regiment, and that camp life wasn't what it had been when a wound had forced him from active field duty, but decided not to. It would be hard enough for Wint when he realized how different things were now without James ruining his cherished illusion. "Where am I supposed to meet Abner?"

"Lieutenant Colonel Couper is awaiting your presence at the Spotswood Hotel, right down there on the corner of Main and Eighth."

James looked to where Wint was pointing. "Did he bother to tell you where in the hotel he'd be?"

"Well," Wint chuckled as he shook his head, "more than likely, he'll be at the bar, swapping stories and rumors with all the other fine officers from the Army departments that're scattered all about this town."

Lifting his right shoulder slightly to shift the weight of his slung rifle on his back, James sighed. "Well, I guess I should be going and find out what Abner wants."

"Yes," Wint added with a wink, "I guess you should too. And while you're enjoying your visit with the colonel, I need to say farewell to a lady friend."

James looked at the other man and gave him the best smile he could manage. "You be careful, you hear. Remember what they keep telling us when we're in town. An unguarded moment with the wrong lady will lay you as low as a Yankee bullet."

"Jimmy," Wint laughed out loud, causing several civilians to turn and look, "I certainly do hope that these tired old bones do get laid low in the next hour or so." Then, still laughing so much that tears came to his eyes, Wint turned and marched, as best as his legs could take him, down the street as women parted to let him go by quickly so that the hems of their skirts didn't touch any part of his body.

James, turning to leave, took one long last look at his reflection in the window. He had come a long way, he concluded, yet still had a long way to go.

Just as Wint had predicted, James found Abner Couper engaged in a heated discussion with two other officers in the bar that was just off the hotel's lobby. Aware of his appearance, James didn't enter the bar but instead stood in the doorway until his presence, and odor, caused enough people to turn and look his way. When Abner Couper did so, James locked his eyes with Couper.

It took Couper a moment to realize whom he was looking at. When he finally did, he turned to one of his fellow officers, excused himself, grabbed his cap, and headed for James. "Mr. Bannon," Couper declared as he neared him and offered his hand, "I am so glad that they found you."

Unsure of the reasoning behind this meeting or Couper's attitude toward him, James felt the need to pull away the outstretched hand. Still, to have done so would have been rude and presumptuous. So James grasped the sling of his rifle with his left hand and took Couper's hand.

This simple act seemed to ease the tension in Couper's face that James hadn't noticed till the very last moment. "Ah, could I speak with you, Mr. Bannon, outside?"

Having no desire to stay where they were, with many of the bar's patrons taking great offense at James' appearance and smell, James agreed and followed his former cadet officer through the lobby and out onto the street. Once there, James came up next to Couper on his left, as military etiquette called for, and waited for him to speak.

Couper did not do so immediately but, instead, placed both hands in the small of his back, one held by the other, and slowly walked down the crowded sidewalk looking about as he did so. "Before the war," Couper began, talking to James without looking at him, "this city had a population of a little over thirty-eight thousand souls. Today, with the government people, the Army and Navy departments, and refugees from every part of the state, there's almost four times that number living here." Glancing over to James, he smiled. "I'll be glad to leave this place."

James, unsure of where this conversation was going, nodded as Couper looked away and kept walking and talking. "It's a different world here, Mr. Bannon. A very different world. The people who walk these streets haven't grasped the notion that the South is dying." Stopping at that moment on a busy corner, Couper looked at everything about him and repeated his statement. "Our nation, our state, is dying."

There was a rather mournful tone in his voice, one that reminded James of a person admitting to a terrible fact for the first time. Then, just as quickly, as the feeling of gloom swept over James too, Couper turned sharply and looked James in the eye. "But if we're dying, we're doing it on our feet." With that, he stepped off the sidewalk and into the paved, brick street, taking as great care to avoid the wagons and buggies being pulled by horses and mules well past their prime as he did to make sure he didn't step in the piles of droppings those horses and mules left behind.

Once on the other side, Couper continued his discussion, this time in a more even, businesslike manner. "I asked you to see me for two reasons, Mr. Bannon."

James felt his guard go up.

Stopping again, Couper turned and faced James, letting his hands drop to his sides. "The first is to apologize to you."

Caught off guard by this announcement, James blinked as he fought the urge to take a step back and look Couper over from head to toe. "I was wrong about you, Mr. Bannon, very, very wrong about you. And I wronged you. You're as much a Virginian as this state's noblest sons. Your conduct over the years has proven it."

Speechless, James didn't know what to do until Couper offered his hand. "Can you forgive me, Mr. Bannon?"

Taking Couper's hand, James couldn't think of anything at first. Finally, he simply said, "James, my first name is James."

The sincerity of Couper's smile told James that this man had meant every word, and that his simple response had been more than adequate. After taking a deep breath, Couper turned and started to walk again, placing his hands behind his back as before. "The second matter is of equal importance, Mr. . . . James. As you know, the adjutant's office is scraping up every man it can in order to rebuild the old Stonewall Brigade. Every man who was detached on other duties, including me, thank God, is going back to their regiment. And though we'll never be able to field anything even resembling the old Fourth Virginia given the dearth of manpower the entire South faces, we're even in tighter straits when it comes to officers and noncommissioned officers. Which is the second, and main reason you're here. I have been authorized to appoint sergeants and corporals to fill vacancies. I want you to be one of those sergeants."

Suddenly realizing what Couper was saying, James stopped in his tracks. Couper took several more steps before he realized that he was alone. Halting, he looked back at the startled expression on James' face. Pivoting about, he walked up to James and stopped before him. "Why not? This promotion is years overdue and, may I say, well deserved."

James was about to tell Couper what he thought of his promotion, but then a voice inside told him to wait. In the past, the idea of being promoted, of taking rank, while never offered was always the furthest thing from his mind. James, ever the responsible brother in a family where his father abused him and his younger brother wanted no part of authority. He told himself time and time again that he was more than content with following the orders of others and going along with whatever everyone else was doing. After a while, he began to enjoy the lack of responsibility, of having to think and worry about this matter or the other. Except for his small band of friends, he was happy to let the world go by.

But they were gone now, he realized, taken from him one by one.

And as he had realized before, he was alone again, leaving him few choices. He could either establish for himself a new band of friends and comrades or . . .

"Will you take it?" Couper asked finally.

In the end, there was no other answer James could give. There simply wasn't enough of his emotional fabric left to tolerate the pain of making new friends and then watching them die or be horribly maimed, one by one. He had already endured much and doubted if he could endure such suffering again. If the war was to continue, and he knew it would, and he was to be part of it, for there was nothing else he could imagine, then he had to do so in a manner that isolated him from the pain and suffering of those about him. "Yes, Colonel," James finally said. "I'll take the stripes."

Couper didn't need to take the men of the brigade who had come to Richmond as part of the prisoner guard force back to the lines just outside the city to rejoin the brigade. Rather, the brigade, now consisting of the remnants of the fourteen regiments that had belonged to Jackson's old division and had been savaged at Spotsylvania, came to them. Together with the bulk of Jubal Early's Second Corps, Couper and his small detachment met the brigade as the Second Corps left the defensive works east of Richmond and marched through the city, headed west. "Looks like we're a goin' back to the valley one more time," Wint commented dryly as he stood about with the rest of the replacements, waiting to take their place in the long line of march. Looking at James with a bland, almost forlorn look, Wint shook his head. "I sure hope we find some of Old Stonewall's magic there."

James, left behind with orders to wait for the adjutant general's office to finish gathering the next draft of recruits and replacements for the brigade, didn't want to think about what they'd find in the mountains and valleys that had become so much of his life. Rather, he yearned to indulge himself in the unexpected joys Abner Couper had made available to him. "While you're waiting, James," Couper told him as he issued his instructions, "take my room at the Spotswood. It's paid for through the end of the month. Take some time, tend to your personal needs, and rest. It looks like you could use some. I have a friend in the quartermaster's department who'll be able to secure a decent uniform and accoutrements. I've also managed to secure a small advance on your pay so that you can survive here in comfort till it's time to rejoin the regiment."

James didn't mention to Couper that he had over one hundred Union dollars, collected from the bodies of Yankees, hidden away in his haversack. It didn't seem appropriate, he reasoned, to share such sordid information with an officer and a gentleman.

Given three days of absolute freedom in a city, even a city as badly crowded, run-down, and expensive as Richmond was in the late spring of 1864, was a novel experience to James. After following Couper to his room at the Spotswood, James left his meager possessions and helped Abner take his to the assembly point. Having no desire to stand around and watch the sorry party of recruits and returning veterans march off, James made tracks as fast as his legs would carry him to the quartermaster's department.

"Let's see that letter," demanded a one-armed clerk at the warehouse he was directed to. Taking the neat, crisp white document that authorized James to draw equipment and uniforms for himself and the expected recruits in his one good hand, the clerk looked at the page for a moment, up at James, then back at the sheet. "Well, now," he announced in a haughty manner. "Can't do too much for you, I'm afraid. We've been picked clean by a Georgia unit that came through here. *They*," he announced with great emphasis, "had an officer with them."

James smiled. Reaching into his pocket, he pulled out a Union five-dollar piece. Careful to make sure that no one else saw it, he let the one-armed clerk catch a slight glimpse of the piece. "Did they have any of these?" James asked coyly.

The clerk's bored expression suddenly changed as he eyed the coin. Glancing this way, then that to ensure no one saw what he did, the clerk cleared his throat. "Ah, well, perhaps there is something I can do for you."

Not wanting to play the same silly game that the clerk had tried, James played down his triumph. "Well, I'd appreciate that." Then, eager to see how far he could push his advantage, James added, "And please, new issue. I don't want any of that stuff taken from the local field hospitals, cleaned in river water without benefit of soap, and stocked for reissue."

The supply clerk gave James a wink. "Oh, no need to worry, Sergeant. I know how to take care of a friend."

James returned the smile as he reached across the counter and shook hands with the clerk, exchanging the coin without anyone else in the room seeing it. "I'm sure you do," James replied as he felt the coin leave his possession.

With fresh clothing in hand, including new socks, underwear, and a stiff, squeaky pair of shoes, James made his way back to the Spotswood and a bath. With small bribes carefully dropped here and there, James was able to turn the disdain the staff showed him into a cozy working relationship that made him the envy of guests who considered themselves his betters. It didn't bother James that he had to use some of his hard currency to secure a hot bath, shave, and haircut. The money, he felt, was best used by him when he could for things he needed. After all, James figured, why hoard it and lug it about, only to pass it on to some total stranger or undeserving hospital steward as they went through his pockets after he had been shot. No, James reasoned, as his mind turned to the serious business of enjoying his hot bath, I'll spend what I need to and enjoy myself while I can.

To cap off his day of great self-indulgence and resurrection of both body and spirit, James paraded through the lobby of the Spotswood in his fresh, newly issued uniform, en route to the hotel's restaurant. And though his blue sergeant's stripes, sewn on by him with great effort and more than a few oaths, were out of place among the gold braid of the officers' uniforms that filled the lobby, James didn't pay any attention to their stares. He had as much, if not more, of a right to be there, that night, as any of them. This embryonic country that they were living in after all was founded on the principle of freedom and individual rights and as a champion and defender of those rights, James felt that he had to answer to no man when it came his time to exercise them.

Forewarned of his liberal tipping with hard currency, the restaurant staff catered to James' every wish. Foods and delicacies that he thought were little more than memories in the Southern Confederacy appeared on his table as if by magic. Even a bottle of wine, a rare sight even in such a place as the Spotswood, suddenly was served to James. "The young woman in blue," the Negro waiter said with a smile when he saw James' questioning look as the waiter served him his first glass. "Her man friend isn't all too excited, but she felt sorry for you and insisted," the soft-spoken waiter explained.

James looked up, across the crowded room to where the waiter had nodded his head, and caught sight of the young woman. With a coy smile and glance, she returned James' stare, much to the displeasure of her escort. Maybe, James thought, as he smiled and lifted his glass to her, good old Dale Wint was right. Maybe there wasn't any difference between the working girls of this town and their betters.

In his efforts to take in every morsel of food that his overextended stomach could hold, and then some, James didn't notice the young man who approached his table. Only when the youth, wearing a hastily mended VMI cadet uniform, spoke did James pay him any attention. "I was hoping I would find you here," Daniel McPherson blurted when he saw that James didn't recognize him.

Only slowly did the voice, and then the face, register in James' wine-clouded mind. Even then, he was slow to perceive what Daniel's presence meant. With a giddy smile, James leaned back in his seat, took his glass of wine in both hands, and studied Daniel. "Well, well, well. Look at what we have here," he said with a voice that was both slurred and a tad too loud. "One of Virginia's finest, fresh from the fields of glory."

Blushing from embarrassment and unsure what to make of James' comment, Daniel moved up to the table, pulled out a chair across from James, and sat down. With a wide sweeping motion of one hand, James all but shouted. "Well, please do, sir, take a seat and tell me and these gentle people how you and your brethren snatched victory's noble laurels from our despised enemy's brow."

Though he was becoming angry at James' loud and cynical comments, and nodded by way of apology to one or two other guests who scowled at him, Daniel held his temper in check. "James," he quietly stated, "I've come to tell you I'll be joining you when you leave Richmond to rejoin the Fourth Virginia."

Like a thunderclap, Daniel's pronouncement sobered James. Sitting bolt upright in his seat, spilling some wine as he did so, James glared at Daniel. "You'll do nothing of the sort," he snapped. "Your sister and I sent you to VMI to keep you out of this war and you're going back there as soon as I can make the arrangements."

Now it was Daniel's turn to smile as he shook his head. "I'm afraid that's not possible, James," the boy stated in a low, even voice. "The Corps of Cadets was marched from Lexington to here. The institute's been burned to the ground by the Yankees. Those of us who could left the corps at the first opportunity and joined up." Holding up a sheet of rumpled paper in front of James' face, a sheet no different than the one that James himself had signed when he had enlisted in the 4th Virginia with Daniel's brother three years before, Daniel added, "It's official. I'm part of the Fourth, just like Will before me. I was told to report to you."

For a moment, James felt the urge to scream, not at Daniel's foolishness, but at himself for being so foolish, so naive as to think he could protect Mary Beth from any further suffering. Slumping down into his seat in defeat, James drank every drop of wine that was still in the glass he held, then glared at Daniel. "You fool," he finally whispered. "You God damned fool. You don't know what you did."

Without any desire to hide his anger, Daniel leaned forward. "Neither you, my sister, nor anyone alive is going to keep me out of this war. I proved I was man enough at New Market and don't have to answer to you or to anyone else when it comes to deciding when and where I'll do my duty."

James was about to tell him that he didn't know a damned thing about what it meant to be a man, much less about war, but didn't. What, he figured, was the point? What was done was done. Now, he reasoned as he poured himself another glass of wine and one for Daniel, the only thing he needed to figure out was how to keep this young fool from following in his brother's footsteps all the way to the grave.

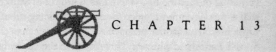

CHAPTER 13

Washington, D.C., June, 1864

STILL AGITATED THAT HIS servants had failed to forward Harriet's telegram to him in New York where he had been tending to business, Edward Bannon all but crashed his way through the crowd of people that always seemed to be camped in the lobby of Willard's Hotel. That his son Kevin had been wounded, despite three years of war and endless discussions with his cronies about losses and casualties, still came as a shock to the old Irishman. As was his habit in times of great distress, he stood before the portrait of his dead wife that hung in his private den. "Oh, Mary," he had lamented while gazing through teary eyes upon the soft, warm smile that looked down upon him, "how could I be so blind? So cruel? Will you ever forgive me, dear Mary, for being the kind of man I've become?"

"Edward!" a familiar voice rang out above the din of countless masculine conversations and bombast of the hotel lobby that filled the air about him. Turning, Edward watched as Judge Shields stepped away from a crowd of gentlemen, whom he recognized as being Democratic party hacks, and started to make his way toward him. Though he wanted only to drop his bags and find the general hospital where Kevin was convalescing, it would be rude not to spend time with the father of his son's fiancée.

"Edward! What a great surprise and pleasure it is to see you here," Judge Shields belted out as he took Edward's hand and shook it vigorously.

The judge's words, spoken with all the sincerity of a politician, put Edward on guard. Instinctively, he lifted his hand to cover his wallet as one would do to protect it from a pickpocket. The judge's manner, and the gathering of men he had walked away from so hastily, could only mean that it was time for the judge to solicit further contributions from him for Little Mac's run for the presidency.

"I was told you were in New York," the judge declared as he continued to pump Edward's hand, "speaking to some fellows about the Union-Pacific Railroad." Then, seeing that his exuberant demeanor wasn't having the desired effect on Edward, the judge let Edward's hand go and straightened himself up. "Do you come here on their behalf or on other business?"

The question was as dumbfounding to Edward as the judge's presence here had been. Shaking his head, Edward stared at the judge in bewilderment for a moment as he tried to make sure that he had heard the man right. Upset by this reaction, and fearful that he might have interfered with some important business matter that would alienate one of the biggest sources of political campaign funds that he had, the judge rushed to ease Edward's concerns, whatever they might be. "Dear sir," he hastened to say, "if I've caught you at an inopportune moment, please forgive me. I just . . ."

Recovering from his confusion and dismay, Edward responded hesitantly, almost apologetically. "I've come down here, I can assure you, sir, for no other reason than to see my son."

Now it was the judge's turn to be confused. "Kevin? Here? In Washington? I thought he was still with the Fourth New Jersey, in Virginia?"

It finally dawned upon Edward that Judge Shields was ignorant of Kevin's plight. This was all the more strange to Edward since it had been the judge's own daughter who had wired him, from Washington, about Kevin. "He was wounded at a place called Spotsylvania some two weeks ago."

Embarrassed by his ignorance concerning an issue so dear to the heart of one of his most prized sources of funds, the judge quickly stepped forward, grasped Edward's arm, and offered his condolences. "I am so terribly sorry to hear of this. I do not know why someone didn't tell me of this before. I would have done something to . . ."

"Your daughter informed me," Edward stated with a cold, even tone. "She's been attending him ever since he was wounded, and accompanied him here to Washington from the field."

Edward's announcement, as well as the accusatory look in his eyes, caused Judge Shields to let go of his arm and back away as if Edward had slapped him in the face. For a moment, the judge stood before Edward, looking down at the floor in embarrassment. Then, recovering his composure, he mechanically straightened himself up, tugged at the hem of his frock coat, and looked at Edward with a blank expression. "I have not spoken to nor communicated with my daughter in the past year, not since she chose to take up the life of a camp follower."

For a moment, Edward Bannon stood riveted to the floor staring at the man before him. Torn between admonishing him for being so cruel and uncompromising with his child, and striking him for suggesting that Harriet had run away from home in order to take up whoring with his son, Edward rocked from side to side as his being pulled one way, then the other. Sensing Edward's distress, the judge backed away again.

Suddenly, as if struck by a bolt of lightning, Edward Bannon realized that he was condemning another man, another father, for sins against his children that he, himself, was guilty of. The image of his older son, James, flashed before his eyes and brought back memories of the heinous manner that he had dealt with both James and Kevin. Overwhelmed by this sudden revelation and the grief that came with it, Edward Bannon turned on his heel and fled from Judge Shields, making no effort to hide the tears that flowed down his cheeks.

With all the excitement and anticipation of children waiting to open a gift, Harriet, Anna Belle, and Kevin watched as the hospital steward secured the straps of the wood and metal artificial limb to the stump of Major Thomas Crawford's leg. "There will be some discomfort at first, sir," the orderly warned as he pulled a strip of leather through one of the small buckles.

Kevin grunted. "That'll be especially true if you let these two women help you out of bed, Thomas."

Anna Belle, put off by Kevin's remark, turned and glared at Kevin. "That'll be enough out of you, Mr. Bannon."

Another wounded soldier across the way whistled and hooted. "Atta girl, Anna Belle. Give 'em . . ."

Shifting her fierce gaze from Kevin to her unsolicited supporter, Anna Belle snapped at him. "And that will be enough of that sort of talk, Mr. Wade. There are ladies present." Then, turning back to Crawford, she smiled as she looked down upon the anxious man. "This is Major Crawford's special moment and we don't want to spoil it for him."

Hushed back into silence, the rest of the men in the ward, as well as the two women, watched and waited while the steward finished making all the adjustments and preparations. When he was satisfied with his work, the steward wiped his nose across the sleeve of his coat, gave the artificial limb one more inspection, then looked up into Crawford's anxious eyes. "We're ready for you to try it out, Major."

Instinctively, Crawford looked up to Anna Belle. "I assume," he stated as calmly as he could, "this dance belongs to you?"

Understanding the major's need to hide his fears and apprehensions with humor, Anna Belle gave Crawford a warm smile. "Sir, it would be a pleasure."

Stepping aside, Harriet watched as Anna Belle helped Crawford sit up in bed. With hands that were as gentle as those of a mother holding her newborn baby, Anna Belle guided Crawford's good leg and artificial limb over to the edge of the bed. All were hushed and some held their breath as they watched every move Crawford and Anna Belle made. Only Anna Belle dared break the silence, and then it was only to give Crawford soft, soothing words of encouragement and advice. "There, now, Major, put your weight on your good foot, slowly," she cautioned him. "There's no need to rush this."

Leaning heavily on Anna Belle, Crawford looked down as he allowed his body to slowly shift from its seated position to standing. Harriet glanced back and forth from his face, taut with concentration and beaded with little drops of sweat, to the floor, where the foot of his artificial limb now rested. "I feel like a child," Crawford nervously uttered when he glanced up and saw Harriet watching his every move.

Harriet smiled. "You're doing splendidly, Major, splendidly."

With a smile and a nod, he thanked Harriet for her words of encouragement, then looked into Anna Belle's eyes. "Well, I guess I'm ready."

Anna Belle nodded. "Then let us procede, dear sir."

Slowly, ever so slowly, Crawford shifted his weight from his good leg to the one with the artificial limb. That this seemingly simple task was accompanied by much pain was obvious by the expression Crawford found impossible to conceal. "We need to take our time," Anna Belle warned. "Don't go any faster or farther than you're ready to go."

Opening his eyes, already blurred by tears brought on by extreme pain, Crawford looked over to Anna Belle and nodded. "I'm . . . about . . . as . . . ready . . . as . . . I'll . . . ever . . . be," he managed to stutter.

Taking him at his word, though she wore an expression as pained as Crawford's, Anna Belle slowly led him to the aisle between the beds much in the same way she and Harriet had done for Kevin. With Anna Belle providing support on the side that the artificial leg was on and Harriet hovering close to Crawford's good side, the tiny procession moved on as all eyes watched. Slowly, the tense expression melted away from Crawford's face as he put a bit more pressure on his stump with each step he took. Anna Belle, judging by the manner that he was shifting his weight and letting up on her shoulder that he was needing her less and less, prepared to let go and back away.

Suddenly, without warning, the silence of the room, disturbed till now only by Crawford's heavy footfall, was shattered by a deep, piercing wail. Crawford's face lost all color as his eyes bulged and his whole body stiffened. Harriet, unsure what was happening, stepped forward with both arms outstretched to catch Crawford as he began to totter, this way, then that. Caught off guard, and unable to support the sudden return of Crawford's complete weight thrown back onto her without notice, Anna Belle tumbled over with Crawford, who collapsed on top of her like a rag doll.

Yet, despite the suddenness of it all, Anna Belle managed to break Crawford's fall with her own body, though this effort knocked the air out of her and twisted her back. "Harriet," she gasped over the pitiful moaning of her charge, "help us."

Having regained her balance by grabbing the post of one of the beds, Harriet was about to comply when she looked down at the floor in order to avoid the slippery spot that had thrown her before. The sight of a pool of blood, bright red and fresh, caused her to recoil. "Oh! Dear God! He's bleeding."

Harriet's horrified gasp, and the expression on her face, caused everyone who could to look down at the floor. Kevin, who had propped himself up as rapidly as he could when he saw the calamity before him unfold, leaned over to see what was happening.

The stump of Crawford's leg, with the new artificial leg still affixed to it, was covered with a stream of blood that shot out from a ruptured artery like a fountain. Helpless as anyone else, Kevin watched as Harriet, recovering from her initial shock, dropped to her knees, quickly unsnapped the straps and buckles that held the useless limb in place, and started to poke about the gaping wound with her fingers. "For God's sake," she screamed without ever taking her eyes away from her desperate search for the artery, "someone get the surgeon. *Now!*"

The hospital steward, still standing where he had retreated when Anna Belle had taken charge of Crawford, bounded past Crawford's bed, avoiding the widening pool of blood on the floor, and fled toward the door. "Is he going for the surgeon?" Harriet called as she caught a glimpse of him disappearing through the door.

"Oh, Lord," Anna Belle wailed as she struggled to sit upright without interfering with Harriet's struggle to save Crawford, "I hope so." Then she saw Harriet as she continued to poke and pry with her fingers in the ugly scar where the blood was spurting from. "What are you doing, girl?" Anna Belle demanded over Crawford's pitiful moans.

"His artery. A bone sliver must have severed his artery. If I can find it, we can . . ." she paused in midsentence when she thought she had found the violated artery. Working her index finger about it blindly, she applied pressure to the spot despite the warm, slippery blood that covered Crawford, the floor, Anna Belle, and herself. Then, as quickly as the geyser of blood had started, it stopped. "There," Harriet announced to no one in particular in a rather matter-of-fact way. "Now," she added as she looked up and searched for assistance, "can someone help us get the major back in bed?"

Ignoring pains that had moments before been crippling, Kevin swung his feet out over the bed and prepared to respond to Harriet's plea. His assistance, however, was unnecessary as the ward steward and several orderlies who had been alerted by the screams of the steward who had fled the room came rushing through the door. With Harriet applying pressure on the ruptured artery and moving carefully so as not to lose it, the orderlies lifted Crawford, his face now as pale as the sheets on his bed, off Anna Belle and back onto his bed.

The surgeon, wearing a look of anger for being disturbed in such a manner, stormed into the room and marched down to Crawford's bed. The orderlies, finished with their duties, backed away as quickly as possible, leaving Harriet alone on one side of the bed as the surgeon took his station on the other. "How in the Lord's name did this happen?" he demanded as if he were a schoolmaster walking in on a prank.

Unruffled by his manner, Harriet spoke quickly in a quiet, controlled manner. "Something, a piece of bone maybe, pierced an artery."

Put off by Harriet's interference in a medical matter, the surgeon looked up at her with incredulous eyes. "And where, pray tell, did you receive your medical training, dear lady?"

Without letting go of the artery, Harriet looked into the surgeon's eyes. "At Fredericksburg, Chancellorsville, Gettysburg, Mine Run, the Wilderness, and Spotsylvania Court House, sir." Then her eyes narrowed into angry, dark slits. "This man is in distress, sir. He needs your help."

Though upset at being spoken to by a woman in such a manner in his own ward, the surgeon looked at Harriet's determined expression for a moment, then down at the wound. Wiping his hand across the front of his white coat, the surgeon moved his head this way and that over the wound before reaching over Crawford's stump of a leg. Another surgeon who had heeded the distress call rushed into the room and came up next to Harriet. Like the first surgeon, he looked at the wound for a moment, then started to probe with his fingers.

Recovering from the initial shock and surprise, Crawford opened his eyes and looked up at the ceiling. "Oh, dear God, what happened?"

Anna Belle, who had been helped off the floor by the ward steward and had taken her post at the foot of Crawford's bed, tried hard to smile as she did her best to look at Crawford and not the bloody wound that three people had their fingers in. "We, ah, had an accident. You'll be all right, though. The doctors are here."

"Oh," Crawford moaned through his pain and delirium. "It . . . will . . . be . . ." Then, as the surgeon in charge of the ward twisted a bone fragment, Crawford's body jerked up in a spasm of pain as he howled like an injured animal. Harriet, though frightened by the sudden, violent reaction, managed to keep pressure on the artery. With a troubled look on his face, the ward surgeon stepped back, looking first at Crawford's face, contorted beyond recognition by pain, then over to the assisting surgeon. "Ah, Doctor, could I have a word with you?" he whispered. "Over here."

Going over to where the ward surgeon had pointed, the second surgeon bowed his head so as to hear and speak to the first in private, hushed tones. As the two doctors consulted, Crawford recovered from his last agonizing bout of pain. Slowly opening his eyes, he looked over to Harriet. "Not doing well, are we?"

Though she wanted to say something encouraging, the best Harriet could manage was a sick smile. Anna Belle, understanding her distress and the amount of concentration she was exerting to keep the artery clamped with her fingers, tried to divert Crawford's attention. "You must not concern yourself with anything right now, Major Crawford. We're doing all that can be done."

Having finished with their quiet discussions, the ward surgeon left the two-man huddle and came up next to Harriet while the assisting surgeon stayed where they had talked. Looking down at the wound one more time without making any effort to probe it anymore, the ward surgeon grunted, then looked at Harriet. For a moment, he pondered what to do. Then, turning his back to Crawford, he leaned over toward Harriet until his lips were an inch away from her ear. "There is nothing we can do for him. The damaged artery is too deeply embedded in the fleshy part of the thigh."

Recoiling, Harriet's face betrayed her horror. Then, realizing that she was still holding Crawford's artery and his only chance of surviving between her fingers, Harriet stepped back toward the surgeon and whispered in his ear. "What shall I do? If I let go, he'll bleed to death."

This time, the ward surgeon took a deep breath. "I'm sorry, girl. There's nothing to be done. Please tell him and then, when you're ready, let go."

The sudden realization that her actions, rather than saving a life would end one, struck Harriet as nothing had ever hit her before. Desperately, her eyes darted first to Anna Belle, then to Crawford, and back to the ward surgeon, who was in the process of backing away from her as quickly and as gracefully as he could.

Understanding what was going on, Crawford reached up and took Harriet's arm. "This is my end, isn't it?"

At first, she couldn't look him in the eyes. All she could do was stare at the hand that kept the artery clamped. "It's all right," Crawford whispered. "I'll be all right." Only after she felt his hand on her arm did she find the courage to turn and face him. After their eyes met, there was a terrible pause. Finally, he asked in a voice choked with emotion, "How long before . . ."

His eyes, blurred with tears, tore at Harriet's heart as she looked into them. "As long as I hold your artery, you'll live. When I let go, you have . . ." She took a deep breath as she looked up at the ceiling with eyes overflowing with tears. "You have only a few minutes." The words, spoken slowly and with great deliberateness, sounded to Harriet as if they had been spoken by someone else. But they hadn't, she realized. She had pronounced this man's death sentence and held its execution in her hand.

"It's all right," he said again, as moved by Harriet's plight as by his own circumstances. Turning to face Anna Belle, who was crying and stood as though rooted to the floor at the foot of the bed, he began to speak. "Dear woman, don't cry, for I go to a far better place than this. Please write my wife and tell her that I died a good Christian and a faithful husband." Finished saying all he intended, Crawford closed his eyes for a moment of silent prayer. When his face, until now twisted and distorted by pain, lost all its tenseness, he opened his eyes and looked up at Harriet. "I am ready now," he stated clearly, calmly. "You may let go."

Though Crawford was composed and ready, Harriet was not. With tears streaking down her cheeks, she shook her head, unable to utter even the slightest sound. She couldn't do it. Though she had the strength to endure the suffering she had witnessed these many months—marching with an army in victory and defeat—Harriet couldn't find the strength to take her own fingers away. Only her fainting spared her from having to make that horrible decision.

Little of the former glory that had once greeted guests of the old hotel was evident to Edward Bannon as he made his way through the treadbare lobby of what was now an army hospital. The tromping of too many boots rushing across the floors and up the stairs, together with the lack of a thorough cleaning every now and then, combined with the passage of years to give the place a shabby, run-down look. Perhaps, Edward Bannon mused gloomily as he made his way to the desk where an orderly sergeant sat, this hotel was but a tiny reflection of the state of the nation, converted to uses for which it was not intended and badly in need of serious attention.

Halting in front of the sergeant, who was busily scribbling in a ledger that was quite similar to a hotel register, Edward lightly tapped his cane on the floor, cleared his throat, and waited. Used to the continual comings and goings of civilians in search of family and loved ones, the sergeant felt no rush to interrupt his labors and respond immediately to the pitiful inquiries of another. Other than a casual glance at the feet of the person before his desk to make sure they did not belong to an officer, the sergeant paid no heed to Edward's subtle call for attention. If this fine gentleman had waited this long to get here, the sergeant figured, as he recorded the deduction of a cavalry major from the rolls of the hospital, he could wait a moment longer.

Edward, however, was not used to being put off in such a manner. The staffs of the finest hotels in New York City and Philadelphia leaped at the chance to tend to even his slightest whim. Being treated like a second-class citizen, a feeling he still could clearly recall from the days before his labors and prosperity elevated him above such petty concerns as waiting in line or having to ask twice for service, bothered Edward greatly. Seeing that the sergeant was not about to halt his methodical inscribing, Edward once again tapped his cane on the floor. "I am looking for a captain by the name of Bannon, Kevin Bannon."

This second inquiry brought as little response as the first, for Edward did not realize that, despite his wealth and power, he was, within these walls, a second-class citizen. Though most soldiers of both armies would claim that they were nothing more than civilians condemned to military service for only as long as their services were required, once in uniform and initiated into the brotherhood of arms, even the meanest private felt himself superior to the noblest civilian. Since their duties and experiences had placed them in situations that required them to face death, all too often their own, they felt themselves separated from the very people from whose ranks they had come and whom they were charged with defending. For the sergeant, this attitude was routinely manifested by his habit of making civilian visitors wait while he executed whatever business was at hand, no matter how trivial.

Knowing that he was involved in just such a game, Edward Bannon, anxious to see his son, placed his two hands on either corner of the desk, and leaned over until his face was even with the sergeant's and only inches away. Unable to ignore this man, now breathing on him, the sergeant looked up into Edward's face. Whispering so that only the sergeant could hear, Edward growled. "I've traveled a long way to find my son, sir, and am in no mood to stand here and be ignored by the likes of you while my boy lies bleeding upstairs." Seeing that he had the sergeant's attention, Edward stood up, his eyes locked on the sergeant's as he did so. "Now, sir, please direct me to where Captain Bannon is," Edward announced in a loud voice, "or to your superior ranking officer."

For a moment, the sergeant studied Edward's eyes, as a gambler would study his opponent's in an effort to determine how much of his threat was bluff. The orderly sergeant, however, was no match for Edward Bannon, a man well schooled in the art of staring down his competition. Breaking eye contact as his way of admitting defeat, the sergeant looked down to the book he had been working on and flipped through the pages until he reached the section he needed. "Bannon, Bannon, Bannon," he mumbled as he ran his finger down the column of names. "Yes, Bannon, Captain Kevin Bannon of the Fourth New Jersey. Right here," he finally stated as he pointed to the entry and looked up at Edward with the best smile he could manage. "He's in the old ballroom, where we place most of the worst cases."

This last piece of news was unsettling, serving only to heighten Edward's sense of foreboding. Sensing the old man's concern, the sergeant saw an opportunity to extract a bit of vengeance for being put down by Edward. "All of us here," he chirped in a cheery manner that was in sharp contrast to Edward's pall of gloom, "think it's rather appropriate to use the ballroom for those poor souls who've been shot with minié balls. Don't you think so?"

Not having followed the sergeant's attempt at dark military humor, Edward shook his head. "Excuse me, but where did you say I would find him?" he inquired as soon as the shock of the sergeant's first statement wore off.

Seeing that it would be pointless to pursue his quest for some sort of vengeance, the sergeant pointed to the stairs with the end of his pen. "Up one floor, then to the right. Can't miss it. Big double doors with a sign above them."

After a mumbled and cursory thank you, Edward made his way through the lobby and up the stairs, bumping into several people as he did so. Only when he reached the double doors that he had been directed to and was greeted by the sight of an orderly carrying a bundle of bloody sheets out of the former ballroom did Edward snap out of his daze. "I'm looking for Captain Bannon," he stated quickly before the orderly was able to rush by. "Where's his bed?"

Eager to dispose of his burden, which was saturated with the cavalry major's blood, the orderly kept going, shouting as he went by, "On the left."

Seeing that he'd get no more help from this man, but satisfied he was in the right place, Edward went in and started to search the faces that looked up at his in the row of beds along the left aisle. Skipping over two vacant beds, one of which was stripped but still bloodstained, without seeing Kevin, Edward searched the faces on the right side of the room and again failed to see Kevin. When he reached the end of this row, a sudden, paralyzing fear gripped him. In the moment that he finally realized that Kevin's face was not among the men in the room, Edward felt his throat close, choking the very breath from his body.

Stepping back, as much from a sudden dizziness that he felt as from the desire to leave the room, Edward moved to the entrance and looked up at the sign to make sure that he was in the right room. Twice he read the word "Ballroom" before he reentered it again. This time, as he surveyed the faces, he did so with great deliberateness. Kevin's wound, Edward imagined and hoped at this point, might have affected his appearance. Still, he saw no one that even vaguely resembled his second son, a lad whose bright eyes, fair complexion, and delicate features had so often reminded Edward of his late wife's.

Slowly, ever so slowly, Edward's eyes were drawn to the bloody bed that lay vacant on the left side of the room as his Gaelic foreboding pushed aside all logic and hope and drew him to the one conclusion that he had been avoiding. Like a man staring at his own open grave, Edward walked toward that bed. When he reached it, he stood at the foot of the bed, looked down, and let out a moan of pain. "Oh, dear God, Mary, I'm too late," he lamented as his eyes began to water. "I've missed my one chance to make good all my sins." Then, looking up at the ceiling as tears began to stream down his checks, Edward continued, "Will you ever find it in your heart, dear girl, to forgive me?"

From the doorway, Anna Belle saw Edward standing at the foot of Major Crawford's bed. Used to such heartrending scenes, Anna Belle rushed to Edward's side and placed her hands on his arm. "I'm sorry, Mr. Crawford," she said in tones that could only come from a heart that was truly in mourning. "Your son is . . ."

Startled by the soft, consoling feminine voice and the sudden embrace, Edward's head jerked down as he turned to face the source of that voice. Startled for a second time by the appearance of a black face, totally incongruous with the voice he had just heard, Edward stepped back.

Used to such reactions, Anna Belle looked down for a moment, bit back her anger, and then proceeded with the sad task at hand. "I'm sorry you have to find out this way, but there's been an unfortunate accident. The major . . ."

"My son was a captain, Captain Kevin Bannon," Edward blurted as soon as he was able to struggle through his double shock.

Now it was Anna Belle's turn to stare at Edward in confusion. "You're not here about Major Crawford?" she asked by way of confirmation.

"No." Edward shook his head. "I am Edward Bannon. I am here in response from a Miss Harriet Shields concerning my son Kevin."

Overcome by joy and relief, Anna Belle grasped Edward's arm with both hands and bowed her head as her expression changed from one of confusion to joy. "Oh, dear sir, you must excuse me," she stammered as she looked up into his eyes. "This is, was, Major Crawford's bed. Your son's bed is over there, the next over," she stated in light, joyous tones.

Though he was still uneasy about being handled by a Negress in such a familiar way, Edward was anxious to find out what was going on. "Miss," he asked quickly after looking over first to the vacant bed and then back to Anna Belle, "if that is so, then where, may I ask, is he?"

Led down the hall by Anna Belle, Edward was taken to the small linen closet that served as Harriet's room. "Our Doctor Gillespie is of the old school," Anna Belle explained as she weaved her way through the crowded corridors with grace. "He still believes that women have no place in medicine. '*They haven't the head for such matters,*' he'll mutter one day, or claim that dealing with wounded men '*defeminizes*' proper ladies the next."

Feeling a twinge of shame for the manner in which he reacted to her at first, Edward felt compelled to say something. "Obviously, miss, you feel that your Doctor Gillespie is wrong."

Looking back at Edward without slackening her pace, Anna Belle smiled. "When I left Boston, there were many who still believed that the Irish are a race fit only for menial labor and working the fields as tenants. Of course," she stated before she looked back to the front, "that isn't true, now is it?"

Though thankful for her help, Edward was uncomfortable in the presence of this woman and prayed that their journey would soon end. "In here," she finally announced as she stopped before a door and nodded toward it. "She's had a difficult day, and your son is sitting with her."

Mumbling a "thank you," Edward stood before the door for a moment, his hand on the knob, and took a deep breath as he steeled himself for meeting his son. Slowly he turned the doorknob and, when he felt it release, pushed the door open carefully till it was wide enough for him to enter. Slipping into the small room, he closed the door behind him and looked about. To his left, he saw a bed partially hidden behind a shelf piled high with crisp white sheets. Tiptoeing over to the end of the shelf, he looked around the corner.

Harriet, fully clothed and lying on her back, was asleep. And though her hands were clean and her face was as peaceful as a sleeping child's, the white apron and hem of her skirt, splattered and smeared with huge blotches of dried blood, showed Edward that Harriet was no more a stranger to the horrors of war than the toughest veteran. As his eyes moved about, he saw a hand lying on the bed, holding one of Harriet's.

It wasn't until Edward had moved farther around the corner of the shelves, into the little cubbyhole where the bed was wedged, that he saw his son, sitting in a worn high-back dining room chair. Edward was taken aback by the appearance of his younger son, sitting at the bedside of his love staring vacantly out of a dirty, narrow window. The face that had always tormented him so because of its likeness to his dear Mary was ashen and haggard. Though he was clean shaven and apparently well cared for, the ravages of war had aged and marked the boy's face almost beyond recognition. As tears began to well up in his eyes, obscuring further inspection of his son's torn body, Edward called out to his son. "Kevin."

Though surprised by his father's voice, Kevin turned his head slowly, almost hesitantly, to face him. In another place, at another time, that voice would have caused him to jump. But too much had transpired since those days, too much had passed before Kevin's eyes for him to be concerned with his father's presence. Without changing expression, Kevin looked at Edward, and blinked once. "Father, how did you . . ."

Edward nodded toward Harriet. "She cabled me. Told me that you were wounded, that you were . . ." Overcome by regret for not having come sooner, for the years of neglect, at seeing his son like this, and for many, many other things, Edward was unable to finish his sentence. Instead, dropping his hat and reaching out with his arms toward his son, he moved across the room. "Oh, Lord," he wept, "I can't tell you how happy I am to find you alive."

Barely able to react in time to receive his father's embrace, Kevin's effort to stand was greeted with pain that drove him back down into his seat and caused his head to spin. The crushing grip of his grieving father did nothing to relieve the pain that emanated from each of his wounds. Still, as his father wept with joy, and Kevin felt the warmth of his father's arms about him, he somehow managed to ignore the physical discomfort of the moment.

Slowly, almost hesitantly at first, Kevin let go of Harriet's hand with his good hand and wrapped it about his father's waist. When the two were joined, they hugged each other for the first time and shared the affection that only two people who have suffered and found peace can know.

Harriet rebounded with the same resilience she always managed after a major battle. "Sometimes," she explained apologetically to Edward on the way to dinner at Willard's, "the horror of it all simply becomes too overwhelming." And though Edward stated that he understood, he knew he never would know the full measure of what this woman had endured in her service with the Army. But he could appreciate the manner in which she threw herself back into her routine of helping in the ward despite the ever-present scowl of Doctor Gillespie. "That woman of yours," Edward told his son one day, "is a fighter. Don't let her go."

Such advice, given in the course of casual conversations and long visits over the next several days, made Kevin uneasy at first. He had never known his father except as a person to be avoided, an ogre who ruled his life and his home. Even the few meals they had shared in the past had always been hastily consumed in the oppressive silence of an elegant, yet loveless home. Still, despite his caution, Kevin found himself unable to resist the attention his father seemed so eager to give him. Every morning, as soon as it was permissible, Edward would be at the hospital, ready to take his son for a walk in a wheelchair. Harriet, working with Edward, would have Kevin up, washed, shaved, and ready. Leaving her to tend to others who needed her attention, Edward and Kevin would spend as much time together as Kevin's condition would permit.

With the skill and enthusiasm of an Irish bard, Edward told Kevin of his past and the past of his ancestors. "Our family's roots are not as noble as most," he'd muse as he walked slowly pushing Kevin's chair, "but they are good, strong roots." Without undue sentimentality but with a note of love that was as unmistakable as his sincerity, Edward told James of his mother and their life together. Everything that he could remember was recounted, with great care, as if he were trying to pass the oral history of his family down to the next Bannon. Only the subject of James seemed to be avoided. Fearful of jeopardizing the budding relationship between them, neither of them mentioned the older brother, except in passing and only when absolutely necessary. "Perhaps," Harriet told Kevin one evening as they discussed the day's events in private, "that wound is still too fresh to air."

Fearing that Edward's transformation was ephemeral, it was almost a week before Kevin was sure enough to respond in kind to his father's efforts at conversation. Even then, his responses were carefully worded, almost guarded. It continued like that until one day when the subject of Edward's marriage to Kevin's mother came up. With great interest, Kevin listened to his father as he recounted, in detail, the circumstances surrounding their courtship and marriage. "Between the two of us," he mused as he walked along the gravel pathway that wound through the hotel's ill-tended garden, "we didn't have two pennies to rub together. It was madness, in every sense of the word, and yet . . ."

"You married her," Kevin finished the sentence with a questioning tone. "Why?"

Thrown off the track of his tale by Kevin's interruption, Edward looked down at the back of his son's head and thought about it for a moment. "Why what?"

"If you were so poor, Father, why did you marry her?"

Still unsure why Kevin was asking such a silly question, Edward hesitated for a moment. Then, with a sigh, he responded in a manner that surprised Kevin. "Because we were in love, lad. We were madly and passionately in love and no man, and nothing, could keep us apart."

The image of his father loving someone was as foreign, despite his recent change, as that of his being passionate about anything, other than money. It was, Kevin thought, as if this man with him were a stranger who looked like his father. "For no other reason?"

Edward laughed. "And here I thought I was the cold-hearted bastard."

His father's laugh, and his frank admission of his cruel nature, broke down Kevin's last barrier. "Father?"

"Yes?"

"I've been thinking . . . I mean, I was, or have been for a long time, considering . . ."

Seeing that his son was having great difficulty, Edward intervened. "And why haven't you married her yet?"

Kevin seized a wheel of his chair with his good hand and gave it a quick spin, yanking it from Edward's hand. "Because of this!" he shot back. "I don't want Harriet to be tied to a man who's half a corpse."

Though startled and somewhat angry at his son's actions, Edward pushed those thoughts aside and studied his son's worried expression. "Do you think that matters to her?" he finally asked. "Do you think that girl is only interested in you because of your fine young body?"

"She has a right," Kevin shot back, "to peace of mind. She has a right to some kind of security, a security that I cannot give her."

"I've talked to your attending physician," Edward countered in an effort to calm his son, "and he seems to think that the worst for you has passed. You've survived the wound fever and now it's simply a question of time before you're up and about again."

Kevin would not be denied, however. "And what happens when I go back to the regiment? What then? My chances of being taken down by another bullet will be no better than the next man's."

This last pronouncement made Edward blink, for he had assumed that Kevin's days of active campaigning were over. "You've done your duty," Edward announced after collecting his thoughts for a moment. "There is no need for you to go back and risk everything again. Let someone else carry on in your place."

"Who, Father?" Kevin countered with a tone that was now even and measured. "You of all people should know that support for this war is waning in the North, that our failures so far this year all but guarantee that Lincoln will be turned out of office and the Copperheads and Peace Party will go to Washington with a peace treaty in hand giving the South everything it wants."

Though much of what Kevin said was true, including his own association with the very forces that would hand the Confederacy a victory it could not win in the field, Edward did not feel like debating that issue with Kevin, not here, not now. Nor did he care to challenge his son's apparent decision to return to active service. There was, Edward believed, a more important issue at hand that needed immediate attention and he intended to stay with it. Lifting his hand, Edward feigned studying his fingers as he began to speak again in soft, unhurried tones. "Have you discussed this with Harriet?"

Thrown by his father's sudden change of tack, Kevin remained mute for a moment as Edward looked at him, and then began to speak. "I didn't think to do so," he announced. "It seems to be a great fallacy among men, especially we Bannons, to assume we know what is best, not only for us, but for others."

Walking over to where Kevin now sat somewhat disarmed and mollified, Edward took the handles of the wheelchair and began to push his son as he talked. "I feel for you, lad, I truly do. And though I never faced the horrors that your young eyes have beheld, my life was not without its trials and tribulations. There was many a night, back in Ireland after your dear mother and I were newly married, that we went to bed without a single crumb in the house for the next day. We had nothing and, even worse for a man such as me, I often found myself with no means of providing for her. So she worked on her knees, a servant girl for an English lord, scrubbing his floors while I seethed with my own failure to do what was right by her."

Suddenly, without warning, Edward let go of the wheelchair and walked away from Kevin. With his back to his son and his face turned upward to the clear blue sky, as if he were looking at something that no one else could see, Edward continued his story, his voice vacillating between mournful lament and bitter anger. "I made a pledge to myself, not to the saints, for I was convinced they had abandoned us, but to myself. I promised myself that I would never, ever allow your mother to go down on her knees in order to put bread on our table. That resolve is what brought us to America, a journey that broke your mother's health. That same resolve was the force that drove me to ignore everything and everyone, including your mother, in an effort to accumulate wealth at any cost. And, may the dear Lord forgive me, that pledge is what turned me into the kind of man I am today, a man so blinded by his own ambitions and dreams that he was willing to throw away his own sons to feed those ambitions."

Turning sharply, Edward lifted his hand and pointed a finger at Kevin. There was fire in his eyes, fire mixed with tears. "Son, don't let your stiff-necked pride and foolish ambitions cripple you. Marry that girl, as soon as you can. Enjoy yourself and let her enjoy your company for as long as you can. Let the future do to us what it may, for it will not matter what we do or try to do."

For the longest time, the two men stared at each other, Kevin looking up at his father who continued to point his sharp finger at him. Finally, without a word, Kevin wheeled himself to where his father stood. Letting go of the large wheels of his chair, he took his father's outstretched hand in his, pulled it toward him, then held it up next to his face as one would a pillow.

The ceremony was as moving as it was simple. Held in the old hotel's seedy, overgrown garden, most of those in attendance were in uniform, hospital gowns, or clothing still soiled with specks of blood from their toils in the wards. A young artillery officer from Rhode Island who occupied a bed near Kevin's and whom Kevin had befriended stood by him. At Harriet's insistence, Anna Belle followed her as maid of honor. And despite the fact that her own father was still in town, Harriet insisted that Edward give her away. "You have been the agent of my happiness and fulfillment these past two years," she explained to Edward as she presented her case over his objections. "And though I do dearly love my father and pray for a speedy reconciliation with him, he is a prisoner of his own conventions. I want to start my life with Kevin free from the tyranny of those ideals that bind and restrict love and life."

And for a moment, they were free of them. Lost in each other's eyes, the worries of a world gone mad were as far away from this place as the far side of the moon. But only for a moment. For even as the Army chaplain lay his hand upon the joined hands of Kevin Bannon and his new wife, the sound of wagons drawing up at the entrance of the hospital began to drown out his solemn words. Their kiss, the first as husband and wife, was to the accompaniment of the moans and screeches of wounded men being brought from a field not far from Cold Harbor. When they parted and looked in each other's eyes again, they both knew that their moment of peace had passed.

As the two stood there, still hand in hand, they looked over toward the garden entrance as the chaplain, followed by Anna Belle, walked through it to where his new charges lay waiting. Then Kevin looked at Harriet. With eyes downcast and a forlorn look on his face, he lamented, "There is still much to be done."

Harriet, despite the sounds of suffering that assailed them, reached up and kissed Kevin again lightly on the lips. Then she smiled as she slowly pulled away and gave Kevin's hand a gentle squeeze. "We *shall* endure this, you and I. Now and forever."

Slowly, he pulled her soft hand up to his lips to kiss it. Yet in his heart, toughened by the murder of his first lover and the still unresolved exile of his only brother, Kevin found Harriet's joyous prediction hard to accept. Even as he looked into Harriet's eyes and returned her smile, he wondered if this act, so sweet, innocent, and pure, was but the precursor to more suffering, more heartbreak, more pain. "The war," a voice from the depth of his mind whispered, "goes on."

PART FOUR

A FINAL
HURRAH

CHAPTER 14

Winchester, Virginia, July, 1864

By the time the resurrected Stonewall Brigade made its way into Winchester, the new uniforms that James had managed to procure for himself and Daniel were thoroughly impregnated with sweat, dust, mud, and grime. Even the lice, the nemesis of all armies, were back, and with a vengeance. New to this universal military experience, Daniel McPherson went to great lengths to find and kill every perpetrator he could. The veterans of the unit watched him and chuckled to themselves as he sat around the fire at night, squinting in the flickering light of the fire as he pored over every stitch of clothing, hunting for the notorious little critters known as graybacks. "Best thing you can do," Dale Wint advised Daniel, "is think of 'em like you would a wife. Ignore their nit-picking and be grateful for their company at night." Not knowing if the older soldier was giving him sound advice or merely mocking him, Daniel thanked Wint and returned to his labors.

Douglas Geddy, happy to have other men in the ranks junior to him, kept to himself. These recruits provided the pranksters in the unit with new targets, and the sergeants more choices when it came time to pick "volunteers" for those dirty little details that no soldier enjoyed and well-schooled veterans always seemed to avoid. Freed, somewhat, from these mundane concerns, Geddy was able to turn his attention to other things. Every day, as they moved closer to the valley that hot, dry July, he calculated and recalculated his chances of slipping away from the Army and disappearing from this war for good while his body and soul were still one. "I didn't ask for this war," he confided in another soldier whom he assumed to be of like mind, "nor did I volunteer to fight in it. If Jeff Davis and all those folks in Richmond truly believe in what they say, about being left alone to go their own way, then I can't see where they'd be upset if I did the same. So first chance I get, I'm going to declare my independence and secede from this Army."

James, the second sergeant for one of the companies that the survivors of the 4th Virginia had been lumped into, suspected as much. Together with the other sergeants and corporals in the company, he made sure that young Geddy was kept close at hand. When Lieutenant Austin Roberts, James' young company commander, asked him why he never sent Geddy out on picket duty or foraging parties, James explained with a sly smile, "There's no need to tempt a sinner."

Several years younger than James, Roberts had been a law student at the University of Virginia when the urge to fight for the Southern Confederacy and its rights became too strong to resist. New to the Army, he was still filled with an enthusiastic and romantic vision of war that many miles of marching and countless bloody battles had purged from James long ago. "What's the point," the youthful lieutenant asked as the two of them stood back from the campfire one night, "of spending so much time and effort keeping a man you claim to be worthless as a fighter in the ranks? As far as I'm concerned, let him be gone, and forgotten. When we go into battle, I only want men with pure hearts and fire in their eyes behind me."

James ignored Roberts' high-minded sentiments that were, to him, out of place in this war that had become little more than a bloody endurance contest between the two armies. Instead, he looked for a moment at Daniel, who was busy searching his clothes for unwanted guests, then over at Geddy, lounging back against a log swapping lewd stories with Dale Wint. Turning to his lieutenant, he looked the young officer in the eyes. "He's not worthless, sir. If that man takes a bullet for someone who is a good fighter, he's done his job."

Unsettled by the cold judgment James had passed on Geddy in a tone that was as dark and cold as his stare, Roberts dropped the subject. "Well," he pronounced as he broke eye contact with James and scanned the men he commanded as they sat circled about their fires, "tomorrow, we'll be in Winchester."

James nodded sadly as he added dryly, "Again."

Anxious to end the conversation, Roberts tugged at the hem of his well-tailored frock coat. "Sergeant, see to the men. I'm going to go see the colonel before turning in to see if there's been any change in our orders for the morning."

James wanted to tell Roberts, two years his junior, to say hello to Abner Couper when he saw him, but didn't. Instead, he just gave his lieutenant a slight nod before turning and walking farther away from the lingering, choking smoke of the campfires.

Once clear of the noise of the soldiers' talking and laughing, James looked up at the clear night sky, drew in a deep breath, and let out a nervous chuckle. "Oh, dear Mary Beth," he whispered, "how am I ever going to be able to explain why Daniel's with me and not tucked away, safe and sound, in school?" That, more than the prospect of another battle or Geddy's desertion, worried James. He had, after all, been the one who had convinced Mary Beth that VMI would be a safe place to send Daniel. "They won't use the corps in battle," he told her with great confidence less than a year ago. "They're the sons from the best families of Virginia. Do you think they'd throw away their own future?"

At first, Mary Beth had fought the idea. "And what about Gettysburg?" she shot back in that defiant manner that added to, rather than detracted from, his attraction to her. "*How* many brave sons of Virginia did they bury there?"

Though well aware that her point was valid, James convinced Mary Beth that if they did nothing, Daniel would find a way into this war. "If he's determined to join up and fight, there isn't anyone or anything that's going to stop him. At least at VMI he'll have the illusion of being part of the war." Persisting with what he thought to be the lesser of two evils until Mary Beth gave in, James had won his point and Daniel had gone off to VMI. Now, as he breathed in the clear, cool night air and gazed at the heavens above, he had little doubt how she would react when he came back to her with Daniel at his side, dressed and armed for battle, just as he had done with her other brother.

For a brief moment, James considered not asking Roberts' permission to leave the unit to visit the McPherson farm, or not going at all. He was, after all, a sergeant. He could always find things to do or duties that required his attention. That, however, wouldn't solve anything, and he knew it. It would only postpone things. As this brief glimmer of hope faded like the tail of a shooting star James happened to glimpse, he looked down and shook his head. He'd have to face her. He knew that. And the sooner, the better. He loved her, loved her more than anything or anyone he had ever loved. He even loved her more than his own brother, now a memory that seemed as distant and almost as faded as the shooting star he had just seen.

Looking up, James studied the stars in the sky, wondering as he did so about Kevin. Where was he? What was he doing? Was he alive? How strange, James thought, this world was. It was so full of people, as full of people as the night sky was full of stars. Each and every one of them, the people he knew and the stars he saw, were bright and alive. Each of them were, at the same time, independent yet part of a universe, all moving about along their own invisible paths. Yet at times like this, they were all so distant, so untouchable. And, James thought, they were all too often hidden by the harsh light of a sun that, like this war, threatened to keep them from him forever.

Somewhere behind him a drummer tapped out the soft, mellow notes of evening retreat. Another day was coming to an end. Tomorrow would be a new one, one in which two of those distant stars would cross, for the briefest of moments, in their indeterminable travels before going their own separate ways again. "I love you, Mary Beth," James whispered to a shimmering star that stood out bright and bold in a sky that was crowded with so many other, lesser lights. "Stay with me awhile," he pleaded as he settled down onto the ground cross-legged without ever losing sight of the bright, pulsating star.

The citizens of Winchester greeted the soldiers of Early's small army with as much enthusiasm as three years of war, and over sixty such reoccupations, would permit. "This place has sure seen the worst of it," Dale Wint stated as he scanned the weather-beaten buildings with barren storefronts, all begging for a coat of paint. Wint, who had not been with the regiment since it left Winchester in the spring of '62, was amazed at the change. "Sort of makes Richmond look good."

James and Daniel, who had been through the town on and off during its slow decline, weren't paying much attention to what Wint, or anyone else, was saying as they paraded through town. "You suppose Sis will be mad when she sees us?" Daniel had asked naively when he finally began to think about visiting home.

James looked at his young companion, still betraying all the signs of a youth out on his first great adventure, and laughed. "What do you think?"

Looking down at the worn roadway, Daniel thought about James' question as they marched along for several minutes. Then, sheepishly, he looked up at him. "Yes, she'll be upset, for sure." He paused, looked down at the ground again, and shook his head. Then, with a quizzical expression, he looked back at James, again shaking his head as he did so. "Though I'm sure she meant well, I still can't understand why she wanted to keep me out of this war?"

James snapped back without hesitation. "Can you blame her? She's already lost one brother and her father. And your mother hasn't been the same since they died. Besides the farm, which is nothing more than some buildings and land, you're all she's got."

Although Daniel took offense at James' statement that the farm was little more than property, he did appreciate his views on why his sister had been so desperate to keep him out of the Army. "You think I was wrong? I mean, after all, Will and Pa are, I mean were, as much kin to me as they are to Mary Beth. Doesn't that count for something?"

James looked over at the youth, then back to the front as they moved through the narrow streets. He gave a slight shake of his head. "It's not my place, Daniel, to judge right or wrong." He wanted to leave his answer at that, hoping to keep from choosing sides, Daniel's or Mary Beth's, in the fight that would surely come when they reached the McPherson farm. But the expression on Daniel's face, like a child looking for some sort of comfort, reminded James too much of the look his younger brother Kevin used to give him whenever a difficult matter was weighing heavily upon him.

Looking up at the bright blue summer sky for a moment, he reflected on how things used to be between him and his brother. Then he looked at Daniel and smiled. "This war's put you, and your family, in a bad place. You've all had to make decisions most people never have to make. Though I have no doubt things were not always easy for them, your father and my father never had to deal with the question of war and what to do. So, the way I figure it, our guesses as to what to do is as good as theirs would be, if they were here to give it." Then, reflecting on his own past, James reached over and gave Daniel a pat on the back. "You could have done worse, I know."

Though he didn't quite understand the cryptic meaning of James' last comment, Daniel felt relieved that, regardless of what happened when he reached home, he could depend on James for support and solace, much in the same way his brother had.

Mary Beth found it hard to be patient. It was, her aunt bemoaned often, a trait that would be her undoing. Her father, unable or unwilling to change his method of dealing with his offspring simply because of their gender, had dealt with his only daughter in much the same way he had when William had been alive. Rather than rely solely on his status as head of the household to discipline his children and educate them in the ways of the world, he used a homespun logic when guiding them along their way to adulthood.

As she crawled forward on her hands and knees along the row of pathetic potatoes she was struggling to grow in the garden, some of his words came to mind. "There are times," he had often repeated, "when things simply cannot be hurried. We've got to wait for nature to take its course and trust in God that all will be well."

Stopping for a moment, she sat up and stretched her back before yanking the weeds that threatened her embryonic crop. Placing her dirty, calloused hands in the small of her back, Mary Beth arched, turned her face to the bright blazing July sun, and let out a groan as her stiff muscles sent tiny slivers of pain throughout her body. She was trying as hard as she could to do as her father had advised her. She was sincerely endeavoring to give nature and the Lord a chance to work their miracles. But as she settled back on her calves and surveyed the jumbled garden of vegetables and herbs, she found it hard to wait until they were fully mature before tearing them from the ground and eating them. The pain in her stomach from incessant hunger, a sensation that seldom left her, always seemed to be more pronounced when she was working in the garden.

Looking up into the cloudless sky, she wiped the sweat off her brow with a backhanded swipe of her worn and soiled dress sleeve. Dropping her arm to her side, she folded both hands loosely in her lap. "Papa, I'm trying to be patient, I really am. But it's hard. Mama's no better. Ever since you and Will died, she's been bedridden. I fear her mind is gone, gone for good. Without Bucky, I couldn't finish the plowing. The chickens are all gone, and there isn't a penny in the house. And even if I had the money, no one for miles around has anything to spare at any price." She paused for a moment, looked around at the garden, then turned her face skyward again. "I know we have to make it, somehow. I just don't know how."

Then, without further ado, she pushed herself up off her haunches, lurched over until she was back on her hands and knees, and went back to the slow, tedious task of pulling the weeds from the dry ground and covering the potatoes. Her mind was as numb from the problems that rambled through it as her knees were from the long hours of work. She didn't notice the approach of two soldiers until, in a sweep of the arc she was working on, her downcast eyes caught sight of their shoes.

At first, there was panic. Recoiling as she glanced up, her right hand shot behind her and began a mad search for the only weapon she had nearby, a small shovel she had been using. "What do you want?" she demanded as her tired eyes tried to focus on the faces of the two figures in front of her. It was, she knew, a foolish question, for regardless of the color of their uniform, the first thing any soldier always asked for was food. Still, she knew she had to challenge them, if for no other reason than to hide her fear.

"Sis?" Daniel asked hesitantly, surprised as much by her haggard and gaunt appearance as by the manner in which she had snapped at them.

Caught off guard again, Mary Beth lifted her left hand to shield her eyes from the harsh sun without giving up her search for the shovel behind her.

Even as her eyes became accustomed to the sun and she could make out facial features, she was slow to recognize her own brother and James. Recovering from his shock, Daniel nervously shifted his weight from one foot to the other, tightened his grip on the sling of the rifle that hung limply over his shoulder, glanced up at James for a second, then back at his sister. "Mary Beth, it's me, Daniel. James and I have been given permission to fall out and visit the farm for a while."

Full recognition brought on the reaction that James and Daniel had been expecting. Without breaking contact with Daniel's eyes, now that she had managed to focus on them, Mary Beth slowly rose. "Permission to fall out from what? Daniel, don't tell me you've . . ."

Though she knew the truth based on Daniel's appearance and his presence here with James, Mary Beth still couldn't bring herself to say it.

Silent until now, James looked down at the ground in embarrassment, then at Mary Beth. "Listen, Mary Beth," he started to explain in a low, mournful tone, "I can explain everything."

With a quick jerk, Mary Beth turned her head and glared at James. "There's nothing to explain. You lied to me," she yelled. "*Lied!* You promised you'd keep Daniel out of the Army. You sat in my house, held my hand, and told me that Daniel would be safe, that sending him to VMI was the only way to keep him out of this war. And now you have the gall to come back, less than a year later, dragging him behind you like you dragged poor Will about. How dare you expect me to believe anything you say?"

James was tempted to step back as he watched Mary Beth, shaking from anger, clutch a small shovel at her side so tightly that her knuckles turned white. She was angry. Now that his worst fears had been realized, James didn't know what to do. Glancing sideways for a moment, he hoped Daniel would be able to say or do something to save them from this terrible dilemma.

Daniel, however, was still in a minor state of shock as he continued to study the pale, thin figure dressed in a threadbare skirt and blouse impregnated with dirt and stained black from her sweat. The effects of stress, hunger, and a long, cold winter had not only conspired to age Mary Beth way beyond her years, but they had also left a harshness in her features that her anger magnified. As lost as James was, Daniel stood mutely as Mary Beth berated the man who had now become a substitute for both father and brother.

Though there was so much more that Mary Beth wanted to say after having held so much back for so long for fear of losing her ability to cope, she checked her anger and ended the tirade she had unleashed on James and Daniel. Yet her rage, though summoned forth by James' appearance, still needed to be played out. In frustration, she turned one way, then another, as her eyes wildly searched for something that she could strike at. Only when she looked down at her feet, at the weeds that had crept into the neat rows of vegetables that would keep her starvation in check in the weeks to come, did she move. Dropping back on both knees before the befuddled men in dirty gray uniforms, Mary Beth took the small shovel she held and started to jab at the soil with vicious, angry thrusts.

As she assaulted the ground furiously with her shovel, Mary Beth grabbed at the weeds before she had hacked them free of the soil and yanked them from the ground, roots and all. Tossing the offending weeds over her shoulder, she created a virtual shower of dirt that began to cover her from head to toe.

Seeing the need to give Mary Beth an opportunity to calm herself, James and Daniel began to back away. Daniel was about to ask James if he wouldn't mind going back to where the brigade was camped when someone called his name. "Daniel McPherson. Oh, dear Lord, you've come home." His mother's weak, wavering voice, in sharp contrast to Mary Beth's shrieks, was almost welcome until he turned and saw the old woman standing in the doorway of a house that had once been his home. "Daniel, oh, Daniel," his mother kept repeating as she moved from one item to the next for support. "Come here and let me see you."

As taken aback as he had been when he had first seen his sister's appearance, Daniel could at least recognize Mary Beth as a person he had once known. The frail old woman now standing on the porch, however, bore no resemblance to the calm, maternal figure who had cared for and nurtured him not so very long ago. Elizabeth McPherson's white, uncombed hair hung about a face that lacked even the slightest hint of color. Her eyes, which had always been so bright, so clear, so expressive, were dull and lifeless black dots almost lost in the deep, dark sockets that surrounded them. Even her stooped frame, shaking uncontrollably, spoke of a weakness he had never associated with his mother. "Oh, Daniel," her quivering voice cooed, "you've come home and you've brought your brother William back to me."

Snapping their heads in unison, the two men looked at each other for a moment. Any doubts that Daniel had as to his mother's state of mind were now gone. Embarrassed, ashamed, and devastated by what his family had become, Daniel lowered his eyes and let his head droop. James, turning to Mary Beth in the hope of finding some aid and comfort at this most difficult time, was ignored by her as she continued to hack madly at any weed that came within her reach.

Unable to find anything else to support her, Elizabeth McPherson stood at the edge of the porch, hanging desperately to a post for support. "You two boys come over here and let me see you. It's been a long time," she ranted in a voice that quivered every time her frame shook, "and I want to hear what you've been up to."

Realizing there was little to do, James slowly began to move to the house. As he passed Daniel, who still stood with his head bowed, he whispered, "Come on, Daniel. We have to spend a little time with her. It's the least we can do."

Daniel didn't move at first. Only after James had passed and he had been able to wipe away the tears forming in his eyes without James seeing him do so did Daniel begin to move. As the two men reached the stairs of the porch and began to climb them with leaden feet, Elizabeth McPherson looked up beyond them to where Mary Beth continued to vent her anger. "Mary Beth," Elizabeth McPherson called, "quit fussing about in that garden of yours and come in the house. You need to fix supper for these poor boys. Why," she added as she looked at James' and Daniel's drawn faces, "they must be starving."

James halted midway up the stairs, in part to allow Daniel to pass him and reach his mother first, and in part to look back to see what Mary Beth's response had been. After his eyes locked on hers, James realized that this had been a mistake. The anger and hatred that he had seen in them moments before were still there. Sadly, he turned away, finished climbing the stairs, and went into the arms of a broken, feebleminded old woman who thought he was her son.

If it hadn't been for Elizabeth McPherson's constant nonsensical chatter, conversation at the table that night would have been as sparse as the food that was served. That chatter, however, clouded by Elizabeth's befuddled grasp of reality, did little to ease the tension James, Mary Beth, and Daniel felt. The two men, with faces and hands clean, but still reeking of the pungent odor that permeated their clothing from hours of sitting about campfires and long marches in the Virginia heat, sat across from each other. As Elizabeth McPherson tripped about from one subject to the next in a totally random fashion, never finishing a thought or story before moving on to the next, James cast hesitant glances from one woman to the other, eyeing them as he would an animal waiting to pounce. Daniel, embarrassed to the point of despondency, sat staring at his plate.

Only Mary Beth moved about freely, though James wished she didn't. Though not as enraged as she had been when they had been in the small garden, her anger was still very much in evidence. While she had been preparing their meager fare, Mary Beth had slammed pots and pans on the cast iron stove whenever she had the opportunity to. As she moved about the kitchen, where James had fled in an effort to avoid Elizabeth McPherson, she did so briskly, pushing James out of her way without so much as a word of warning or apology. Torn between fleeing from the house altogether and staying in the hope that she would eventually vent all of her anger and at least try to reason with him, James opted to retreat to one corner of the kitchen where he could watch and wait without being in the way.

"Daniel!" Elizabeth suddenly snapped as she stopped in midsentence and turned her attention to her solemn son. "You haven't touched your meal."

Jumping from his mother's sudden and unwanted attention, Daniel glanced up at her, then back at the immature potato that sat in the center of a plate that seemed far too large for the pitiful portion of food it held. With a series of quick, jerky motions, Daniel raised his hand, snatched the tarnished fork off the table, and jabbed it into the center of the potato without ever looking back at his mother's withered face.

"The two of you," Elizabeth McPherson continued as she looked away from Daniel and over to James, "have been acting like a pair of mules." Though he didn't want to, James looked up at Elizabeth. When, he wondered, as she carried on about their conduct, would it finally dawn upon her that he wasn't her son Will? Would she ever? Either way, one thing James was certain of, when that did happen, he didn't want to be there.

From across where her mother sat, Mary Beth watched this performance. And though she was still angry, angry at everyone and everything that had anything to do with the war, she felt herself feeling sorry. At first, this sudden glimmer of sympathy was for James, for she could see the agony that he was enduring as her mother continued to speak to him as if he were her long lost son. Earlier in the day, she had reveled in James' plight. Now, the pathetic misidentification was becoming as difficult for Mary Beth to suffer as it was for James.

Turning her eyes away from James, Mary Beth looked down at her plate. Her potato, as small as all the others at the table, sat before her untouched. She should have used them in a soup, she thought. In a soup, with other greens and herbs, their size would have been immaterial. Sitting there alone on the plate like this only served to accentuate their puniness. They would have been nice potatoes, she thought, if they had been allowed to grow a little longer. Nice potatoes that would have truly been a meal in themselves, had they been left alone, had James and Daniel not come back.

Like a thunderclap, the selfishness and lack of concern for the man she loved and her younger brother struck her. With eyes that were as big as saucers, she looked up, first at Daniel, then at James. Without a word, she quickly rose to her feet, tipping her chair back and over onto the floor. This caused everyone to stop what he was doing and turn to face Mary Beth. Mary Beth, standing at her end of the table, still wide-eyed and glancing from person to person, found it impossible to deal with their stares. Torn by her own shame, confusion, and anger, she turned and fled the dining room.

Slowly, James followed her to the darkened barn. Though he was familiar with it, he halted at the door. "Mary Beth?"

He waited for a moment in the dark silence before calling out again when she didn't answer him. "Mary Beth?"

From a corner of the barn, where the stalls for the horses were, she finally answered. "Please, James, go away."

The plea was more of a sob than a command. Having seen, time and again, people on the brink of snapping, James knew that Mary Beth needed comforting. Carefully inching his way into the darkness, he felt his way forward till his hand fell upon the half door of the stall that used to belong to Mary Beth's favorite horse. Stopping at the opening, he looked into the pitch blackness without seeing her. "Mary Beth, I'm sorry."

In the silence that followed, James wondered what he was sorry for. Was he sorry that he had allowed Daniel to stay with the regiment? No, he wasn't, for he knew that if he had chased Daniel from the ranks of the 4th Virginia, the eager youth would have simply found another unit. Then, he wondered, was he sorry for having become involved with the decision to send Daniel to VMI in the first place? Again, as he waited for Mary Beth to respond, he dismissed that thought. She had come to him for advice and to have said nothing would have been wrong. Why, then, James wondered as he nervously shifted his weight from one foot to the next and peered into the darkness, was he sorry?

He was, he finally realized, sorry for Mary Beth. Of all the people he knew, of all the devastation he had seen and been a part of, James couldn't think of anyone who had suffered more, and still stood to suffer even greater hardships, than Mary Beth. And although he had no idea how much of her suffering she held him responsible for, James knew that by any measure it was too much.

"Sometimes when it's dark like this, I can almost imagine he's still here, in his stall with me," Mary Beth finally stated in clear, even tones. "I can almost smell him, as if he were standing just out of reach, but still there." There was a slight chuckle. "Every now and then, I even reach out to touch old Bucky." With eyes that were finally able to discern faint images in the darkness of the stall, James could make out the shape of a hand, white and wavering, as it desperately grasped for something in the darkness that was not there.

Softly, he stepped into the stall, reached out with his own hand, and took Mary Beth's. Without a word, he used it as a guide, following it till he found her. Dropping on his knees before her, James took his free hand, reached out, and touched Mary Beth's cheek. His rough, calloused hand could feel the moisture that tears had left on her cheek.

Anxious to feel someone who was warm and near, Mary Beth took James' hand from her cheek, and pulled it over till she held both his hands, together, between her own. "What is to become of us, James?" she asked.

James didn't answer, not at first. Instead, without letting go of her hands that were blistered though still gentle, he managed to ease himself until he was seated next to Mary Beth. Only then did he let go of one of her hands so that he could reach around her and pull her close to him.

On Mary Beth's part, there was no resistance, no awkwardness. Settling into a comfortable position, with her head on his chest and one hand still grasping one of his, Mary Beth continued to stare into the corner of the stall where Bucky used to lie. "What is to become of us, James?" she slowly repeated.

James Bannon mechanically pondered this question, though he knew it would do no good. "You know," he began slowly, "for years I've gone through life without a plan, without any direction. Others have always provided the push or pull needed to drag me this way or that." He paused for a second and thought a little more as he slowly stroked Mary Beth's hair. "First there was my father. His bullying left me with no choice but to stand up to him in order to protect my brother. From there, I went to VMI, where everyone told me what to do, twenty-four hours a day. When the war came, I followed your brother Will without hesitation, without thought. And when he was gone, there was the Fourth Virginia. Now, I guess I've come full circle, since I'm looking out for someone again. The only difference is that it's your brother Daniel this time and not my own."

Though she desperately wanted to ask him where, if at all, she fit into all of that, she didn't. She already knew. She would be what he would turn to when the 4th Virginia and the war were but a memory. Then, and only then, she lamented, would there be time for them. Squeezing James' hand, she pressed herself against his chest. "I don't know how much longer I can hold on to this farm, James. It's not the work. Lord knows, the work is the only thing that keeps me from going . . ."

She was about to say "crazy," but then thought better, especially in light of her mother's performance at dinner. "What I mean, James, is that things just always seem to get worse and worse. Sometimes I just feel like giving up and quitting, I get so frustrated."

James knew how she felt, for he felt the same. They were both rational enough to see that things were going downhill fast. Yet neither had the ability to change either the shape of things to come or their petty roles in the events that would shape their futures. Even here, in a silent, darkened barn that had once stored the abundant harvest from their land and labors, they could not escape the cold, cruel hand of war.

"James?"

Daniel's pleading voice shook James from his scattered, dark thoughts. Without letting go of Mary Beth, he responded with a simple, "Yes?"

"I . . . I'm headed back to camp. I'll see you there," the youth announced.

James started to rise, but Mary Beth tightened her grip on his hand. "Please," she whispered in his ear, "stay a little longer."

Torn between the two, James called out, "Daniel?" But there was no response. "Daniel?"

"He's gone, James," Mary Beth finally stated after they both waited in the darkness for a response.

"I should go catch up with him," he told Mary Beth. "We march in the morning and there's . . ."

"There'll always be things to do, James," Mary Beth shot back. "Right now, I need you more than Daniel does. That might be selfish of me, because I know how poor Daniel must be feeling right now. He hasn't seen Mother since she lost her mind and I know it was a shock to him. But I have needs too. And right now, I need you."

Though he didn't quite know how she meant this, James understood what she was asking for. So he eased back, relaxed, and returned to stroking her hair. Perhaps, he thought as he slowly began to drift off to sleep, he needed her too.

Only an eerie, low moaning drifting through the open barn door brought an end to their time together. Sitting upright before the second low, mournful wailing, Mary Beth turned to James. "She's come out of it," she stated as she prepared to stand up.

"Who? Who's come out of what?" James asked, not understanding this sudden change in Mary Beth's demeanor.

"Mother. Every now and then, she has a moment or two of clear thought." Standing up, Mary Beth brushed away the old straw from her skirt. The suffering of her mother, very much a physical manifestation of the emotional turmoil that she had experienced, brought back the anger and frustrations she had felt earlier in the day. "When that happens, she remembers everything," she responded coldly.

"Do you suppose," James asked hesitantly, "that she realizes what happened tonight, I mean about me not being Will?"

"Yes," Mary Beth responded without any hint of emotion in her voice.

"Should I come with you? Maybe I can . . ."

Not wanting to deal with James, or her feelings toward him at that moment, Mary Beth stepped away. "No. You'd best go back to your war." As she walked through the open doorway of the stall, she added curtly, "It's best you leave this to me."

Stunned by this sudden rejection, James walked out of the stall and watched Mary Beth as she walked briskly to the house. He had hurt her, he realized. For years he had rebuffed her affection for him and now, when he needed her, she was unable to put aside the suffering the war had laid at her feet and embrace him as she once wanted to. All he could hope for, he realized, was that someday he would have the chance to make it up to her.

After watching her disappear into the house, James slowly made his way to the porch where he retrieved his equipment and rifle. Heavy-hearted, he turned his face away from the McPherson farm and started down the long, dark lane alone, toward the uncertain future.

CHAPTER 15

Washington, D.C., July, 1864

"IT'S MADNESS TO LEAVE that man in command of the armies, after what he's done to them," a bewhiskered gentleman with beefy jowls insisted as he poked his finger into his companion's protruding stomach. "Grant's a drunken, stumbling butcher. His conduct since he crossed the Rappahannock proves it, beyond a shadow of a doubt."

Ignoring the finger of his animated friend as it was thrust repeatedly into his portly midsection, the second gentleman took a long sip from the brandy snifter he was slowly swirling. Both men ignored the comings and goings of the people rushing about the lobby of Willard's Hotel. "I tend to agree with you," the portly man finally concluded as he finished savoring his drink. "Grant's no military genius, by any measure. But what choice do we have?"

With eyes aglow, the first gentleman straightened his back, took in a deep breath, and announced triumphantly, "McClellan!"

Edward, who had been sitting near these two men, trying hard to ignore them, let out a groan. Though he had not intended it, the sound was heard by both the gentlemen involved in the debate. Automatically, the McClellan man turned toward Edward. "You disapprove, sir?"

Though he didn't want to enter into another pointless discussion with armchair strategists, especially when the subject was McClellan, Edward found he couldn't resist. He might have been approaching old age, but he was still a scrapper, a fighter who found it hard to turn his back on a

challenge. "Oh, dear Lord," the pudgy man groaned. "We've tried Mc-
Clellan twice before. And both times, he's managed to snatch defeat from
the jaws of victory. Are you gentlemen willing to offer him a third
opportunity?"

"As I recall, General McClellan saved the capital twice," the gentleman with beefy jowls asserted triumphantly. "After the First Bull Run and
at Antietam. Have you forgotten that?"

Edward smiled and shook his head. "No, sir, I have not. But did he
win the war?" Edward paused while his opponent, caught off balance by
Edward's cool manner, pondered the question. Edward, with the advantage now, took it and verbally lunged at his foe. "No," Edward announced
as he slapped his hand on the soft leather arm of the chair he was seated in.
"When Richmond lay open before him," Edward continued, making a
wide, open-armed gesture, "Little Mac hesitated, stumbled, and stopped,
allowing Lee to come out of nowhere and chase him back into the sea.
And when he had Lee cornered and on his knees at Antietam, *our* Little
Napoleon let him slip across the Potomac, unmolested and unpursued.
No, sir," Edward declared as he slammed his clenched fist on the arm of his
chair, "we do not need someone who can merely save this capital. We
need someone who can bring this war to an end."

Edward had become so focused on the beefy jowled gentleman and
his response that he was unaware that his tone of voice had risen in pitch
and his manner was both excited and aggressive. Others in the lobby,
many of whom were in the process of checking out and fleeing the city,
could not ignore Edward. One man, a colonel with hat in hand and a
sweaty brow, stopped for a moment in his quest for an important guest at
the hotel and cheered Edward on. "Hear, hear! Let's not speak of changing
commanders when all we've worked for is finally coming to pass. Damn
any man who is willing to settle for half measures and let us get on with
bringing this detestable war to a close."

Stung by Edward's challenge and this new assault on his cherished
position, the beefy jowled gentleman turned to the colonel. "And would
you have us run from Early's rabble and abandon our capital?"

The colonel smiled. "I'm with Grant. Let's trade queens and see who's
the worse for it."

The idea of allowing Lieutenant General Jubal Early's army to advance through western Maryland toward Washington unchallenged by

the Army of the Potomac had been the subject of debate for days. Many, like the colonel, favored letting Early do as he liked, so long as Grant and the Army of the Potomac were allowed to stay in place before Petersburg and keep their stranglehold on that place and, in turn, Richmond. Others, such as the beefy jowled gentleman, were less sanguine, and unwilling to take such a chance.

Finding himself in a difficult spot, the beefy jowled gentleman glared at the colonel. "Sir, only a coward would suggest we tuck our tails between our legs and flee from our very own capital."

The flinging of the colonel's rich, black hat on the floor, the angered expression that distorted his face, and the swift, forceful advance through the crowd and toward the beefy jowled gentleman told Edward the gentleman had made a mistake. When he was toe to toe with the beefy jowled gentleman, the colonel thrust his face into the gentleman's. "*Coward?* You sit here, stuffing your face and wagging your tongue like a woman while men are dying, and you dare call me a coward? How *dare* you. I've given an arm and my son for the cause, and I'll gladly give another of each. What, *sir*, have you given to the cause other than idle chatter?"

For the first time Edward, and everyone else in the crowded lobby, looked and saw the empty right sleeve that was neatly tucked under and pinned. "All we want," the colonel pronounced, "is to be allowed to get on with it and finish it, *once and for all*."

Who the "we" was that the colonel spoke of wasn't clear to Edward. What was clear was that the colonel had no intention of backing down. Seeing this, the beefy jowled gentleman lowered his eyes, took a half step back and away from the enraged colonel, and pushed his way through the crowd as he fled.

Feeling the need to do something, Edward stood up, walked over to the colonel, and took the colonel's good hand in his. "Well spoken, sir. And I agree. My son is with the Sixth Corps, and I pray God and General Grant see him through."

Edward's appearance and words provided the colonel with the diversion he needed to recover from his outburst and retreat from the scene gracefully with an appreciative nod to Edward and a few others who came forth to heap their praise on him. Satisfied that tranquillity had been restored and a minor victory scored for the voice of reason, Edward turned and was prepared to take his seat again when he saw Harriet across the sea of faces, standing and smiling approvingly at him. Returning her smile, Edward reached down to recover his hat, conscious that just the sight of his son's young wife was enough to cause his heart to skip a beat with joy.

Though business in New Jersey demanded an occasional trip back to Perth Amboy, Edward Bannon was spending as much time in Washington as he could, to be with the son that he seemed to have discovered. But it wasn't easy, for either father or son. After years of ignoring his younger son, Edward found that there were great chasms that still divided them and even threatened to bring the fledgling relationship to an end. Harriet, Edward quickly realized, could serve as a bridge across the gulf and the troubled waters that still threatened to keep him and his younger son apart. So he took every opportunity he could to spend time with her, talking about Kevin and what he thought, as well as making his own feelings known in the hope that Harriet would represent them to Kevin for him. Besides, Edward thought ruefully as he walked toward Harriet, she is a lovely girl, the type of woman whose beauty matures as she grows older. He had even caught himself regretting the fact that it was Kevin, and not he, who had found and married such an enchanting woman.

"Well, Father," Harriet beamed as he drew close, "it seems you've vanquished another foe of reason and the Union and sent him scurrying for cover."

Though Harriet's comment could just as easily have been a barb, rather than a compliment, Edward didn't mind. Everything about her manner was disarming. The soft sweetness of her voice, the ease with which she addressed him as "Father," and her warm approving smile caused Edward to blush with pride. "Well, ah, that fellow was becoming a bore, a real bore." Stopping a few feet from her, Edward paused to study Harriet from head to toe. She was dressed in a smart outfit consisting of a bright red Zouave jacket ornamented with dark blue trim worn over a crisp white blouse with billowing sleeves. Her skirt of dark blue was worn over full hoops and smartly decorated with red piping and trim, making her appear smaller and seem more fragile than Edward remembered her. "Well," he said with approval, "this is a far cry from the bedraggled, careworn girl I first laid eyes on a month ago."

Reaching out to close the final gap between them, Harriet lightly touched Edward's arm as her face lit up in a warm smile. "And I have you to thank for that. Though I was reluctant, at first, to accept your kind offer to move into the suite of rooms you arranged for me, I am glad I did. I can tell you, in private, I do not miss that dreadful hospital."

"Sleeping well?" Edward asked as he stepped closer to Harriet and accepted a light kiss on his cheek.

"Like a baby, though I do feel guilty about not being at the hospital for Kevin and the others all the time," Harriet confessed.

"Nonsense," Edward responded as he took her arm in his and led her out the door into the bright sunlight. "You've done more than most women have done and ever will. You deserve to be taken care of. Besides, it is important to me to preserve the health and well-being of my very first daughter."

Edward's comment, though it made Harriet blush, caused a pang of regret. How strange, she thought for a fleeting moment, that her own flesh and blood could not accept her and love her in such a manner for who, and not what, she was. Sensing her momentary distress, Edward led her onto the street.

For several minutes, Harriet didn't say anything as they made their way down the street and headed up Pennsylvania Avenue. Both she and Edward looked incredulously at the number of wagons, carriages, and buggies, bulging with trunks and suitcases, headed north. "Is the capital really in danger of falling?" Harriet finally asked as she watched one woman about her age with a distressed look on her face leaning from the window of a carriage to see why they weren't moving faster.

Edward, his gaze fixed on a man dressed very much like him who was arguing with a soldier in a wagon about who had the right of way, just shook his head without looking back at Harriet. "I cannot say, dear girl. I simply do not know enough about military matters to properly judge such things."

Taking her eyes off the woman whom she had been watching, Harriet took a tighter grip on Edward's arm and looked down at the pavement before her. "Someone seems to be taking the danger seriously," she finally said.

Edward, scanning the snarled traffic and comings and goings of the people about them, nodded. "Oh?" he responded halfheartedly.

"Word in the hospital is that the Sixth Corps is being brought back to bolster the capital's defenses," Harriet announced without looking up from the pavement. "One division is already on the way to western Maryland."

This revelation caused Edward to turn his face quickly toward Harriet. "That's the corps Kevin belongs to."

Without changing her expression or looking up, Harriet nodded.

"And," Edward added as his expression clouded over, "my son is talking about joining his regiment."

"Yes," Harriet replied weakly, then added, "of course."

For several minutes, the two walked down the street, each lost in his own dark thoughts. "I had intended to talk during this trip to some people I know in the War Department about securing Kevin a position here, in Washington. I noticed the last time I visited him, he was becoming restless, anxious to . . ."

Harriet gave Edward's arm a tug as she slowed her pace, then let go of it altogether. Stopping, Edward turned to see what the matter was. Harriet, holding both hands together before her and resting on the billowing hoop, stared down at the pavement. "You may not understand this, and you might think me terrible for asking this of you, but please, don't do that. If we truly love him, we must let Kevin do what he will and trust that God will see him through."

"Regardless of possible consequences?" Edward asked.

Slowly, Harriet tilted her head up and looked at Edward from beneath the brim of her hat. A quick nod, a momentary closing of her eyes, and then a long, hard stare through moist eyes was the only response Harriet could manage.

Feeling a pang of regret and sorrow, Edward took Harriet's arm and began to lead her on. "And you? You will follow the Army again?"

"Yes," she responded as she cleared her throat and sniffed back a tear. "Despite what General Grant has declared."

Edward had heard that Grant had ordered that all women working in the field hospitals of the Army of the Potomac be sent back to the Army's supply base at City Point. He was about to ask how she would manage to duck that restriction, but then, looking over at her, decided not to. She was a strong-willed woman, as strong-willed and determined as any he had known, including his own Mary. Like Kevin, she would make her way through this conflict, on her own terms, come what may.

Still, Edward couldn't give up without at least a try. "I, ah, had been hoping that now that you were married to Kevin, and you have already done so much, much more than anyone would dare ask of a young lady, that you would . . ."

Harriet smiled and responded without looking over at Edward. "Move back to New Jersey where I could take up the duties of a good, loyal wife waiting patiently for the return of her brave husband?" Her response carried a note of sarcasm that Edward had never heard from her before.

"Well, yes, I guess something like that," he replied haltingly.

"My father, though he's still quite angry at me for having run off as I did, and then marrying your son, has already tried that ploy with me." Harriet, her face set in a determined expression, looked straight ahead as she shook her head. "He's a foolish man, more foolish than I ever imagined." She paused as she thought about her father for a moment. "I had always thought that he was the kindest, wisest, most intelligent man on earth. Like so many little girls, I wanted to marry a man just like him." Her melancholy words were spoken almost in a whisper that was all but lost in the noise of people and animals scurrying about the streets of the capital. "None of us," she added, "not you, Kevin, my father, or me, can go back to what we were before this war. It would, I think, be foolish and wasteful to try."

"And so," Edward countered, "your solution is to blindly plow your way forward, without looking back."

Harriet looked over at Edward and studied his expression for a moment. She had hoped to discuss the issue of his older son, James, with him this day. It was, she suspected, an open wound between him and his son Kevin that Edward refused to let heal. The secret that was at the root of Kevin's brooding manner, one that he always seemed to keep hidden from her, was more closely guarded now than ever, even in the afterglow of their marriage and the partial reconciliation with his father. Harriet, more through intuition and guessing than fact, suspected that until this issue was resolved, neither she and Kevin, nor Kevin and his own father, could find true accord and happiness. This, she finally concluded as she looked at the concerned expression Edward wore as he waited for her answer, was not the time to bring that subject up. Edward's mind was already fixed on one issue and that one issue was all Harriet was prepared to deal with at this time.

With a squeeze of Edward's arm, Harriet smiled. "I do hope that you realize that neither Kevin nor I intend to turn our backs on our families.

No one can escape his past, not entirely. In time, I hope that we will all become reconciled with each other, what has been done, and get on with the business of building our future."

Taking what he wanted from Harriet's astute assessment, Edward missed entirely the deeper meaning that Harriet attached to her statement. James, though a major part of Edward's past, was more often forgotten these days than previously. Edward had managed, through the efforts of this bright young woman, to regain one of his sons. And though he did not relish the thought that Kevin might soon be placing himself in harm's way again, he was sufficiently trusting in luck and providence to allow things to go as they might, for now. There would, he thought as he and Harriet slowly made their way to the hospital where Kevin still lay, be plenty of time and opportunity to take a hand in shaping his son's future and fortunes. Plenty of time.

East of Frederick, Maryland

FROM THEIR POSITIONS BEHIND the lead brigades, the troops of fourteen different Virginia regiments, now collectively known as Terry's brigade, watched attentively as their clothes dried and the battle before them developed. After wading through the waist-deep water of the Monocacy downriver from the major crossings, Terry's brigade had deployed into line of battle and passed through John McCausland's dismounted Virginian cavalrymen. General John B. Gordon threw one of his brigades, Leroy Stafford's Louisianans, across an open field against a Union position atop a ridge while sending Clement Evans' brigade of Georgians through a patch of woods to the right in an effort to turn the Union right flank. Terry's brigade, which included the 253 men of the resurrected Stonewall Brigade, followed in support of the Louisianans.

Dale Wint managed to keep up with the men of the old 4th Virginia despite a painful limp that caused him to grunt with every other step he took. "Damn," Wint lamented as he looked up from the ground before him and over the solid ranks of the Louisianans to the rail fence atop the ridge. Above those bobbing heads, on the ridge at a greater distance, he could clearly see angry red flashes and billowing puffs of white smoke spewed out from the fence, lashing at the advancing lines of Confederate troops. "I kind of forgot how much I hated all this," Wint moaned to no one in particular between grunts and pants.

"What's the matter, Dale?" Keith Atkerson, a tall, stringy man with a mouth full of yellow teeth, shouted back to him from the rear rank. "Missing Richmond already?"

"Well," Wint snapped back, "ya gotta admit that trading in all those whores for the likes of you is sort of a raw deal."

Despite the severity of their current situation, James shook his head and chuckled. Wint had always been a complainer when he had been with the regiment before. "Two years in Richmond," James shouted out as he looked down the line, "have made you soft, Dale."

With a sideward glance, Wint glared at James. "I could match you, and any other man in this regiment, step for step, back in '62 and I can still do it."

Though the men between and around James and Wint enjoyed the diversion from the grim task that faced them, their company commander did not. "Quiet in the ranks. Pay attention to your alignment and keep it quiet."

From his post on the far left of the company, James leaned forward as far as he could and looked down the company's front to where Lieutenant Austin Roberts was doing the same, in James' direction. Roberts' angry expression reminded James of a schoolteacher trying to stare down an errant student. James responded by masking his feeling of frustration and indignation with a bland expression. Roberts took this as a sign of submission. Satisfied that he had restored order and discipline in the ranks, he stood up while James continued to survey the ranks between them.

Taking his time, James made sure that Douglas Geddy was still where he had personally placed him just before stepping off into the attack. Geddy, as if alerted by some sixth sense, glanced over at James. For a moment, their eyes met, causing Geddy's expression to sour. As he had with Roberts, James hid all emotions behind a bland expression. Satisfied, James straightened himself up, but still kept looking down the ranks, this time at the second rank, until he caught sight of Daniel McPherson. Following Geddy, Daniel's tense face was focused to the front. James watched as Daniel's eyes darted from side to side as he kept his head erect and his chin tucked in, just as he had been taught at VMI. Were it not for the fact that this was Will McPherson's younger brother and they were moving forward against a strong enemy position, James would have found Daniel's expression and pose comical.

"You'd think those Louisiana boys would wanna pick up the pace some or get out of the way or somethin'," Wint grumbled as more fire came boiling out of the covered Union position.

"Quiet in the ranks!" Roberts yelled.

"Oh, calm down, sonny," a voice from the packed ranks responded. "Ya making me nervous."

Stung by the laughter that followed the comment as much as by the audacity of the man who had uttered it, Roberts all but forgot where he was and took a few quick steps out and in front of the regiment. Walking backward, he shouted at the raggedy collection of men before him. "Who said that?" he demanded. "Who was the scoundrel who sassed me?"

The angry red face of their lieutenant caused most of the men to chuckle, and few tried to hide it. Colonel J. S. H. Funk, commanding the five small regiments of the old Stonewall Brigade, cut this farce short. "Lieutenant, back in ranks," the colonel snapped. "We have serious matters at hand and no time for such foolishness." Unbowed, but obedient, Roberts resumed his position, though he continued to look down the ranks in a futile effort to find the man who had belittled him.

For Daniel, this bantering in the ranks between the men and the scorn with which they treated their conscientious commanding officer was confusing, almost disconcerting. In comparison, the attack at New Market by the Corps of Cadets had been conducted in almost utter silence. All his fellow cadets, as he recalled, had worn a stern, determined expression that had been appropriate and fitting for the occasion. And although he had never been in battle before, all he had seen that day fit nicely the picture of war as he imagined it should be.

The advance of Terry's brigade, on the other hand, lacked anything resembling precision or smartness. When the order to advance had been given, the line of men had more or less simply lurched forward rather disjointedly, as a train does when it leaves the station, jerking one car after the other until all of them are in motion. Many of the soldiers, though the order had been given to advance at shoulder arms, carried their rifles pretty much as they saw fit. And the talking by some of the men, even by several of the sergeants, was incessant. More than once an officer had to snap, "Quiet in the ranks. Keep it down," so they could hear the orders of their superiors. This, Daniel concluded, was not at all what he had expected of a crack unit. Not at all.

Up ahead, James watched as Stafford's brigade of Louisiana regiments closed on the split-rail fence that marked the Union line. As was customary, the Union soldiers, seeing that their efforts to stop the Confederate advance had been for naught, gave way and yielded their position before the two opposing lines actually collided. In three years of war, and dozens of fights, James could count the number of times an attack resulted in hand-to-hand combat. "It's all a question of nerve and determination," he explained to Daniel. "You seldom find a unit so determined to hold a position that it's willing to take on an enemy, hand to hand, that's dead set on seizing it. At some point, one side or the other decides, without any officer saying so, that the task they've been given just can't be done."

Despite James' effort to teach him everything that he'd need to survive, Daniel's head was still too filled with romantic notions of war, clouded with patriotic sentiments, and driven by the concepts of manhood that were grounded more in fantasy than fact. When he saw the Union soldiers before them give way, he didn't appreciate what was happening. War, to him, was still rather black and white, a contest of right versus wrong, and the strong and brave against the weak and cowardly. "Look at those blue bellies run," he shouted with glee. "Just like at New Market!"

James didn't pay Daniel any heed. He, as well as the other noncommissioned officers and company officers, weren't concerned with what was happening in front of the Louisianans. Instead, they were busy dressing their ranks and preparing for what was bound to come next. They didn't have long to wait. Even as they were in the midst of sorting out the alignment of their units, General Gordon was ordering General Terry to throw his brigade against another line of Union troops that had been formed behind the one that had just given way at the fence. Whatever relief the men near Daniel had felt about having made it thus far without having to fight or suffer was quickly forgotten as the units wheeled and moved nearer the river.

"Oh, damn," Wint muttered as the line of Union troops, firing from behind another fence lining a road leading up from a bridge on the river, came into view. "We're gonna catch hell now."

Anxious to see what concerned Wint so, Daniel moved his head one way, then the other, in an effort to see around Geddy's head. Unlike the line that the Louisiana brigade had seized, this one ran along a winding and twisting road, half hidden in deep cuts. Even worse, this time they were the ones out in front, making the attack instead of simply supporting one.

Still, Terry's brigade went forward. Their pace, at first, was deliberate, steady. Yet, Daniel noted, it was neither a smooth nor neat advance. In part, this was due to the terrain. In this, his second fight, it finally dawned upon him that battles weren't fought on flat, grassy parade grounds. At New Market, they had crossed plowed farm fields, gone up and down hills, and around houses and barnyards. Here, they were moving through cuts and gullies, across fences, in and around small clusters of trees. This made it almost impossible for the officers and sergeants to keep the long, thin brigade line straight as it moved forward.

A new force that Daniel saw at work here was friction within the ranks, friction between those who wished to rush forward, as quickly as possible, like him and Lieutenant Roberts, and those, like Geddy, who truly wanted no part at all in what they were doing. At New Market the VMI Corps of Cadets had gone forward willingly, as one, with cadets falling behind only when their wounds were too severe to permit them to stay with the rest. In this advance, Daniel began to appreciate why corporals and sergeants were posted to the rear, rifles more often than not held level with the ground at waist height, ready to nudge the faint-hearted back into the ranks.

All of this resulted in a slower advance, much slower than Daniel had expected, and a great deal of shouting, shoving, and jostling in the ranks. Daniel himself contributed to this. Geddy, one of the more reluctant participants, tried mightily to fade back, out of the front rank. Daniel, however, wedged in tight between Keith Atkerson and a swarthy youth from Lynchburg, had no choice but to bodily push Geddy along or lose his place in the ranks. Geddy's response, whenever Daniel pushed up against his back, was a quick jerk of the head, first around at Daniel, then down the ranks at James. The look of anger in Geddy's eyes tinged now and again by fear, together with his actions, reminded Daniel of an animal that had been cornered.

Caught up in this pushing match and his own thoughts, Daniel was slow to perceive a sudden surge forward when the line was still a hundred yards from the Union line. We're charging, he thought. This is it. Tightening his grip on his rifle, he tucked his head down, swallowed hard, and pushed his way back forward between Atkerson and the dark-skinned youth who hadn't been caught by the stepping up of the pace.

This surge, a tradition of the old Stonewall Brigade, was short-lived. General Terry, anxious to preserve his alignment and cohesion, slowed the advance back to the steady, if somewhat disjointed, pace it had been moving at. For the men in the ranks, this was difficult. James knew they were suffering as he responded to the order "Close it up toward the center" by leaning to the right and forcing the men to that side to angle over and close the gaps left by dead and wounded comrades. As the company's second sergeant, this, and keeping the front rank aligned between him and Lieutenant Roberts, was his primary task. The company commander set the pace and direction, James kept the rank closed up on the commander and even, and the file closers behind the company, the third and fourth sergeants, made sure that the company stayed together. Will McPherson, when he had commanded the company, had often half jokingly compared the officers and noncommissioned officers to sheep-herders. Though bothered by this comparison at first, James began to realize that it was all too often applicable. And in his case, given the habit of letting random events and others decide his course, the analogy was all too true.

The Union soldiers along the fence-lined road gave way long before the first member of Terry's brigade reached it. Some of the old 4th Virginia, including Dale Wint, couldn't resist the urge to break ranks, rush forward, and take at least one shot at the blue-clad devils who had been punishing them with their fire during the long, tortuous advance. He was standing there, fully exposed, loading his rifle for all he was worth when James and Daniel came up to the fence, shoved their rifles between the split rails of the fence, and fired their pieces.

"Damn them," Wint muttered as his nimble fingers twirled the steel ramrod over his head and returned it under the barrel. "I hate fightin' militia. They fight when they feel like it and scatter before you can get a piece of them."

James, busy loading his own rifle, caught sight of a discarded Yankee kepi. Reaching over with his ramrod, he picked the bloody cap up with the end of the ramrod and brought it closer. As he took the hat off the end of the ramrod, he could still feel the warmth from the sticky blood that had soaked one side of the hat. Turning it over, he looked at the blue Greek cross for a moment, then held the hat up to Wint. "These boys aren't no militia."

Wint, still busy slipping a cap onto the cone of his rifle, glanced over. His eyes narrowed. "Sixth Corps," he said with a whistle. "Looks like Old Jubal's got them fellas in Washington a might concerned, pullin' their best corps up from Petersburg and all."

"Second Corps is their best," Corporal Tim Lawrence countered as he lay on his back, talking between sips from his canteen. "Toughest Yankees in the attack or the defense. Sixth Corps always manages to be someplace else when the serious fighting is going on."

"Ya crazy," Wint responded. "I'll take the Yanks in Second Corps any day of the week." Without waiting for a response, he lifted his rifle to his shoulder, took aim at something in the distance, and fired.

Daniel was both amazed and appalled at the easygoing and almost lackadaisical manner that these hard-bitten veterans went about their tasks. In the small knot of men around him he could see just about every possible range of emotion being displayed. James, at one end, was coolly, methodically loading and firing his rifle as if he were popping off at paper targets. Dale Wint, his hat off and his dirty, unkempt stringy hair dripping with sweat, stood fully exposed at the rail fence, cursing a blue streak as he continued the debate about which Union corps was the best while firing his rifle at the Yankees who were busy reforming in the distance. Douglas Geddy, not at all anxious to take any more chances than he needed, pressed himself against the ground without even bothering to look through the split rails at the danger that threatened them all. Keith Atkerson, unable to find an opening big enough for him at the fence, passed the time by lying on his back while chewing on a chunk of rancid bacon and staring up at the blue sky. Glancing behind him, Daniel looked out over the field they had advanced across and watched as wounded men, who had been shoulder to shoulder with him moments before, struggled to crawl off in search of help or lay where they had fallen, dead or too badly injured to move.

A sharp kick in his shoulder caused Daniel to yelp like a dog. Rolling over, he looked up at Roberts, towering over him with his sword in one hand and his smoking pistol in the other. "You best not be thinking about running off," he yelled down at Daniel, mistaking the boy's study of the unit's rear as a sign of imminent flight.

His lieutenant's insinuation that he might be thinking of running infuriated Daniel. He wanted to tell his young commander off, but wasn't given the chance. With a thrust of his sword toward the fence, Roberts yelled, "Get up there and start shooting, damn you." With that, he turned and walked off, stepping over Atkerson without saying a word and paying not the slightest bit of attention to Geddy. Why Roberts had picked on him and not the other two bothered Daniel. Was he afraid of saying something to the old-timers? Daniel hoped that wasn't the case, but didn't give the matter another thought at that moment.

Instead, he turned his attention back to the front just as James, in his calm, steady voice, called down the line, "Here they come, boys." Looking beyond the fence, through the thin veil of dirty white smoke lingering from the discharge of rifles, Daniel could see a line of blue come surging forward. A mass volley, followed by the deep-throated Union "hurrah," announced the beginning of a counterattack.

"Okay, you scum-sucking swine," Wint yelled as he prepared to fire. "This is more like it."

No, Daniel thought as he pushed his way past Geddy up to the fence, this was nothing like it was supposed to be. As Geddy gladly gave way and crawled back away from the fence, Daniel began to join in the general firing as the first of two unsuccessful Union counterattacks came forward in what Daniel would later regard as his first true day of battle.

CHAPTER 16

Fort Stevens, North of Washington, D.C., July, 1864

ONLY A FEW OF the men deployed in the skirmish line in front of Fort Stevens understood Kevin Bannon's nervous parading from one end of his company line to the other. It wasn't the dull pain in his side or occasional twinge in his partly healed leg, though annoying, that bothered him. Kevin found he could tolerate these physical discomforts. What he wasn't sure of was the ability to face enemy fire again. His wounds, not yet fully healed, served to remind Kevin of the costs that many soldiers pay for doing little more than following orders and performing their duty. Together with the apprehension that always gripped Kevin before a battle, this new fear of mortal harm all but threatened to paralyze him.

Still, from the moment he was given command of this motley company, made up of other convalescents and Army clerks quickly armed with ancient smoothbore muskets, he had mechanically executed his orders. From his first order to form up in the same shabby garden in which he had been married, Kevin found that only his long service and training enabled him to push aside his personal fears as each step, each movement, brought back the memory of the agony of his wounds.

"You know, Kevin," Harriet had told him as he watched his men draw weapons and cartridge boxes, "you don't have to go."

Kevin had turned to Harriet and studied her pleading eyes before answering. Did she know, he wondered, what he was feeling? Had she guessed that he was seriously considering resigning his commission rather than face the horrors of battle again? Was this her way of offering him a graceful escape from this insanity and telling him it was all right, with her, to do so? Or was she merely trying to boost his courage? He didn't know. Though she was now his wife, he still found it difficult to penetrate her heart and soul and understand all that she said and did. Women were still very much a mystery to him, a mystery he was as unprepared to deal with as he was with his newfound fear. Which was why, when he looked down at his motley collection of troops, he had to go with them, if for no other reason than to prove to himself, one way or another, that he had not lost his nerve completely.

The presence of someone coming up next to him shook Kevin from his unnerving gloom. "Given a month and a few stands of first-class rifles, sir," the haggard sergeant who was serving as his first sergeant choked out, "I might be able to make something of this sorry lot. As it is, it'll take every ounce of strength you and I can muster just to keep these clerks and cripples in line." Then, as he eyed the extended skirmish line those clerks and cripples were deployed in, the sergeant mumbled in his gravelly voice, "I sure hope those bloody big guns in the forts can keep Johnny Reb at arm's length, 'cause if they don't, we'll be swept aside like so many dry leaves in a windstorm."

Kevin looked at his first sergeant's weather-beaten face, tanned from years of hard campaigning, and grunted. At the moment, he couldn't recall the first sergeant's name. Not that it mattered much. Both men were used to putting their trust in the hands of strangers based on little more than a quick study of the way the other man returned his stare or carried himself. After no more than a salute that morning, each man had judged the other to be worthy of his trust and respect and that was that. With a quick glance over his shoulder at the new copper dome rising up above the trees, Kevin responded to the sergeant's dire prediction. "With the Rebels in Silver Spring and our backs to the walls of our own Capitol building, seems we don't have much of a choice." Then fixing his gaze on the sergeant's eyes, Kevin added, "Does it?"

The first sergeant looked over to the Capitol building, little more than six miles distant, then back at Kevin. "No, sir. I guess we don't."

Kevin nodded. "If we keep the men's minds on the task at hand, we'll do all right."

With a quick glance to the northwest, the direction in which the enemy would be coming, the sergeant returned Kevin's nod. "Yes, sir, I suppose that's the way things will have to be."

"Yes," Kevin snapped with little conviction, "exactly." Pivoting about on his heels, Kevin began to pace toward the right end of the line. Just back of the center of the line, midway to the earthen ramparts of Fort Stevens, a group of a dozen men, Kevin's reserve, stood about or knelt in a tight formation. A few of the men watched Kevin with a keen eye, as if they were trying to gauge the mettle of their newly appointed commander. Off to one side, a corporal was busy going over the finer points of loading the 1842 caliber .69 Springfield with two of the clerks who had been flushed out of the War Department and added to the ranks at the last minute. Of all the men he had, these clerks, and a few others scattered here and there, were the most visibly shaken by the prospect of the coming fight. "Must be a terrible thing," one grizzled old veteran mused to another veteran in the ranks as the two watched the white-faced young men from the War Department join their ranks, "to wake up one morning and find out all your conniving and whining is for naught."

The other veteran smiled a big toothy grin as the two watched the clerks clumsily adjust cartridge boxes and belts. "Yeah. A sight like this sort of makes you thank God for old Jubal Early."

Too concerned about his own state of mind and readiness to face fire again, Kevin didn't respond to such remarks. Everyone was already on edge and lost in his own private hell of fears and concerns. There was, he figured, no need to add more stress to an already tense situation. Besides, the way he figured it, no one intended for this thrown-together collection of half-crippled, half-green soldiers to be anything more than a temporary breakwater, a minor obstacle meant to keep the oncoming Confederate tides away from the big guns of the earthen forts. "The guns," said the colonel commanding the stretch of front Kevin's men were deployed along, "they're the real backbone of this defense. I just need you and your boys to keep the Rebels at a respectful distance while the siege guns do the serious killing."

Simple, Kevin thought, then and now. All so simple, just like everything in this war was till it came time to do it.

From along his line, a scream came out. "Outpost coming in!"

They were coming, finally and for real. Drawing his pistol, Kevin took up his position behind the skirmish line with the small reserve and looked down the long, thin row. "Steady, boys," he shouted. "Hold your fire till they're in range." This last point, Kevin knew, would be the hardest for his men. They would have to wait for battle-hardened veterans of Lee's Army, armed with first-class rifles and in tight, disciplined ranks, to close within seventy to eighty yards before his men had even a prayer of hitting them with their ancient smoothbore muskets. One good enemy volley, Kevin knew, from one hundred meters could scatter his whole line without any of them having even the slightest chance of inflicting any punishment on the enemy. Looking behind him, he watched as the gunners on the fort's ramparts scurried about in preparation to fire. "Lord," he prayed, "let their aim be true and their hands be swift."

With that, he turned back to the front to watch and wait.

Unlike their response to the constant haranguing from officers to keep moving, every man in the 4th Virginia complied instantly when the order to break ranks and rest was given. Some, worn out from the incessant marching and oppressive heat, simply fell right on the Seventh Street road without bothering to seek shade from the merciless early afternoon sun that beat down upon them like a blacksmith's hammer. James Bannon, as worn as any of them, kept to his feet for a few moments longer as he looked about, trying to determine who had fallen out since their last break several hours ago.

Dale Wint, he saw, was gone from the little cluster of men his lieutenant called a company. That, James faintly recalled, had occurred around midmorning when Wint's legs, still unaccustomed to hard marching, had finally given out. "Well, Bannon," he lamented as he fell back behind James, "you've gotten the better of me this time." With no more than a nod, James had let Wint slip away from the company and into the growing mass of stragglers that were soon to outnumber the main body of Early's small army. From his spot under a small tree, Keith Atkerson shouted out to James, "How far do you make it to Washington?"

James didn't answer at first. He was still trying to collect his thoughts and focus. Taking his time, James wiped his brow with a new handkerchief he had foraged from a discarded Union haversack and looked down the road. He'd lost track of Geddy, he finally concluded, somewhere along the way. "Damn," James muttered. "Damn it all." Keeping Geddy in the ranks and protecting Daniel as best he could had become his reason for being, for staying with the Army. And though he knew there had been, in truth, little that he could have done to keep Geddy going when he himself was pushing his own limit, James still cursed this failure. Finally, with a great sigh, he tucked the handkerchief into his dirty haversack and reached for his canteen. After taking a long sip, he looked over at Atkerson and forced his parched lips into a smile. "If those folks back there at that schoolhouse were right, we should be in the District of Columbia now."

Daniel, who had been lying flat on his back, lifted his head, looked about for a moment, then gave James a quizzical look. "You mean we're in Washington?"

Swallowing a drink of water, James looked over at Daniel and gave him a wink as his tongue ran along his lips in an effort to capture every drop of water it could find. "We're not in the city yet, but we're about as close to it as any Confederate unit's been to it since '61. This road," he stated, pointing down at the hard-surfaced street under his feet, "turns into Seventh Street. If we follow it for another couple of hours, it will take us right onto Pennsylvania Avenue."

This revelation caused some of the men to stir and look about. "You think so?" the swarthy youth from Lynchburg asked.

"What happens when we get there?" Daniel asked as James finally managed to get moving again and slowly limped over to join the others in the shade.

"We win the war and we all go home," someone on the other side of the tree responded with a sneer.

Turning to James, now easing his aching body down next to him, Daniel asked in a serious tone, "Do you think we can end it right here, today, just like that?"

James, however, hadn't heard Daniel's question. His mind was on something else as he looked away from the young man, out across the road where a group of officers were gathering around General Early's lathered horse. The idea of going home had been a new idea that James had only recently allowed to enter his troubled mind. His last visit at the McPherson farm had been a sorry affair, one which had diminished his hopes of finding a new home, and a new family, to replace the one he had been exiled from so long ago. And though he had never discussed this with Daniel, James had the feeling that Daniel shared many of his feelings. While it was true that the land was still there, as well as the house, and barn, and other buildings, the family that had made the McPherson place so attractive, so warm and comfortable before the war was gone, gone for good. The McPherson family had been mortally wounded. Those who survived did so out of habit, for their very heart was gone. James had seen that in Mary Beth's desperate, sad eyes. No victory, he thought, no matter how stunning or complete, would ever change that fact. Like so many of his friends, the McPherson family was now little more than a memory.

A sudden boom, echoing up the road in the distance, caused everyone to look up. "A cannon," Daniel snapped, as if he were in a classroom rushing to beat other students to the correct answer.

"A siege gun," James responded in a low voice. "Guess some of Rhodes' boys are at the outerworks."

"And we'll be there soon enough," Atkerson moaned as he got up on his knees to watch General Early spur his frazzled horse into a gallop toward the sound of the guns.

"Well, boys," Lieutenant Roberts shouted out as he managed to push himself up off the ground and onto his feet, "looks like we'll be in Washington before nightfall."

"Or," a sad, reflective voice responded, "we'll be in hell."

For James, with his mind filled with dark thoughts about the future, there didn't seem to be much of a difference.

It was hard to tell who had been more frightened by the thunderous report of the massive siege guns, Kevin's own men or the raggedy line of Confederate skirmishers who were deploying along his front. "The men are worried, sir," the first sergeant had told Kevin when he reached his part of the line.

With a nervous smile and a chuckle, Kevin winked at the first sergeant. "I'm worried, First Sergeant."

This caused the weathered face of Kevin's senior noncommissioned officer to break into a smile for the first time. "Then, sir, I guess that makes it unanimous."

With a pat on the first sergeant's shoulder, Kevin repeated his orders before turning to walk back to his position with the reserve behind the center of the line. "Keep the men down and have them hold their fire till the Rebels are within fifty yards. It'll be hard as hell to do so, but we've got to do the best we can."

Looking down the line as one of the War Department clerks squeezed off a round at a target well beyond the range of his ancient musket even before Kevin finished giving his warning, the first sergeant bowed his head, shook it, and sighed. "I'll try."

Kevin nodded as he gave the first sergeant another pat on the back. "That's all I ask. That's all anyone can expect. Good luck."

By the time Kevin reached the dozen or so men who made up his reserve force, screaming at the men he passed as he went along to hold their fire, the corporal who had been giving instructions to two clerks had them and the rest of the reserve down and lying flat on the ground. When Kevin walked up to them slowly, the corporal started to get up. "I figured it was better to get the men down and out of the line of fire before . . ."

With a downward motion of his hand, Kevin signaled the corporal to resume his position on the ground. "You figured right, Corporal. Now just stay down there out of harm's way until . . ."

The earsplitting report of a siege gun drowned out Kevin's words and caused him to tuck his head between his shoulders. Kevin shook his head, and gave the side of his head a quick smack in the hope that this would stop the ringing in his ear. Instinctively, he took a quick glance around to make sure that the explosion was in fact friendly cannon firing at the enemy and not a near miss or enemy fire. He had been around cannons as they fired before, even guns firing overhead. But the huge Columbiads of Fort Stevens were a new experience. He only hoped the Confederate infantry before his thin skirmish line was as impressed by them as he was.

Seeing that the corporal was as concerned about the firing of their own guns, Kevin continued where he had left off as he slowly surveyed his line and the enemy skirmish line off in the distance. "Keep the men down until I call them forward to fill in gaps."

The corporal looked up at Kevin. "What about you, Captain? Shouldn't you get down?"

Glancing down at the corporal, Kevin thought about his exposed posture for the first time. The zing of a Rebel bullet zipping past his head highlighted the mortal danger that, until that second, had escaped him. All his concerns and apprehensions concerning his ability to face enemy fire again seemed to have evaporated without his ever having noticed. Dropping to one knee next to the corporal, Kevin took a deep breath as a wary smile crept across his face. Though he no longer understood what was driving him to risk whatever the future held for him, Kevin knew now that he would be able to see this war through, until the end, whenever that might be.

"I'll be just fine," Kevin finally said in response to the corporal's concern. "All we have to do is keep the men together here, let those guns behind us do their work, and this will all work out."

Though the corporal considered simply keeping body and soul together a daunting task in itself, he took comfort in Kevin's calm demeanor and cheerful prediction. It was good, he reflected, to have a man like this in command. Very good indeed.

Re-formed and moved forward as quickly as their aching muscles could carry them, the soldiers of Terry's brigade formed up into a line of battle well behind the skirmish line that General Rhodes' division had thrown out to probe the Union defenses. For young Daniel the wait for what might be the last and most glorious battle in the whole war was unbearable. "When are we going to go forward?" he repeatedly murmured from the ranks. "When are they going to get on with this? I don't understand what's going on."

He had hoped James would answer, but his brother's old friend seemed to be lost in deep thoughts, totally divorced from what was going on about them. Keith Atkerson, tired of listening to Daniel, finally told the young man to hush. "Ain't no use, boy, in wishing for something we're bound to get anyway." Just then a pair of siege guns fired in quick succession. "Hear that? You gonna stand there and tell me that you're in a hurry to rush out and tangle with guns that can spit out a ball the size of a house?"

Not having the depth of experience most of the men around him did, all cannon reports were still equally loud and ominous to Daniel. Looking off down the road where trees and distance obscured the skirmishing that was well under way, Daniel didn't respond. Instead, he just looked down at the ground, shuffled his feet, and waited in the oppressive July heat with everyone else.

Lieutenant Roberts, now animated by the same prospects of rushing into the enemy's capital that so excited Daniel, paced back and forth. "He's got to at least try, damn it! We've come too far not to at least give it a shot."

In the rear rank, Daniel heard Atkerson as he leaned over and whispered to the man next to him. "Can you imagine that? Our boy lieutenant hasn't even worn out his first pair of boots and he's yipping about how far we've gone."

The swarthy soldier from Lynchburg smiled as he looked down the line to make sure Roberts was out of earshot. "Yeah. Next he'll be tellin' us all about our past and glorious victories and how we've earned the right to be given this chance."

This caused Atkerson to laugh a little too loudly. Spinning about, Lieutenant Roberts caught sight of Daniel looking at him with an expression he took to be one of guilt. Walking up to Daniel in quick, short strides, Roberts stopped before Daniel and glared at him. "I find nothing at all funny about this, boy," Roberts shouted, though in truth Daniel and Roberts were less than two years apart in age. "This regiment and this brigade have a long and glorious past, one any man would be proud of. And given a chance, we'll add another shining victory to it."

Predictably, Roberts' bombastic statement caused Atkerson and the man from Lynchburg to grin. But they neither laughed nor were caught by Roberts. Daniel pulled away from Roberts' angry face. He wanted to utter an excuse, a few words of apology, or something. But nothing came to mind. He was tired, frustrated, hot, hungry, and totally unprepared to deal with Roberts' undeserved wrath.

Seeing no challenge or point in punishing Daniel, and anxious to return to his nervous pacing, Roberts turned away and started to move back down the line. Atkerson chuckled. "Well, Danny, I guess you really showed him."

With a quick jerk, Daniel looked over his shoulder at Atkerson. "Shut up, will you. Just shut up. I'm tired of listening to your yapping."

"Relax," the man from Lynchburg countered. "We're only having some fun."

Daniel turned his head to face him. "I'm tired of your idea of fun. I just want to go forward, fight this damned fight, and be done with it."

For the first time that day, Atkerson spoke with a seriousness that took the edge off Daniel's anger. "Don't be in a rush to go up there, or anywhere else where there's shooting, Danny boy. You'll soon enough see all the fightin' and killin' you'll ever want to see."

It wasn't so much what Atkerson said; it was the way he said it. The slow somberness of his words carried a weight that left no doubt in Daniel's mind that they came from the heart. With a deep breath, Daniel shuffled about, looked off into the distance again, and continued to watch and wait in silence for the order to advance.

At the far end of the line James, tired of standing, dropped to his knees, then eased himself back onto the ground next to Dale Wint. Wint, having just joined the ranks after catching up, was lying flat on the ground with his hat covering his face. "Ever think of what it would be like, Dale," James started without any sort of preamble, or even checking to see if Wint was awake, "to go home again?"

Wint reached up, took his hat off his face, and looked up at James. "You mean when the war is over, or just to visit the missus?"

"For good," James responded softly. "When all this is over and the armies are disbanded. Ever wonder what it would be like?"

"Huh," Wint scoffed as he replaced his hat on his face. "Wishful thinking."

"You think so?"

"Jimmy," Wint answered slowly, without picking up the hat this time, "we've seen too many a good lad laid low in his grave to play with such silly notions." Animated by the subject, Wint finally took the hat off his head, propped himself up on one hand, and waved his hat at the direction of the firing. "We ain't gonna go stormin' down this road, into Washington, no more than Early and Ewell went chargin' up Cemetery Hill last year. If Early was serious about attacking, he would have done so hours ago.

No," Wint concluded, "we're gonna let this one slip by, just like so many other chances, and we're gonna go marching away back south, again. And after we've licked our wounds, and waited for Billy Yankee to catch up, we'll be at it again, just like before. No, my friend, we ain't goin' home. Not today, not next month. This war's gonna go on, and on, and on, till there ain't a single soul left standing."

James studied Wint for a moment without responding. Dale Wint didn't speak much. When he did, it was usually to tell a lewd story or an off-color joke. James hadn't ever thought Wint capable of making a serious statement such as the bitter pronouncement he had just uttered. Noticing James' amazed stare, Wint averted his eyes, looked down the road for a moment, then eased himself back down with a groan. "No," he stated calmly after he had placed his hat back over his face to keep the sun off, "I figured there's no point for a man to drive himself crazy wondering about things that just might not happen. I left a good woman back home, a fine, healthy girl that can cook up a storm all day and still keep a man entertained all night. I suppose unless a fever or somethin' else has carried her away, she's still there, waitin' for me to come back. But it wouldn't do me no good to sit and pine all day wonderin' and worryin' about her. No, sir, that's not my style." Then he pulled his hat up and away from his eyes so that he could look James in the eyes. "And it ain't healthy for a man to do so. It's not natural, if you know what I mean. So, I just take what the Lord and our featherbrained generals give us and deal with it each day as it comes."

Wint's view of the war and how best to deal with it wasn't novel to James. He had known many men who had dealt with their fears and apprehensions about their futures by hiding behind humor or some other means. He himself had tried to keep such thoughts at bay simply by ignoring them. But it was impossible to do so all the time. He had seen it many a time while they were on the march or in camp. Something, often obscure and unrelated to what they were doing, would catch a man's eye and trigger a thought, a memory, a cherished dream. Then, like a gush of water let go by a collapsing dam, all defenses would melt away and the man would be lost, for hours, sometimes even days, in deep, thoughtful melancholy about home, family, or his future.

"Back there," James started saying, not even knowing if Wint was paying attention, "I started to think about what it would be like to go back home, to New Jersey. I haven't thought about that, oh, in years."

Sensing that James needed to talk to someone about a matter that was on his mind, Wint eased his hat back till his eyes were exposed and he could see James. "You got troubles, though, back home, don't you?" Wint injected.

James looked up at the pale blue sky. "I got troubles, Dale, the likes of which I never even told Will about."

Recalling the close, almost brotherly regard with which James and Will had held each other, Wint nodded, though James didn't see him. "Got a woman in trouble?"

That Wint was able to guess that a woman was involved was not at all surprising. It was a common practice for respectable Southern families to solve illicit affairs involving the two sexes by exiling the errant son. Most of the men in the regiment, both when Wint had been in it before and now, suspected that there had been a woman involved in James' dark, secret past.

"Yes," James responded as he looked down at the ground between his feet and absentmindedly began to dig into it with a small twig. "There was a woman. Both my brother and I wanted her, but . . ."

"He got her," Wint added.

Though Wint had meant one thing, James took the comment differently. As had happened so many times before, the sudden image of the girl he loved, eyes bulging in shock and her body falling away from him and his brother Kevin as they struggled for the gun that had just fired, flashed through James' mind. James jabbed the stick in the ground, gave it a quick twist, and jerked it up, sending small clods of dirt flying all about.

Sensing that James was not willing to tell all, Wint tried to divert the conversation. "Any chance of you and he, or you and your father, ever making amends?"

James looked over at Wint and smiled. "You see, that's just it. I don't know." Then he looked away, back at the tiny hole he was digging with the stick, before continuing. "I haven't written or spoken to anyone back home since the day I left four and a half years ago. Though I don't think my father's changed his mind, it's not knowing, for sure, that's been bothering me lately. I had hoped to settle in Virginia after all this was over but . . ."

Wint sighed. "Yeah, I know. A lot of boys have seen their homes burned and families scattered. Some of 'em, just like you, have been wondering where they'll go after it's all over." Sitting upright, Wint looked around. Another quick series of reports from the siege guns, followed by a sharp increase in rifle fire, caught Wint's attention. "It's been a terrible war, Jimmy, and it ain't gettin' any better."

James halted his digging for a moment and looked in the same direction that Wint was staring in an effort to determine if the sudden increase in activity had some significance. "Think we're gonna do anything here today?" Wint finally asked, in part to change the subject that neither man really cared to pursue too far.

After a quick glance up at the late afternoon sun, James shook his head. "No, I doubt it. If we were going to go, we would have gone in hours ago. I think Old Jubal's just waiting till the sun goes down before slipping away."

"Too bad," Wint lamented. "It would have been nice to see if Washington whores were any better than those Richmond has to offer these days."

With a laugh, James threw away his stick and lay down to wait for the order to re-form into columns and retreat, as both he and Wint expected.

Kevin was quite happy to turn away from the uneven contest he had been watching between his line of skirmishers and those of the better-armed Confederates when someone tapped him on the shoulder. "You in charge here?" a young lieutenant in a dirty, faded uniform shouted to Kevin.

"Yes," he responded as his eyes fell on the white Greek cross of the Sixth Corps' Second Division that decorated the lieutenant's sweat-soaked hat. A smile lit Kevin's face as he extended his hand to greet the commander of the troops that had come to his relief.

The Second Division lieutenant, however, was in no mood for niceties. He was under fire and anxious to get the rabble under Kevin's command out of his way so they could begin the serious work of pushing the Rebels back. "My men are in line behind you and coming up," he announced sharply, paying no heed to the difference in their ranks. "If you can manage, somehow, to keep your men under control for a few minutes longer, and then take them out of our way once we're through, it will help."

There were no badges on Kevin's uniform, other than his rank, to mark him as an experienced officer. All the lieutenant from the Second Division saw was a captain, wearing a newly issued clean, crisp uniform, which stood in sharp contrast to his own faded uniform and worn boots, both still caked and soiled with the dirt of the Petersburg trenches. Kevin himself had been contemptuous of the dandies who garrisoned the forts of Washington, and now being mistaken for one upset him.

This, however, was neither the time nor place to stand on one's personal pride. Slowly, with steady pressure, the Confederate skirmishers had pushed his line back, ever closer to the dirt ramparts of Fort Stevens. In the process they had picked away at it, leaving a string of fresh corpses to mark its rearward progress. All the while Kevin's concern about holding grew as he waited for the enemy's main attack to be launched by massed troops hidden in the woods behind the Rebel skirmishers. With a forced smile, Kevin gave way, consoled by the knowledge that he and his men together would escape that storm. "It will, sir, be my pleasure. Good luck."

The Second Division lieutenant simply nodded, then turned to wave his line of troops forward. The Second Division men, as contemptuous of the assorted convalescents and War Department clerks who had been holding the line all day as their lieutenant was, jeered and threw insults at the soldiers of Kevin's ad hoc command as they made their way forward. "Back to your desk, sonny, before the Rebs get ya," one Second Division veteran sneered as he came up alongside a young man wearing spectacles.

Though he felt sorry for the clerk, since neither he nor anyone else who had been on the line that day deserved such ridicule, Kevin did nothing. In a few days, once the immediate threat to Washington was over, his tiny command would be disbanded and scattered to the four winds. Everyone in his company would either be returned to his previous duties or go back to a nice, clean hospital bed. Kevin, however, had no intention of waiting for that to happen. As soon as he could gracefully do so, he was determined to leave this thrown-together company of Washington's lame and lazy and find the First Brigade of the Sixth Corps' First Division, the Jersey Brigade. He would, he decided then and there, rejoin his unit and go with it, no matter what. If nothing else, today's inconclusive little skirmishing proved to Kevin that he hadn't lost his nerve. And his wounds, though still painful, were not enough to keep him from seeing this war through, until the end.

"Should we be moving back, behind the fort, sir?" the first sergeant asked as Kevin watched the experienced soldiers of the Second Division move forward and trade shots with the Confederates.

Kevin stood up, turned to the first sergeant, and smiled. "Yes, by all means, do so. I am going to find the colonel. There is something I need to discuss with him."

The first sergeant, used to officers running off whenever they got the chance, said nothing. Instead, he simply saluted and walked away, as anxious as Kevin to be rid of this motley collection of clerks.

When darkness finally brought an end to the oppressive heat of day and the indecisive skirmishing, word came down to form into columns facing north, the direction from which they had come that morning. To the soldiers of Lieutenant Roberts' small company, this order was a sign that all their hard marching and efforts over the past few weeks had been for naught. "This makes it three times," Keith Atkerson mumbled as he shuffled out onto the roadway into formation, "we've been up here and have gone back with our tails tucked between our legs. Three times."

James, who had been with the Army on each of those occasions, said nothing. There was no need to discuss what it meant, no use in moaning or complaining. Just as before, they had been led north, to the brink of victory. Each time, they had done their best to cinch that victory, and each time, at the very last minute, found out that their best hadn't been good enough.

Sore and tired from over three weeks of hard marching and the perpetual hunger that always seemed to accompany the Confederate Army even in a land as rich and plentiful as Maryland, Lieutenant Roberts stood silently at the head of his small command while he waited for the order to move. James, standing near the rear of the company, and just off the road, leaned against a tree and gazed off to the north. It would be a long time, he thought, before he would be this close to New Jersey again, if ever. His mind, unable to focus on anything else, kept turning all his thoughts back to a home he hadn't known in five years. Had everything back there changed? Was his brother alive and still serving with the same army he only knew as the enemy? Would it ever be possible, his tired mind mulled over and over again, to go back and start over?

It was only the exhortations of an officer, whose voice he did not recognize, that made James aware that the old 4th Virginia had moved out. Slowly, almost casually, he looked over at the long column of tired men, their faces hidden in darkness and their heads bowed low between their shoulders as they trudged along in silence. They were going back, back to a state devastated by war to wage more war. If they didn't stop or have to fight, they'd be back in Winchester in nine days, maybe less.

Turning his face back north, James looked up at the stars in the night sky. Mary Beth was still in Winchester, but that was all. Everyone else he had cared for in Virginia was gone, dead, or broken. Everyone. Will. Marty Hazard. Matthew Hazard. Even old Jack, Thomas J. Jackson, a drier than dust professor at VMI who had risen to the pinnacle of fame and glory, was gone. And although Mary Beth, a girl who had once been as free and as lively as the horse she had so loved, was still alive, she was now, in spirit and body, as downtrodden as the once vibrant McPherson farm. Gloom, despair, devastation, and death, with nothing but the promise of more to come, were all that waited back there, in Virginia. For better than three years, James thought, he had blindly marched in the ranks of this ragged army with nothing but the vague hope that somewhere, off in the distant future, there would be a place for him in Mary Beth's heart and Virginia.

But, he wondered, as he stood there alone, if there was still a place for him in New Jersey. There was only one way of finding out for sure, he realized, as rank after rank of Early's small army made its way past him, redeploying into new lines of battle that would never move any closer to Washington than they were now. With his company already well down the road and no one paying any attention to him, there would be no tears shed if he didn't answer the roll call in the morning. Not even Mary Beth, he reasoned, already used to hardship, would miss him much.

Still, he thought as he crossed his arms, his fingertips lightly touching the light blue sergeant stripes on the sleeve of his dusty gray jacket, would he be welcomed back there? Could he really go back home? Gazing at the distant stars, James wondered about this and many, many other things as the rear of his division came up to where he stood and went by without so much as noticing him.

CHAPTER 17

Winchester, Virginia, August, 1864

IN THE SAME MANNER that her father used to know that a storm was coming, Mary Beth sensed that the armies that had been stalking each other for the past weeks were about to come to blows right there, in Winchester, again. And despite the fact that the coming contest would involve two of the people she most cared about in the world, she had little time to worry about their safety and well-being. As heartless as this attitude seemed during those few moments of rest when her mind was free to address concerns not connected to the running of her failing farm, her survival and the survival of her invalid mother demanded Mary Beth's full and undivided attention and energies.

It wasn't so much the actual danger of fighting, she tried to explain to her aunt, that compelled her to stay on the farm and work day and night till she dropped from exhaustion. In three years, previous battles fought over the possession of Winchester hadn't come close to their place. Nor was it the armies themselves, though they sometimes suddenly transformed themselves from bodies of organized, disciplined soldiers into swarms of locusts when they spied an inviting orchard or cornfield along the side of the road. Instead, it was the refuse of an army, especially a broken one, that most concerned Mary Beth and other farmers in the area.

Inevitably, soldiers who either had enough of fighting or never had the urge for it separated themselves from their units and officers and wandered about alone or in small groups. Like wolves, they would roam freely, hiding when their freedom was threatened by the enemy or provost guards, boldly coming out in broad daylight when there was no danger in the air. Their freedom from the watchful eyes of stern sergeants and demanding officers also meant that they were separated from their normal source of food and supplies. This left the free-roaming bands little choice than to beg, or more often than not, steal what they wanted and needed. Having already left the authority of their officers, and thus becoming fugitives and deserters, these men seldom saw any harm in adding theft and other depredations to their growing list of sins. With the exception that Southern soldiers added an occasional "please" or "thank you" after taking the food right out of a farm family's mouths, the color of the uniform they wore made no difference.

"You must stop thinking about yourself and your precious little farm, Mary Beth," her aunt scolded as if Mary Beth were still a girl of ten. "Your mother, the poor dear soul, just isn't up to this sort of thing. With her mind already gone and her body not far behind, I can't see how she can survive out there, alone with you, in the middle of nowhere, with a battle coming."

Biting her tongue, for her aunt was truly trying to help, Mary Beth patiently explained that the farm was not exactly in the middle of nowhere. "We're less than three miles from town. Besides," Mary Beth countered, "the chances of a battle taking place right there, in our own front yard are small. Why, Auntie, I'm willing to wager that you're in more danger, there in town, than we are here. After all, anyone trying to get through the town has to pass right by your house while no one in their right mind would want to bother our little place so far off the beaten path."

Making a face, as she often did when someone she considered her junior talked back to her, her aunt said, "At least let your mother come back with me. Then you're free to go out and dig in the dirt all day long while I give my sister the attention her delicate condition demands."

Mary Beth, offended at the implication that she was incapable of caring for the farm and her own mother, felt the hair on the back of her neck begin to bristle. "I can manage, thank you," she responded slowly, stiffly. "Mother will do much better here, in her own bed, than . . ." She was about to say "in town with you nagging and lording over her" but didn't. At the last minute, Mary Beth caught herself and ended instead by saying, as sweetly as she could, "adding to your already overwhelming burden."

Catching her niece's sudden pause and change in demeanor, Mary Beth's aunt stood up and prepared to leave. "If you change your mind," she barked, "you're free to come to town with us, both of you."

Standing up, Mary Beth pulled away from the door as her aunt made for it. "I know that, Auntie dear. And I do appreciate your concern, I really do."

Looking at Mary Beth out of the corner of her eye as she adjusted her hat before leaving, the older woman said nothing. She was not used to not getting her way and always took any objection to her views and opinions as a personal affront. She began to leave, but hesitated at the door for a moment as she turned her head sideways and called over her shoulder. "Don't wait," she cautioned, "until the last minute. Your mother's health is failing and she can't take as much as she used to."

Irritated by the way her aunt always had the last word, Mary Beth found it all but impossible to bite her tongue. But she did. "If things get out of hand, we'll come."

For the longest time, Mary Beth stood where she had been when her aunt had left, looking at the closed door. Finally, with a hint of a tear in the corner of her eye, she looked up at the ceiling and shook her head. "If things get out of hand?" she asked as if she were talking to someone upstairs. "*If?* Dear Lord, what more can you heap upon me? *What?*"

Though she seldom gave in to tears or self-pity, the harsh realities that faced Mary Beth every day sometimes were too overwhelming to ignore or keep penned up inside. At a time when farms all around hers were still prospering, despite the war, the farm that had belonged to their family since the days before the First War of Independence was failing miserably. It wasn't because she hadn't tried. On the contrary, every waking hour of every day not taken up in caring for her mother was spent in the fields and small garden she had nursed through the long, hot summer. It was cruel, backbreaking work, made harder by the lack of a plow horse of any kind or another pair of skilled, helping hands. Added to this was a dearth of new seed, no animal manure to fertilize with since there were no more animals, and a genuine lack of knowledge on her part.

"Why," she pleaded to her long-departed father, "didn't you teach me something useful, instead of reading? Why," she now demanded, "did you let me fill my head with silly dreams and notions about a world that doesn't exist? *Why?*"

When the faint, weak voice of her mother finally penetrated Mary Beth's gloom, she shook her head and looked around. It wasn't fair, she suddenly realized as she wiped away the lone tear that had managed to escape from the corner of her eye, to blame her father. He had been a good man, who had done well for them all as long as he could. But he was now gone, gone for good and beyond caring. It was up to her, Mary Beth knew, to see herself and her mother through this terrible ordeal. It was up to her to pull in all the crops that were ready for harvest before the armies of lost soldiers descended on her little farm and helped themselves to the fruits of her labors. It was up to her to hide it as best she could. And, she knew, it was up to her to endure. Like her mother's summons, there were only the realities of life, as they presented themselves to her daily, and the task of dealing with them as best she could.

Though Kevin Bannon's unit was deployed in a skirmish line south of Winchester, much as the ad hoc force he had commanded two months before had been at Fort Stevens, all similarities ended there. Everything about the small band of men, from the casual manner in which the soldiers of his old company carried themselves to the worn and faded, but comfortable, uniforms, told all who saw them that these men were veterans. Even the new faces that Kevin wasn't familiar with, bountymen and conscripts who had joined the units in his absence, went about their tasks as if they had been with the rest since the beginning.

There was no problem in rejoining the regiment north of Washington after the engagement at Fort Stevens. Fact was, most of the officers and men treated Kevin as if they expected him to come back, as they would if he had been gone for a short walk in the woods. This didn't disappoint Kevin, who was never one to be fawned over. Rather, he was quite glad that he was allowed to slip back into his old comfortable routine without fuss.

As Sergeant John O'Keeth walked with quick and purposeful strides to where Kevin stood, he studied the thin line of men facing to the south. Most were lying prone on the ground, watching to their front as they cradled their rifles under them. Others, unfazed by the firing on the right, where the 15th New Jersey was engaged in a lively fight with Confederate skirmishers, busied themselves with other activities. Some were on their backs or sitting upright, looking about, chatting idly, or digging in their haversacks in search of a cracker or hunk of bacon to nibble on. O'Keeth, like Kevin, knew the men and their abilities, so he didn't bother to correct those who were being less than vigilant. When the time came, even those who were obviously sound asleep would be up and firing for all they were worth.

Reaching a point close enough to Kevin where he could speak and be heard with a normal voice, O'Keeth began to render his report. "Neither the Tenth New Jersey on the left nor the company on the right has anything to report, sir. Seems the Rebs aren't in any particular hurry to push us aside."

Kevin didn't respond immediately. Instead, he looked over the heads of his men out into the distance. Then he took a quick, nervous glance to the rear. "Well, I hope that's the case. I don't much care for this game of bluff we're playing without a single regiment in support." The eight hundred men of the Jersey Brigade, even with the 3rd New Jersey Cavalry, was not much of a rear guard. Kevin, and practically every officer in the brigade, knew this and was anxious to pull back and be done with this duty. "I can understand Sheridan's desire to keep the Rebs in check," he mused more to himself than to O'Keeth, "while he finishes moving the Army north. It makes sense. I only wish he would have left a bit more here than what he did."

Sharing his company commander's concern, O'Keeth looked toward the setting sun. "Well, we won't need to fiddle about out here, in the open like this, much longer."

Turning to face the west, Kevin nodded in agreement. "Yes, praise the

Lord. If the enemy can be a little patient just a little longer, they can have Winchester, with both my compliments and General Sheridan's."

O'Keeth laughed. "Not much left in that town that's worth defending, is there?"

"No, Johnny, not much at all. I suppose that's why it's changed hands so many times." A sudden flareup of fire over in the 15th New Jersey's area caused both men to look in that direction. Kevin listened as he watched attentively.

"Why not pull out now?" O'Keeth asked slowly. "We've done our job. We've delayed the enemy most of the day. I'm sure the rest of the Army is well on their way to being ready north of town."

Turning his head slowly, Kevin smiled. " 'Theirs not to reason why.' "

Though he had heard those lines somewhere, O'Keeth couldn't place them. Seeing the quizzical look on his second sergeant's face, Kevin decided not to finish the line of poetry. An old Irish brickyard worker had once told him and his brother, James, that if you talk about something bad too much, it will come true. Instead, Kevin turned his attention to other things. "Corporal Miller ready with the reserve?"

"Yes, sir, he is." Then, as an afterthought, he added, "I hope you don't mind me putting Miller in charge there. I thought it was more important to have Yonts up on the line rather than with the reserve."

"Oh, there's no need to explain. I wish I had thought of that myself. Miller's a good soldier and will do well where he is." Kevin made a face. "He's a little on the quiet side, but he seems to do well."

"Yes, sir, he does. Fact is," O'Keeth hesitantly added, "I wish more of the men were like him, keeping to themselves and being a little more respectful of others, I mean."

"You know," Kevin said almost absentmindedly, "my wife has said the same thing, several times."

The mention of Harriet made O'Keeth blush and look away from Kevin. News that his commander had finally married her had crushed a long-held and cherished notion that O'Keeth had harbored since he had first laid eyes on Harriet in late 1862. Though he knew the odds were nil of a high-born woman like her seeing anything in a common man like himself, O'Keeth had always dreamed, that maybe, somehow, she would see that he was just as good a man as Captain Bannon was. Such fantasies, however, were foolish and, O'Keeth knew, a waste of effort. Still . . .

A shout from Corporal Yonts, down on the line, drew both men out of their own private thoughts and back to the situation their unit faced. Looking beyond the thin blue line of skirmishers, Kevin caught sight of two lines of Rebel skirmishers closing fast toward his own. "It seems, Johnny, they're not going to wait till sundown."

Swallowing hard, O'Keeth nodded. "Well, I guess we expected as much, didn't we?"

"That we did," Kevin agreed. "Now get back down to the left and keep an eye on the flank for me. If the Tenth starts to move back, you let me know right away."

Without responding, O'Keeth took off at a fast trot. Along the line, the men who had been asleep or doing other things were quickly turning their full attention to the closing enemy, though some of the harder cases continued to stubbornly chew the last piece of bacon they had started on. Those who had been up and alert, studied their opponent.

The appearance of the enemy skirmishers was, in itself, bad enough. Kevin's men, like the rest of the 4th New Jersey, were spread out ten paces and, in some places, were apart even more. The enemy, on the other hand, not only had two lines of skirmishers coming at them in much tighter ranks, with no more than five paces between men as Hardee's book on tactics prescribed, but they were also backed by two solid lines of infantry deployed in line of battle. With luck, Kevin reasoned, they would be able to hold them till dark. But only, he knew, if the enemy didn't get too aggressive and pitch right into the 4th New Jersey.

As the firing opened along the line, Kevin moved over to the shelter of a tree that was midway between his firing line and the small reserve Corporal Miller was holding back behind the cover of a stone fence. Glancing back, he stared at Miller until Miller, scanning the front, locked eyes with him. "Send no one forward," Kevin warned, "unless I tell you. You may have to cover our retreat." Miller, understanding Kevin's concern for their predicament as well as his orders, gave his commander a nod. Satisfied that all was in order, and with little more to do, Kevin, as much concerned about what was going on to either side of his small command as what was to its front, watched as the two uneven lines of skirmishers began to trade shots.

Slowly the fight began to take shape. From their positions behind any convenient rock outcropping, tree, or depression, the soldiers of his company fought their own private war with the oncoming horde of Confederate infantry. Each of his men, Kevin noted, went about their tasks in slightly different manners and at slightly different speeds. There were some, mostly the older veterans who, it seemed, had been with the company forever. They took their time with everything. When firing, they'd rise from behind their cover, slowly, smoothly, as they brought their rifles to bear on a target. Then, once they had their mark, there would be a moment of hesitation as the rifleman took his bead. The flash and telltale puff of smoke from firing came only when all was ready. Even then, the old fellows would take their time as they drew back behind cover to begin the process of reloading. They, James knew from hard experience, were the real killers. Those who were excitable, who did things quickly, were more often than not simply fillers in the ranks, men to add to the mass of a unit and little more.

As his eyes swept down the line, pausing here and there, he could pick out, without any trouble, which of his command were the fillers. Unlike the steady, methodical movements of the killers, these men were quick, almost jumpy in everything they did. One man Kevin watched reminded him of a chicken as the soldier's head popped up and down around the edge of the rock he was using for cover in rapid, jerky moves. When he did fire, it was done in the same quick manner, and usually with the muzzle angled so high over the rock that the odds of hitting something even near the enemy had to be less than nil. While doing no physical damage to the massive number of enemy soldiers before them, their rapid, wild shooting at least added to the appearance and credibility of the Union's line.

Others, Kevin knew, and sighed, as he spied a soldier here and there cowering behind his cover, were doing little or nothing to contribute to the unit's effort. The bolder of the slackers would, with great trepidation, attempt to peek around the corner of their concealment. More often than not, a near miss, smacking the nearby ground and throwing up dirt, or zinging menacingly overhead was more than enough to dissuade these timid souls from continuing any activity that was remotely hazardous. Usually, their attention was drawn to the rear, where safety lay. Every now and then, Kevin's eyes would meet those of one of these men for a moment. Though he was never quite sure what his own eyes and expression betrayed to them, there was little doubt that most were mortally embarrassed by their performance, and perhaps, even by their own thoughts. With few exceptions, these brief exchanges ended when the soldier, unable to stand the glare of his commanding officer, averted his eyes and bowed his head.

It was during one of these staring contests that Kevin became painfully aware of a feeling that had, for years, eluded him. After watching one particularly fidgety individual, whom Kevin suspected of preparing to bolt for the rear as soon as he could, Kevin decided to go over to him for the purpose of either steadying him or putting the fear of God in him. He had done that many a time. At Crampton's Gap, he had led the company up South Mountain without ever feeling his feet hit the ground of those precipitous heights. At Chancellorsville, he had pushed, and dragged, and boldly led a ragtag unit of Dutchmen in a last-ditch effort to stem the smashing Confederate flank attack. And at Spotsylvania Court House, he had stood in a grueling fire, serving an abandoned field piece.

But something had been missing then, something that Kevin now found he had rediscovered. Fear. Fear of physical harm, so keenly missing on those other occasions, that his recent wounds had awakened. The chill he felt, as he tried to stand upright in preparation for dashing over to the errant soldier, was like nothing he had ever felt before. For a second, he paused, as if to determine if that chill was, in fact, imaginary or if he had really been hit again.

After thinking about what had just happened, Kevin found himself wishing he had been hit. He had often been told that, once wounded, many men lose their nerve and are no longer fit for combat. Rumors, rampant after Spotsylvania, hinted that General Winfield Scott Hancock, Second Corps' commander and the hero of Gettysburg, suffered this, which was why his performance there was so lackluster. That he, Kevin Bannon, should be stricken with such a fear was, once he thought about it, almost horrifying. Why, he wondered, hadn't he felt this way at Fort Stevens? Why now, when so much was at stake?

Stuck between trying to go forward and dealing with a sudden mental panic, Kevin didn't hear Johnny O'Keeth's frantic calls at first. Only when O'Keeth rose and began to run to where Kevin crouched behind the cover of his tree did Kevin snap out of his troubling thoughts.

"The Tenth is giving way!" O'Keeth yelled as calmly as he could, so as not to unsettle the men on the firing line. "The Rebs are rolling up the flank."

With a quick jerk to the left, Kevin looked over in time to see scattered blue figures, the remains of the 10th New Jersey's skirmish line, making their way to the rear with all possible speed. Snapping his head to the right, Kevin listened to the volume and direction of the firing coming from the 15th New Jersey's fight, which told him that they, too, were giving way. Only to his immediate right, where the rest of the 4th New Jersey was, and in his own front, was the line still holding. But that, he realized, was a mixed blessing.

"They're gonna take us in the flank if we don't refuse it, sir," O'Keeth blurted between pants as he tried to catch his breath.

"I know," Kevin snapped as he looked to where his regimental commander should be. "We're losing the right, too."

"Then it's time to go," O'Keeth responded without shame.

"From the sounds of it, it's well past that time. Now," Kevin commanded in as calm and controlled manner as he could manage, "get back there with Corporal Miller and have him deploy his men to cover our retreat. Quickly."

There had been, Kevin realized as soon as he had said it, no need to add the word "quickly." O'Keeth, almost anticipating what Kevin was going to do, was gone, headed over to Miller and the reserve, to carry out his commander's orders even before he had finished giving them. With that taken care of, Kevin again looked to the right, seeing what he hoped he would see. Other companies of the 4th, aware of the mortal danger that was rapidly enveloping them, were already beginning to pull back. "Thank God," Kevin muttered out loud. "I'm not the one who's starting this rout." Why that particular thought would be so important to him at that moment escaped him. What did not was the imperative to get moving.

"COMPANY J!" he shouted as he left the cover of the tree and stepped out into the long shadows of early evening. "Rally on the colors! Rally on the colors!"

No one had to be told twice. Even the dullest had already become painfully aware of the tight spot the collapse of flank units had put them in. A few of the older steady soldiers who had been in the final stages of taking their next shot, hesitated then finished. But most of the men, with the same deliberate purpose that had sustained them throughout the afternoon, responded with speed. A few, reluctant to give ground despite their plight, insisted on firing on the advancing enemy as they fell back while others helped wounded comrades who lagged behind. "Come on," Kevin shouted as men went streaming past him. "Get back with Johnny O and keep heading back to the rear."

One man walking up to where Kevin stood, his rifle resting on his shoulder as if he were returning from a hunt rather than battle, smiled and winked at Kevin. "I was wonderin', Captain, when you'd pull us back."

Kevin nodded at the grimy-faced veteran but said nothing as he nervously waited for the last of his command to pass where he stood. "Come on, men. At the double quick. Get back there and rally on the colors."

A zing followed by another, closer zip left no doubt that the Confederates were as aware of who he was as his own men. As unnerving as this was, Kevin forced himself to stand his ground. He would be the last man back, by God. He was going to face his fears down and do what was expected of him.

Two more near misses, one cutting a neat, clean furrow in the sleeve of his coat caused him to waver, but only for a second. "*Come on*, damn you! Get back here."

The last of his men having finished taking a shot as he stood in the middle of the open field, exposed to every Confederate rifle in sight, finally turned and came up to Kevin. "Why so excited, sir? As I recall, this ain't nothin' compared to Gaines' Mill, now is it?"

Stifling a sudden urge to smash this man's face, Kevin contented himself with a sharply barked order to move and proceeded to follow him to where Miller and the reserve, now acting as rear guard, were opening up a lively fire. Reaching the wall and bounding over it in midstride, Kevin realized that Miller and the reserve were all that was there. Coming down with a heavy thump that sent a stream of pain from his old wounds throughout his body, and fighting the urge to scream in pain, Kevin turned to Miller. "Where's everyone else? Where's O'Keeth?"

"Gone," Miller responded in a husky voice. "The rest of the regiment has already taken off down that road to our rear and O'Keeth, leading the rest of the men in search of the colors, followed."

Though he had intended to rally the company here, and then move back in order, Kevin quickly realized that O'Keeth's mistake had been a fortunate one. Smelling blood, the previously cautious Confederates were up and running, for all they were worth, at them from every direction of the compass except the rear. With no time for anything fancy, no time for explanation, Kevin turned to Miller. "Everyone to the rear, *now*. And run like hell. Hear me," he repeated and he turned his head to shout to the rest of his small reserve, "run like all hell's behind ya."

When the last of his men were up and headed back, Kevin pulled his pistol from his holster for the first time that day, took careful aim at the closest Confederate soldier he saw, and fired. With great satisfaction, he saw the man tumble over backward before he himself turned to join the fleeing remains of his command.

With the close of another battle, and the reoccupation of Winchester by Confederate forces for the umpteenth time, Mary Beth sat in her dark, dingy kitchen, wondering how much more of this she could take. Slowly, she looked about the room, which was lit by a single candle sitting in the center of the table. The deep shadows added an air of gloom to the room. For the first time in a long time Mary Beth realized just how far she had let everything in the house go.

The walls and ceilings, smudged with soot from candles and lamps, were badly in need of cleaning, or even painting. Stray chips of old paint flaked off here and there. The tabletop, lying bare before her except for the lone bowl that had held the watery soup she had managed to fix herself, was spotted and marked where water or food had been spilled and not cleaned for days. And the floor, even in this poor light, betrayed clods of dirt and streaks of mud, dragged in on the soles of Mary Beth's shoes from the fields that had become her entire world.

For the first time, the idea of leaving this house, for good, popped into her mind. How wonderful, she thought, to be rid of the terrible burden that her once-beloved farm had become. How grand it was to imagine herself free to lie in a clean bed, warm and rested, with nothing to do but dream about the future and far-off places as she had done so many times before as a child. What a blessing, she thought, total destruction of this house, this prison of hers, would be.

A sudden shot from somewhere outside snapped Mary Beth back to the harsh realities of the present. Soldiers, Union and Confederate, were out wandering about in the darkness, hunting each other like animals. Standing, Mary Beth was about to leave the kitchen and rush to her mother's room to comfort her when a painful yelp from outside, like that of a stricken animal, caught her attention. Against her better judgment, she took the candle from the table, moved to the back door, opened it, and stepped out onto the porch.

"Damn," Miller hissed.

Surprised to hear his mild-mannered corporal curse, Kevin turned to find out what was wrong. The sight of a woman, standing on the porch of the house, holding a candle up high, however, explained Miller's indiscretion. Turning to the two other men who were holding a third man, squirming and grimacing in pain, Kevin whispered. "Can't you keep him quiet?"

Exasperated, one of the pair, Amos Flatherly, turned to Kevin. "Sir, we're doin' the best we can, but the lad's in a great deal of pain."

A twinge, feeling more like a sympathetic pain than a real one, shot through Kevin's exhausted and weary frame. Heaving a sigh, Kevin nodded. "I know, I know." Then he turned to watch the woman. He hadn't quite decided whether it was better to keep going and hope his man survived the ordeal or stop and seek help from one of the local farmers.

"Think she saw us?" he asked Miller after a moment.

"Well," Miller responded blandly, "she definitely heard us."

Together, the two lay as still as they could in the tangled foliage that had grown up along the roadside fence and watched as the woman continued to scan for the source of the noise.

Having spent her entire life on a farm, Mary Beth knew the difference between an animal's cry of pain and a human's. The one she had just heard had been, without doubt, human. Standing on the porch, she looked about in the dim light provided by the flickering candle and the moon as she listened for another telltale sound in the still summer air. The question of what she would do when she heard it only slowly began to creep into her brain. There wasn't much, she knew, she could do. The Army Colt pistol that had once belonged to her brother Will would be of no use to her. She hadn't touched it since she stuffed it away under some old sheets in a dresser the very same day James Bannon had given it to her in May, 1863. Only once, when some of Mosby's men had taken her horse, had she been tempted to use it.

A rustle of the bushes along the side of the road startled her and caused her to step back, toward the door of the house, as she turned to search for its source.

"Please," a male voice called out, "don't be afraid. We won't harm you."

Even in the faint light, Kevin Bannon could see that the look on the young woman's gaunt face was more of concern than fear. Still, she was already halfway back to the door and ready to flee the rest of the way if she had to. "Miss, please don't run. We need your help."

"There's nothing I can do for you," Mary Beth shot back instinctively. The voice had a Northern accent, not unlike that of James'. "Your men have already taken everything worth taking and there's precious little left for us."

"We're not here for food, miss," Kevin hastily explained as he slowly took a few steps closer. "We have a man, a wounded man that . . "

"I'm no doctor," Mary Beth snapped as she took another step back toward the door to counter his advance. "If you need help, best you give yourselves up to the provost guard. They'll have a doctor with them."

Despite his exhaustion, Kevin chuckled. "Ma'am, it was the provost guard that shot my soldier. And, besides, I'm not about to give myself up just so I can be locked away in Richmond. I've been there once before as a prisoner and don't intend to go there again."

Though she was still on guard, Mary Beth felt that there was no real danger and relaxed some. "Seems to me," she countered, "if you're truly concerned about the well-being of your wounded soldier, you'd swallow your pride and do the right thing."

Kevin shook his head. "I'm not asking a whole lot, miss. All I'm asking you to do is let us leave him here, on your porch if need be, till the Reb . . . I mean Confederate provost guard comes by here. I'm sure they'll be along soon, seeing as they're looking for us and the rest of our brigade."

Mary Beth shook her head. "I'll not take responsibility for your soldier. What if he dies before someone who knows what they're doing comes? Then what do I do? Who's going to help me bury him? You? My sickly mother? And what happens if the provost guard doesn't believe my story about you just up and leaving him? They'll burn my house for harboring the enemy. No, sir. I'm really very, very sorry about your friend being hurt. But I just can't. I can't."

A moan from the bushes, where Miller and Flatherly still lay hidden, spurred Kevin on to keep trying. "Listen, miss, we all have a couple days' rations with us, in our haversacks. Fresh coffee, sugar, bacon, crackers, and such. If you just watch my soldier until some of your people come by, we'll leave all the rations we have with you."

She was about to turn down the Yankee's offer without a second thought when it dawned on her that coffee and sugar, commodities that were more valuable, pound for pound, than gold in the exhausted Confederacy, would make wonderful trading material when the starving time came that winter. As hazardous as taking the wounded Yankee might be, the offer of such treasures was simply too good to turn down.

Seeing her eyes lower as she weighed his offer, Kevin stepped closer to the porch, coming into the small arch of light that her candle threw out. When she finally looked up after having made up her mind, she looked into his eyes, started to speak, then without any explanation, gasped. Fearful that he had frightened her by inching forward, Kevin froze. "Please," he pleaded hastily as he raised his right hand to show he meant no harm, "I didn't mean to . . ."

Leaning back against the door frame, Mary Beth lifted her hand up to her chest and took a deep breath. "Oh," she exclaimed as soon as she could. "No, that's not it. It's just that you . . ." Another moan from the bushes cut through the still night air before Mary Beth could explain that, for a moment, she thought that the Yankee officer was her dead brother's best friend.

"Please," she called out as she regained her senses, "have your people bring the poor soul up and into the house. He can use my brother's room."

Not quite sure what had just happened and concerned that he not offend the woman, now that she was giving way, Kevin stayed where he was as he directed Miller and Flatherly to carry their wounded comrade out from the bushes and into the house. As they passed where he was standing, he whispered to them to leave all their rations with the woman and hurry out. After they had disappeared into the house, he took off his own haversack and emptied it of those personal items he wanted to keep, stuffing them into his pockets. When he was finished, he advanced to the porch, laid his haversack up against one of the posts, and stepped back to where he had been to wait for his men to reappear.

Without a word, both Miller and Flatherly came out of the house, followed by the woman who stopped in the doorway. "I left my haversack and rations there," Kevin told the woman as he motioned toward the post. "It's all we have."

Mary Beth, despite herself, forced a smile. "I'm much obliged. I'll tend to your man until someone comes by. Then it'll be up to them." As an afterthought, she added, "Make sure you tell your people that I did the best I could and that I'm no doctor. I don't want your cavalry coming by here when your army comes back, looking to revenge your friend if he should pass on."

Kevin nodded. "Fair enough. I'll do what I can." Turning, he began to walk away followed by Miller and Flatherly, then stopped. Removing his cap, he gave a slight bow. "I thank you, miss, for all your kindness. And who, shall I say, was of such assistance?"

For a moment, Mary Beth hesitated. Was it, she wondered, a good idea to give this man her name? After all, she thought, he was lost and probably had no way of directing anyone back to her house. Still . . . "McPherson. This is the McPherson farm."

Satisfied, the officer nodded, replaced his cap, and disappeared into the darkness, leaving Mary Beth to marvel at the resemblance that the young captain bore to her own James.

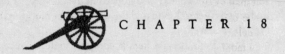

CHAPTER 18

Winchester, Virginia, September, 1864

STILL GRUMBLING THAT THEY had not been allowed a day's rest after their grueling march the previous day, few of the handful of men who still called themselves the 4th Virginia paid heed to the rumble of cannon and rifle fire in the distance. "Nothin' more than our daily brush with the Yank skirmishers," Dale Wint confidently told Daniel McPherson, who kept stretching his neck out of the ranks in an effort to see toward the head of the column. "It'll all be over before we even get close."

"And praise the Lord for that," a former seminary student from Washington University by the name of Fielding Spencer called out. "We don't need to go poking our noses into every fight this Army gets itself into, now do we?"

Daniel looked over at Spencer for a moment. He wanted to challenge him, as he often did when someone even mentioned shirking what Daniel took to be their duty, but hesitated. Instead, he looked behind him, down the ranks to where James Bannon marched, head bowed low and eyes glued to the dirt road, bringing up the rear of the company. For a moment, he thought about making his way back to where James was, and asking him what he thought. Then as quickly as that idea came to him, he dismissed it. Since breaking off their attack just short of Washington, D.C., James had been in a dark, forbidding mood. Whenever Daniel, and practically everyone else in the company, approached James to talk about something, anything, James either snarled or simply turned and walked away.

"Leave him alone," Wint cautioned Daniel one evening after James had snapped at him. "That man's carrying three years of war all penned up inside of him," Wint tried to explain, "and a whole lot more." When Daniel asked Wint to explain, Wint simply turned and stared into the fire for a moment before responding. "Perhaps," Wint mused, "someday he'll feel ready to share his burden with someone like he used to do with your brother Will. And maybe, he'll keep it with him, all the way to the grave. There's no way of knowing these things, boy." Then Wint looked at Daniel with the same stern expression that Daniel's own father had used when he was trying to make a point. "I'll tell you straight up, Danny. It's best to leave such things alone, 'cause no amount of prodding, even by a man's dearest love, can shake out the ghosts that haunt a man's soul, not till he's ready to let them go. If you value your friendship, you'll leave him be."

Though Wint's conversations seldom concerned anything of significance, Daniel somehow knew that what he said on the matter of James was right. Having seen fewer than a dozen battles and skirmishes, and their ugly aftermath, Daniel was able to appreciate that they were nothing in comparison to what James had endured. "Do you think," Daniel asked after a few moments of silence, "James will ever be the same after all this is over?"

With a twinkle in his eye, Wint was about to laugh, but then cast his eyes down. When he looked up at Daniel again, Daniel thought he could see the hint of a tear in the crippled old soldier's eyes. "Boy," Wint responded softly, "there ain't none of us that will ever be the same again, ever."

Daniel continued to stare at James, thinking about what Wint had said and wondering what horrors had turned a man who had been so much like his own brother into such a wreck of a human being. These thoughts and the idle chatter of tired men all about him drowned out the slowly rising crescendo of cannon and rifle fire to the east.

At that moment, it wasn't past battles or lost friends that tormented James' troubled mind. It was Douglas Geddy. Shortly after turning their backs on the Federal capital, Geddy had reappeared in the thin ranks of the brigade. Everyone, especially James, was quite surprised by this. "What's the matter," Dale Wint had chided, "forget which way the rear was or 'fraid of the big bad Yank cavalry?" While Geddy chafed under these, and other blistering remarks, it dawned upon James that as much as he despised Geddy, he shared a common trait with him. They were both cowards.

That thought, when it first popped into James' head, struck him as odd. After all, his performance over the past three years seemed to indicate otherwise. Hadn't he, James rationalized, stood shoulder to shoulder with the best and bravest Virginia had to offer in battle after battle without flinching, without giving an inch till all hope was lost? Hadn't he stayed with his comrades, through the worst of times, starving and freezing near to death for a cause that wasn't even his? And hadn't he come back to his regiment, time and time again, when logic dictated that he do otherwise?

While these were all true, and those who knew him admired him for having done so, the reason, James realized, he had stayed with the 4th Virginia was no different than the reason that kept Geddy coming back, again and again. After giving the matter serious thought, James concluded that they were both afraid, afraid of what would happen once they strayed from the narrow confines of duty prescribed by military law and the society they lived in. "It's a hard thing," James had muttered to Dale Wint over a picket fire one night while they stood watch, "to figure out what is right and what is wrong." Not sure he followed what James was driving at, Wint had simply nodded and let James go on. "But even when a man finally does realize what's right for him and what needs to be done," James concluded as he stumbled slowly through his one-sided conversation, "it seems it's even harder to do something about it. All my life," James continued to muse, "I've found it so easy to shut my mouth and do what was expected. While I fought everything from my father and the whole Union Army to my feelings, I was fighting out of anger, not conviction." Turning to look into Dale's incredulous eyes, James ignored the vacant stare he was being given and continued. "I've done everything that was expected of me, and nothing that was right. Every time I came face-to-face with a real decision, a real choice, I buckled." He almost added "just like Geddy," but didn't. Such a confession, spoken out loud, would have truly confused a friend who was already befuddled by James' ramblings.

• • •

Since that night, these thoughts, and what to do about them, had never been far from James' mind. Neither had Mary Beth. In all his trials, personal as well as physical, the memory of her had always come through, like a shining beacon, to calm his worst fears and give him the courage to carry on. That he had ignored her for so long, that he had denied his true feelings about her, especially after his last disastrous visit to her in early July, troubled James now as much as his self-comparison to Geddy did. He would, he decided, do more than make simple amends to the one person who touched his heart. He would, he realized as he trudged along through the choking dust kicked up by hundreds of feet, have to make a commitment, one unlike any he had ever made before in his life. At that moment, he decided, for better or for worse, he would ask Mary Beth to marry him.

James didn't have much time to reflect on this decision, however, as his trained ear, like an alarm, detected a change in the battle's tenor. Picking his head up, he looked to one side, then the other. His eyes followed a staff aide who whipped his lathered horse along the side of the long column of troops to the rear. Straightening up, he waited for the order to pick up the pace that followed as surely as he had expected it.

"All right, boys," Lieutenant Roberts bellowed after General Terry rode by, repeating the order to close up and step off smartly. "There's a fight up ahead and we're needed."

"Ah, hell, Lieutenant!" Douglas Geddy moaned. "Why us? How come we always have to rush in and save the day?"

"Ha!" Wint snorted. "When in blazes was the last time you ever rushed anywhere with this here Army, Geddy, except when it was time for chow?"

The chorus of laughter was cut short by Geddy's angry reply. "You shut your mouth, you gimpy old coot, or . . ."

Wint did a sharp about-face and pushed his way back through the ranks till he faced Geddy, who had stopped in the middle of the road when he came face-to-face with Wint. "Or you'll what, boy?" Wint demanded.

James, though he would have loved to see Geddy knocked on his rear, was just as anxious to save Wint from himself. Pushing up the ranks, James shoved his arm under Wint's and spun him around without stopping. "This isn't the time, Dale."

Angry at being handled so, Wint stopped, pulling his arm free from James. "I'll be the judge of that, Jimmy. You hear?" Then thumping his chest, he repeated his proclamation. "*I'll* be the judge."

Roberts, who had been busy trying to see what was going on up front, heard Wint's second cry of defiance. Not knowing what was going on, and determined not to let anything interfere with the movement of his tiny command into battle where he could lead it forward into glory, Roberts cocked his head back to the rear and shouted over the growing noise of battle, men grunting under their burdens, the shuffling of feet and clanging of loose equipment. "Keep it closed up and keep the noise down in the ranks."

Though not mollified completely, Wint shook himself off, brushed the arm James had grabbed, and stepped off before the rear of the company had passed him. Though James couldn't understand the words Wint mumbled under his breath, he was satisfied that his old companion was over his fit of anger and ready to carry on.

Toward late morning, Gordon's division, with Terry's brigade in the lead, reached the fringe of the battle already well progressed. General Terry maneuvered his brigade of Virginians on a plateau crowned by the fields of an old farmstead owned by a Revolutionary War hero, deploying them behind the cover of a stand of trees that separated his men from the Union. Making their way south past and around batteries firing furiously to the east, James could see the end of another division, Rhodes' division someone said, ahead. Just as they came out from behind the cover of the trees, not far from the end of Rhodes' left flank unit, the brigade was halted, given a left into line, and halted. Brigadier General Zebulon York's brigade of Louisianans, following the Virginians, did likewise, forming up to the left, or north, of Terry's men.

When the order to lie down was given, James and most of the rest of the old 4th Virginia dropped to the ground without a mutter while skirmishers were shaken out and sent to the woods. Lieutenant Roberts, excited by the prospect of battle, nervously paced back and forth in front of the line, his gauntleted hands held tightly together behind his back. "It's going to be a standup fight, by God!" he cheerfully exclaimed. "No hiding behind breastworks and waiting for them to come at us. A real standup fight."

Finished sipping from his canteen, James looked over at his enthusiastic commander and made a face. Fielding Spencer, who had belonged to another company of the 4th before being brigaded together with James' old company, saw the look James gave Roberts and chuckled. "Kind of makes one wonder," Spencer said in a low voice, "where he's been these past few years." Then, as he looked around the barren hill they were perched on, Spencer shook his head. "Call me a yellow-bellied coward, but I'd gladly give a whole month's pay, all eleven worthless Confederate dollars, for one good log to snuggle up behind."

Looking around, James caught sight of their division commander, General John Gordon, mounted upon a splendid black charger. With the same cool, detached demeanor that he perpetually wore, Gordon watched the Union troops deploy under the steady fire of Confederate guns and the sniping of numerous skirmishers. Spencer, seeing James studying their general, moaned. "Oh, Lord, I hope he doesn't speak."

Surprised by this statement, James asked Spencer, "What do you mean?"

"Well, you know what I mean, Jimmy. Seems like every time that man opens his mouth, he makes the dead want to rise up and follow him to the gates of hell itself."

Wint, lying flat on his back as he always did when given the chance, spoke through the hat that covered his face. "Yeah, that one does seem to have a way with words. I'll bet he could even get old Geddy excited enough to whistle 'Dixie.' "

Both Spencer and James looked at each other and grinned. "Dale," James responded, "I don't think even the Lord on high could manage that one."

As James and some of the others chatted away the idle time, ignoring the growing battle that promised to swallow them up, Daniel found himself mesmerized by it. Tightly gripping his rifle, the sixteen-year-old boy watched the masses of blue as they maneuvered and began to press forward against the lines of gray deployed to their left. How strange, Daniel thought, to be sitting here, doing nothing while men, just like him, were fighting for their lives a few hundred yards away. It all seemed so unreal, so contrived, as he watched individual shells from the batteries behind him streak overhead. The burning fuse of each shell traced its arc across the pale blue sky, descending on the tight Union formation like a shooting star. Then, just as it was about to drop out of sight, it burst in a brilliant star explosion of black smoke and flaming red and yellow fire, raining grape and shrapnel down on the hapless victims below. Even from this distance, Daniel could see men scatter as comrades, who a second before had been beside them, were struck down by the ugly death from above. Men were dying over there, he told himself. Real men, just like him, just like his brother Will. Yet somehow, at this distance, he felt nothing, nothing at all, except a strange fascination for the spectacle that was being played out before him.

Douglas Geddy, lying flat on the ground in front of Daniel in the spot James always placed him, watched too. Like a deer faced with danger, Geddy watched, his only motion being to mechanically tear away at the grass that lay under his hand. It seemed, Daniel observed, that everyone in the company, except for him, Geddy, and Roberts, was uninterested in what was going on out there. It was almost as if none of the others understood what was about to happen to them.

Daniel, of course, was wrong. It only took the scurrying back of the line of skirmishers who had been fighting stubbornly in the woods covering Gordon's division to transform the mass of idle men into a line of battle. James, pushing himself up off the ground and looking toward the woods where dense clouds of smoke spewed, studied the scene for a moment. "Well, boys," he said to no one in particular as he watched groups of Atkerson's brigade flee the burning woods, "looks like we're in for a hot one."

Wint cocked his head, spat on the ground, and shook his head. "It's not a good sign, not in my book, when the Georgians run like that."

Unlike the other two, a strange grin lit up Fielding Spencer's face. "Guess you know what that means."

Looking behind, James caught sight of Gordon, his horse literally straining to surge forward as if it sensed its master's next order. It wasn't long in coming.

"Forward," the command rang down the ranks. Like a surging tide, regiment after regiment, starting with those closest to the center, with their brigade commanders stepped off toward the woods. Advancing, grim-faced and determined now, the men of the 4th Virginia watched the Union officers before them struggle with the milling mass of blue soldiers as they attempted to re-form their scattered and winded commands back into some semblance of order before the wave of butternut and gray broke upon them. The urge to pick up the pace and storm forward at a dead run was checked by individual soldiers as well as their officers. To have done so too soon would have exhausted them before contact, thus losing the momentary advantage of their numbers and sheer weight of attack. As tempting as it was to move forward with all possible haste in order to take advantage of the confusion in the Union ranks, Gordon, Terry, and every commander knew this fight was just beginning. To exhaust their commands now, in the first rush, would be foolish.

Even after the order was given, the restraint that only a well-disciplined veteran unit could muster kept the men together. For some, this discipline came from the realization that all of them, smashing into the Union in mass, were far more devastating than the impact of individuals flinging themselves into their foe's midst. For others, the reason for holding back was more utilitarian. There is, even when advancing fully erect and exposed to enemy fire, the comfort of knowing that you are one of many, just another faceless figure in an onrushing avalanche of flesh and bone. For a soldier to go out in front of the others, or to lag behind, would be to call unwanted attention to himself. Far better, the old soldiers knew, to stay with everyone else.

Long before the impact came, James knew they had won the day. Unwilling to listen to their officers and convinced that death was only a hair's breadth away, the more timid of the Union soldiers to their front turned and made for the rear as quickly as their legs would carry them. Those in the ranks who were of slightly sterner stuff, but still unsure of the outcome, found themselves being instinctively influenced by those whose courage wasn't equal to the task at hand. Though they gave ground more grudgingly, they gave ground nonetheless and added their numbers to the leaderless mass of refugees streaming back to the rear. Only those with more pride than common sense, or simply unaware that the issue was already beyond salvation, stood their ground and met the irresistible wave that carried them back into the woods or cut them down where they stood. There, along with the men who had quit the field earlier, they broke through the ranks of friendly units rushing forward to their support, thus frustrating the efforts of these new units to form an effective defense.

For a moment, James was blinded as he went from brilliant daylight into the dark shade of the woods. Stumbling forward, more by feel than sight, he felt his boot fall upon a prostrate body. Had it been dead or severly wounded and not moved, James wouldn't have given the event second thought. But the figure, far from being dead, suddenly began to rise just as James was bringing his full weight onto it. This threw James off balance and backward. "God damn you," James shouted as he struggled to hold on to his rifle and keep his balance.

The Yankee, a man who had feigned death to escape the fury of the Confederate charge, made it to his feet while James continued to thrash his arms about in an effort to keep from falling over. Had the man taken advantage of this and run for all he was worth, he would have survived, at least for a little while longer. But instead, the Yankee soldier, a blond-haired boy with striking blue eyes frozen open as wide as saucers, stood before James in sheer terror.

Without any conscious thought, without the slightest hesitation, James lifted his rifle up and over his left shoulder as high as he could once he had regained his footing. Then, in a single, smooth motion, he brought it smashing down, butt first, into the unarmed Yankee's face with all the might he could muster. The blond-haired Union soldier crumpled under the impact like a rag doll. By habit, more than out of necessity, James brought the bloody butt of his rifle up high again and rammed it down into the skull of the writhing figure that, once more, lay at his feet. Even through the deafening roar of battle that echoed throughout the smoke-choked woods, James could hear the crunch of bone as he drove his rifle down with all his might. Satisfied that he had done all that was needed here, James hoisted his rifle to the ready and went forward in search of his company, which was already deep in the woods and engaging the next enemy unit.

From her perch on the seat of the hospital wagon, Harriet listened to the familiar sounds of battle. The old worries, and the old fears, all came back to her as if she had never been away. Was it Kevin's brigade, she wondered, that was bearing the brunt of the fight that seemed to treble in intensity with every passing minute? Or was the 4th New Jersey off to one side or the other, waiting to be committed or in reserve? It was, she knew, impossible to know one way or the other.

"Miss Shields . . . I mean, Mrs. Bannon, Dr. White's compliments, ma'am," the orderly sergeant called up from the ground. "He requests your presence, up at the house yonder, immediately."

Happy for the diversion, Harriet looked down at the sergeant and forced a smile. It seemed whenever dear Dr. White was confronted with a particularly delicate matter that he deemed better handled by a woman, he sent for Harriet. She, of course, didn't mind, most of the time, for it gave her value. Still, she often reflected, she did wish that more male doctors learned how to tell other men that they were about to die. "What seems to be the problem this time?"

"Well, ma'am," the sergeant started, barely able to suppress a smirk, "seems there's a crazy old woman keeping the doctor and the other surgeons out of the house they intend to use as our hospital."

Looking ahead, along the column of stalled wagons and ambulances, Harriet could see men waiting, patiently, while the white-coated figure of Dr. White stood at the bottom step of a porch, facing a woman in black holding a broom at the ready. Harriet always found it amusing when the doctors and medical orderlies of the First Division's field hospital found themselves confronted by people that were not overawed by their rank or credentials. *"I think it is wholesome,"* Harriet wrote in her diary, *"that even the noblest of men should, on occasion, be so humbled."*

Easing herself down off the seat and over the wagon wheel, Harriet straightened her plain dark blue skirt, pushed a stray hair back into place, and marched to the head of the stalled column with the orderly sergeant. As they approached, Dr. White caught sight of Harriet and turned to the woman he often complained about but always regarded as essential. "Mrs. Bannon," the exasperated doctor barked even before Harriet was before him. "That woman over there," he stammered as he pointed to the old woman on the porch, "is being more stubborn than an Army mule."

"Oh," Harriet said coyly. "Then that would make her almost as stubborn as you."

Shaking his head, Dr. White stared at Harriet for a second. Throwing his head back and closing his eyes, he stood there for a second before he opened them toward the clear blue sky. "Excuse me," he softly stated, "Mrs. Bannon." Then, with the apology dutifully rendered, he looked back down at Harriet with eyes livid with anger. "Would you be so kind as to explain to that woman that it is of the greatest military necessity that we borrow her house for a while."

"And if she continues to refuse?" Harriet asked playfully.

Dr. White all but jumped. "*I'll* shoot the old hag," he exclaimed as he flapped his arms at his side. "*Personally*, if need be. *Now* tell her!"

Having pushed the good doctor as far as she dared, this time, Harriet threw her head back, turned to the house, and walked slowly up the steps. The woman, while she had been prepared to swat the first soldier in blue who dared approach her, hesitated when Harriet appeared. Still, she didn't yield her position. "It won't do you a bit of good," the old woman rasped. "I told those other *people* over there that I had no intention of letting them in here and the same answer holds true with you."

Pausing for a moment, Harriet studied the old woman in black. To say that she was haggard was an understatement. Worry, hunger, illness, and of course, age, had wiped away any traces of youth or beauty that she may have once boasted of. Her skin, even that of her hands, was pale beyond belief with a tinge of gray. And her white hair, disheveled and hanging down about her face as if she had just risen from her bed, reminded Harriet of long, dry grass.

Forcing a smile Harriet looked into the old woman's eyes. "I am truly sorry for all this inconvenience, Mrs. . . . ."

"McPherson," the woman choked out as her eyes narrowed.

"Yes, thank you, Mrs. McPherson," Harriet continued slowly. "But you see, we have need of your house. There is a battle, over there," Harriet indicated pointing to the west, toward Winchester, "and we are a hospital, a field hospital."

"Take your sick and wounded to Winchester, like they did the other boy," Elizabeth McPherson snapped.

Though Harriet knew the old woman wasn't in control of her senses, she hadn't realized it was this bad. "Well, I wish we could, but it's not that easy. You see, we don't have Winchester. The Confederate . . . your Army has the town. We're stuck out here, in the open country and we have to make do with whatever facilities we find. Your house happens to be ideal for our purposes."

Quivering from the exertion needed to hold the broom up, Elizabeth McPherson still managed to shake it at Harriet. "No!"

Slowly the smile left Harriet's face as she looked down for a moment. "I do wish you would reconsider. You see, the surgeon in charge of our field hospital has no choice. We'll have wounded boys, both Union and Confederate, coming back from the front soon. We need someplace where we can care for them."

Unbowed, Elizabeth McPherson barked back in defiance. "Go find some place else. Leave now, or I'll have to go fetch my sons, Will and Daniel."

Frustrated, and realizing that there was no way to reason with this woman, Harriet was about to turn away and admit failure to Dr. White when another woman's voice bellowed across the field next to the house. "*You leave her alone!*"

All eyes turned to watch Mary Beth McPherson as she came charging through rows of high corn, across the narrow space that separated field from house, and pushed her way past Harriet to her mother. Grabbing the broom with one hand and reaching around her shaking mother with the other, Mary Beth turned on Harriet. "What do you people think you're doing?" she screeched. "Can't you see this woman's sick? Don't you have any decency, any compassion?"

Stung by Mary Beth's bitter accusations, Harriet fought her urge to respond in anger. Instead, she took a deep breath and started to explain. "We need to use your house as a field hospital. I was trying to explain that to this woman when . . ."

"We don't want you here," Mary Beth screamed. "None of you or your damned war. You've killed my father and brother and took everything we had until there wasn't anything left for us. All we've got is this farm and each other and I'll not let you take them."

"Well," Harriet snapped, tired of being circumspect, "you don't have much of a choice, I'm afraid. You either give way, and let us in, or these gentlemen behind me will have to remove you and your mother and take the house and do with it as they please. There is a battle going on," Harriet shouted as she pointed toward the sound of the guns. "My husband is out there, with his company, risking his life and those of his men. Some of them are going to be coming back this way soon, wounded. And I'll be damned if the likes of you are going to keep me and the men of this hospital from doing all they can in the best possible facilities we can manage. Now step aside or I'll brush you both aside myself."

The force and viciousness of Harriet's anger startled Mary Beth, impressed Dr. White, and surprised everyone who had been standing behind her watching. As Mary Beth stood on the porch, staring down at Harriet on the ground, it became obvious that she would be forced to yield. Still, she simply could not step aside and let the Yankees take the very last refuge she had. "You keep your men out of my momma's bedroom, you hear," she finally conceded. "And there isn't anyone who's going to run me from my house. So long as you're here, I'm staying to look out for things."

Though she knew Dr. White would like to have been rid of the two Rebel women, Harriet realized that she needed to leave them something, if nothing else than their pride. Managing the best smile she could, Harriet nodded. "That will be most satisfactory. I will help you keep your possessions safe as best as I can."

Though she didn't believe the Yankee woman, Mary Beth knew that she had managed to come off with the best deal she could have managed, given the circumstances. Turning, she led her mother into the house, followed by Harriet and a flood of surgeons, orderlies, medical assistants, and hospital stewards. The wounded would soon be coming back in search of aid and comfort and they needed to be ready.

Long before the orders made their way down to the 4th New Jersey, Kevin Bannon knew he and his men were going to be committed in a desperate bid to save the Union center. The advance by Ricketts' Third Division, which had begun not more than an hour before, had failed miserably, just like an earlier advance by the Nineteenth Corps in some woods farther to the right. And like that fight, the Confederates were following up their bloody repulse of the Union advance with a counterstroke of their own.

Drawing his pistol for the first time that day, Kevin aimed the .44 caliber Army Colt at the ground, pulled the hammer to the half-cocked position, and gave the cylinder a quick spin as he checked to make sure the caps for each of the six individual chambers were still in place. Satisfied that he was ready, he looked at the surging mass of blue, hotly pursued by a wall of gray, as it grew nearer and nearer. He had seen all of this so many times before.

With a deep breath, he stepped out of line and looked down the ranks to where Johnny O'Keeth stood at the far left. "Sergeant O'Keeth," Kevin bellowed above the growing roar of cannon fire, musketry, and hoots and hollers from advancing Rebels, "don't worry about the regiment to the left. That's the field officer's concern. You just keep the ranks closed up toward the center. Understand?"

Kevin, of course, knew that O'Keeth understood. He had, after all, been in almost as many battles as Kevin had himself. The admonition was more a reminder to the men in the ranks who, often in the heat of an intense fight, became so fixated with firing and reloading that they often lost track of what was going on around them. Even old-timers like Thomas Yonts and Amos Flatherly needed an occasional shove from a noncommissioned officer this way or that to keep them closed up and aligned. Stepping back until he could see beyond the rear rank of the company, Kevin caught the attention of Corporal Miller, posted back there to keep an eye open for stragglers and shirkers as well as to help anyone who needed a hand with a fouled rifle. Miller, as was his style, locked eyes with Kevin, gave him a deep nod that he was ready, and then looked away. A good soldier, Kevin thought as he resumed his post, but still, after three years, an enigma.

With forced deliberateness, the order "Forward" rippled down the line from brigade commander to regimental to company officers. Together with the First Division's Second Brigade to the right, the entire New Jersey Brigade stepped off and moved slowly, steadily forward toward the maelstrom that was speeding toward them. Men of Ricketts' division who were fleeing from that fury ran into the Jerseymen at a ravine not long after the advance had begun. Anxious to make their way through the wall of fresh troops coming up and escape the fury of the pursuing Rebels, the panicked men threw themselves at the 4th New Jersey's line. With few exceptions, the ravine, the solid front of the Jersey Brigade's steady units, and the efforts of their own officers checked them. Though they were far from being effective combat units, Kevin watched with great relief as the officers of the shattered commands led their men to the rear to rest and to re-form them. After all, Kevin reasoned, if things didn't go well on the other side of the ravine for the Jerseymen, the very same shirkers that his own men were still jeering at just might be the source of their salvation.

There was little time to dwell on what might happen. No sooner had they managed to climb out of the ravine that had served to break the momentum of the rout of Ricketts' division than the advancing Confederates, flush with victory, were upon them. Fortune, for once, favored the 4th New Jersey and the rest of the Jersey Brigade, for the Confederates' counterattack had left them winded and somewhat disorganized. Staggering through rows of corn that were taller than most of the men, the Rebels were brought to a halt as volley after measured volley slammed into their haphazard ranks.

The enemy, however, did not waver. Even as Kevin watched his men inflict a terrible execution upon the enemy's stalled masses, he could see field officers and senior commanders directing the deployment of supporting forces in preparation for a continuation of the advance. The enemy units already facing Kevin's command were not idle, either. At ranges of less than two hundred yards, they matched the Jerseymen's fire with controlled volleys of their own.

With the range simply too great for his pistol to be effective, and certain that he would need all six shots in due time when one side or the other decided to end this stalemate and close, Kevin contented himself with stalking along the rear of the company. It had been a long time, he realized, since they had been engaged in such an open, standup fight. All the battles in the spring and summer had been deep in thick woods, or had involved assaulting or holding massive breastworks. This battle, he realized, was more like those of 1862. But not quite, he thought, as he looked up and down the ranks of his tiny company. Then, he had a body of men that could reasonably be called a company. Now, he commanded little more than a handful of men. Though they were good men, and the smattering of a few conscripts and bounty men here and there didn't seem to affect their steadiness, they were, nonetheless, a mere shadow of the proud force that he had first drilled near Trenton, New Jersey, three years before.

A hand touched Kevin's sleeve. He turned to face Miller, who stared calmly at him. "The general!" Miller shouted over the din and pointed to a cluster of staff officers that had gathered to the rear. Peering through the whiffs of smoke that drifted over the field, Kevin looked to see what had caused the unflappable Miller to become excited. Then, as one captain turned away and stepped aside, he saw the reason. Brigadier General David A. Russell, a man beloved by the entire brigade and much of the division, was down on the ground. And though Kevin admired Russell, for he had been a good brigade commander, he felt little sorrow. Wasn't it fitting, after all, he reasoned, that the great should share the same fate as those they command? Turning his back on the commotion to the rear, he focused his whole attention on the enterprise at hand, stepping over the body of one of his own men whom no one, as yet, had found time to weep for.

For the better part of half an hour, the two lines of infantry stood their ground, neither giving way as the Confederates, fighting in small knots like Indians rather than using standard infantry tactics, attempted to press forward. Casting a wary eye to the rear every now and then, Kevin could see Ricketts' division taking shape again. Perhaps, he thought, Sheridan was waiting till they were ready to go forward again before pressing his attack. That, however, seemed unlikely, since the entire Eighth Corps, still making its way along the crowded Berryville Pike, had yet to make its appearance.

Deliverance, however, from the building Rebel pressure didn't come from either of these forces. Instead, it was the First Division's own Second Brigade, commanded by Brigadier General Emory Upton, that changed the face of the battle. Deployed earlier to the right, and a little apart from the rest of the division, Upton had held his mixed command of New Yorkers and Connecticut men out of the fray. Only after the Confederates were about to make their way around the right flank of the New Jersey Brigade and unhinge the line the brigade had managed to stabilize did Upton unleash his command. When the head of the enemy column came popping out of the cornfields less than two hundred yards from where he held his men in waiting, Upton himself gave the command. "Ready, aim, fire!"

While these results were devastating, it was his next order, the order to charge, that cinched the victory on this part of the field. As if he were nothing more than a spectator, Kevin watched Upton as he personally led the triumphant sweep of blue that pushed the Confederates, caught off balance by this sudden stroke, before them. Some of Kevin's own men, noticing the enemy fire slacken as more and more of the Rebels turned to retrace their steps, ceased fire and began to cheer. Others, like Amos Flatherly, continued to calmly load and fire his rifle for as long as a target worth shooting at presented itself. Even Miller, frustrated by having to stand idly by all afternoon and watch without firing, took this opportunity to push his way forward, through the ranks, and open fire on the enemy that had tormented them so long.

With the range between them and the enemy increasing, Kevin considered issuing the order for his company to cease fire. It was almost a waste of powder to keep up the fire. Almost. Taking his eyes away from the scene playing itself out before his ranks, Kevin looked down at his pistol. It was still as clean and shiny as it had been when he had drawn it almost an hour before. Looking back up, Kevin decided not to give the order. The men, he knew, were venting their anger, the same anger he himself was feeling. Rather than make the effort to stop them, he decided to let them go. Besides, his mind coldly rationalized, even if just one Rebel went down from all their efforts, it would be one less they would have to face when it came time for the 4th New Jersey to rejoin the fray.

Accompanied by a rousing cheer that echoed across the six hundred yards that separated Gordon's division from them, two fresh Union brigades broke out of the tree line, into the sunlight, and began their advance. With grim expressions that betrayed nothing, James and the hardened soldiers watched them in silence. Only the dry, emotionless pronouncement "Fresh units," muttered by someone near James Bannon, broke the hushed silence in the ranks.

Daniel, having managed to work his way along the ranks every time they had been re-formed until he stood by James, turned to him. "They can't expect us to hold against them, too, James. Can they?"

There was no need to look behind. Even if he could have seen through the smoke-filled carnage of the woods they had fought over, through, and from all afternoon, it would have done him no good. There were no units behind them to come up and relieve them. Like the units to the south of them, now reeling back from a renewed effort by the same Sixth Corps that they had earlier routed, Gordon's men would need to weather the new storm rising from the east with the strength they had. Looking over at his friend's brother with sad eyes, James shook his head slowly. "There's not a thing we can do except hope and pray day gives out before we do."

Though he trusted James implicitly, Daniel's youth would not let him accept such a forlorn forecast. Desperately, he looked from man to man, hoping to find some glimmer of hope, some sign that they were not as yet doomed to an inevitable defeat. Yet as his eyes darted from face to face, filthy and grimy from all their exertions and bitter fighting, he could find nothing of promise to grab on to. Even their enthusiastic young company commander, always ready to burst out in patriotic slogans and preposterous exclamations, stood quietly as he leaned forward on his sword and stared blankly at the coming Union hordes.

Still, as Daniel quickly came to realize, such resignation did not portend submission. On the contrary, when the order "Ready" came, each man still with the regiment brought his rifle up waist high, cocking the hammer of his piece in unison. Only after the enemy had moved well within range did regimental commanders cry out the command "Aim," an order that was echoed by the few company commanders that still stood with their units. With the same cool skill that had marked the old Stonewall Brigade as something special, the men sighted down their long barrels with great deliberateness, intentionally aiming low. Only when the order "Fire!" rang out did the soldiers of Terry's brigade squeeze back on the trigger and let fly a thunderous volley that scythed down scores of Yankee soldiers.

Though effective, the Confederate volley was not enough. Halting only long enough to return the Rebel volley with one of their own, the men in blue let out a deafening cheer and pressed on.

"Right about-face," the command came. "Right about-face and march, quickly." Unlike previous occasions when he had protested such orders with contempt, Lieutenant Roberts pushed his men along through the tangled and body-strewn woods. "Be quick," he repeated as he glanced furtively over his shoulder every time he heard a Union yell behind him.

Coming out into the open, James looked over to his right to see what was going on where the Louisianans and Georgians were deployed. The sight of their lines, already doubled back out of the woods and facing to the north as well as east, told him why they were so quick to give up their hard-won position in the woods. Grabbing Daniel's sleeve, he jerked the young man near to him. "Stay close," he commanded without preamble or explanation. "When I tell you to move, boy, you do as I say and move where I go without looking back. Hear?"

Dumbfounded by James' behavior, Daniel stared at James for a second. In the past, even when the odds were high of their becoming involved in a serious fight, James had always kept him in the rear rank, out of harms way, while he had recklessly exposed himself time and time again. And even though it was obvious to everyone, including someone as inexperienced as he, that things were not going well, Daniel couldn't explain the desperation he suddenly saw in James' eyes.

Though he sensed Daniel's confusion, and in part understood it, James didn't have the time or inclination to spell it out. Instead, he gave Daniel's sleeve a jerk. *"Do you hear me?"*

Almost as frightened by James as he was by the rush of Union troops, Daniel nodded dumbly. "Yes, James, yes. I hear you."

Without another word, James turned away from Daniel and looked out over the open field to the woods they had just evacuated. Already a wall of blue began to come surging out of the trees, first here, then there. "Look to your front," James shouted, in part to Daniel, in part to the rest of the exhausted command. "When you get the order, aim low and keep up your fire."

At other times, hardened veterans would have shot back with snooty remarks that they weren't recruits or that James didn't need to tell them something as obvious as aiming low. But there was none of this. Even the enthusiastic Lieutenant Roberts was silent as he sheathed his sword and drew his pistol, for the first time that day.

Without waiting to reform, the Union units came on as if victory were theirs for the taking. They were met, however, by the devastating fire directed at them not only from Gordon's division, to their front, but by Confederate troops to the right of Terry's who had angled back, to conform with Gordon's retreat from the woods. Wracked front and flank by incessant fire, one valiant effort after another died on the slopes leading up to the plateau where James and Daniel stood, blazing away without let up.

This grim and determined stand against daunting odds was not without cost. Even in the maelstrom of shot and shell, Daniel could not help but catch glimpses of the little horrors that were being played out, literally, at his feet. In the midst of reloading, Daniel watched as Edward Hobson, a quiet, freckle-faced boy not much older than he, jerked upright as if hit by a stone, then collapsed in front of him. Squirming on the ground and howling like a wounded animal, Hobson clutched savagely at his groin in a desperate attempt to stem the flow of blood from a devastating wound. "Oh, Jesus, God! Oh, Jesus!" he shrieked above the clatter of musketry. "Oh, God, Danny," he implored as he looked up at Daniel with eyes alive with agony, fear, and desperation. "I'm killed, Danny. I'm killed. Dear God in heaven," he shrieked, "shoot me, please, *shoooot meee!*"

Of all the horrors and misery he had seen up to that moment and had been a part of, this was the most unnerving, most abhorrent thing he had ever witnessed. Frozen in sheer terror, Daniel watched helplessly as Hobson took one bloody hand off his hemorrhaging wound and grabbed Daniel's ankle. *"Damn you, Danny! Shoot me! Please."*

In all the stories he had heard about the war, in all the books he had read about great battles, in all the classes he had sat through on tactics, nothing and no one, nowhere, had ever spoken to him of things such as this. To kill an enemy soldier, at a range that made him look more like a rag doll than a human being was one thing. To turn your rifle on a man whom you had marched next to, shared your last morsel of food with, huddled together with on cold, miserable nights was simply beyond him. Still, as Daniel's mind blocked out everything around him except the terror and pain in Hobson's eyes and his desperate cries for relief, Daniel felt he had to do something, anything. But what? a voice deep inside screamed. *What?*

Then, like a spear piercing through the blurry bubble that his field of vision had narrowed to, Daniel watched as a long silver barrel appeared from out of nowhere. With one, smooth motion, the muzzle of the silver barrel, gleaming brightly in the late afternoon sun, fell upon Hobson's forehead for a second, then spewed out fire and death that slowly faded away in a fine mist of white smoke tinged with red.

As horrified as he had been at the sight of Hobson writhing about at his feet in agony, Daniel found this sudden and unexpected execution even more repulsive. Jerking his head to the side, Daniel's eyes locked onto James' cold, piercing stare. For a moment, the older man looked into Daniel's eyes as he slowly brought his rifle up and began to reload it in the same methodical way that he always used. To Daniel, stunned that James was capable of such an act, regardless of how justified, it seemed as if James were daring him to say something. Daniel, however, could not. With a single violent convulsion, Daniel doubled over. Dropping his rifle and falling to his knees, Daniel came down on top of Hobson's still body and emptied his stomach in a single heave.

Busy with her own duties, Harriet didn't take notice of what had become of the young woman who had so stoutly defended her home. The wounded waiting to be examined and worked on by the surgeons had quickly swamped the once-prosperous farmhouse. As was normal under such circumstances, these men were laid out in long rows on whatever straw or blankets could be had, if any, and left until their turn came. Making her way along those long rows, carrying a bucket with drinking water and a rag to clean and cool their faces, Harriet closed her heart and mind to the suffering that surrounded her as best she could. "*It is often so very, very hard to turn one's face away from a boy,*" she lamented in her diary, "*that you know no power on earth will be able to save. There are times, too many as of late, when all I want to do is to drop to my knees and scoop up one of these poor, wretched souls, and cradle him in my arms until his time has come. But there are so many, so, so many of them. And there is so little time and, in truth, so little of me left.*"

After writing that last passage, Harriet wondered about what she had said. It was her habit to write whatever came to her mind, to vent her fears, frustrations, anger, and sorrows in words that no one would ever read. Only on occasion, when she had written something as troubling as that one passage, did she reflect on her daily entries. What, she wondered, had she meant by that? Had it been a silent cry of pain, or a warning?

Such personal concerns, however, no matter how troubling, could not be allowed to interfere with her pressing duties. With a heave, she lifted herself off the ground, turning her back on a man with his left forearm lying across his chest, hanging on at the elbow by a few bloody strands of skin and sinew. Turning her attention for a long moment to the next man in line, she studied a boy whose face had been obliterated by a volley of canister. Without needing to give it much thought, she decided that there was little she could do for him. With a sigh, Harriet moved past him. As she did so, she noticed her water bucket was near empty. This, she decided with a quick glance up at the late afternoon sun, was a good time for a break. It would be, she reasoned, as her head came back down and scanned the crowded yard, a long, tiring night.

With the cries and moans of the wounded ringing in her ears, Harriet made her way to the well. It took her a moment to realize, after she reached it and paused to wait for someone already there pumping the handle madly, that the person she was waiting on was the Southern woman she had confronted earlier. Not sure whether the woman had calmed down any after they had parted, Harriet stood patiently behind her, watched, and waited to be noticed.

When the bucket was filled to overflowing, Mary Beth stopped pumping. With a sweep of her hand, she brushed away the strands of hair that had worked their way loose and fell across her face. Ready, she grabbed the rope handle of the bucket, went to lift it, but suddenly found that she didn't have the strength left to do so. Taking a step backward, she lost her balance, struggling with the bucket in a vain attempt to hang on to it. Stumbling on the hem of her own skirt, she finally let go of the bucket and flailed about in a desperate effort to grab something to keep from falling.

From out of nowhere, a hand grabbed hers. Turning, she threw her other hand about and latched on to the arm connected to the hand that she now held. Only after she had managed to plant both feet firmly on the ground did she look up into the eyes of the Yankee woman who had served her notice that she was to lose her house for the Union cause. Though grateful, Mary Beth drew away. "I . . . I'm sorry," she stammered breathlessly. "Lost my balance."

Harriet forced a smile as Mary Beth drew away. "No need to apologize. I'm always stepping on my hem or struggling to keep my skirt out of the way."

Pausing, Mary Beth looked into the warm eyes that betrayed a hint of sadness. Forgetting her earlier anger with this Northern intruder, Mary Beth looked down at the ground, then over to the gaggle of wounded Confederate prisoners she had been fetching water for. "It . . . must . . . be hard," she whispered without taking her eyes off the blood-soaked coat of a painfully thin soldier lying listlessly on the ground. Slowly, she brought her head around till her eyes met Harriet's. "How do you ever manage to get used to it?"

Harriet didn't answer at first. Rather, she looked to where the woman had been staring, then over to the rows and rows of newly arrived wounded. She thought about the passage in her diary that had been troubling her so. Then she looked down at the ground between her and the Southern woman. "You don't. At least," Harriet said, raising her head till her moist eyes met Mary Beth's, "I haven't been able to." Looking back to the wounded, Harriet took a deep breath. "It would be a sin, I think, for anyone to allow themselves to become so hardened to this that they no longer can feel the pain. A sin."

Mary Beth stood watching the woman for a moment, not knowing what to do or say. Only when she saw a stray tear running its wild course down Harriet's cheek did she move. Reaching into the pocket of her apron, Mary Beth pulled out a torn handkerchief and presented it to Harriet.

Glancing up at Mary Beth, then taking the handkerchief, Harriet forced another smile. "Thank you," she muttered, dabbing one eye, then the other, as she held the handkerchief tightly in one hand. "I suppose I shouldn't go on like this," she babbled in her embarrassment. "It's not supposed to be ladylike to let one's feelings show so."

Without thinking, Mary Beth placed her hand on Harriet's. "There has been many a night that I wish I had someone I could share a good cry with." Looking about the yard, past the throngs of wounded, at the shabby house and weed-choked farmyard, Mary Beth sighed. "Many a night," she repeated as she squeezed Harriet's hand.

Then, as if suddenly realizing what she had said and done, Mary Beth withdrew her hand and stepped back. "I . . . I'm so sorry. I didn't mean to . . ."

Now, for the first time, Harriet smiled with sincerity as she reached out to return the handkerchief. "Again, no need to apologize. I think everyone needs to cry a little, now and then."

That she had found such deeply felt common ground with this

woman so soon after cursing her with all her might befuddled Mary Beth. Not knowing for sure what to do or say, she smiled shyly, nodded, then turned away to retrieve her bucket and try, once again, to draw water for the wounded.

"Here," Harriet volunteered as she stepped forward to the pump, "let me help you."

Without resistance, Mary Beth moved away from the pump's handle. After placing the bucket squarely under the spout, Mary Beth drew off a bit, folding her arms across her chest, and watched the Yankee woman.

"You know," Harriet said as she labored with the pump, "when you mentioned your name before, I didn't realize, at first, that this was the same place where my husband left one of his wounded men last month after a skirmish south of the town. I try hard to keep track of my boys and would appreciate knowing what became of the young man."

"Oh," Mary Beth responded, "the provost guard took him off to one of the hospitals in town the next day. When he left, he seemed to be doing better, more rested." After a moment, Mary Beth, bemused by the coincidence, added, "That officer who was here that night was your husband?"

Harriet smiled. "Yes, that was Kevin, Kevin Bannon from Perth Amboy, New Jersey," she responded as if his entire name and city he was from were a title.

Rocking back on her heels as if she had just been hit by a great invisible stone, Mary Beth's eyes and mouth flew open. Harriet, not sure what she had said to startle the poor woman so, stopped pumping and stood upright, unsure what to do. "Did . . . did I say something to offend you?"

At first, all Mary Beth could do was shake her head as her mouth tried to form a word but couldn't. Finally, after taking three quick breaths, Mary Beth blurted, "He has a brother named James, doesn't he?"

Surprised that this Southern woman knew that, Harriet smiled. "Why, yes, yes he does. How did you . . ."

"James, he's . . . he's," Mary Beth was hesitating now, in truth, she didn't know where she stood with James, search for a word.

"You know James?" Harriet all but shrieked.

Still struggling for breath, Mary Beth nodded. "Yes."

Dropping all pretense of decorum or appearance, Harriet threw her arms out, rushed over to Mary Beth, and embraced her with an unrestrained hug. "Oh, thank God," Harriet muttered over and over again as she began to cry.

Only slowly did Mary Beth realize what this meant. When it finally did begin to seep its way into her consciousness, she lifted her limp arms, wrapped them around Harriet's heaving shoulders, and returned the hug.

Few of the busy hospital attendants, and none of the wounded, paid any heed to the two women embracing each other at the water pump. Knee deep in human carnage, they were too concerned with surviving that moment to ponder what strange event had caused these women, from two alien worlds, to find comfort in each other's arms. And even if they had known, none would have believed that in the midst of such suffering and misery, the seed called hope could find a place to take root.

Slowly, with little more than brute force and sheer weight of numbers, the Jerseymen of the Sixth Corps' First Division made their way up the crest of the plateau against unrelenting and unbowed resistance. Kevin, having witnessed enough battles to know that even the surest victory could be thrown away by the bungling of a single inept general, nevertheless felt that this fight was theirs as he looked about the field. To the left, the Sixth Corps' three divisions were moving forward in unison against a receding Confederate line. To the right, the Eighth Corps, finally on the field and deployed, was making both its numbers and freshness felt as it cleared the patch of woods the Nineteenth Corps had won and lost so many times that day. Now clear of the woods, the troops of the Eighth Corps stretched out as far as Kevin could see, around and behind the crest of the hill where the Rebels, flushed from the woods, continued to stand and deliver a devastating fire at their tormentors.

From down the line, a cheer rose, growing louder and louder as one unit after another took it up in succession. Turning, Kevin saw General Phil Sheridan, spurring his jet-black horse, Rienzi, for all he was worth as he rode down the line, shouting one thing or another to the units he passed. In Kevin's own command, some of his men reacted to this by joining the cheering. Johnny O'Keeth, always ready to give in to any excitement, stepped back, tore the hat from his head, and let loose a bellow that drowned out the shouts of half a dozen men around him. Others, like Corporal Miller, didn't respond to the hoopla at all. With the steady gaze with which he viewed everything, Miller simply continued to watch the rear rank of the company as others, like Amos Flatherly, calmly went about their business of loading, taking slow, careful aim, and firing. Those men, Kevin knew, needed no false heroics, no generals to whip them up to a fight. They were machines, killing machines, intent on doing what they were trained to do and getting on with the task at hand.

That it would soon be over was obvious to all who took the time to look about. Though it was late in the afternoon, and evening was fast approaching, Kevin slowly became convinced that nothing, not the setting of the sun or the exhortations of their own generals, was going to save the exhausted Rebels before them from defeat. Somehow, somewhere along the line, something was going to break the bloody deadlock they were locked in and end this brutal execution.

The terrible final act that Kevin felt was coming fell upon Gordon's battered command with a swiftness that was as devastating as it was unexpected. Behind earthworks for the first time, the men around James Bannon watched in muted silence as line after line of mounted Union horsemen deployed to their front. At a walk, they started forward, unfazed by the shot and shell that hastily deployed guns along the Confederate line hurled at them. "Dear God," Dale Wint muttered as he stared open-mouthed at the mass of horsemen that appeared to stretch from horizon to horizon. "Ain't that the most beautiful thing you ever did see."

Above the growing rumble of thousands of beating hooves, sharp notes from dozens of bugles took the Union horses from a walk to a trot. Daniel McPherson watched in awe, wondering how anyone could even imagine something so terrible as beautiful. That he himself had often fantasized about being in a cavalry charge little more than a year ago never occurred to him. Instead, the image of poor Edward Hobson, tormented by pain beyond belief, together with this new terror unfolding before his eyes, unnerved him to the point of near panic. All Daniel could think of was ending this day and getting away from this place. That the beloved fields, and forests, and hills of his childhood could host such horrors and depredations as he had been witness to that day staggered the young man's imagination. Glancing at the setting sun, Daniel prayed that this day would end, soon.

That it would end was never in doubt. But there remained one, unstoppable act to be played out. Again the cavalry bugles blared a new order, one that took the Union troopers from the trot to a full gallop. Standing in silence, the ragged remains of the 4th Virginia braced itself for that final act by fixing bayonets and closing up ranks so tightly that Daniel had to struggle to keep from being squeezed out. Yet even as they watched the cavalry charge unfold, many knew it was over. Their brigade commander, General Terry, was one of the first men to go down, wounded and knocked out of the saddle before issuing a single order. And despite their best efforts, which equaled those that had succeeded in turning back attack after attack all afternoon, the soldiers of the Stonewall Brigade could do little to stem the avalanche of men and horseflesh that slashed though their ranks as if they weren't there.

With a suddenness that was both terrible and shocking, the Union Cavalry burst through the tight, but paper-thin Confederate ranks at a dead run. The slow, agonizing wait was instantly transformed into a blinding swirl of blurred images. All around the small knot of men that James had quickly formed, men and horses collided. Riders, alive with a bloodlust that bordered on madness, tore through the disintegrating ranks, swinging and slashing with their sabers as they went. Desperate infantrymen, knocked loose from their own small knots of comrades or abandoned by them when they had fled, scurried about aimlessly searching for safety. Some, overwhelmed by the confusion that had engulfed them, stood rooted where they had been left, with only their heads jerking this way and that in a manic effort to make sense of a scene that was utter chaos. More often than not a horseman, riding by, ended the confusion of these pathetic figures by leveling his pistol and firing on the lost souls at point-blank range.

In the pandemonium, James caught sight of one blue rider, his eyes alive with the wild fire of combat, singling him out. Jerking his horse's head toward James, the Yankee cavalryman dug his spurs deep into the flank of his mount, let out a scream that was drowned out by the din of battle that filled James' ears, and leveled his pistol at him. Firing as he closed, the Union trooper's aim was as wild as his frenzied charge. Still, the horse soldier managed to hit the left shoulder of the man behind James, a stray who thought he had found refuge in the 4th Virginia's tight little clump of men.

With only one shot, James had to be more deliberate, more precise. Bringing his rifle up at the ready, he tried desperately to remember what they had been taught, years before, when rehearsing the "repel cavalry" drill. Unable to think clearly, he finally decided to try for the larger of the two targets, the horse. With a single quick, smooth motion, James brought his rifle up to his shoulder, sighted down the long barrel till the muzzle was aimed squarely at where he thought the horse's heart was, and fired.

The result of his round was both spectacular and disastrous. Though he had hit his mark with unerring accuracy, the momentum of the horse and its own weight carried it and its rider forward. Collapsing to its knees, the horse began a wild somersault that literally launching its master high into the air. As if in slow motion, James watched the cavalryman, his look of rage now transformed into one of sheer terror, as he flew up, over James' head, and down into the pack of men James had tried to defend. The impact of a thousand pounds of dead horseflesh, still sliding forward on its back, knocked James off his feet.

Knowing that his survival depended on getting back up and reforming the knot of men as quickly as possible, James scrambled to find his rifle and push himself up off the ground. It was, however, too late. Other riders, having seen what had happened, took advantage of the breaking up of the clump of Rebel soldiers. Like hyenas, they closed quickly to ride down the scurrying refugees. Helplessly, James watched as Douglas Geddy, confronted by a tall Yankee sergeant waving a saber over his head, threw his arms up over his head and bowed his head to avert the coming blow. The cavalryman, with all his might, brought his saber down as he rode past Geddy. Biting deep into Geddy's arms till it met bone, the saber continued to slice its way downward as the trooper leaned out of his saddle and followed through, raking the edge of his weapon down across Geddy's face and chest.

That this man, who had always been little more than a nuisance, was gone didn't bother James. Rather, he turned his attention to finding Daniel. "*Danny!*" James screamed in a vain effort to be heard above the roar of battle. "*Danny!*"

A bump caused James to spin around, bringing his rifle up to the ready as he did. He stopped though, when he stepped back and saw Daniel McPherson, wavering wildly from side to side, before him. His eyes were wide with terror. Hatless and without a weapon, Daniel had a gash on his left ear that left a thick trail of blood running down into his collar. James could not tell whether he was hit somewhere else, or if there was more to the wound than he could see. A beating of hooves and the brush of a horse's flank across his back didn't leave any time for James to find out more.

"Come on, Danny," James shouted in the boy's right ear as he grabbed his sleeve. "We've got to run."

Dumbfounded, Daniel staggered forward and followed as James weaved his way through the melee that had lost all form. He didn't even hesitate when Lieutenant Roberts caught sight of the two and yelled for them to stop. With his eyes alive with terror, Roberts stood, alone in the middle of the field, sword in one hand and pistol in the other, demanding that they stand and fight. "You men," Roberts shouted as he pointed his sword at James, "over here and form a line."

James didn't even bother to look to where Roberts had swung his sword to indicate where he wanted them. There was no one else left to form Roberts' line and James was not about to sacrifice himself and Daniel in a futile effort. James followed a captain whose head was bowed low and who had his sheathed sword tucked under his arm in resignation. Roberts, incensed by this disobedience, bellowed, "Come back here, you cowards. Come back and stand."

There was nothing to be gained, and everything to be lost, James knew, by delaying any longer. They had both done their duty, he and Daniel, and then some. And if nothing intervened between now and when they reached safety, wherever that lay, James knew they would be asked to do more.

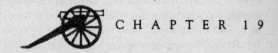

New Brunswick, New Jersey, October, 1864

"AH, BANNON," THOMAS HOWORTH called out. "There you are."

Looking up from his meal, Edward Bannon hid with a smile the displeasure he felt at having been found by Howorth. "Thomas, how good to see you."

Pushing his way between the seats of other well-dressed diners, who made no secret of their contempt for the fat man who was disturbing their meals, Howorth made his way to Edward's table. The man was out of place in an elegant restaurant such as this. He had few manners, no sense when it came to his choice of clothing, and little concept of personal hygiene. Edward chuckled as he recalled that he had stepped across the bodies of some of his drunken workers in front of saloons in Perth Amboy who were better dressed and groomed than Howorth.

Yet while it was true that Thomas Howorth was not the type you'd want respectable company to find sitting in your front parlor, he was a man who no smart businessman in the state of New Jersey could ignore or take lightly. His domain was the back rooms, where bankers, politicians, even the state legislators made deals that were never meant to see the light of day. There, he and a select few held court, assuring a politician's future with a single nod of his head or sealing the fate of a great financial empire with the shrug of his beefy shoulders.

"When I heard you were in town, I came looking for you," the fat man announced as he pulled out a chair and plopped down without any further greeting or invitation. Placing his elbows on the table, he leaned forward. "I can't let you do this, Edward," he whispered. "You'll ruin yourself and any chance that your son would ever have of making a name for himself in this state."

Edward, struggling to control his temper, ignored Howorth's comment for a moment as a waiter came up behind him. "Thomas," Edward beamed, "would you care for some dessert? The pastry chef here is excellent."

Making no effort to hide his anger, Howorth growled and slapped his hand down on the table. "Stop toying with me, Edward. I'm serious, damn it."

Ignoring the disapproving glances of other diners, Edward turned to the waiter. "Nothing for my friend. As for me, I'll just have coffee, thank you."

Angered by Edward's show of contempt, Howorth nonetheless hesitated until the waiter withdrew before starting again. "Bannon," the big man hissed, "you're a fool. You always have been, you always will be."

Edward leaned back in his seat, affecting a mock look of surprise as he did so. "Why my dear sir. Less than a week ago you were hailing me as a financial genius and a visionary."

Ignoring Edward's use of his own words, spoken before an assembly of prominent businessmen and politicians, Howorth continued his straightforward attack. "When I heard that you were going to declare for Lincoln, I gagged. I mean, I literally fell out of my chair and choked on my meal."

It took all of Edward's strength to keep a wisp of a smile from creeping across his face at the image of Howorth's obese body rolling on the floor.

"Edward, this state is going to stick with McClellan, regardless of what happened in Georgia or Virginia. We're committed to stand by the only man who can make sense out of this disastrous war."

"Well," Edward responded, warming up to the purpose of Howorth's visit for the first time, "since it's not your funeral, I don't see where it's any of your business."

Stunned by this rebuff, Howorth sat back and stared at Edward. After a moment, Howorth shook his head. "My God, man, I don't think you understand."

"No," Edward shot back as he leaned forward for a moment, then settled back in his seat again. "It's you who doesn't understand. Everything has changed," Edward announced with a wave of his hand. "Everything.

This war has become more than a simple argument over states' rights or even slavery. It has become a struggle for the soul, the soul of every man and woman, the soul of this nation. We cannot, in all good conscience, turn our backs on the sacrifices that our sons have made and expect to live in peace with ourselves and the two mongrel nations that will emerge from a war ending with this country divided. Anyone who believes that is a bigger fool than your beloved McClellan."

Howorth stared at Edward for several seconds in disbelief. "You've become a dreamer," he declared. "I don't believe it. The man who I once looked up to as the most ruthless, most unscrupulous businessman in the whole state is a dreamer."

Looking down at the table, Edward chuckled as he slowly wrapped his fingers around the delicate handle of the china cup before him. "You know something, Thomas," he said as he glanced up, "I think I've always been a dreamer. Who else would have married a girl who had nothing to speak of other than a warm smile and a heart full of love? Who else would have turned his back on the only world he had ever known and ventured across the ocean without a penny in his pocket and a pregnant wife to care for? And who else would walk down the street with the finest houses and say, out loud to God himself, 'Someday, I'll live in a house like that'?" Edward shook his head and chuckled again. Then his expression grew serious. "If the truth be known, it was when I stopped dreaming, when I refused to listen to my heart and started listening to the likes of you that I lost my soul. And for what?"

"Power, Edward. Power. Don't you see?" Howorth stated with a sweep of his hand. "We are the people who have the power to do as we please. Those of us who choose wisely are the ones who make the policies and the wealth of this state. It's not the dreamers who run things in America. It's us! We're the ones who say what is to be done and what is not to be done. While Mr. Lincoln's ideas of freedom and democracy yield marvelous speeches, it is the power wielded by men like you and me that really matters. I appeal to you as one businessman to another. For your own sake, listen to logic and not the ranting of a man more concerned with freeing ignorant slaves."

With a hard, uncompromising expression, Edward stared into Howorth's eyes. "I have listened to your logic, and the logic of cynics like you for too long. I spent so much time trying to be like you that I forgot who I was. If there is any listening I need to do, it's to my own heart, and not the *clink, clink, clink* of coins as they pass from one corrupt man's hand to another's."

Angered by Edward's retort, Howorth stood up. "You've been reading too many Dickens novels, Bannon. Men like you and I don't have any souls worth saving. We sold them, along with everything else we dearly loved, long, long ago."

"Perhaps," Edward mused for a moment. "And if that is the case," he continued, "so be it. I've had a good run of it. But the least I can do, while I still have the presence of mind to do so, is make a difference so that my sons can live in a better place than I have had to."

Determined to get one last swipe in, Howorth smiled. "If it's a better place you're looking to build for your sons here in New Jersey, then you're going about it in the wrong way. If you turn Republican, the doors of power and success in this state will be closed to you forever."

Edward was unfazed by Howorth's feeble threat. "Perhaps that is a good thing. Perhaps it will be time, after this war is over, for my sons to turn their eyes west, as I did when I was their age."

Frustrated, Howorth stared at Edward for a moment, trying desperately to think of a suitable response. When he was unable to do so, he turned away with a huff and bullied his way through the crowded dining room. When the busy chatter of diners and the clank of silverware settled back upon the room after Howorth's rude departure, Edward leaned back and took a sip of his coffee. Despite his well-measured responses to Howorth, he was still uncomfortable with the thought of throwing away all the power and prestige that he had so carefully amassed in the state over the years. Yet he kept telling himself, if it had been done for his sons, then he owed it to them to allow them the freedom to follow their own dreams, and not his. Kevin, after all, had matured in strength of character and abilities beyond his wildest dreams. He was a man in his own right, a man who needed the freedom to make his own choices, to make his own way in a world that would be so different than anything he or Howorth had yet imagined.

Still, Edward smiled as he looked about the room, it wouldn't hurt to nudge his son a little here and a little there. When afforded the chance, Edward Bannon was unable to resist making massive investments in the Union Pacific Railroad with the understanding that his son would eventually be offered a seat on the company's board of directors. In time, he hoped to be able to find common ground where he and his sons, both of them if that was still possible, could come together. Until then, there was nothing wrong with squirreling away a little here and there for their future.

Winchester, Virginia

AS SHE WALKED SLOWLY from one bloodstained room to another, it was not the future that Mary Beth McPherson was thinking of. Rather, it was the past, a past that the stench which permeated her house made hard to recall. Visions of mutilated men lying on the floor on blood-soaked blankets, burned into her memory during the last few weeks, obscured the images of the happier times that these rooms had once been witness to. The parlor, where the family shared so much time together, was barren. Even the rocker that her father had so enjoyed was gone, for good, just like its former owner. All that was left were the bloodstains that no scrubbing could remove, a stench that permeated the walls and floor, and the memory of shattered men, writhing in agony. It had been far too long, Mary Beth thought as she stood in the doorway and looked into that vacant space, since she had felt the warm glow of a loved one sitting before a fire and heard the carefree voices of a family's idle chatter. Too long. And too much suffering had come her way.

Turning her back on that room, she continued her journey. When she reached her mother's room, she placed one hand on the doorknob and another on the door itself. Pausing, she leaned her head forward until her forehead also rested on the door. This room had always been very special to her. How many mornings, she wondered, had she crept out of her own room and into this one while her mother was busy fixing the morning meal and her father was out tending to his morning chores? Snuggling up under bed covers still warm from her parents' long slumber, Mary Beth would lie awake and look around the room, dreaming of the day when she would have a bed of her own such as her mother's, in a room that was just like this one.

That the room was now hers, if she chose to take it, no longer mattered. What had made it so special, so alluring to the mind of a little girl, had been the warmth and love that it had represented, a warmth that now seemed as stone cold dead as her very own mother. Even as she had stood at her mother's graveside, next to a woman whom she hoped one day to call sister-in-law, Mary Beth found it difficult to mourn the passing of her mother. She had already done that, many times before, as she watched the woman she had once looked up to fade away into madness and grief. Letting go of the doorknob, Mary Beth backed away from the door and looked at it one last time. Even tears, it seemed, were in short supply.

Turning quickly, she made her way to the kitchen where she grabbed her bonnet, a small bag made of carpet, and her shawl as she passed the bloodstained table. Without taking the time to put the bonnet and shawl on, she passed through the kitchen door and into the brisk predawn cold. Behind her she closed a door that had never been locked and stepped away from the only life she had ever known.

From the road, Harriet Bannon watched. "I do wish you would reconsider your decision and accept my offer to go north and stay with James' father," she pleaded as Mary Beth drew near her. "He's very much a changed man from what James remembered and would be more than happy to share his house with you."

Struggling with her bonnet and shawl, Mary Beth didn't answer at first. Harriet took this hesitation as a sign that perhaps the destitute girl would reconsider. But a quick nod of Mary Beth's head and a look of dejection dashed this fleeting hope. Reaching out, Mary Beth touched Harriet's hand. "As long as James and my brother are still with the Army, I cannot leave the South."

"You know that conditions in Richmond are bad. It's overcrowded, expensive, and not at all a healthy place for a young woman to be going to on her own," Harriet offered in argument.

With a squeeze and a sad smile, Mary Beth cut off Harriet's efforts. "It seems, with the valley so devastated by Union forces, the only place left where I can go and have any chance of fending for myself. Many others, I am told, have done so." Then, with a sigh, she added, "I cannot tell you how touched I am by your concern for my welfare. And I promise I'll keep your father-in-law's address in a safe place should things ever become too . . ."

Reaching up, Harriet cupped Mary Beth's calloused hand between hers. "I wish there was more that I could do."

"You cannot imagine how much you have already done," Mary Beth responded softly. Glancing back over her shoulder for a moment at the now-abandoned house, Mary Beth sighed, then looked into Harriet's eyes. "You have given me hope at a time when I needed it. Hope and love. Now I must see if I can pass some of that on to James."

Harriet smiled. "For his sake, for all of ours, I pray you succeed."

Unable to respond for fear of bursting into tears, Mary Beth threw her arms open and embraced Harriet. Unused to such public shows of affection, Harriet hesitated at first to return the hug. But when she did, it was with all the warmth that her heart could muster. "Take care, Beth, and please come north as soon as you can."

Letting go and stepping back, Mary Beth dropped her head as she wiped a tear away. "I will, I promise."

The snort of a horse and Albert Merrel's forced cough reminded Harriet that they needed to go. "Albert here can only take you as far as the Union picket lines. Then I'm afraid you're on your own."

"I'm sure I'll be all right," Mary Beth responded as confidently as she could. "Between the food you've given me and the hard currency, I should have no trouble making it to Richmond. Don't worry about me."

Biting her lip, Harriet reached out and grabbed Mary Beth's hand again as she lost her struggle to hold back her own tears. "Oh, Beth."

The two women were about to embrace each other again when the sound of cannon fire rolled through the early morning air like distant thunder. In an instant, they froze as they listened to the continuing sounds of the war that had brought them, if only for a moment, together.

Middletown, Virginia

WHILE THE COMPANY FIRST sergeants held parade in the early morning mist, calling out the names of their charges from the company rolls, Kevin Bannon and several other officers of the 4th New Jersey stood around a cook fire, drinking coffee. After listening to the sound of scattered musketry to the south, a lieutenant raised his cup and waved it in that direction. "The lads in the Eighth Corps seem to be rather feisty this morning."

A captain, looking in the direction of the lieutenant's cup, which gave off steam that slowly curled up until it merged with the cold morning air, grunted. "It takes two to dance, you know."

Another lieutenant laughed. "Well, I'd be willing to bet that some Rebel brigade commander, with nothing to offer his boys for breakfast, decided to pick a fight with some of ours just to ruin their breakfast." Just then the youngest of the gathered officers spied a cook passing with a basket of fresh-baked biscuits. Reaching around the cook, the officer snatched one of the biscuits before the cook had time to react. With great show, the officer held the piping hot biscuit before his face. "You, sir, are my prisoner, and I shall show you no mercy." With that, he took a huge bite from the biscuit as the other officers gathered about laughed at his antics.

The thunder of a mass volley, rolling up the valley through the fog, cut their merriment short. One by one, the officers fell silent as their eyes once more turned to the south in a vain effort to penetrate the fog that obscured everything beyond a hundred yards or so. At irregular intervals, the boom of a cannon punctuated the growing volume of rifle fire.

Finished with his duties and having dismissed the company, Sergeant Johnny O'Keeth came up next to Kevin and joined his company commander. While Kevin sipped coffee, he looked down the row of tents that trailed off into the gray morning mist in the direction where the noise of battle was growing by leaps and bounds. Johnny, a man who always found it hard to stay quiet, finally broke the silence. "You suppose Old Jubal Early means to attack us?"

Kevin turned and looked at Johnny. Before he could say anything, the young officer who had snatched the biscuit waved his hand above his head. "Nonsense," he proclaimed. "How could he after the beating we gave him last month. Why, he'd have as much success taking us all on, gathered again as we are, than a fly has of eating a cow whole. It's nothing more than the daily skirmish between picket lines."

Johnny, unconvinced, shook his head once as he looked at the officer, but kept his response brief. "I don't know, sir," he muttered. "Sounds pretty serious to me."

That others took the situation seriously was readily made apparent as bugles began to blare, first in the camp of a brigade a little farther south of the Jersey Brigade, then over in another unit that was closer to the valley pike. Not having to wait for their own brigade staff to come to life, Kevin and his fellow officers emptied their cups by flinging the contents on the ground and made for their separate commands. "Re-form the company, Sergeant O'Keeth," Kevin barked in his official voice.

O'Keeth, however, didn't hear him. He was already headed back to where he had just finished dismissing his men, calling for them to reassemble. Whatever the cause of the fight, Kevin concluded, he hoped that the Eighth Corps would be able to sort it out before his brigade was pitched into it. As much as he wanted to see the war come to a quick and speedy close, Kevin decided that he just was not up to a major battle today. "Getting too old," he muttered to himself as he made for his tent to retrieve his pistol, belt, and haversack.

Hearing him, Captain Baldwin Hufty, acting commander of the 4th New Jersey, turned to Kevin. "What? What's that you say, Kevin?"

Without pausing Kevin grumbled as he reached into his tent. "I'm twenty-three years old and I already feel like an old man."

Despite the nervous tension that was building as the sounds of battle continued to grow and more bugles and drums sounded all about them, Hufty laughed. "Bannon, you've always been an old grouch. Now see if you can manage to limp over to your company and get them ready to move."

With his pant legs still dripping from their crossing of the Shenandoah at the base of Massanutten Mountain, James Bannon didn't wait for Lieutenant Roberts to echo General Terry's order to advance. With a great leap, he was up and moving forward, screaming "Yip! Yip! Yip!" for all he was worth. Daniel, taken aback by James' sudden burst of enthusiasm, took off at a run in an effort to catch up with him. In this way, James led the company forward and into the midst of the stunned Union soldiers.

Before he realized how close the enemy camp had been, James found himself confronted by rows of white canvas tents laid out in regulation company streets. With little warning, the men who had been lounging about moments before in those tents were pouring from them, some fully dressed, others only partially so. Few were armed and even fewer were equipped with cartridge cap boxes and ready for battle. Stunned by this sudden vision before him, James slowed, then halted as the men who had been struggling out of the brush that they had been deployed in came up next to him and fell into line of battle. Lieutenant Roberts, thankful for this pause, came up behind them, took one look at the situation, then quickly issued his first orders of the battle. "Ready! Aim! Fire!"

While few Yankees went down with wounds, the quick volley shattered the efforts of the handful of officers and sergeants who had been trying to form their men up to make a stand. "Reload and come to the ready."

Yet by the time the men gathered around James were ready, the fleeing Yankees had disappeared into the fog and the units to the left and right were surging ahead. "Forward."

Having vented the fury he had been harboring as the brigade had marched throughout the previous night, James settled down into this familiar routine. With his rifle held at the ready, he responded to both the orders from the officers and the ebb and flow of the battle line as it moved forward, shifted to the left or right, or gave way because of an obstacle or row of tents. Occasionally, the line would halt as a knot of Yankees, massed by officers desperately trying to form a line, became visible in the early morning fog. A quick volley, sometimes delivered spontaneously, was all that was necessary to break up these fledgling attempts to stop the Confederate onslaught.

Caught up by the euphoria of what appeared to be the start of a spectacular victory, Daniel began to scream insults at the fleeing Union soldiers. "*Come back here and make a stand, you yellow-bellied trash!*" Daniel shouted whenever he lost sight of an intended target. "Come back and get your due."

Looking over his shoulder at Daniel, James remembered how his brother, Will, had behaved so when things were going well. They were an excitable, moody family, James concluded, both men and women alike. Perhaps, he reasoned as he moved along almost absentmindedly now with the next forward rush, that was what he had always found so endearing about the McPhersons. They were alive, every one of them, and their actions, their manner of doing things, even their speech had shown it.

"Halt and come to the ready!" Roberts shouted. Men, like James, who had been thinking of other things or looking for inviting items to pick up as they went by, overshot the line Roberts wanted. Quickly, James and the others backed up and found their place in line. Clear of the first row of tents, James looked up once he was settled back in the ranks. To their front, barely visible in the early morning gloom and fog, a substantial line of Union troops was formed and facing them. "Fun's over boys," Fielding Spencer volunteered as he finished loading his rifle. "We have a fight on our hands this time."

But it turned out to be not much of a fight at all. The Ohioans and West Virginians, members of Colonel Rutherford B. Hayes' division, were too few and totally unsupported. With Terry's brigade in the front and Pendleton's Louisianans on their flank, the Union line buckled and cracked. Efforts by their brigade commander to hold his men together as they retreated were for naught. As so many of their companions had already done, these men took to their heels and sought safety in flight to the north.

It was more the completeness of their success, rather than enemy action, that slowed the Confederate advance. Yet while fighting continued to erupt all around them, the lure of the bountiful Union camps, abandoned while many of their former occupants had been preparing their morning meal, carried more Confederates out of the ranks than enemy bullets did. And even though the majority of the men who did so realized that there was more fighting to be done, empty stomachs proved to be much more compelling than their officers' exhortations.

Daniel, though fast becoming a seasoned veteran, still found the practice of looting uncomfortable. Despite all he had seen, and the knowledge that the enemy they were taking from had shown no mercy when it came to burning crops and destroying public and personal property throughout Virginia, he couldn't bring himself to do so in return. "Thou shalt not steal!" his father had repeated in stern, uncompromising tones with each swat on his bare behind every time Daniel had been caught taking something from his brother or sister. Even today, in the middle of a full-scale battle, those words, "Thou shalt not steal!," rang out as clear as if his father were standing beside him whenever Daniel's eyes fell upon something inviting.

James, however, had no qualms whatsoever about taking immediate, and frequent, advantage of the situation. With the sense that only a well-seasoned soldier possessed, James knew when it was possible to slip out of ranks, grab something here or there, and slip back in without being missed for very long. This frustrated Lieutenant Roberts. Excited by the spectacular success so far, he was forced to divide his attention in many different directions. As a company commander, he had to pay attention to what the regimental commander was saying and doing and what the enemy before them was up to, not to mention keeping his own unit aligned with those to the left and right. All of this, with the fog that refused to disperse and the smoke of battle, made keeping his men in the ranks almost impossible. When he had turned to James to solicit his assistance in this endeavor, he couldn't find him. When he did finally lay eyes on this errant second sergeant, James was wandering back to the ranks, rifle slung, as he busily stuffed his mouth with fresh-baked biscuits wrapped in bacon while cradling an armful of them for the rest of the boys in the ranks.

"You're supposed to set the example, Sergeant Bannon," Roberts bellowed.

Undeterred, James finished stuffing the biscuit he held into his mouth. After it was half eaten, he smiled. "But I am, sir," he responded as crumbs of food tumbled from his mouth. Then, in a show of utter contempt, he took another biscuit from the hoard he was holding in the crook of his arm, and held it up to Roberts' face. "Want one?"

Though his first inclination was to scream at the top of his lungs, the smell of the warm biscuit being held beneath his nose was too much. Dropping his eyes, Roberts snatched the biscuit from James' hand, turned, and stormed off to the other end of the line, hungrily tearing away at the first food he had eaten all morning.

Any hope that Kevin Bannon had held that the fight which had disturbed their morning routine was a local affair was quickly dispelled by the flood of panicked refugees that flowed to the rear as the New Jersey Brigade pressed forward. A self-taught expert on routs and military disasters, Kevin knew that salvation, if it was possible at this stage, would come only after hard, bitter fighting. "Six hundred," the young lieutenant that Kevin had been chatting to that morning shouted to Kevin. "The brigade adjutant said there were six hundred of us present for duty, just like the Light Brigade."

Kevin found this officer's selection of analogies, given their current circumstances, rather odd. "Well," he responded after looking up and down the line of grim faces of the First New Jersey Brigade, "let's hope more of our six hundred see this day through than those other fellows."

Johnny O'Keeth, normally the most talkative soldier in the whole regiment, was silent as he read the same omens Kevin had picked up and listened to the exchange between Kevin and the lieutenant. "You suppose the Nineteenth Corps will hold 'em?" Johnny finally ventured as they started their way up a hill.

Kevin didn't need to think much on this one. With a nod, and disgust in his voice, he responded immediately. "No, more than likely not." Like most of the men in the Sixth Corps, as well as the Eighth Corps, Kevin didn't think much of the Nineteenth Corps, a unit that had taken part in Nathaniel Banks' ill-fated Red River campaign. "It'll be hard fighting for us, Johnny. Hard fighting."

As if to underscore the seriousness of the situation and the confusion that swirled all about them, the brigade was brought to a sudden and rather disjointed halt just as they started up a hill that lay south of Meadow Run. The commanders were unsure what was going on and what should be done, he guessed, as he moved down the ranks of his halted company in an effort to hide his own nervousness. All the signs were there for anyone who could read them to see. Senior officers, mounted on skittish horses, turned this way, then that in an effort to assess the situation or find someone who knew what was going on. Staff officers and messengers, spurring their horses to and fro, shouted as they passed someone who looked as if he were in charge, "Have you seen Colonel So and so?" they would ask. Some responded with anger when they were given a negative response, while the concerned expression others wore grew deeper with every "No" they heard. Even the soldiers, listening in silence to the sounds of battle muffled by the morning fog but growing closer with each passing minute and watching the demeanor of their nervous officers, knew that all was not going well.

With nothing better to do, Kevin watched the brigade staff. Their commander, Colonel Penrose, as well as several of his staff officers, kept casting fugitive glances to his right, where sporadic rifle fire could be heard. This could only mean, Kevin concluded, that there was a very real danger that the enemy was coming up that way or that a unit that should have been on the flank wasn't there. Then, with a snap of his head, he faced his stalled brigade, ordered a right about-face, and spun his own mount to face the rear.

"Lordy," O'Keeth lamented. "Another retreat."

"Better a retreat when we want to," Thomas Yonts chuckled, "than a rout when Johnny Reb finds us wandering out here all alone."

"We ain't alone, Thomas," O'Keeth protested. "Just listen to the fighting all about."

Watching a pair of hatless Union soldiers with panic on their faces, stumbling along the length of their column toward the rear at the double quick, Yonts snorted. "Well, give the Rebs another hour or so and they'll take care of that."

Already uneasy with his own dire thoughts of gloom, Kevin was in no mood to listen to such defeatist chatter. "Quiet in the ranks," he snapped. "Close it up and keep moving."

Except for the clanking of cups and bayonet scabbards on canteens and rifle stocks, the column silently slipped back across Meadow Run, through their recently abandoned camp, and up another hill, farther north, in search of a place to make their stand. Only the sounds of battle, drifting all around them like the early morning fog and mist, broke the muted stillness that engulfed the Jersey Brigade.

Even James was surprised at how quickly he and Lieutenant Roberts were able to gather the handful of soldiers in their care and re-form them for a continuation of the march. Not that the conscripts, dumped in the 4th Virginia after the disaster at Winchester, had been doing anyone much good that morning. "Why don't we just let 'em go?" he suggested to Roberts as they looked about in search of men whose names they barely knew. "They'll just get in the way when we get into a serious fight."

For once, Roberts was tempted to follow James' advice. Shouts from his commander and every senior officer riding by to close up their ranks and move on were becoming too much for the young officer. Still, his stubborn pride kept him from turning his back on men who were flagrantly defying his orders to re-form and move on. Pointing to a group of soldiers standing around an abandoned Union cook fire, Roberts yelled to James. "Go get those men back into the ranks, *now*."

The prospect of going into part of the ransacked camp that he hadn't been in before didn't bother James at all. With a nod and an expression that hid his satisfaction, James sent Daniel and Fielding Spencer along with Roberts to keep him out of trouble while he walked over to the merry group of scavengers. Coming up to a tall red-headed boy who was almost as thin as his rifle, James planted his rifle butt down on the ground and smiled at the circle of faces that turned to greet him. Some of the older soldiers knew James' smile was just a put-on. Self-consciously, like children who had been caught in the midst of some mischief, they began to stuff their pockets with whatever food they could before being ordered back into the ranks.

The red-headed boy, however, innocent and buoyed by the spoils of an easy victory, returned James' smile. "Hey, Sergeant. Ain't this some fun? I never thought this fightin' would be so easy."

James looked down at a pot of coffee, left unattended on the cook fire and all but boiled away now, then back at the enthusiastic youth. "Well, maybe so. Maybe so. But there's a whole lot more daylight left, and a whole lot more fighting to be done before we can kick back and enjoy ourselves." Then he turned to the older soldiers and glared at them, "Wouldn't you boys say?"

Nodding glumly, their expressions at this prospect mirrored James' own feelings. Still, he was a sergeant, bound by his duty, and they were soldiers bound by theirs, no matter how grim it might be. "You boys know what's right and what's wrong," James pointed out without trying to sound like he was scolding them. "And you know what needs to be done. Now finish up here right smartly and get on back into the ranks before I turn you over to the provost as deserters."

Knowing full well that James was serious, the older soldiers shouldered their rifles without a word and made their way through the thinning mist to where Roberts was re-forming the command. The young conscripts, seeing the manner in which the veterans reacted, scrambled with their gear and rifles, left scattered around on the ground or leaning against crude camp tables, and beat feet to catch up with the others. In his excitement, the red-headed boy tripped, sprawling on the ground, crushing the biscuits he had stuffed in his pockets. James, though he tried hard not to, laughed at the poor lad. Not knowing whether to be angry or embarrassed, the boy picked himself up off the ground, rubbing his shin as he did so.

Feeling sorry for the boy, James walked over to where he was gathering himself, and handed him another biscuit. "Here, munch on this while you catch up. And be careful. A body can get hurt out here if he's not careful."

Finally deployed in line of battle north of the mansion that had, less than an hour before, been the headquarters for the Nineteenth Corps, Kevin watched the flood of refugees stream through his lines. Few were fully dressed and turned out. Some were barefoot while others were bareheaded. Many had no rifles while all wore a look of bewilderment or panic. They weren't beaten men, Kevin concluded as he watched a group of six men slink away from him when they saw him studying them. They were just badly frightened. They were confused, demoralized, and lost. Given a little time, and some hard work on the part of their officers, these men would be right as rain and ready to do their part. The question, of course, was whether or not the Sixth Corps, untouched so far that morning, could buy that time. With the diminishing number of stragglers coming out of the fog, and the growing clatter of rifle and cannon fire to their front, Kevin suspected he would soon have his answer to that question.

Slowly, as the sun inched its way into the sky, the fog and mist began to thin. Their position was far from solid or reassuring. A gap of some two hundred and fifty yards yawned open between the right of the Jersey Brigade and the left flank of the corps' Third Division. To the immediate left of the Jersey Brigade, Upton's old Second Brigade, now commanded by Colonel Joseph E. Hamblin, was jackknifed back almost at a ninety degree angle as it stretched east toward the valley pike. While two batteries from the corps' artillery rolled into the gap to their right and deployed, Kevin was far from comfortable with their positions. "We'll have to hold them here for a while," Baldwin Hufty told Kevin as he paced back and forth along his regiment's front. "Need to give the lads in the other two corps a chance to sort themselves out."

Kevin didn't respond to Hufty's pronouncement. With nothing more than a blank stare, he nodded and turned his attention to watching the beginnings of a vicious fight off to their left.

The two batteries to their right, supported by the Third Division, let loose a hot fire at masses of figures he hadn't noticed before, as they made their appearance out of the morning haze. His fear that the gunners might be firing into the rear of another Union unit was quickly dispelled when the indistinguishable mass responded with a ragged volley. This and subsequent volleys seemed to do nothing to slow the intrepid gunners, even as their limber horses and caisson teams staggered, bucked, and kicked as round after round smacked into them or their companions. Whether the Rebels were intentionally trying to kill the horses of the two batteries didn't matter. In time, Kevin realized, as he watched the uneven exchange between the gunners and the Confederates, the artillerymen would be left with no choice but to manhandle their guns back or abandon them.

The Third Division, under the command of Colonel William Keifer, composed of regiments from New York, New Jersey, Pennsylvania, Ohio, Maryland, and Vermont, was not idle, either. Pressing forward, past the pair of batteries that continued to deliver a punishing fire, the Confederates attempted to maintain the momentum of their attack by breaking the Sixth Corps' line. The Third Division refused to give way. Instead of buckling under the weight of the Confederate attack as earlier stands had, it actually counterattacked, twice. From his position in line, Kevin watched as the Third Division went down into the shallow valley where Meadow Run lay, driving the Rebels back before them. It was a vicious and confused fight, made more so by the white smoke of rifle and cannon fire mixing in with the lingering morning fog, as the soldiers in gray, with the taste of victory fresh on their tongues, lashed out at the blue-clad men, who were equally intent on holding their line.

With all going well on the right, Kevin, like the other officers in the 4th New Jersey, turned his attention to the front and left, where the newly reorganized Confederates were slowly pressing forward. The first inkling he had that there was a serious problem on their flank was when Colonel Penrose issued the order "Right about-face."

With the order normally a precursor to a retreat, Kevin looked this way and that to see what had prompted this sudden turn of fortune. His search for the answer came to an end when he saw men in blue, infantry and gunners, struggling to drag off the guns that stood between the First and Third divisions in the face of massed Confederate infantry.

"We're going to save those guns" came the cry, followed quickly by "Left wheel, march."

As he kept his eyes glued to the right and leaned to the left during the intricate turning movement, Kevin wondered about the wisdom of throwing an entire brigade away for nothing more than the honor of saving a few cannon. Stories of gunners fighting to save their guns from capture rivaled those the infantry told concerning struggles for regimental colors. Seizing, or keeping guns from being seized, was a matter of pride, not only for the artillerymen, but also for the commanding generals. No battle report was complete without the number of guns captured from the enemy being prominently reflected. Still, there was a point where pride became foolishness. And being a practical person, Kevin would have just as soon accepted a little humiliation rather than throw good men away in such a foolish enterprise. But like the men of the Light Brigade in Tennyson's poem about their ill-fated charge, his was not to reason why.

When the brigade had wheeled about far enough, Colonel Penrose gave the order to advance on the guns, abandoned by gunners unable to spirit them away, and was promptly shot out of the saddle. Recovering as his brigade came up behind him, Penrose shook himself out, found that he had only been nicked in the heel of the boot, and started forward again. His second wound, a minié ball in the right arm, broke that arm and sent him to the rear for good.

Losses continued to climb as the brigade went forward. Hunching down, as if he were walking into a hailstorm, Kevin thrust his right hand forward, holding his pistol pointed toward the enemy, yelling for his men to keep their alignment as they pressed forward. Major Lambert Boeman, commanding officer of the 10th New Jersey that day, was doing likewise when he was hit in the lower chest. Slumping out of the saddle and onto the ground, he called to his passing troops to carry him off the field, but no one heard him. With the enemy around the guns realizing that they were in for a hot fight and redoubling their efforts to hold them, the men of the 10th had little time for their stricken commander.

It was the 15th New Jersey that reached the guns first, with the 4th New Jersey coming up on their flank. Together with some of the gunners who had followed in the wake of the advancing Jerseymen, the soldiers of the 15th began the arduous task of pushing and pulling the two-ton cannons back uphill to safety while Kevin and the other officers of the brigade directed a withering fire on the masses of Confederates that hung just out of arms' reach. The punishment that they received for their efforts was staggering. Lieutenant Colonel Campbell, elevated to command of the brigade when Penrose left the field, shared his predecessor's fate within minutes when his left arm was shattered between the elbow and the wrist. Kevin watched only briefly as Campbell turned and rode off toward Winchester and safety.

Turning his attention back to his front, Kevin surveyed the scene before him. The defiant line of Rebels, as thick if not thicker than their own, was standing less than a hundred yards off, pouring heavy fire into their shredded ranks. His own company, still closed up, was returning the fire for all they were worth. At the far end, Johnny O'Keeth, grim faced and determined, bit deep into the base of his cartridges, spilling powder down his sweaty chin, leaving streaks of black ghoulish drool that ran all the way down his neck into his collar. Corporal Miller, unable to stand idly in the rear and watch as a good file closer should, pushed his way forward when he was ready to fire, bringing his rifle down with a smooth, graceful sweep before taking careful aim and firing. Amos Flatherly, kneeling next to the still body of a messmate, threw obscenities at the enemy as he frantically twirled his ramrod about in his rush to complete the long, involved process of reloading his rifle. Even Kevin, caught up in the frenzied and mindless bloodlust that swept up and down the ranks, found it annoying when he had to stop and reload the empty chambers of his caliber .44 Army Colt.

How long they stood their ground, no one knew. And how, in the midst of all the chaos and pandemonium, made more confusing by the smoke of rifle fire and lingering fog, the brigade got the word to move back was an even bigger mystery. All Kevin knew was that at some point in the fight Captain Baldwin Hufty, now acting brigade commander, told Kevin to take charge of the regiment and move it back up the hill and to the rear. Straining to make himself heard over the roar of battle, Kevin fell in beside the regimental colors and began the slow, tedious process of pulling the regiment back, out of contact, without losing alignment with the other regiments of the brigade. Of course, the fact that the 4th New Jersey now numbered well under two hundred men made this easy. Still, nothing in combat is easy, and when an army is in retreat, everything becomes harder. Much harder.

James Bannon took no great pride in the fact that he had been right about there being a lot more battle to fight. "It would have been better if we'd hit the Sixth Corps first," he repeated as they stumbled back from their last failed effort to break up the Sixth Corps' new line north of Middletown. "That was when we could have rocked those devils back on their heels. Not now, though," he shouted to Daniel as he watched his jaded soldiers stumble about in an effort to re-form behind a stone wall after their last abortive attempt. "We'll never budge them now when they're all closed up together and ready."

Though he was as disappointed as James that their easy victories over the other Union corps in the early morning hadn't been repeated when they came face-to-face with the last of them, Daniel was still pleased with what they had achieved. "What are you complaining about?" Daniel asked James as he sat down with his back to the wall when it became apparent that they weren't going to make another attack. "We whipped them, whipped them good. Now all we have to do is wait till night, when they'll slink away down the valley, just like they always do. And in the morning, after a good night's rest in their camps, we'll follow 'em all the way to Winchester."

Daniel's breezy pronouncements didn't sway James. "They're not whipped," James replied in disgust as he thrust his hand in the direction of the Union line. "Gordon knows it. I know it. I'll bet even Early's horse knows it. The only one who doesn't know it is that damned, bald-headed old fool."

Too tired to care, much less argue, Daniel closed his eyes. "All right, James, all right," he moaned sleepily. "But even if they aren't whipped, what can we do? We've been up since midnight and on the move. We fought from dawn till past noon, almost nonstop, and we've pushed the Yanks out of their own camps like so many sheep. We've hit the Sixth Corps twice and have only been thrown back once. It'll be hours before they sort themselves out and longer before they can come at us, even if they have a mind to. By then, it'll be dark and the day will be ours. Simple."

Seeing no point in pursuing this line of discussion, James let the matter drop. It was pointless, as pointless as a victory at this late date would have been. Atlanta was gone, seized by one of Grant's protégés. Now the valley, once the breadbasket of the Confederacy, was all but gone, laid waste and spoiled by another protégé. Dispirited by these grim thoughts, a sudden exhaustion fell over James like a heavy wool blanket. Looking around, he saw that everyone, even the officers, was struggling to stay on their feet. Those who did moved about like drunken sailors. They had shot their bolt, James decided as he eased himself down on the ground next to Daniel. Again, they had done their best and, again, they had come up short.

Closing his eyes, James began to block out the noise of a sputtering battle. Slowly, the random rifle fire, scattered reports from cannons, and even the pitiful screams of wounded, faded away. Daniel was right, it seemed, as James let himself slip away into a well-deserved sleep. There was nothing to do now but wait to see what happened next. Within minutes, nothing could penetrate the deep sleep that enveloped James. Not even the rousing cheers that rolled across the open ground from the re-formed Union lines.

Word that Sheridan was back spread down the line faster than the diminutive general's horse could carry him. Riding at a jaunty pace, Sheridan whipped up an enthusiasm in his shattered command like no other general could have at this stage of the war. "Never mind this morning, God damn it," he shouted as he rode by Kevin's tiny regiment. "We'll lick 'em like hell before night and sleep in our own camps."

All around Kevin, men who had gone about their duty all morning and afternoon grim faced and tight lipped gave way to wild cheering. Even Corporal Miller, a soldier whom Kevin had never seen show any emotion, tore the cap off his head and flung it into the air as the commanding general rode by, waving his arms in wild gestures and pronouncing success as if it were all but guaranteed. "We're ready to go back and give 'em what for," Johnny O'Keeth bellowed as he stepped out of ranks and followed Sheridan's horse for several paces. "We're ready, General. Just give us the word."

Phil Sheridan, however, wasn't a man who rushed into anything. It took time to turn an army around from defense to attack, especially one that had been as soundly beaten as his had been during the long, bitter morning hours. Units had to be sorted out and re-formed. Stragglers and shirkers who had undergone a change of heart needed to find their commands. Gun batteries had to be moved and massed all along the line to support the coming advance. And orders that would propel this entire host forward needed to be formulated and given an opportunity to trickle down from Army to corps, corps to division, and division to brigade. Only when all was ready, and General Sheridan felt all that could be done had been accomplished, was the order given to start the attack.

For the men of the First New Jersey Brigade, the initial part of the advance was easy. When the bugles announced the commencement of the general attack just before four o'clock, the Jerseymen stepped off in support of the New Yorkers and Pennsylvanians of the Second Brigade. Still fired up with the enthusiasm from Sheridan's impromptu trooping of the line, there was no hesitation in the ranks of either brigade.

To Kevin, the sensation of leading a regiment, even if it was a small one, was quite exhilarating. Marching down the gentle slope where they had stood while the Army rearranged itself, he found himself lost in the wonder of how he had emerged, over these past three and a half years, from a boy who had been content to cower in the shadow of his older brother to a proven leader of men. So much of it, he realized, had been nothing more than sheer accident, a simple matter of luck and fate. Nor had he always been a willing subject, he realized, when he recalled how often he had fiercely resisted that which he now saw as inevitable.

Turning his head, he looked at the thin blue line of determined faces that now followed him like a shadow. All of these men, he realized, were different men than they had been not so terribly long ago. They were veterans, men who were determined, confident, sure of who they were and what they were about. Johnny O'Keeth, who had helped him along by doing nothing more than providing a smiling face and a cheerful greeting even in the worst of times, was back there, as he always was. Even Amos Flatherly, caustic and rude to the point of insubordination, had been there, helping him by rising to the occasion and soldiering on when lesser men gave way. Turning back to face the front, images of men who were no longer with them, such as Frederick Himmel and countless others, flashed through his memory like a deck of cards being cut and shuffled.

Moving ahead, Kevin's thoughts were momentarily distracted from his solemn reflections as the Second Brigade staggered, for a moment, under the weight of the enemy's first volley. It wasn't going to be easy, he concluded as he watched the blue ranks before him continue to move on, shedding heaps of dark and sky blue cloth in their wake. The Confederates, secure behind a stonewall not far ahead, had been stopped, but not broken, not yet. There was still hard fighting to be done.

Taking a deep breath, Kevin Bannon looked up into the pale autumn sky. There was something he needed to do, he thought, before . . .

He looked behind him, shouted for the ranks to close up, then looked over his right shoulder, first at the brigade commander, then up at the sun as it sank in the west.

The words of an old saying, one that claimed it was better to live one day as a lion than a thousand years as a lamb, came to mind as the roar of rifle fire drowned out the shouts of officers all about him. Kevin suddenly felt the need to thank someone for all that he had become. Though his experiences of war had often been brutal and painful, he realized that for him, as well as for the nation, they had been necessary. As cold, inhuman, and selfish as that thought was, Kevin accepted the idea that all life leads to death, and death, in turn, inevitably gives way to new beginnings, new lives.

With a snap of his head, he looked to the front. Unable to press its attack, the Second Brigade staggered to a halt under the galling fire of a desperate enemy.

Resurrection! Kevin thought with a start as his mind shifted from the brutal hammering that was grinding up the Second Brigade to his wandering thoughts. That was the answer he had been looking for, the answer that put all of this insanity into focus, that gave it meaning and purpose. The answer was as pure as it was simple. Resurrection. What had been before had to die so that something new could come forward, something better. His father had left the old country, ending his life as he had known it so there could be a new one for his children. The old social order that had been the prison of Harriet's father and his own would need to die so that the son and daughter could build a new society, a new nation from the shambles of the old personified by the hostile Confederacy. Resurrection!

With his mind speeding along as fast as his feet in response to Baldwin Hufty's order to advance at the double quick, Kevin felt his whole soul start to burn with a passion, a drive that he had never felt before, with everything so clear, so self-evident. Every step he had taken had been a clear path to this point in his life, this moment. All that remained for Kevin to do was to crush the last remains of the enemy that stood between him and the rest of his life. Spinning about, Kevin ran backward as he waved his pistol over his head. "Come on, Fourth! Come on!" he screamed. "Pitch into them! Pitch into them and give them hell."

As fired up as their commander, the double ranks of the 4th New Jersey let out a hasty "hurrah," pressed through the shredded ranks of the Second Brigade, and joined the hot fight already well under way.

Nowhere along the stonewall where the 4th Virginia was making its stand was the heady euphoria of that very morning evident. As he lowered himself below the edge of the stonewall and began to reload his rifle, James reflected upon this awful transformation. Over near the center of the regiment stood young Lieutenant Roberts, leaning heavily upon his sword to keep from falling over from a leg wound that left his powder blue trousers streaked with blood. Like so many other fine young Virginia gentlemen, he had come into this war convinced of the righteousness of their cause and the purity of their purpose. And like so many others before him, Roberts was bewildered by the realization that, perhaps, God was not on their side. James had watched Will McPherson struggle with this dilemma. Now he was watching Will's brother, and Roberts, come to grips with this ugly truth. Even James, who was determined to harden himself to foolish hopes, couldn't help but feel his heart break a little for all those who had given so much, including their lives, for a cause that he was watching die before his very eyes.

Moving along the rear of the line, James watched the few remaining field-grade officers and generals survey the long line of blue arrayed against them. Grim faced, they would turn and look at the sun for a moment. Discouraged by the determined host that continued to flail at their thinning lines and saddened by the painfully slow progress that the setting sun was making, the officers would bow their heads, turn away, and walk on.

A hand on his sleeve caused James to turn and face Fielding Spencer, leaning against the wall, white faced, inches from James' face. "Jimmy," Spencer stammered, "I've got to ask you a favor."

Closing his eyes, James suppressed the urge to curse, for he knew what was coming.

"Jimmy, I'm serious. I'm not going to make it this time, I swear I'm not. I can see it all as plain as day. I'm going to . . ."

"Now damn it, Fielding," James shouted to make himself heard above the discharge of rifles all about them, "you do this to me every time." Reaching over, he pulled Fielding's hand off his arm and threw it back. "You're not going to die, damn it, and that's that."

"What if you're wrong and I'm right, this time, Jimmy?" Spencer countered. "What if I really do die in this fight?"

"Did you die when you saw your body laid out, all stiff and cold before Wilderness?" James countered.

"No."

"Were you shot down like a dog at Spotsylvania Court House like you kept shouting you were going to be before we went forward with Gordon's attack?"

"No."

"Did your body wind up floating down the Monocacy, all the way to the sea, like you thought it would during that battle?"

"No."

"And did grapeshot rip you to tiny pieces as you claimed it would in the middle of our last fight at Winchester."

"No."

"Then shut up," James howled as loud as he could, "and stop telling me how you're going to die. I promise you, as soon as it finally does happen, I'll tell you."

Undeterred by James' anger, Spencer continued. "It's different this time."

"It's always different," James screamed. "You never seem to manage to die the same way twice."

"No," Spencer countered. "The feeling. It's real, I can tell you, it's real. I know it."

Seeing there was no point in arguing, James closed his eyes and reached out with his open hand. "Here, give me the God damn letter."

James' acceptance of his judgment pleased Spencer. "Thank you,

Jimmy, thank you. Please make sure my mother and father get this letter after I'm gone. They'll be so thankful."

"Fielding," James replied as he stuffed the letter in the pocket of his shell jacket, "I'll put it with *all* the others. Someday, Fielding, I swear, I'm going to make you read each and every one of them *aloud*."

Ignoring James' snide remark, Spencer smiled before returning to the grim task of killing Yankees.

For better than three quarters of an hour, Kevin and his men stood their ground, hammering away at their enemy with a deadly rifle fire that chipped, but did not break, the gray line before them. Walking back and forth behind his own lines, Kevin stopped his incessant pacing only when he came across a body that had been knocked back out of the firing line by a Rebel bullet. If it was the face of a man he didn't recognize, a man from the Second Brigade, he would continue on. If it was one of his own, from the 4th New Jersey, he'd bend over, to see if there was any sign of life. If there was, he'd allow a couple of men a few minutes' break from the firing line to haul the poor soul out of harm's way. If there wasn't, he'd close his eyes, mutter a silent prayer, and continue on down the line.

On one of the legs of his journey, Baldwin Hufty stopped Kevin. "They can't take much more of this," Hufty shouted over the clatter of rifle fire.

Confused, Kevin looked at his brigade commander. "Who, our men or the enemy?"

Surprised by Kevin's question, Hufty blinked. "Why those people," he shouted, pointing in the direction of the stone wall. "We've about got them whipped."

Knowing, after having watched some of his more energetic fighters pause while they emptied the contents of dead men's cartridge boxes that his men were coming close to exhausting their ammunition, Kevin was about to inform Hufty of his concern when a series of hoots and hollers caught both officers' attention. "What's going on?" Hufty demanded.

Pushing his way forward through the ranks, Kevin peered through the smoke. "What's going on?" he demanded of no one in particular.

"They're runnin'," O'Keeth shouted. "Runnin' like whipped dogs. Look at 'em go."

Faintly, at first, Kevin could make out the forms of one, then two men in gray, their backs to the 4th New Jersey, as they fled for all they were worth. Jutting his head out of the ranks, he looked this way, then that, to see which Union division had managed to gain the wall and unhinge the enemy line. "The cavalry," a shout came down the line as the rifle fire tapered off. Looking back in the distance, Kevin caught sight of mounted men, blue horse soldiers, spurring their mounts on as they rode down the fleeing enemy. As they had at Winchester, the once-maligned Union horsemen provided the decisive stroke that broke the enemy's back.

From behind, a hand fell on his shoulder. "Take the regiment forward," Hufty shouted in Kevin's ear before turning to issue that order to the rest of the brigade.

Kevin, however, didn't have time to give any orders, for his regiment, seeing with their own eyes what was happening, took it upon themselves to advance and join in the pursuit.

Suddenly tired from his exertions, Kevin hesitated for a moment. Left standing in a line of dead and dying in a farm field, he looked about the shattered landscape for a moment. From right to left, he could see the Union line surge forward, prying the stubborn Confederates away from the wall they had held so tenaciously. It would be another grand victory, even more spectacular than that of a month before in Winchester. Together with Sherman's adventures in Georgia, he realized, these back-to-back successes would wipe away any doubt in the minds of voters up North that a Union victory was theirs for the taking. Lincoln, Kevin knew, would surely be elected, and with his reelection, they would be free to go on, not only with the ending of this godforsaken butchery, but with the rebuilding that he and Harriet would take a hand in.

"Just one more push," Kevin's corps commander's plea from earlier that afternoon rang in his ears. "All we need to do is give them one more push and it'll be over."

Pleased with himself, with the efforts of his command, Kevin shoved his empty pistol in his holster and began to go forward.

Exhausted, and unable to bear the burden of Lieutenant Roberts another step, James ordered his small stretcher party to move off the road and set the lieutenant down. He meant to tell them to be careful, to set the captured stretcher down slowly, but he was too late. Daniel's arm gave out, allowing his side of the stretcher to drop before the other's. Neither Fielding Spencer, James, nor a stray Yankee prisoner they had impressed into service were able to react in time to compensate. Only the softness of the ground and the delightful state of delirium that Roberts had slipped into prevented him from feeling the pain that radiated from his leg wound.

After mumbling an almost incoherent apology, Daniel threw himself down on the ground and fell instantly asleep. James and Spencer eased themselves down with their backs against two trees, facing the road choked with the refuse of a beaten army. "You suppose," Spencer said after several minutes of watching exhausted men drag themselves and their wounded comrades by in the darkness, "the Yank cavalry has given up the chase?"

Not having thought about anything for the past few hours other than placing one foot in front of the other, James listened for a moment. When he heard no telltale sign of rifle fire in the distance, he answered. "Seems so, Fielding. I expect those boys are about as tuckered out as we are."

Spencer, already asleep, didn't respond. Looking over at the Yankee prisoner who had been carrying the fourth corner of the stretcher all night, James debated whether he should tie the man up, just in case he fell asleep too and the Northerner got it into his head to escape. But James was too tired. Besides, he reasoned, he didn't have any rope, at least none that wasn't being used for something. There had been plenty of rope, he recalled, back in the Union camps. Ropes were all over the place, there for the taking. But that had been earlier in the day, before the final Union attack.

As James closed his eyes, he tried hard to remember if he had even seen a Yankee horseman when the line broke. He had heard the cries that they were flanked. He had watched helplessly as his half-trained recruits took to their heels and fled for their lives. He had seen cannoneers whipping their horses into a lather to escape certain death. But he couldn't remember seeing a single Union horse soldier before he, too, turned and ran.

Opening his eyes with a start, James looked around. In groggy puzzlement, he realized that he had fallen asleep. The road, which had been crowded with men and wagons, was empty and silent. The Yankee, who he had remembered sitting across from him, was gone. Only he and his small party of survivors who called themselves the 4th Virginia were there, in the cold, still darkness. At first, James thought about waking everyone and pressing on, down the road in an effort to catch up. That idea, however, was quickly discarded when he found he didn't even have the strength to push himself upright, away from the tree he was leaning against. Looking around, he saw everyone about him, including Lieutenant Roberts, rock sound asleep, despite the cold. Deciding it was best to leave things as they were, for a little longer, James allowed himself to relax.

Cocking his head back, he looked into the sky through the barren tree branches above him. The stars were out in force that night, filling the cold, quiet night sky and keeping him company. Sleepily, he searched the heavens for the star he had decided would represent Mary Beth. He had to move his head, which proved to be rather painful for his aching muscles, before he finally caught a glimpse of it. When he had it, he felt a rush of relief. Though it was only symbolic, and a very tenuous symbol at that, James imagined that all was safe, now that he had found Mary Beth's star. He was too tired to look for the one that he had given to his brother, though he knew with an unfailing certainty that it was there. Content, he folded his arms across his chest, closed his eyes, and fell off to sleep.

To the north, Kevin Bannon was doing likewise, snuggling up next to the cook fire where he and so many of his fellow officers had started the day, ignoring the moans of the wounded and dying that kept those already dead company. Less than a mile away, his wife, Harriet, went from room to room of the makeshift little field hospital, checking to see that every man had a blanket and that all their needs that she could manage to provide for had been tended to. Off to the east, Mary Beth, huddled in a blanket and a comforter she had salvaged from her ravaged home, tossed and turned uncomfortably in the bed of the small buckboard while Albert Merrel, ever fearful of being taken by Mosby's men, tried hard to get some sleep.

Slowly, without any of them knowing, the Bannons and those intimately associated with them were pulling away from each other, again.

PART FIVE

CLOSING THE CIRCLE

 CHAPTER 20

Richmond, Virginia, December, 1864

IN THE EARLY EVENING darkness, Mary Beth didn't see the figure emerging from the shadows until it was too late. Smelling him before she saw him, Mary Beth jumped back, almost dropping the bundles of gray cloth she was carrying. "Scuse me, miz," the soldier stammered. "Didn't mean to scare ya."

Shaking, Mary Beth continued to back away even though the man had stopped, still half in the shadows. The man raised his right hand till it came out of the dark shadows where she could see it and his ragged gray sleeve. "Please, miz, all I need is li'l' somethin' to get me by. Lost my arm, ya know. Can't make it home 'cause the Yanks are there, don't ya know. And I can't fight 'em with only one good arm."

Keeping her distance, Mary Beth saw that the right sleeve, barely visible in the dim light, was indeed empty. Still, she didn't want anything to do with the beggar. "I haven't anything for myself, let alone . . ." She was about to say "the likes of you," but caught herself. For though he was obviously drunk, and didn't seem to have a shred of pride left, it was wrong to assume that the man was a total malcontent. No doubt he was like so many other unfortunates that were becoming more and more evident. Crippled soldiers, no longer able to serve in the ranks but too well along in the physical healing process to be left occupying a badly needed hospital bed, had been turned out into the streets in the expectation that they would return home. Too many, however, had no homes to go back to. And too many carried wounds in their souls and minds that prevented them from rejoining a society they had once defended. The man before her, Mary Beth assumed, was one of them.

Still, Mary Beth herself was as much a stray, a refugee, as the pitiful figure before her. "I have nothing of value that would be of use to you, sir," she stuttered, still struggling to catch her breath. "Everything they pay me at the munitions factory goes right into room and board." The miserable wages she earned just covered the cost of what passed as lodging and meals in a private home. Only by sewing uniforms at night, earning ten cents a jacket or pair of trousers, could Mary Beth afford anything extra, such as candles for her little room in the attic. Of course, Mary Beth didn't mention the money Harriet Bannon had given her before they had parted in October. That money stayed hidden under a floorboard under her mattress. In a world that was falling apart, that money represented a hope, a tiny reserve that needed to be preserved for a time when the war was over and it was the moment to start again.

From his haven in the shadows, the crippled beggar looked Mary Beth over. The plain skirt hanging beneath the threadbare cap marked her as a working girl. Bare hands, still smudged black from handling cartridges all day, confirmed her claim. "Sorry to upset ya so, miz," the man finally muttered. "I was only hopin' . . ." Then, without finishing, he turned and limped down the alley he had been hiding in, dragging his left foot behind him as if it were little more than excess baggage.

For a second, Mary Beth's heart went out to him. Then, as the wind whipped down the street and tore savagely through her thin cap, all thoughts of charity disappeared as she bowed her head, turned away, and hurried on.

Walking as quickly as her tired legs could carry her, Mary Beth tried to push the ugly incident with the soldier from her mind. Though she felt for the man deep in her heart, as she did for those, like her, who had become the human flotsam and jetsam of this war, Mary Beth had little left she could offer anyone, even, at times, a kind word. Over and over she reviewed her decision to come to this abhorred place, crowded with refugees, like herself, and populated by more prostitutes and drunken soldiers than she could ever imagine. Still, she told herself, at least there was food to be had here, so long as she was willing and able to work. Back in the valley, Sheridan and his victorious army had ravaged the land, leaving only devastation and hunger in their wake. Besides, Mary Beth reminded herself in an effort to prove that she had made the right choice, James was in Petersburg, only thirty miles south of Richmond. That, if nothing else, was reason enough for her to be here.

Entering the home of Colonel and Mrs. Barrett J. Westerfield III, Mary Beth did not pause to look for anyone or even undo her cape. Instead, she tucked her head down as if she were about to force her way through a crowd and headed right for the stairs.

"Don't touch *anything*, young lady," a shrill voice from the parlor called out, "until you've washed those filthy hands."

Disappointed that she had not managed to make her way to her attic room before being caught by Amanda Westerfield, who took great pride in being referred to as "the colonel's wife," Mary Beth meekly slowed as she responded, "Yes, Mrs. Westerfield." Then, as she ascended the stairs, Mary Beth rubbed her hand back and forth along the entire length of the banister with great exaggerated sweeps in the hope that some of the black powder that permeated her hand would eventually find its way onto the soft, milky white hands of "the colonel's wife."

Reaching the top of the first flight of stairs, Mary Beth turned and hurried down the hall toward the next flight as quickly as she could but, again, she didn't make it in time. From a room at the end of the hall, just in front of the door that led up to the attic, a weak, quivering voice called out. "Bethy? Is that you, Bethy?"

Again, Mary Beth let her head droop for a moment as she realized she had failed to clear another obstacle. "Yes, Catherine, it's me," she replied despondently.

The door, already partially open, swung fully open as a young girl her age, dressed in a night shirt, stepped into the doorway. The girl leaned listlessly against the frame as limply as the unkempt, knotted hair that hung about her pale white face. Though almost two years her junior, Catherine Westerfield looked ten years older than Mary Beth. With sunken cheeks and dark circles about dull, listless eyes, the eldest Westerfield daughter struggled to smile. "Hi," she sighed breathlessly.

Mary Beth lifted her chin and forced a smile. "Feeling any better today, Catherine?"

With a barely discernible nod, the willowy figure responded. "I think so. I was able to join Mother for lunch downstairs."

"Oh, Catherine," Mary Beth replied with a slight widening of her forced smile. "I'm so glad you're feeling better."

"Yes, Bethy, I think I am." Then, after a pause, she asked hopefully, "Can you join me, later, and tell me how your day was?"

Lifting the bundle of gray cloth cut into various uniform parts, Mary Beth shook her head. "I'm sorry, Catherine, but I have so much sewing to do tonight. I need the money, you know."

Disappointed, the sickly girl let her head drop as her smile faded as quickly as her strength. "Yes, well, I suppose it's better you do such work for our boys rather than spend time gabbing with me."

For a moment, Mary Beth nonetheless felt a pang of sympathy for the poor creature. The death of the dashing young cavalier she had married at Brandy Station in June, 1863, followed by the miscarriage of her unborn child during her mourning had left Catherine a mental wreck. Efforts on the part of a friendly doctor to relieve Catherine's anguish through the liberal administration of opium not only failed to lift her torment, but slowly robbed her of her physical well-being.

For Mary Beth, the plight of Catherine, wasting away from grief, bore too striking a resemblance to the insanity that had claimed her mother and had made that dear woman's last days on earth a living hell. Already emotionally bankrupted by her own years of trials and tribulations, Mary Beth had little in the way of comfort and understanding to offer another. Besides, she reasoned as she tried to defend her decision to turn her back on a human being so desperately seeking help, Catherine has a mother. Let her tend to her own. "I need to wash up, Catherine," Mary Beth muttered softly in an effort to break off their conversation, "before your mother scolds me again."

With an understanding nod, Catherine Westerfield turned and retreated into her room. Leaving the door to the attic ajar in the hope that some heat from the house would find its way up the narrow stairway, Mary Beth struggled with skirts, crinolines, cape, and bundle on her way up to her little room. In the darkness, lit only by the faint moonlight that made its way through the tiny window in the house's gable, Mary Beth lay her bundle down on the mattress she slept on and reached for the jar containing matches. Carefully striking one, for matches, like everything else in

Richmond, were rare and not to be wasted, she lit the end of the long, spindly candle made from wax and strips of cloth sewn together for the wick. Unable to stand on its own, this ungainly candle had to be wrapped around an empty bottle. Nor was it much of a light, burning so quickly that a new one seldom lasted the night. Still, they were cheap to make, since Mary Beth was able to forage most of the materials needed from the cartridge factory where she worked.

Turning to the neat bundle of gray cloth, she carefully folded back layer after layer until she found the small brown package she had secured in the middle of it. Though she was tempted to rip the paper away to get at the bread and chunk of cheese it covered, she took her time, for even the often-used crumpled paper could be used again. Even when she had uncovered what would be her dinner, Mary Beth didn't grab it and start eating as she so wanted to. Noticing her hands were still quite filthy, she set the meager parcel of food aside and walked over to where a basin sat with water she had retrieved that morning. After paying better than half a day's wages for that food, Mary Beth was determined to enjoy every morsel of it. And that meant scrubbing away as much black powder from her hands as was possible.

Kneeling on the floor before the basin, for she had no furniture other than the mattress she slept on, she balled her hand and cracked the thin layer of ice that covered the surface. After pulling the thick pieces out and dropping them in the cracked porcelain pitcher she used to fetch water, she wet her hands quickly in the frigid water. Also quickly she took the crude bar of lye soap and rubbed it in her dripping hands before running them through the water again. Lacking a proper towel, she wiped her hands on a rag that served that purpose and others, then returned to her mattress to enjoy her meal.

Settling down on her mattress cross-legged, Mary Beth carefully took the bread and gingerly lifted it to her mouth so as not to lose a single crumb. How wonderful it would be, she thought, just to have a single swipe of butter to liven up the dry, crusty bread. After taking another bite, she exchanged the bread in her right hand for the cheese. The old freed Negro who had sold it to her claimed it was goat's cheese. Though she couldn't prove it, Mary Beth trusted the old man, a wonderful source for food whenever there seemed to be none anywhere else. And though it was quite expensive, it was always fresh and filling. The only thing she refused to buy from the man were the thin strips of meat he often offered her. "Ain't no rat, missy," he'd promise her as he held it before her face. "I don't deal in no rat meat, no, ma'am. Not me."

Despite this, she didn't give in to temptation. Finishing half the chunk, Mary Beth lay what was left next to the bread, then carefully folded the brown paper over the two. She would save some for later, since chances were better than even that the dear Mrs. Westerfield had, again, failed to save anything from the meager offerings she presented Mary Beth and two other female refugees for their board. "Young lady," she often admonished Mary Beth, "if you can't be punctual, as all well-bred ladies in Richmond are taught, then I can't be expected to be held accountable for what becomes of your share of the meals we serve in this house." That Mary Beth was the only one of the women in the house, besides the Negro servants, who worked, was never taken into consideration by Mrs. Westerfield. "The sign of a truly great society and culture," she told her friends in Mary Beth's presence, "is the steadfast way it holds to its customs and teachings, even in the worst of times."

Putting all thoughts of that woman out of her mind, Mary Beth brought her hands up to her lips, blew on them to warm them up some, then rubbed them together. Ready, she bent over, retrieved a needle already threaded from the previous night, and took up the first item to be sewn. Though she could have gotten by without doing this extra work, the sewing at night helped her pass the time. Being a farm girl from the sticks, she didn't fit in at all with Mrs. Westerfield and the other fine ladies of the city she cavorted with. No, Mary Beth thought as she placed the two sleeve halves together, she'd never know the pleasures of being asked to join sweet Mrs. Westerfield for an afternoon of tea at Mrs. Mary Chestnut's or a chat with the president's wife at her home. Even the other two boarders, the wife and daughter of a once-prosperous Fredericksburg merchant named Taylor, weren't of the proper pedigree for such honors, not anymore. "It's so dreadful," Mrs. Westerfield had lamented to Mary Beth once when she didn't have a suitable audience to perform for, "that so many fine, fine families such as the Taylors should fall so far."

Still, while the work kept the hands busy, the mind was left free to wander. In the quiet loneliness of her attic room, Mary Beth's thoughts ran far afield. More often than not, her thoughts took her back to more enjoyable times, filling her mind's eye with pleasant images of her family and life on a farm that had, until just two months ago, been her entire world. Like reciting a lesson in class, she recalled each and every animal and pet she had ever grown attached to and had claimed as her own. All too often, when she came to the horses, and the recollections of her large brown chestnut came to the fore, Mary Beth would be forced to stop sewing until the mist that clouded her vision at the mere thought of that noble beast cleared.

Only rarely did the future figure into her reflections. With no compass to guide her, no clear idea what the next day held in store, and nothing of any substance as a moor for security, any time spent in thinking about the future was, in Mary Beth's mind, useless and dangerous. The haunting image of Catherine Westerfield, a woman who had mortgaged her entire future on the expectation that the man she loved and married would always be there, was an all too visible reminder that dreams in times such as this were too dangerous to harbor.

Yet Mary Beth's consciousness wasn't totally impervious to such thoughts. Sometimes, after finishing a jacket, she would hold it up in the dim candlelight to inspect her work. If she was particularly pleased with the job she had done, inevitably she'd wonder what the chances were of finding a way of holding that one jacket back for James. That she always thought of James first, and without any effort, rather than her own brother, bothered Mary Beth for a while. But then she finally realized that somehow it was right and proper that a woman should put her chosen love first and foremost, even before her own brother. Daniel, Mary Beth reasoned, had always been there, and even in these uncertain times, she somehow thought he always would be. But James . . .

With one side of the sleeve sewn up, Mary Beth let the work drop into her lap. Taking a moment to pull her mother's comforter up over her shoulders before rethreading her needle, Mary Beth looked around the cold, barren attic. She listened to the wind as it whistled over, past the roof and into tiny cracks and crevices. Only the periodic creaking of one of the exposed wooden beams above her interrupted the winter night's harsh song. It would be horrible in the trenches, she thought. Even in the fantasy world that the gentlepeople of Richmond had erected about them, stories were being circulated of the deprivations being suffered by Lee's Army under siege at Petersburg.

James would be there now, she thought as she took up the sleeve again to start on the other side. Word that Early's shattered corps had rejoined the main Army a few miles down the road had brought no comfort to Mary Beth. The one last hope she had held for her beloved James was that he would be spared the experience that, rumor said, was breaking the Army of Northern Virginia bit by bit.

A sudden, mournful wail from down the stairway made itself heard above the whining of the winter wind. It was Catherine. Like her own mother, whenever Catherine floated from oblivion back into reality, a long session of weeping and wailing ensued. Catherine's sorrow reminded Mary Beth of her other concern as she began to run her needle through the coarse gray wool.

With James so near, it was inevitable that he would, if he truly cared for her, come to Richmond and find her. She had sent Daniel a letter, in November, telling him that she had left the farm and where she had settled. The thought of not doing so had crossed her mind, simply because she knew Daniel would tell James, even if she asked him not to. But with William's death, Daniel would inherit the farm. He had to be told.

Tugging away carefully at a knot in her thread, for she didn't want to break it and waste such a valuable commodity as thread, Mary Beth wondered what she'd do if James did make the trek to Richmond. Would she open her heart to him, as she had been tempted to do so many times before? Or would she keep him at arm's length, fearful that if she did tie her fate to his and he died . . .

Looking up, Mary Beth peered toward the small window as freezing sheets of rain started to pelt it. So little, she thought, separated James from becoming a wretched beggar like the one that had accosted her early that evening. So precious little. A foolish act of bravery could bring him down in the twinkling of an eye. Even a simple, innocent peek over the top of the trench's parapet right into the sights of a Yankee marksman would end, forever, the love that was unlike any love she had ever known before.

Closing her eyes, she let her head drop as her aching hands fell to her lap. Outside, the storm lashed at all that stood in its way, thrashing a city and a nation struggling to hang on to the only life it had ever known, had ever understood. In the silence of her room, Mary Beth prayed that it wouldn't wash away the one thing that kept her going, hope.

A spasm of shivers woke James Bannon with a start. His first reaction was to bring his knees in closer to his chin and pull tighter the water-logged wool blanket that he had wrapped around himself. When this did nothing to stop the paralyzing chills that wracked his body, James shoved his face through a small opening in the blanket and looked around.

It was still raining, a cold, bone-chilling rain. Looking down, he saw that the pile of scrap wood he had perched himself on the night before was now totally immersed in the muddy water that covered the bottom of their trench, allowing the water to lap about his feet and buttocks. Shaking off another violent round of shivers, James pulled his blanket down around his neck, freeing his head from the cocoon that he had tucked himself into. Looking about, blurry eyed, with a mind as numb from the lack of a decent night's sleep as his feet and bottom were from the cold, James tried hard to imagine how things could possibly get any worse than they were at that moment.

From outside the trench, James heard a distant *crump* that announced the firing of a heavy mortar shell. Having no way of telling which side had fired it, he was tempted to take a peek over the edge of the parapet, but quickly discarded that idea. Terry's brigade was too new in the line to have established an unofficial truce with their counterpart across the desolate no-man's-land that separated the two armies. Until they had a working "understanding" with the Yanks over there, it was almost suicidal to expose any part of one's body over the muddy rim of the trench.

Unable to track the mortar shell from its point of origin, James would have to content himself with merely sitting where he was and looking up in the hope of catching sight of the ugly black sphere as it passed over the trench. He was not disappointed. Within seconds, he caught a glimpse of the shell, hanging almost interminably as it reached the highest point of its exaggerated arc. Then, as if the invisible hand of gravity reached up and grabbed the spinning black ball, the mortar bomb began its precipitous descent. The burning fuse, so predominant against the dark gray winter sky, let off a hissing, spitting sound that grew louder as the mortar bomb spun around and around and grew larger and larger as it raced overhead to find its target somewhere in the Confederate rear. Without much guessing, James could tell that neither he nor any part of the trench his small command was in was threatened by this particular bomb. Still, he continued to sit quietly where he was until he heard the thunderous explosion and felt the earth under him quiver, then still.

"Well, that's a fine way to wake a fella up," Fielding Spencer moaned from farther down the trench. "Whatever happened to drums and the smell of fresh coffee boiling over an open fire?"

"I recall seeing a drum lying on the side of the valley pike," Daniel responded. "If James can finagle a pass for me, I'll go back and get it for you, Fielding."

Spencer laughed. "Capital idea. I'll go along, just to make sure you don't lose your way. After all, if there is one thing I learned during my short tenure at Washington College, it is that you can't trust a cadet alone on such an important mission."

James shook his head. "If I manage to wrangle a pass for anyone to escape from this madman's idea of hell," James shouted from his woolen cocoon, "it'll be for me. And," he added as he inched his way higher onto his small pile of boards, "it won't be in search of some damned drum."

"God," Fielding quipped, "I hate it when the acting company commander wakes up in a grump. Sort of ruins the whole day."

James looked down the narrow gash in the earth that passed for a trench. Spencer, stooped below the lip of the trench, was busy wringing out his water-logged blanket. It was a truly miserable stretch of earthworks that James was responsible for. Dug in haste during the frantic July battles, there were no provisions made for drainage. Logs used then to shore up the dirt walls were sagging under the weight of enemy bombardment and winter rain, giving rise to the need to constantly reinforce them with crossbeams that stretched from one side of the trench to the other at head level. James managed to bump his head on these crossbeams at least twice a day.

Still, they did have their good points. Enterprising soldiers, using scraps of canvas or blankets taken from dead comrades who would have no need for them in the next world, used the crossbeams as supports for makeshift roofs. James, Daniel, and Spencer had rigged one of these up shortly after arriving in the front line trench several days ago using a tarp Spencer had "found." "Those damned boxes in the wagon didn't need to be covered," Spencer explained. "They were half empty, anyhow."

Though he should have protested the stealing of government property, James said nothing. Everyone these days, it seemed, was looking out for himself as everything in the Army began to break down, from the supply system, which was always a cobbled-together affair, to the discipline that held units together. So James had let that little theft pass without comment, and enjoyed the benefits that their ad hoc shelter had given them. That is, until their ill-gotten canvas roof collapsed, with a great splash, in the middle of the night under the weight of the sleet and rain that had accumulated in it. Too disheartened by the failure of their efforts to waste time stumbling about in the darkness trying to reassemble it, each of the former occupants had gone his own way, in search of whatever cover he could find. James, too exhausted from the stress of being under the threat of imminent death day in and day out, had withdrawn to the lee of the trench wall, perched himself on the wood they had hoped to use for a fire in the morning, and wrapped his blanket about him without any thought of what the others were doing.

For a moment, as he watched Daniel begin to move about, picking at an edge of canvas that stuck up out of the muddy brown water that covered the bottom of the trench, James pondered his lack of concern with anyone other than himself. Though he had only become aware of it recently, he realized that it had been in the making for years. Ever since his separation from his younger brother, in December, 1859, he had been wandering about, mostly on his own, doing little to find a place for himself in the world and in society. Even when circumstances forced him to make a decision, he always did so with great reluctance, and all too often, half-heartedly. His two true efforts to find friendship and emotional attachment with another human being had both ended tragically. Will McPherson was taken from him, as were so many other young men he had known over these past three years plus. And Mary Beth . . .

James sighed as he let his head hang down, ignoring the driblets of rain that fell from his strands of hair and ran down his neck. The day, he thought, was as gloomy as his thoughts. At times he felt like he was the poor fellow from "The Rime of the Ancient Mariner," doomed to walk the earth with a dead albatross hanging about his neck as repentance for a wrong he had committed long ago. At least, James chuckled grimly to himself, the old mariner had taken a hand in his deed. He, on the other hand, tried and found himself guilty of omissions, rather than commission. He had meekly submitted to his father's exile and allowed himself to drift south when he should have struck off on his own. He had followed Will McPherson into the Army out of habit more than loyalty. And he stayed with that Army when common sense told him that all was lost, simply beçause he couldn't motivate himself to do otherwise. Like Geddy, he had found it easier to do nothing than to muster the courage to follow one's own decisions.

Looking around the muddy trench, James wondered if it wasn't his fate to be the ultimate follower, someone who had no will of his own, depending on others to push or pull him one way or the other. He didn't like that idea, for it was not at all flattering. Still, from where he sat, he could see nothing to disprove it. Like the animals on the McPherson farm, he was allowing himself to be corraled and kept till it was time for the slaughter.

Whatever the reason, he concluded, the results were the same. It didn't matter anymore. What mattered was that in the process of bouncing from one crisis to the next over these past few years, he had lost the love of the one woman who might have been his salvation. Mary Beth, so free, so vibrant, had come to represent a new future, something that now lay in mud just like their feeble shelter. Unable to accept wholeheartedly or return that love, James realized that he had become lonely, bitter, and selfish. Even his self-proclaimed task of doing all he could to protect Daniel McPherson was forgotten when it was convenient to do so. Lost in his own self-pity, James continued to huddle under his blanket as the ragged remnants of the 4th Virginia began to come to life all around him and sort themselves out after another long, miserable night in the trenches.

"You gonna call roll this morning, Jimmy," Spencer called out, "or do you want me to do it for you?"

Shaking his head and looking up, James threw his blanket off his shoulders and stood up, forgetting that he would be half a head taller than the height of the trench due to the pile of wood he had been squatting on. "No, no," he responded absentmindedly. "It's my duty and . . ."

The searing pain that cut across the top of James' head stunned him. With eyes opened wide in shock, James stumbled backward, against the trench wall he had been sleeping in front of all night. Stunned, he threw his arms out in a wild effort to grab on to something. His stiff fingers, however, didn't find anything but loose mud to claw into.

When others finally heard the *crack* from the rifle report, few turned to see if anyone was hit. Such things were annoyingly routine. Rifle fire and death had become grim realities that the trench dwellers had learned to live with. It wasn't until James slowly began to sink into the mud, slime, and filthy water that lined the bottom of their trench that anyone noticed he was in trouble. Even when Spencer finally did stop and look to see what was wrong with his friend, it wasn't until the thin rivulets of blood seeped out from under the brim of James' hat and streaked his face that Spencer realized that the sniper bullet had found its mark.

Slowly settling in the cold, muddy water, James was only dimly aware of the shouts of those around him as they rushed to his aid. Closing his eyes as he felt the warm blood on his face mix with the cold winter rain, James let go of the wall he had been trying to grasp and slumped forward into a ball.

"Miss McPherson," Amanda Westerfield called in the haughty voice that so annoyed Mary Beth, "there is a *soldier* here to see you."

Stopping in midstride, Mary Beth spun around and made for the parlor where Amanda Westerfield had called from. She didn't, however, make it that far. "Stop!" Amanda Westerfield announced as she advanced to the doorway to block Mary Beth's passage. "You know better than to come into the main part of the house before you wash up."

Though she was angry, Mary Beth was anxious to see James. Bobbing up on her toes, she tried to catch sight of him over Amanda Westerfield's shoulder. "*Dear* child," Amanda Westerfield stated, "you don't think I'd let a soldier *like* that, fresh from the field with filth dripping from him like a coal miner, in *my* house."

For the briefest of moments, as she settled back on her heels, Mary Beth wondered if Amanda dealt with *the colonel* in the same manner. "Where is he? You didn't turn him away, or make him stand outside in the cold, did you?"

Amanda Westerfield gave Mary Beth a look of disdain. "Of *course* not, young lady. What kind of a woman do you think I am?"

Mary Beth didn't answer that. Instead, she went back to her un-answered question. "Where is he?"

"In the cookhouse, of course."

Knowing better than to go through the dining room and out the rear door to the cookhouse, Mary Beth spun on her heel and flew out the front door. Making her way down the brick path that circled the house, Mary

Beth approached the cookhouse, a warm place she frequented when the bitter cold in the attic became too much. Flinging the door open, she rushed into the room, startling the Negro cook who was finishing up the last of her chores for the day. "Dear Lord, girl," the thin slave screeched, "you near scared the daylights out of me."

Ignoring the woman's protestations, Mary Beth blurted, "Where's James?"

"In the big hospital, at Chimborazo," Daniel McPherson responded with a mouth full of food. "Took 'im there myself before coming over here."

In a panic, Mary Beth froze where she stood. "Is he . . ."

Licking the fat that coated his finger before answering, Daniel swallowed what he had in his mouth, then smiled. "James? Oh, he's all right. Just another near miss that was more near than it was a miss."

Confused, Mary Beth cocked her head. From across the room, the Negro cook scolded her. "Girl, shut that door. This is a cookhouse, not a barn."

Obediently, Mary Beth reached behind her and slammed the door shut. "Here," the Negro slave ordered her. "Come on over here, take a seat, and visit with your brother while I find somethin' for you to eat. You look just famished."

Too involved with her line of questioning to respond, Mary Beth obeyed the cook and moved to the chair the slave had pulled out from the table across from her brother. Of all the white women in the house, Mary Beth was the only one any of the three Negro servants went out of their way to help and talk to. In part, this was because Mary Beth, never having been around slaves in her life, treated the Westerfield servants in the same manner she dealt with all God-fearing Christians. And in part, the servants saw little difference between Mary Beth, a working girl, and themselves, though they didn't dare say this to Mary Beth.

Turning her full attention to Daniel, she waited for her brother to tell her more. "We were in the trenches, this morning, when James forgot himself, stood up, and, *pow*, got himself shot in the head," Daniel recounted in a matter-of-fact manner that horrified Mary Beth.

"In the head?"

Daniel raised another small chicken leg, but stopped to answer his sister before bringing it to his mouth, passing off Mary Beth's concern in a casual tone. "Oh, it wasn't bad, no worse, some of the older fellows say, than the last shot he took in the head."

"He was shot in the head before? When?" Mary Beth screeched.

"Over a year ago, I think, in October '63 during the Mine Run affair. You didn't know?" he asked before bowing his head and sinking his teeth into the warm chicken leg.

Mary Beth desperately tried to remember why she hadn't noticed any scars when James had last visited her in July, before marching north. Unable to recall any marks, and ashamed, now, of the manner in which she had behaved then, Mary Beth bit her lip. From behind, the cook reached around her and placed a plate with a small piece of baked chicken, corn bread, and rice before her. "Eat this, child, 'fore *the colonel's wife* comes out here and gives me what for."

Though anxious to find out more from her brother, who was more interested in eating his first real meal in civilized surroundings in months than answering her questions, the plate of food before her was too tempting to ignore. It had been a bad day at the marketplace where she foraged for food from its pitiful offerings.

Daniel looked up from a bone he was picking at. "You eat like this all the time?"

To his surprise, the colored cook answered. "Oh, Lord no. Beth here is lucky if she sees this much food in a week. The *colonel's wife* wouldn't think of wasting a single crumb of the precious stocks of food she and her sister have squirreled away somewhere, let alone hold a meal for the likes of your sister."

Shocked, Daniel looked over to his sister, who didn't even raise an eyebrow as she attacked the meal before her. Noticing that Daniel's expression of dismay was slowly turning into one of disgust, the cook turned away from him and went back to her cleaning without another word.

When she finally did speak, Mary Beth did so as she ate, an act that would have resulted in a quick slap in the face had she tried doing so in front of her mother or father. "Well, just how bad is James? I mean, it must be bad if he was sent all the way back here."

Daniel winked as he gnawed away at a chicken bone in order to scrape away every bit of meat he could. "No, he's not bad, not at all. Fact is, I expect they'll throw him out in a day or two and send us back down to Petersburg."

"Then how," Mary Beth came back, as she brought her finger up to catch a bit of food hanging from the corner of her mouth, "did you manage to get them to let you bring him here? Or did you . . ."

"No, Sis, I didn't desert. An old friend of James', an officer by the name of Abner Couper who's on Gordon's staff, 'arranged' to have James sent back with me." Then, he smiled. "As for me, I'm a temporary hospital steward. I'll get to stay with the guards over there at the hospital. That'll be good for a bath and a couple of nights' sleep without the fear of waking up to find a mortar bomb in your lap or having rats run up and down your pants leg like they were the valley pike."

Though disturbed by the harsh images of life in the trenches, Mary Beth forced a faint smile. "That was nice of him. I'm glad he was able to help." Turning back to her meal, Mary Beth reflected about her feelings for James as she finished the piece of chicken she had been attacking. Done with that, she dropped the bones on her plate and grabbed up the corn bread. Behind her, the black cook heaved a great sigh. "My, my. You two have worse table manners than my Jerome, and he's four years old."

Mary Beth turned her head. "Prissy," she retorted with a friendly tone in her voice, "sometimes you're worse than my mama."

"Well, child, we mothers have to stick together and look out after each other's children, now don't we?"

As he sat silently eating, Daniel watched his sister and the Negro slave as they exchanged verbal jabs. Since leaving home, first attending VMI and then serving in the Army, Daniel had come across many Negroes. Most were either servants still dutifully following their officer and sharing the risks and hardships of military life, or slaves, used on occasion to dig earthworks or do other menial work for the Army. He had only come across a few freemen and had never spoken to any of them. Like Mary Beth, his experiences with Negroes while growing up on their farm outside of Winchester had been few and fleeting. Unlike Mary Beth, he had learned from his fellow cadets and comrades in the ranks how to deal with the "darkies." Making a mental note, Daniel told himself that he'd have to talk to Mary Beth about carrying on with a slave girl in such a manner, even if the girl was kind and very, very forthcoming with such fine food.

"Daniel," his sister asked as she turned her attention back to him, "can we see him tonight?"

Shaking his head, Daniel dropped the clean bone on his plate. "James has had a really, really rough day. Besides," he added as he lifted his cup and shoved it toward the black cook, indicating he wanted more coffee without bothering to ask, "it's late, his brain is still a bit scrambled, and they don't like visitors poking about the hospital at night."

Disappointed, Mary Beth's head drooped. "I'm not sure I'll be able to get off from work. They're awfully hard on absenteeism at the factory. And if I lose that job, I'm not sure I can find another that's as well paying."

Reaching across the table, Daniel placed his hand on Mary Beth's arm. "It's better if you don't show up, at least not right away."

Taken aback by Daniel's statement, Mary Beth pulled away. "Why?"

Taking a deep breath, Daniel eased back in his seat, took a sip of the coffee he had been given and not bothered to thank the cook for, and thought a minute. "James, is, well, not sure about how things are between you two. When we were at the farm last, you . . ."

Closing her eyes, Mary Beth bowed her head in shame. "I know, I know."

"Well," Daniel continued after waiting a few seconds, "I think it would be better if I told him you were coming. You know, sort of give him a chance to sort out his feelings toward you and, well . . ."

"Daniel?"

"Yes, Beth?"

"What are his feelings toward me?"

Coldly, Daniel eyed his sister for a moment. "What," he asked slowly, deliberately, "are your feelings toward him?"

Without needing to think of the answer, she looked into her brother's eyes as tears began to well up in hers. "Danny, I love him, I love him more than I could ever imagine was possible. I think I always have."

Smiling, her brother reached out and patted her hand like her father used to. "Well, then, Beth, you have nothing to worry about."

After managing to get herself lost twice in the sprawling 125-acre complex of one-story wooden hospital wards that made up the Chimborazo military hospital, Mary Beth finally found James. The late afternoon sun threw its dying light through the small, dirty windows of James' ward, brilliantly illuminating everything that it fell on while hiding all else in deep, dark shadows. Scanning the rows of beds in her search for James took time, for Mary Beth's eyes had to continually adjust and readjust themselves as they moved from light to darkness, and then back into light. A woman, whose youth was hidden by the same haggard and careworn expression that marred Harriet Bannon's beauty, stopped when she saw Mary Beth slowly walking down the aisle, looking at the face of each man as she passed. Having witnessed this scene a thousand times, she walked up to Mary Beth, stopping before her. "Excuse me, but perhaps I can be of assistance."

Surprised by the young woman, for her eyes were in the process of adjusting as she turned to focus on a patient lying in the sunlight, Mary Beth came to an abrupt halt. "Oh, excuse me, I . . ."

The woman smiled. "I'm sorry. I didn't mean to startle you. I just thought that perhaps I could help you find the soldier you were looking for."

Having managed to settle herself, Mary Beth glanced over at the face of the man whose bed she was standing next to. Seeing that the one-armed blond-haired youth bore no resemblance to James, she looked back at the woman before her. "James Bannon," she uttered without preamble. "He would have been brought in . . ."

The smile that lit the woman's face told Mary Beth that she had finally found him. "That one, yes," the woman responded cryptically. "He's hiding over here, in the corner." After pointing to a bed behind her, hidden in the dark shadows of the opposite row, the woman turned back to Mary Beth. "Best spend as much time with him as you can. The doctors are on to him and he'll be out of here and on his way back to his unit in another day or so."

"Then he'll be all right?"

The woman smiled, cocking her head. "Oh, I suppose he'll feel like his head's about to split open for another few days or so, but compared to these other poor creatures," she announced with a sweep of her hand, "he's the picture of health."

Recalling Daniel's explanation that he and a Colonel Couper had conspired to send James back to Richmond for a few days of comfortable recovery rather than keeping him in the overcrowded and less comfortable hospitals at Petersburg, Mary Beth understood. Feeling embarrassed by this duplicity in the light of the suffering of men who bore worthy wounds, Mary Beth hastened to apologize for her brother's and James' action. "I hope he hasn't been a bother. I'm sure they didn't mean any harm."

Again, a smile lit the woman's face, this time with a sweet sincerity, as she reached out and touched Mary Beth's arm. "Oh, he's been no bother. In fact, I can't blame him, not one bit." She spoke slowly, mournfully, as her eyes scanned the long rows of filled beds. "I've heard all the stories of what it's like, *down there*. And I've seen how they come in, day after day, ragged, filthy, gaunt." She paused. Mary Beth felt her shiver. "I can tell you in all honesty," the young nurse continued looking into Mary Beth's eyes, "I can't blame your James for not passing up a chance for a few days' rest in a nice, warm, clean bed. Besides," the woman added with a glint in her eye as she tilted her head down while a sheepish expression lit her face, "if it hadn't been for Sergeant Bannon's coming here, I'd never have been afforded the opportunity of meeting his charming companion."

Caught off guard again, Mary Beth's eyes opened wide. "Daniel?"

"Why, yes. Daniel McPherson. Even with all the mud that covered him from head to toe when he first came tromping through here, I don't think I ever laid eyes on such a handsome, more exciting young man. It will be a shame to see him leave before I am afforded the opportunity of a proper introduction."

Taken aback at first by the love-struck look in the young girl's eyes and her words of hopeless adoration for her brother, Mary Beth didn't know what to say. Then, with a comforting pat on the girl's hand, she smiled and looked into the nurse's eyes. "Oh, I think that can be arranged. You see, I am Daniel's sister."

Now it was the nurse's turn for embarrassment, which quickly gave way to hope and joy when she saw the warm, friendly look in Mary Beth's eyes. With a blush that was quickly followed by a wide, beaming smile, the young woman squeezed Mary Beth's arm. Then, excited by the prospect of meeting the object of her affections in an appropriate manner, she hurried out of the room as if she remembered something important was waiting to be done. Left alone, Mary Beth shook her head and smiled to herself before walking over to James' bed.

Approaching, she saw that he was asleep. Not knowing what else to do, she paused before reaching his bedside and looked about for something to sit on. A rickety old straightback chair that had three good legs and one that looked questionable, even at this distance, stood near the door by James' bed. With no one around to ask, and seeing no harm in borrowing it, Mary Beth walked over, took the chair, and quietly set it next to James' bed so that she could sit facing him.

For a moment, she arranged her skirt, fretting at all the street stains along the hem as well as numerous splotches of black here and there from the powder she handled all day. With a sigh, she bowed her head and started to brush futilely at one of the more obvious stains, rubbing her hand back and forth across it. She was in the process of moving her attention to another spot when she looked up and caught James staring at her with one eye half open and the other half shut.

"Mary Beth?" he whispered.

"Yes, of course," she responded with a smile. "Who were you expecting?"

Quickly, James lifted his finger to his lips and tried to hush her while looking around to see if any of the nurses or ward stewards were around. "Sssh! Not so loud."

Despite the bandage on his head, the dark circles about his eyes, and the shallow gauntness of his face, James' childlike behavior reminded Mary Beth of her brothers when they were trying to hide something. Canting her head to one side, she gave him a sly look. "You're trying to fool these people into thinking you're really hurt bad, aren't you?"

"Well," he countered in his own defense, "I am wounded. You try taking a Yankee minié ball straight down the center of your skull and see how you feel."

Reaching across, Mary Beth lay her hand on top of James' hand. "I'm sorry to present you with bad news, but they're already wise to your little game."

Astonished, James lifted his head off the pillow and looked at Mary Beth for a moment. Then he relaxed, easing his head back. "Daniel! I'll bet it was Daniel and that nurse he's been making eyes at since we've been here."

"She is the one who told me, James. And she's been watching my baby brother too. Haven't they met or talked?"

James chuckled. "Her? Not likely. Don't let the fact that she works in this hospital fool you. She's still very much the proper Richmond lady, all manners, frills, and respectability. All hell itself could be knocking at the door and she'd open it because it would be impolite not to. Still . . ."

"Still what?" Mary Beth asked incredulously.

"She is a charming lass, one well worth shedding my feigned insensibility for if it weren't for . . ." Pausing, James looked at Mary Beth's smiling face, thin and careworn but still glowing with the rich, wholesome beauty that had stolen his heart the first time he had laid eyes on her.

Feeling the mood change, Mary Beth went to pull her hand away from James', but she wasn't fast enough. Quickly flipping his over, he caught her rough, black smudged fingers in his hand and brought them up to his lips. Without even noticing the smell of gunpowder or scent of lye soap she had used in a vain effort to scrub them clean, James kissed her fingers, then pulled them over next to his check.

Breathlessly, Mary Beth let him do with her hand as he pleased. Teary-eyed, she smiled as he rubbed his rough, stubbled cheek across her hand. "James," she finally uttered, "I've been wanting to tell you so much, for so long, I just didn't . . ."

Reaching up with his free hand, James touched a finger to Mary Beth's lips. "Please, my dear Mary Beth. Say nothing. Too much has already been said. Too much, yet not enough."

Mary Beth followed the finger he let fall from her lips, lightly kissing it. With eyes too blurred by tears to see, she lowered her head and brought it to rest on James' heaving chest. Wrapping both hands about the one she had been holding, Mary Beth brought it up to to her lips, kissed it, then laid it to rest before her face.

In the gathering darkness, lit only by the weak flicker of candles brought into the long ward, the two outcasts clung to each other. Emotionally scarred beyond recovery by a war that knew no end, logic dictated that each of them should pull away, that they should protect themselves from any further sorrow by avoiding entanglement with another. Yet their love, like the war, no longer responded to logic or reason. Right or wrong, sane or mad, both realized that their future was now, and forever more, bound to the other. For better, or for worse.

For the longest time, both men contented themselves with listening to the clicking of the wheels of the train as it made its way south along the dilapidated rail line that connected Richmond with Petersburg. James concerned himself with trying to keep clean the uniform Mary Beth had somehow managed to procure for him. Though five minutes in a forward position would leave it indistinguishable, except for its lack of patches, from any of the others around him, by keeping it clean he would be able to preserve the caring, loving thought that Mary Beth had sewn into every seam.

Lost in his thoughts, James didn't hear Daniel try to get his attention. It wasn't until Daniel had called his name out for the third time that James turned to face his companion. "Did you say something?"

In a voice that betrayed his frustration at having been ignored so long, Daniel repeated his question. "I said, do you think it's foolish to get married?"

Shaking his head as if to clear old thoughts from it in order to accommodate new ones, James wondered how Daniel knew what he had been thinking about. For the longest time, he stared at the brother of the woman he loved. Just how much did he know, James wondered, about the long, quiet conversation he and Mary Beth had had over the past four days and how much was simply guesswork? Was this a trick question of some sort?

Frustration soon gave way to budding anger. "Damn it, James," Daniel asked bitterly, "I'm serious. Do you think it's wise for me and Helen to, well, you know . . ."

James' bewilderment gave way to relief. Daniel wasn't even thinking of his sister and him.

Mistaking the grin on James' face, Daniel let his anger show. "Well, if that's the way you feel about something that's so important to me, then the hell with you."

"Oh, no." James hastened to calm his friend down. "I wasn't laughing at you. I was just thinking about something else and thought . . ."

"Well, I'm glad one of us is enjoying himself," Daniel snapped.

Assuming a more concerned expression, James leaned forward. "Sorry, Daniel. Now, what is it that's bothering you?"

"I told you," Daniel responded peevishly. "Helen and I, we're really serious about each other. I truly do think we're in love and I'm not sure what to do. I was hoping for some advice, serious advice."

James thought about the issue for a moment. Helen, the nurse on James' ward, had received the formal introduction to Daniel that she had been craving, and more. Daniel, jaded about everyone and everything after having witnessed, firsthand, the death of all his dreams of military glory and honor in one shattering battle after another, found comfort and joy in Helen Marie Hanson's unquestioning adoration of him. That she was, herself, seeking escape from the horrors of dealing with the broken and disfigured wounded that flowed through her ward in an unending stream didn't matter to either of them. What mattered was the same thing that seemed to propel James and Mary Beth to each other. In a world in which all that had gone before was slipping away, where it seemed that everyone was cast adrift and left to fend for themselves in an endless nightmare, and the only thing that was certain was that the next day would be worse than the one before, uncompromising and unadorned love between a man and a woman was the only comfort that eased the suffering. It was, James reasoned, as if the entire Southern way of life were being reduced to the lowest common denominator. Like an onion, the Confederacy and all its trappings of culture and civilization were being peeled away, one layer at a time, until there was nothing left, nothing but one man, one woman, and a mysterious, unquestioning love for each other.

Adam and Eve, James imagined, would fit in well in Virginia. That he had found this biblical truth before it was too late was, in many ways, a relief, a form of redemption. "I do not know how we will make our way in the world," James confessed to Mary Beth as they lingered outside the train station waiting for the whistle to signal their parting. "I have no real skills, other than being a soldier. Nor do I have any property, other than the clothes I am wearing. I am about as wretched, destitute, and forlorn as they come."

He had watched a slow, confident smile creep across Mary Beth's face as he spoke those words of hopelessness. And though he was anxious to know what inner strength or knowledge gave her such confidence, James chose not to shatter the warmth of the moment with such worldly concerns. Instead, he brought her cold, powder-stained fingers up to his lips and kissed them. Unconcerned with issues of propriety, Mary Beth pulled her hands away and lunged forward. Wrapping her arms about his neck, she reached up and kissed him on the lips as other passengers waiting to board the rickety train looked on in smiling admiration or gasped in feigned horror.

"Helen's mother was all flustered," Daniel went on as James' thoughts wandered about, "when she found out I was only a private. It wasn't till she found out I had been a cadet at VMI that she even considered talking to me."

James grunted. "Good Tidewater stock?"

Daniel beamed, "Oh, the best. Helen says she has ancestors who are counted as part of the original founders of Richmond."

"Impressive," James responded with a nod. "Is she equally impressed by your farm in Winchester and the prospects of becoming a farmer's wife?"

Daniel's expression soured noticeably as he looked down at the floor of the boxcar they shared with crates and sacks. "You haven't told her," James finally said, "have you?"

"Well, sort of," was all Daniel could respond.

"You exaggerated," James came back, smiling now. "Told her you had a mansion and all, I'll bet."

"Yes," Daniel responded defiantly. "One with two dozen slaves."

The mention of slaves caused the corners of James' smile to droop. Of all the questions that he had wrestled with in the past five years, the issue of black slaves had been one he had never fully faced. Though raised to take his place as part of the very aristocracy that rejected his father, James found he identified better with what was known by "proper society" as the common sort. It was the Irish laborers in his father's Perth Amboy terra-cotta works and the farmers of Virginia, both still on the land and in the ranks, that he felt at ease with, that he admired. Lording over another, taking on airs simply because of an accident of birth bothered James like nothing else.

"You think I'm a fool," Daniel asked as he watched his friend closely, "don't you?"

Pushing the slave issue out of his mind, as he usually did, James turned his full attention toward Daniel's problem. "This war is going to come to an end, and soon," James started slowly. "But not before there's at least one more long, bloody campaign. What we saw at Winchester in September and at Cedar Creek in October will be repeated, here, in central Virginia come spring."

"Lee," Daniel challenged, "wasn't in the valley. He'd never let a chance slip like Early did. He'll never . . ."

"The Army we're going back to isn't the same Army that Lee led in '62, '63, or even last spring. There's only so much we can do, only so far we can go before everything, body and soul, gives out. I'm telling you, Daniel," James concluded, "that moment's at hand."

For the longest time, Daniel said nothing. Though he would have loved to have challenged James, though he would have loved to say that there was still hope, the image of Union horsemen, sunlight shining on upturned pistols and sabers, riding them down like animals, was still too fresh. The reality of those images and James' words were simply too compelling to deny. Squirming, Daniel shifted about on the sack he had been sitting on. "Even if that's all true, even if all you say comes to pass, why should I have to deny myself, and Helen, whatever happiness we can find while we're both alive? Why should I live in total despair of what could be?"

Mary Beth had used the same argument when they had talked about marriage the previous night. "We're here, James, together, now," she had pleaded. "Isn't that enough?"

He had no answer then, and he didn't have one now. Dumbly, he looked at Daniel and lowered his head. "I've come to the conclusion," he stated slowly, "that we're neither victims of circumstances nor masters of our own fates." Looking up, he fixed his gaze on Daniel's face. "Rather, dear friend, life is just as Shakespeare once claimed it was in his play *Macbeth*."

"And what was that?" Daniel asked, half skeptical, half curious.

" 'Life's but a walking shadow, a poor player/That struts and frets his hour upon the stage/And then is heard no more: it is a tale/Told by an idiot, full of sound and fury,/Signifying nothing.' "

"You think all this," Daniel countered with his hands stretched out, "has been for nothing?"

James shook his head. "No, it's not been for nothing. But this," he said as he pulled on his uniform, "isn't what we are. And it isn't what life is all about. If you love Helen, then go ahead, marry her. In the end, there is no right, no wrong."

Confused, Daniel thought about James' comments for the longest time. It wasn't until the train was slowing to stop at Petersburg that Daniel finally broke the silence the two men had fallen into. "You're right, I think, James. I'm going to marry Helen."

James smiled and nodded. "That's good, Daniel. I'm happy for you."

Glad to hear that he had made the right decision, Daniel came to life. "Do you think I'll be able to get a pass to go back to Richmond, soon?"

Having no desire to dampen the boy's spirits, James nodded. "We'll see what we can do."

As the two gathered up their meager possessions and prepared to hop out of the dilapidated boxcar, Daniel looked over to James. "Thanks, Jimmy."

For the briefest moment, the fading light, the expression on Daniel's face, and the tone of the boy's voice reminded James of Daniel's dead brother, Will. The chill that it sent down his spine stayed with James all that night, and for days to come.

 CHAPTER 21

Outside Petersburg, Virginia, New Year's Day, 1865

ONLY THE SCRAPING OF shovels biting into freshly exposed earth and the splattering of raindrops on Kevin's water-logged hat broke the silence. Looking up from the foot of the narrow slit of earth that was beginning to take on the appropriate dimensions of a proper grave, he glanced around the circle of long faces of the men gathered about watching two of their companions as they dug the hole deeper.

It had been a hard day and night for them. You could see it in their eyes, Kevin thought, eyes that saw and remembered everything, for later recall when one was on the verge of a peaceful slumber. Only then, like the long roll that roused them out of the miserable collection of tents and shelters that passed for a camp, would the mind allow the full impact of what the eyes had seen to strike home. Bringing his head down, Kevin forced himself to look over at the corpse tightly wrapped in a muddy gray blanket as it waited for the men in the hole to finish digging its final resting place.

It was only now, with the danger of the previous day receding, that the tense, fearful hours that greeted the last day of 1864 could be viewed clearly, objectively, by Kevin.

"Captain Bannon!" his acting regimental commander had called out as he stood watching his men scramble out of their tents, into the darkness, and rush to recover their stacked arms as the clatter of rifle fire grew. Still struggling to pull his pistol belt around his waist, Kevin headed for Captain Ebenezer W. Davis at the double. "That's more than a simple squabble between pickets," Davis shouted.

"Trench raid?" Kevin ventured.

In the dim light of watch fires struggling to stay alive in the rain, Kevin watched as Davis stared into the darkness in the direction of the sound of gunfire. Finally Davis nodded in acknowledgment of Kevin's estimate. "Yes, I think so, Kevin," he mumbled without taking his eyes away from the flashes just off to their left. "Looks like it's Third Brigade that's catching the brunt of it. Still . . ."

His words trailed off as he thought about what he should do. In the meantime, Kevin turned to watch the regiment as it fell in. Though he enjoyed his new position as regimental adjutant, there were times when he missed his company, times when he felt he was no longer doing all that he could be doing to bring this war to an end. Tonight, however, was not one of them.

Snapping his head about, Davis began to issue his orders. "I want you to go forward with a skirmish line over toward Third Brigade. If possible, push out to the picket line."

Though thankful for something to do, the prospect of going forward in the darkness, made more impenetrable by pelting sleet and rain, into a fight already in progress against an enemy force of unknown size made Kevin hesitate. For a second, he considered offering a suggestion that he wait until the entire regiment was up and ready to go forward. The thought of a thin line smacking into an alert, fully deployed and prepared enemy line of battle in the darkness was bad enough. But to be in line of skirmish, sandwiched between that enemy force and your own troops coming up behind you was even more appalling. Kevin had seen friendly units take fire from other friendly units in the confusion of battle, under better conditions than these, too often to take his assignment lightly.

After a moment's hesitation, he looked off toward the sound of the growing battle, then back at Davis. "If you don't mind, I'll take my old company and one more from the Fourth. I don't want any of the boys from the Fortieth stumbling out there in the darkness getting excited or lost."

The 40th New Jersey, not yet formed, was sending its companies south from its training camp in New Jersey one company at a time until there were enough ready to become an independent command. Until that happened, they fell in as part of the 4th New Jersey, now the senior regiment in the brigade. Taking one of the two new, untried companies, though they were much bigger than any the 4th could muster, would be foolish and dangerous. Understanding Kevin's decision to take his old company as one of the two, with men familiar with and confident in him, Davis nodded. "Okay, get to it."

With a sharpness that his old first sergeant would have admired, Johnny O'Keeth moved the company forward quickly and into skirmish order. Kevin kept himself in the center, where the two companies met and a little to the rear. Their movement forward, difficult in the broken and scarred landscape under the best of conditions, was slow, halting, and agonizing. Here and there, above the report of rifle fire, Kevin could make out an occasional splash or thud, usually followed by a scream of pain or an uttered oath as men fell into holes, bumped into shattered tree stumps, or tripped over debris scattered about. Only the compelling fear of what lay ahead kept Kevin from chuckling when a familiar voice called out to bemoan an accidental run-in with an inanimate object.

"Look sharp, boys," Kevin called out as they approached the rear of the trench.

The warning served to slow those who had surged ahead or had been fortunate enough to pick a clear, unobstructed path forward. It also caught the attention of some of the 4th New Jersey who had been on duty up in the trench itself. "Don't get excited, lads," a voice from up ahead called out. "We're still here. The Fourth New Jersey. The Johnnies have pulled back and we're still here."

"Dale," Kevin responded recognizing the voice, "we're coming through and going up to the picket line."

"Don't be in too much of a hurry," the voice responded as Kevin covered the last few yards to the trench. "Things are still sort of mixed up all over the place."

Seeing the edge of the trench only at the last second, Kevin barely managed to stop himself from falling in. Crouching, he called out, "Dale, where are you?"

"Right in front of you, you damned idiot," a voice called out from less than a foot in front of him. "Another step and you'd be sitting on me."

Peering into the darkness, Kevin slowly began to see the outline of a form, moving from side to side, before him. "Any you boys hit?"

"Hit?" Dale shot back quickly as if he felt he needed to say something while he thought about the answer. "No, I don't think so. But it's too damned dark and confused to know for sure. I do think they captured some of my lads though. Heard some shouting and fussing as we came up to this side of the line. Found some boys from the Eighty-second Pennsylvania firing away but not my men who were supposed to be here." Then, shifting his weight from one foot to the other as he nervously looked about, Dale added, "Haven't found their bodies yet, either."

"Captured?" Kevin concluded.

In a sick, reluctant tone, Dales responded. "Think so."

"Okay," Kevin responded. "Pass the word to your boys. The rest of the regiment's coming up and I'm taking this line forward, up to the pickets. Have everyone hold his fire, especially the Pennsylvanians."

"Fine, fine," Dale stuttered. "I'll get on that, right away."

When he heard his friend begin to pass the word throughout the trench to his men, Kevin stood up. "Skirmishers," he ordered in a voice measured to be heard by those that needed to hear it, "we're going forward. Take it slow, keep track of the man to your left and right, and don't shoot unless you're sure it's a Reb you're shooting."

Under ordinary circumstances, an anonymous joker in the ranks would have shouted a witty reply to Kevin's stern warnings. But too many, if not everyone, who stood in the thin line on either side of Kevin felt the same near-paralyzing fear of what lay ahead to do anything but take a firmer grip on their rifle and draw in a deep breath before stepping off when the order came.

Whether the enemy actually saw them coming or were simply firing blindly at the noise Kevin's skirmish line was making didn't much matter. They were under fire now, with little doubt that it was enemy fire. Slowing their pace, and stooping over as far as possible, they went forward, stopping only when they reached the pickets who clung to their posts and prayed for daylight or deliverance. For Kevin, this was a great relief. He had done as he had been ordered without major incident, without apparent loss. Satisfied all was in order, and taking the initiative, Kevin withdrew his skirmish line after checking to ensure all the picket posts were fully manned. Like his men, he had no desire to be out there, in the open, when day finally broke. By the time he managed to make his way back through their own abatis and into the trench, Davis was there with the rest of the regiment. "Everything appears to be in order," Kevin reported cheerfully. He was elated, as were many of his old company, that their task had been accomplished so quickly and without cost. "Went all the way up to the picket line without making contact or losing a man," Kevin beamed. Of course, it would be some time before anyone realized that he was wrong.

Finished with their solemn duty, the grave diggers threw their shovels up and onto the pile of fresh dirt, now turning into mud. Tilting their heads back, each reached a hand up in search for help in pulling themselves out of the shallow hole. While a few stepped back, two of the spectators reached down and gave them a hand. Finished with their part, the men who had dug the grave wiped their muddy hands on their trousers and moved to the rear of the small crowd of men. "Let someone else do the rest," one mumbled to his companion in a voice meant to be loud enough for all to hear.

Looking about, Kevin watched as one man turned to another, searching for a volunteer. Occasionally, a man would glance over at the blanket-wrapped body as if he were deciding whether he wanted to step forward and do his part or hang back in the hope someone else would rush in and do it for him. As each man looked about and pondered the question, Kevin walked over to the end of the bundle and lowered himself onto one knee. A creaking noise, followed by a pop and aches made this effort painful, far more painful than it should have been for a man who was only approaching his twenty-fifth year.

Ignoring his discomfort and the coldness of muddy water his left knee dipped into, Kevin reached over and pulled back a corner of the blanket that was covering the face. When it was exposed, Kevin straightened up and gazed down at the ashen gray complexion framed by locks of unruly, wet hair. A man deserved better than this, he thought, as his right hand fished about in his haversack in search of a handkerchief. When he found it, he pulled the rag, damp from the wetness that seeped into every stitch of clothing and article he wore, and bent over the body. With the same gentle ease that he had seen Harriet use when cleaning the face of the wounded, Kevin wiped away the splattered mud and flecks of blood that spotted Albert Merrel's face.

He would have to tell her, he thought. As much as he hated spoiling one of his visits to her at the general hospital back at City Point, he owed it both to his wife and to the boy who had been in his command for less than a week. "Take care of him," Harriet had pleaded to Kevin as Albert, decked out in a fresh uniform and the full accoutrements of an infantry-man, looked on and waited impatiently to be off to a war he had waited to join for so long. "He's young, Kevin, too young to waste on this war."

Kevin, with a sigh, looked behind him, at the anxious boy, then back at Harriet. "They're all too young to die, Harriet. Every one of them."

Finished, Kevin let his hand with the handkerchief fall away to his side as he straightened and stared down at the boy's face. In the aftermath of the trench raid, their sweep forward, and the relief everyone felt that there had been no hard, bloody fight, no one had missed Albert for several hours. He was too new to the regiment, too easily overlooked. This, and the attachment that Harriet had for the boy, made Albert's death harder than most for Kevin.

Not knowing what to do, and feeling reluctant to simply stand up and inter the boy in the same offhanded, impersonal manner that he had witnessed so often, Kevin looked at the faces staring down at him. "I guess a few words would be fitting," Kevin muttered.

From across the open grave, Amos Flatherly surprised Kevin, and everyone else gathered there, when he removed his hat and looked up at the sky. "Lord," Flatherly called out as the rain streaked down his face and mixed with the tears running down his cheeks, "wherever you're hiding, we pray that you help this lad find a gentler, more kindly world, wherever he's gone to, than any man ever gave him here on this earth." Finished, Flatherly lowered his head, wiped his face on the sleeve of his uniform, pulled his hat back onto his head, and walked away.

In the silence that followed, without a word, half a dozen hands reached down, nudging Kevin out of the way. Gingerly, Albert Merrel's comrades scooped up his body and lowered it, as carefully as they could, into the ground. Unable to hold back his own tears, Kevin stood up, turned his back to his men, and walked away.

City Point, Virginia

FOR THE LONGEST TIME, Harriet didn't say a word. Rather, she sat staring down at the blouse she had been mending and at the needle and thread she had stopped pulling through almost a minute ago. Not knowing what else to do, Kevin tried to be as quiet and inconspicuous as he could as he pretended to read a book. Without bothering to even scan the page, he would glance up as he flipped from one page to another to see if Harriet was finally ready to come to terms with a grief she was trying so hard to master. It was a terrible way, he thought, to start the New Year, the fourth new year to be ushered in by the sound of the guns.

Depressed by this thought, and the grief that Harriet seemed so determined to keep to herself, Kevin gave up all pretense of reading. Instead, he lowered his book to his lap and gazed out the window. Even the weather, he thought, was conspiring to add to the oppressive, funereal mood that covered the land like a wet wool blanket. The hastily built docks, groaning under the weight of stacked barrels and crates, were distorted by sheets of rain that slashed at the tiny, rattling, one-pane window. Between these mountains of provisions and ammunition that poured off the rickety wharves and covered the landscape as far as the eye could see, Kevin could make out the forms of rain-whipped sentinels slowly treading their way between those stores, in the mud and muck churned up by countless wagons and corrupted by the waste of their mule teams. Like the room Harriet and another nurse shared, everything in City Point was simple, utilitarian, and overcrowded.

That Harriet and the hundreds of females of every sort who followed the Army of the Potomac and provided every imaginable service were able to ignore such personal discomforts and privations was a source of wonderment to Kevin. Glancing back at the silent, motionless figure of the woman he loved, Kevin couldn't imagine what drove her to sacrifice everything that she had known, a future that had promised her nothing but comfort and wealth, to follow in the wake of an army that now produced nothing but destruction, devastation, and death without end, without pause. How much of it was love and devotion for him? he wondered. How much of it was "For the Glories Cause," an idea scoffed at these days when mentioned? And how much, Kevin wondered, was simply out of habit, a determination to see something through, until the end?

Turning his head back toward the window, he caught a reflection of his face. Gazing into his own eyes, Kevin realized that the same questions he pondered concerning Harriet's motivation applied to him. Too many times, he recalled, he had reflected on this very issue in an effort to justify his actions, his very existence. All too often, he had left the matter stand with the simple conclusion that there was no answer, let alone one that was right or wrong. Like a dream that came and went of its own accord in random, almost whimsical fashion, never called for and at times unwanted, the forces that drove him, and he guessed, Harriet, to endure this life and carry on with their duties would never become apparent, let alone be understood.

Bowing his head, Kevin looked at the book in his hand. The fading light of the gray day draped the room in darkness, telling him it was almost time to go. And though he had hoped to pursue other, more pleasurable pastimes with Harriet during this brief visit as a way of greeting the New Year, Kevin was not disappointed. In a world denied every joy, even the blessing of the sun itself, it was comforting to know that there was someone who loved him and was there for him in his time of greatest need, just as he was there for her now.

CHAPTER 22

East of Petersburg, Virginia, March, 1865

ALL ALONG THE LINE, the collection of Virginians once revered as the Stonewall Brigade stood shivering in the early morning cold, waiting their turn to go forward. Officers, feeling the need to be doing something even though nothing more needed to be done, paraded nervously up and down the line of troops, repeating orders for the third, fourth, or sometimes fifth time. "When we move from here," Lieutenant Roberts announced in the solemn, stern tones he used whenever delivering instructions, "there's to be absolute silence in the ranks. I'll *personally* deal with *any* man who so much as utters a peep." Pretending that he did not hear a loud "Ha" that came from somewhere in the second rank, Roberts continued. "We're to wait until the special assault groups have opened a path through the Union abatis and fraises before we go forward."

From behind James Bannon, Joshua Major leaned forward and whispered in James' ear. "Fraises?"

James chuckled. When he saw Roberts turn his back and start pacing down the line toward the other end, expounding on how important this attack was, James tilted his head back and whispered over his shoulder. "The sharp pointy sticks stuck in the ground in front of earthworks to slow us down."

Annoyed, Joshua Major straighten up and huffed. "*Well!* Then why in tarnation didn't he say so?"

Daniel McPherson, standing next to Joshua Major, laughed. "He did, you idiot. Fraises is the French word for that type of obstacle." •

Annoyed more by Daniel's comment than by Roberts' haughty manner, Major turned on Daniel. "Well, what's that got to do with anything? We ain't the French Army, are we? We're the Army of Northern Virginia, by God. Maybe if some of our feather-brained officers spoke to each other in plain English, this war would be going a whole lot better for us. Ain't that so, Fielding?"

Not feeling up to what was coming that morning, and having no desire to become involved in a pointless discussion, Fielding Spencer snapped back harshly, "Leave the boy alone, will you?"

Ignoring them all, James looked down to rearrange his accoutrements and wipe the early morning mist from the well-polished barrel of his rifle with the sleeve of his jacket. Everything about this moment was so familiar, so commonplace for him. Letting his mind wander free, James could almost imagine that this was an earlier time, a time when his world, even though it was at war, seemed a much brighter place, a place where there was room for hope and a good laugh every now and then. The bickering voices behind him, sounding much like the Hazard brothers, brought back a flood of memories from other such mornings spent in other fields doing exactly what he was doing now.

Regardless of how desperate things were, James realized, no matter how hopeless it all eventually turned out to be, these moments always seemed to be magical. Everyone who was supposed to be there was there, in the ranks, ready to go forward despite all the hardships they had endured up to that moment, all the meager rations and lack of sleep that was as much a part of a soldier's kit in this army as his rifle. In the ranks, men bound together by proximity and a common purpose were left to themselves to prepare, in their own fashion, for what was about to happen. There were many who passed these moments as Joshua Major did, wrapping themselves in humor as if their verbal wit were armor that would protect them from the horrors they were about to witness. Others, like Spencer, withdrew into themselves, insulating themselves with a hard, impenetrable shell of isolation in the hope that by doing so they would be protected from the suffering of those gathered about them. No one, from the lowliest private in the ranks to the commanding general himself, was without feelings born from fears and hopes that mingled together freely in these last few minutes before stepping off into an attack.

Satisfied that all on his person was in order, James pulled his rifle back into his side and glanced up and down the ranks. Lieutenant Roberts, still carrying on about some damned thing or another, was now headed back down toward his end of the line. This silenced the bickering behind James and left him free to ponder his own feeling about what they were about to do.

Despite the intricate plans and preparation of their corps commander, General John Gordon, James found it hard to put any faith in the enterprise they were about to undertake. Even if they did manage to seize the Union forts and gun batteries along the entrenchments, he doubted if they'd be able to keep a gap in the Union lines opened for long. And what if the cavalry did manage to make it through the breech? What if their cavalry did make it all the way to the Union supply depot at City Point? What good would that do? The North had seen many, many reverses and disasters before without backing down from its quest to crush the Southern rebellion. The Army of Northern Virginia had, on so many occasions, rocked the Army of the Potomac back on its heels without ever being able to follow through and crush it, or its will to fight. In the end, James concluded, the best they could hope for was a postponement, a delay of a fate that every one of them knew would not favor the South. Why then, James wondered, did Lee, or anyone else who claimed to be in a position of leadership, believe that this attack would make any difference?

Behind him, Joshua Major started up on Daniel as soon as Roberts had begun moving away from their end of the line. "Hey Danny, you suppose your Helen's daddy, 'the Major,' will bring us something back from City Point?"

"Shut up, Josh," Daniel shot back. "He's a good man."

"He's a cavalryman, Danny. Since when have you taken a liking to manure spreaders?"

Daniel smiled as he turned to Joshua a wink. "Since I married the daughter of one, that's when."

The laughter of several of the men around Daniel was drowned out by the order "Attention," followed quickly by "Shoulder arms" and "Right face." Their mechanical response to these commands ended Daniel and Josh's bickering as every second man turned and took one step forward and to the right of the man he had been standing next to in ranks. When the order "Forward march" launched the long, four-man-wide column forward through the darkness, James found himself looking over at Daniel every chance he got. He'd gotten careless, James thought. He'd forgotten his pledge to Mary Beth that he would look out for the last surviving member of her family. In dealing with his own problems and concerns and worries, he'd become sloppy and lazy.

What to do about this, however, was a good question. After he felt his body fall into the steady rhythm of the march, James let his head drop down, as was his custom, and fixed his eyes on the heels of the bare feet belonging to the man to his front. Freed for the moment of the necessity of having to think about fighting, James pondered this problem. It was one thing to look out for a friend or companion in camp. That was easy. You could steer him away from bad influences, advise him where to go and how to do things, even physically intervene, on occasion, when a bully and his friends were threatening to sucker your charge into an unfair fight. But out there, on the battlefield, there was no way James could protect Daniel, or any other person, from the ravages of war. As the only noncommissioned officer in Lieutenant Roberts' little company, he had duties he was obliged to tend to. Plus, he had to be fair, evenhanded. He couldn't keep Daniel in the rear rank all the time, throwing others forward as he had tried to do in the beginning. Not only did the other men resent this but Daniel would not permit it. "I'm out there to fight, James," Daniel had protested, "not hide behind another man's back."

Taking a quick sideward glance, he caught sight of Daniel as he moved along, in step with the man to either side. Strange, James thought. Even when there was no cadence being called, even when they were simply walking around camp, soldiers sort of naturally took up walking in step with their companions. How long, he wondered, would that continue after this was all over?

Shaking his head, James turned his face back to the head down position that was his favorite marching stance and went back to the question at hand, what to do about Daniel.

Through the darkness, James and the handful of ragged veterans who answered up as the 4th Virginia marched on. They followed the rutted roads to the east of Petersburg until these disappeared and branched out onto trails. The trails, worn smooth by the passage of hundreds of feet over nine months of use, eventually narrowed until they were little more than beaten footpaths as they neared the front lines. The men in the ranks maintained their silence, a silence that only served to heighten the fears and apprehensions that they carried like a well-worn article of clothing into every battle. The evidence around James told him that they were in the midst of a greater host. This, he concluded, was to be a big effort, perhaps as intense as Pickett's ill-fated charge had been, but without the fanfare, without the drama. There was no more room in this war for such gaudy spectacles or grand pageants like the grand Union assault at Fredericksburg. Those who still stood with the colors that morning were determined to get on with what needed to be done and be finished with it, one way or the other.

Though he had never been in this part of the line, James could peer off into the darkness and make out images and forms that told him they were halted just beyond the main line of trenches. Up ahead a couple hundred yards, maybe less, was their front line trench. Beyond that, just below a horizon that was beginning to lighten as day approached from that direction, were the enemy works. An advance of a thousand yards, a ten minutes' walk at a leisurely pace, would carry them through the bulk of the Union obstacles and works. Covering that ground, however, would be no easy feat, and James knew it. Pickett's charge, launched in broad daylight across a mile's worth of open, rolling fields with no obstructions, against an enemy hiding behind a knee-high wall, had been disastrous. The Union assault that had shattered the Stonewall Brigade at Spotsylvania, though initially successful against works not unlike those they were about to face, had faltered under its own weight and been stopped by decisive action by Gordon himself. What made that man think that he could do what so many others had failed to do so often before?

The thought of Pickett's charge brought a new thought to James' mind. Kevin was out there, some place. He knew it. In his heart, he knew it. Mary Beth had sent the news that she had actually met Kevin's wife, a lovely, generous woman, according to Mary Beth, with noble bearing and an easy grace that highlighted everything she did. "Your brother still loves you," Mary Beth announced with a hint of hope in her voice. "Harriet, his wife, doesn't know what, exactly, led to your separation, but she does know that he still longs to see you, to make good whatever wrong he or your father brought upon you."

Her words, James thought, sounded so much like Lieutenant Roberts.

Promising, hopeful words totally divorced from the reality of the world they lived in.

"I wouldn't know where to start," James had responded after the impact of Mary Beth's news had sunk in. "So much has happened, so long ago."

"But you can try, can't you?" she responded in a tone that was pleading, almost desperate. "The least you can do is try."

Along the forward edge of the Confederate works, standing next to a lone rifleman, General John Gordon waited to launch the 11,500 men he had massed for this desperate assault. A Union soldier on picket duty, hearing the sound of Confederate soldiers clearing the obstacles away from the front of their own works, called out, "What are you doing over there, Johnny? What's that noise? Answer quick or I'll shoot."

Gordon felt a moment of panic. The rifleman at his side, however, responded without hesitation. "Never mind, Yank. Lie down and go to sleep. We're just gathering a little corn. You know rations are mighty short over here."

Satisfied with the answer, for it was a common practice for soldiers of both sides to sneak out into no-man's-land and gather the corn growing wild in the abandoned fields that separated the armies, the Union soldier relaxed. "Okay, go ahead."

Relieved by this narrow escape, both Gordon and the soldier went back to their waiting. Finally, word came to them that the obstacles were clear and the special assault teams Gordon had organized were ready to spring into action. Turning to his lone companion, Gordon ordered the rifleman to fire the signal shot that would send them forward. The soldier, however, felt a pang of conscience for having lied to the Yankee, and hesitated. "Fire your gun, sir," Gordon demanded.

Seeing no way out, the Confederate rifleman called out. "Hey Yank. Wake up. We're gonna shell the woods. Look out, we're coming." Satisfied he had done the honorable thing, the rifleman squeezed off the single round.

A commotion along the line stirred James from his confused, whirling thoughts. Looking up from where he had settled onto the ground to rest, he was startled to see a group of Union soldiers pass him, headed for the rear under an armed guard. "They got the Union pickets, Jimmy," Joshua Major announced as he slapped James on the shoulder. "Got 'em all without firing a shot. Danny says that'll leave the boys with axes and such to clear the pointy sticks and stuff before we go forward. What do you think?" he asked, as his enthusiasm trailed off and his voice slowly betrayed his concern. "Think we'll be able to make it, all the way through?"

James turned his head and caught sight of Daniel, smiling ear to ear as he watched the Yankees disappear down the line of animated soldiers. How strange, he thought. Here we are, on the brink of an attack that's nothing short of being desperate, and he's behaving like we were about to march into Washington and accept the entire North's surrender. Dropping all other thoughts and concerns, James pushed himself off the ground with the aid of his rifle. He needed to turn his full attention to the one matter at hand that he could do something about, keeping Daniel alive. How he would manage that, as they prepared to go forward into an attack of this magnitude, was beyond him.

The sharp report of cannons, followed moments later by sporadic rifle fire, shattered the silence that had hung over the waiting mass of soldiers. Now the fretful anticipation was replaced by an anxious, driving desire to press forward, to move out into and across no-man's-land before the entire Union line was up and ready for them. "What's he waiting for?" Daniel muttered as he stood on his toes, trying to look over the heads of the men in front of him. Even James was wondering as he caught sight of an occasional flash of distant cannon fire. Though confident that Gordon knew what he was doing, James knew there was always a chance that things might have gotten out of hand before Gordon had everyone in place.

That fear was forgotten the moment the order to move forward, at the double quick, made its way down the densely packed ranks. "All right," their regimental commander shouted, free for the first time that morning to shout out his orders. "Keep it closed up and keep moving."

Once over their own trench line and into the dead space between the lines, James and the tumbled mass of men about him squeezed through the breaches cut through their own obstacles. Free of them, they surged forward, stumbling through the darkness until they reached the Union obstacles where they slowed again. "What's keeping us?" Daniel shouted to James, excited now by the rush of events.

Without having to see ahead, James looked at the expression of alarm on the young man's face. "We're at the Union obstacles."

"Well, damn it," Daniel shouted. "Can't they hurry?" he cried, first to James, then ahead over Josh Major's shoulder as he pushed Josh. "Can't they hurry?"

James didn't answer as he felt the men in front begin to give way to his nudging, then finally move forward. "Keep moving, Fourth Virginia," Roberts shouted as he squeezed in behind James just before they reached the gap in the Union fraises. Once clear of them, there was a moment of confusion while the units poured out of the last constriction and into the open space before the ominous parapets of the Union line. Officers, freeing themselves from the press of men that they had been forced to join while moving through the gaps, rushed out to their posts, glancing this way and that, to assess the situation before them while keeping an ear open for orders from their superiors.

What fire the startled Union defenders were able to pour into the rolling mass of Confederate assailants at this point was sporadic and ineffective. Even before they were forced to deploy into line of battle, the 4th Virginia went up and over the Union positions. Those charged with defending the works who hadn't fled when they realized what was happening were engulfed by the advancing host. Here and there, James caught sight of Yankees, alone or in small groups, being disarmed and ordered to the rear, unguarded.

"By the right into line," the order finally came. "Into line," Roberts echoed as he dropped the tip of his sword into his left hand, held it at arm's length before him, and turned to walk backward so as to guide his men where they were supposed to be.

Coming up to Roberts until his chest was inches from the flat of Roberts' sword, James slowed, then snapped his neck down to the right. "Come on," he shouted as Roberts started to move down the line, still holding his sword up for other men to guide on as they formed to James' right. "Close it up and dress the line."

Daniel, squeezing forward into the front rank, turned and looked into James' eyes. There was a smile on his face, an excited and satisfied smile that reminded James of a kid who was very pleased with himself. He wanted to push Daniel back into the rear rank, behind him, when he saw the flash of a ragged volley fired by a shadowy mass of men before them. Their aim was high, serving only to sober up the 4th Virginia and alert them to the danger ahead. Hoisting their rifles to the ready position without needing to be told, those who hadn't done so slipped a cap onto the cone and waited for the order to advance or fire.

The desultory fire from the little band of Yankees was soon joined by the thunderous clap of Union cannon from an earthen fort some five hundred yards to their front. "*Damn!*" Daniel shouted. "I can't see a thing."

Blinded by the muzzle flash, too, James looked about in the darkness, trying hard to make out what was going on around them as a blaze of bright, dizzying dots burned into his eyes from the unexpected blast, obscuring everything. "Just keep close to me, Daniel," James cried over the roar of cannon fire, "and listen up. I think we're about to catch hell."

James' prediction was both timely and accurate. With the light of a new day beginning to peek over the eastern horizon to their left, the units of Terry's brigade went forward in an effort to seize the earthen fort. The easy, though sometimes confusing, rush that had delivered the 4th Virginia here, inside Union lines, came to an abrupt halt. It was to be a fight now, as the Union forces, fully alert and responding rapidly to the crisis at hand, began to gather.

James looked about as he nervously waited to go forward. Behind them he could see the outline of another earthen fort, this one crawling with Confederate troops who had been in the storming parties. Together with the men of Grimes' division, who had come forward when James' own division had advanced, they were picking through the rich Union camps and dugouts, as officers struggled to reform them into line of battle. James looked at them enviously while he and the rest of Evens' division went after the next fort along the Union line.

The force of a near miss pulled James' full attention back to the offending fort to their front. He could see that if they didn't seize that fort, whose parapets were now alive with cannon and rifle fire, their efforts that morning would come to naught. Fire from the big guns along its walls would not only keep the cavalry from riding off into the east, but it would also sweep the dead space in front of the fort now held by the division behind them. They, and not the Yankees, would be in a bad spot.

"Forward," Brigadier General Terry yelled, for the last time. Haltingly, the line started forward. Yet even before it went more than a few paces, James noticed that a disproportionate number of men were falling. Leaning backward and turning his head to the rear as the line went forward, James quickly realized that most of those going down hadn't been hit. They were going to ground. All along the line, men who shared the same thoughts regarding the futility of this effort that James had entertained earlier were dropping out of the ranks.

The growing daylight, and the steady fire from the enemy fort packed with its own defenders and fugitives from the abandoned stretch of line connecting it to the captured fort, was too much. That, and the defection of its own men from the ranks, brought the attack to a halt. Despite exhortations from their officers, the men went to ground, seeking shelter in any fold in the ground or any handy earthwork.

James, waiting far too long to do so himself, finally grabbed Daniel by the arm and flung him into a shallow ditch. "What'd you do that for?" the boy demanded.

"Look around you, you idiot!" James bellowed. "We're not going anywhere. The attack's failed and it's pointless to stand up there, getting shot at."

As if he had just been shaken awake from a sound sleep, Daniel looked around. In the pale light of dawn, he could see men scattered all about them, some dead or wounded, most hugging the ground for all it was worth. Officers, giving in to the inevitable, had abandoned their efforts to rally their men for one more try. Even Lieutenant Roberts seemed to be content hiding behind a shattered tree stump. Finally convinced that what James was saying was true, Daniel looked at the older man. "What are we going to do?"

James didn't answer, not at first. Glancing this way and that, he looked for a covered route that would take them back to the shelter of the abandoned Union line to their rear. If they made that, he figured, they'd stand a good chance of making it all the way back to the safety of their own lines. It would be hell, he reasoned, and a lot of men would go down, but waiting to be blown up or captured was . . .

Suddenly, an idea popped into James' head. While Daniel nervously looked about, James pulled a note Mary Beth had sent him and turned it over onto the side she hadn't written on. Fishing in his haversack, his fingers found the stubby pencil he had recovered from a Union prisoner weeks ago and began to scratch on the piece of paper.

"What in the devil are you doing?" Daniel asked incredulously when he saw James writing away.

"Shut up and see if Lieutenant Roberts is still in sight," James ordered. "He was over to our right."

Obediently, Daniel turned away and slowly raised his head above the edge of the hole they were hiding in and looked in the direction James had mentioned. "I see him," the boy shouted. "He's waving his sword and pointing it to the rear. I think we're retreating."

"Keep your eye on him, Daniel," James shouted as he finished the note and folded it over. Holding it in his left hand, he withdrew his bayonet from its scabbard.

"James," Daniel called back over his shoulder, "whatever you're doing, you better hurry. Everyone is making his way . . ."

A searing incredible pain that started in the calf of his left leg and ran up his spine like a bolt of lightning changed Daniel's warning to a shrill screech. At first, he was too paralyzed by pain and the shock of being wounded to move. Only when he felt the excruciating pain and pressure let up did he turn to see what had happened.

As devastating as the sight of blood running down his ripped pant leg was, it was nothing compared to that of James, lying against the side of the hole they shared, holding a bloody bayonet in his hand. The expression on James' face, half apologetic, half worried, told Daniel everything. *"Why?"* he stuttered as a new wave of pain, accompanied by nausea, began to sweep over him.

Unable to speak, James reached out and handed the paper to Daniel. "Here! This is the name of my brother and his regiment. First Division, Sixth Corps. Try to contact him. Maybe he and his wife will be able to help you."

Reaching down, Daniel wrapped his hands around his wounded leg and began to cry. "Damn you, James Bannon," he shouted as the tears of pain and betrayal flowed down his cheeks. "Damn you and your brother to hell."

Unable to stand seeing the boy suffer, James leaned forward, stuffed the folded paper in Daniel's pocket, and turned to flee. It had been a foolish idea, he thought. Stupid, and perhaps dangerous. Daniel could die from that wound. He could get wound fever and die from a clean cut just as easily as he could from a bullet wound or amputation. But at least this way, James reasoned as he ran for all he was worth for the relative safety of the stretch of Union lines still in Confederate hands, Daniel had a fighting chance to live to see the end of this war. Neither his foolish notions of courage or honor, nor the stupidity of their own generals, would ever put him in danger again.

 C H A P T E R 2 3

City Point, Virginia, April, 1865

THOUGH IT WAS LATE and the hours in the hospital had been long and, at times, trying, sleep was the furthest thing from Harriet's mind. Flying into her small room, she barely took time to tear the shawl from her shoulders and fling it onto the bed before reaching over and grabbing her journal off the shelf where she kept her private things. Turning to the small table, she lit the oil lamp that took up most of the table, sat down, and began to write as fast as her hand allowed her.

"I hardly know where to start," she scratched without even bothering to record the date, April 1st, 1865. *"After so many months of inactivity and foreboding, everything is happening so quickly, so unexpectedly. The air is alive with excitement and activity. Since the Confederate repulse at Fort Stedmen some six days ago, from here at City Point all the way to Five Forks, west of Petersburg where Sheridan now is fighting, the Army has been in motion. All doubts as to how this war will end, and whether it will end soon, seem to have evaporated like the morning mist when exposed to the bright brilliance of the morning sun. Even Kevin's notes speak to me in tones of hope and cheerfulness that I haven't heard in a long time."*

Pausing, Harriet looked out the window where, despite the hour, men were busy on the docks and along the streets of the depot, loading supplies or whipping the teams of their heavily burdened wagons in an effort to get them to move faster. She wondered what her mother's friends would think if they knew that she and Kevin used wounded men sent to City Point hospitals from Kevin's unit as letter carriers. She smiled. They'd be suitably appalled, she thought. Of course, they wouldn't understand that the men, despite the wounds, did so gladly. Kevin always imagined that they did so out of the kindness of their heart. Harriet, however, knew better. Men who had done so in the past and returned to the unit, bragged about how Harriet had showered special attention and fresh baked goods on them while they were in her ward. Lonely men, far from home and suffering from fear and the deprivation of the company of loved ones as much as from physical wounds, needed little encouragement.

Looking back at her journal, she took up where her writing had stopped. *"Today I learned that James Bannon is still alive, at least he was on the 25th of March. This morning an officer of the provost guard brought me a scrap of paper bearing Kevin's name and unit, saying that one of his wounded prisoners had handed it to him, stating that he had served with Kevin's brother. I found the man with a group of other wounded prisoners who were about to be shipped north and spoke to him. He not only knows James, but he is the brother of the girl I met in Winchester who is in love with James. Having no desire to see him go north, to a prisoner of war camp, which I hear are simply beastly, I managed to drag the wounded man, Daniel McPherson, to Dr. White and have the good doctor declare Daniel unfit for transport. The provost officer, of course, didn't believe the doctor but, already having more prisoners to handle than he could manage, seemed glad to be rid of at least one."*

"The wound, I am glad to say, is healing nicely, with the pus flowing clear and freely and no redness yet evident at the knee or above." Again, Harriet paused. She marveled at how well she could now manage the sight of even the most horrible, ghastly wounds. Lately, this had become both a point of pride, for she was far more useful now to Dr. White and the other surgeons, and an issue that caused her some concern. Was she, Harriet wondered, becoming callous to the suffering of fellow human beings? Had she seen so much death and pain that they no longer touched her heart?

With a shake of her head, she went back to writing. *"Daniel McPherson spoke disparagingly of James. Apparently, at the height of the attack, James ran Daniel through with a bayonet. Though Daniel continues to plead that he cannot understand why a man whom he had called friend would do such a thing, I believe he knows. I most certainly do. We are, I think, seeing the beginning of the final act, the true beginning of the end. Though no one speaks of it, at least not yet for we have all seen far too many dreams of final victory dashed, in their hearts I think every man in this Army, from the greenest private to Grant himself, can see that the end is in sight. It is this vision that is animating this Army with a drive that I have not seen since it pitched its tents last May and crossed the Rappahannock."*

Feeling the effects of her lack of sleep and hard work for the first time, Harriet laid the pen down on the page. Rubbing her eyes, she folded her arms across her chest and held herself tightly. Though she had always let her thoughts spill freely as they came to her onto the pages of her journal, she hesitated to continue, for the one that had been lingering in the back of her mind all day was frightening. It was as if, she imagined, to do so would give the dark thought a chance to come to life. With victory would come peace, and a new life for her and Kevin. And while she had no idea what that life held in store for them, she was confident that it would be one of great promise and happiness. It had to be, she told herself. She could envision no other future. They had suffered together, and apart, for too long, through too many nightmares, not to be afforded the freedom and happiness that so many had fought and died for these four long years.

The rattling of the single pane of glass, followed by a distant rumble of artillery coming from the direction of the siege lines, drove home the growing fear that now gripped her. Despite all the good news, despite all the promise of success, fighting still remained to be done. And fighting, Harriet knew, meant killing. Kevin had told her, not long ago, that when Grant went forward the next time, he would do so with everyone. That, she realized, meant one more opportunity for Kevin to meet a fate that he had so far avoided. One more chance to join the legions of the silent dead who lay in row after row of graves across this shattered state.

Unable to continue, Harriet pushed herself away from the table. Reaching over, she turned the oil lamp down till it was all but extinguished. Letting her hands fall listlessly onto her lap, she sat and watched the distant flashes light up the western sky, and tried hard not to think, to close out all thoughts of what could be and, in a way, isolate herself from a war that she, and her husband, were still very much a part of.

West of Petersburg, Virginia, April 2, 1865

KEVIN PULLED OUT THE pocket watch that Harriet had given him at Christmas from his vest pocket. It took him several seconds to make out the fine Roman numerals that adorned the gold watch crafted by hand. The bright moonlight that had accompanied the Jerseymen earlier that evening when they had started their march to Fort Fisher was now shrouded in a heavy mist that clung to everything it touched. "You know," he had told her jokingly when he inspected the German-made watch for the first time, bouncing it lightly in his hand as if trying to determine its value by weighing the gold, "it's almost a waste to carry such a fine instrument into battle knowing full well some Johnny who can't even tell time stands a fair chance of inheriting it one fine day." Though the remark was meant to be humorous, Harriet was appalled by this bit of graveyard humor that was so much a part of camp life around Petersburg. In a flash, the look of joy and delight that had made her face shine like the sun itself had been transformed into a distorted, pained expression of fear. And though he eventually managed to laugh off the matter, Kevin could never wipe away that image, which haunted him every time he looked at his gift.

Closing the lid of the watch with a snap, he looked up into the early morning darkness while he slipped the watch back into his vest pocket. From behind him, Johnny O'Keeth whispered. "Much longer to wait?"

Kevin, letting the image of Harriet's face fade away, turned and smiled. "No, not much at all. Ten minutes at the most."

"I'd give anything if those guns would start hammering away at the Reb works again," O'Keeth lamented as he shifted his weight from one foot to another. "Standing here like this gives me the shivers, you know, like when you're in a graveyard at night."

This analogy made Kevin shudder. In an instant, his mind filled with the memory of another night not too different from this one spent in a graveyard, a long time ago. Then it had been only him and his brother. Kevin shivered as he struggled to push all thoughts of that wretched night from his mind.

"I can't say that I much like the idea of being stuck here between the Fortieth, up there, and the Tenth behind us," O'Keeth continued.

Glad to have something to talk about and occupy him as he waited, Kevin tried to explain things as he understood them to O'Keeth. "I think the idea is to put the Fortieth New Jersey in the very front, where they'll find it hard to run. I think the general wanted them to think that the only choices they had were to go forward into the Rebel works or face *our* bayonets."

O'Keeth replied with a sarcastic laugh. "That's not what the boys were thinking when they heard of this arrangement. According to Amos, the reason they put the greenest regiment up front was so that they would catch Johnny's bullets and not us, leaving the veteran units to do the fighting."

Kevin nodded, but said nothing. For a long time, now, the Army of the Potomac had become nothing more than a heartless, mechanical grinding machine whose sole aim was to wear down Lee's Army until there was nothing left. That someone up the line might have considered the very thing that O'Keeth proposed was not at all unreasonable. God, he thought as he lowered his head and shook it, he'd be so glad to be done with all this.

"I see you and the colonel don't put much faith in those lads in the Fortieth making it all the way," O'Keeth continued.

"You mean Corporal Miller and the detail with the axes to clear the Rebel obstacles?"

"Yes, sir, that's exactly what I mean," O'Keeth replied.

"Well," Kevin answered with a smile, "we've been down this road too many times before not to prepare for just about every contingency that we could imagine, now could we?"

O'Keeth returned Kevin's smile. "Aye, sir, that we have. Going on four years now. And it's been a good four years, when all is said and done, hasn't it?"

There were many, Kevin knew, who had seen all he had seen, endured every misery imaginable, and yet, like O'Keeth, still felt that this war had been something special, a great adventure, the greatest adventure that they had ever lived through and would ever know. Instead of seeing the end as something to be thankful for, some, like Johnny, were saddened.

Behind them, from the parapets of Fort Fisher, a cannon, quickly followed by another, shattered the silence. Reaching down, Kevin unsnapped the flap of his holster, drew his Army Colt, and shouted out to his section of the regiment, "All right, Fourth New Jersey, we're going forward. Dress on the center and don't fire unless you hear the order."

Slowly, at first, Major Baldwin Hufty led the 4th New Jersey forward, keeping the distance between his regiment and the 40th New Jersey, to his front. Charged with leading the left wing of the line that morning, Kevin kept glancing back and forth between Hufty and the shadowy images of the rear rank of the 40th to his front. A smattering of rifle fire, from Confederate pickets, brought the 40th to a halt. Conforming to this sudden action, the 4th paused, allowing the officers of the 40th to exert themselves and drive their men on with every imaginable oath as well as physical force.

Anxious to keep moving, for none relished the idea of being caught in the open to face the fire of a fully alerted enemy host, Hufty called out for the 4th to pass through their stalled sister New Jersey regiment. "Clear the way," Kevin shouted as he came up behind the rear rank, which was already dissolving, with some men going to ground and others turning in preparation for dashing for the rear. "Clear the way, you sorry bastards, or we'll cut you down ourselves."

Coming up on Kevin's heels, the men he had once commanded pressed forward, freely using their rifle butts and elbows to force their way through the milling confusion that the 40th had degenerated into. "God in heaven," Kevin heard O'Keeth shout, "must we fight our own in order to get at the Rebs?"

Turning his head as soon as they were through the 40th, Kevin snapped, "Quiet in the ranks! Dress on the center and keep it closed up."

With the ease that only a veteran unit could muster, the 4th New Jersey came through the 40th, reformed on the move, and pitched into those Confederates still defending along their picket line. "Left wing," Kevin shouted, "halt." Scampering to one side, he lowered his pistol to the front. "Ready," he screamed so that all could hear.

"Aim." To the front, voices came out of the darkness where moments before menacing rifle flashes had lashed at them. "*Yank!*" a chorus of anxious voices called out. "Don't shoot! We surrender!"

Kevin's order "Fire!" came as no surprise to any of the men in the ranks of the 4th New Jersey. Their blood was up and they were going to finish this, right here and now if they could. With a thunderous clap, the left battalion under Kevin's direction cut loose a volley. Just how many Rebels fell to their fire was impossible to tell. What was obvious, even before the smoke cleared, was that all resistance along the picket line was at an end. "*For the love of God!*" voices screamed, as Rebels ran toward them, rifles held high as a sign of their submission, "don't shoot. We surrender. *Don't shoot.*"

Anxious to keep going, Kevin waved his pistol menacingly at those

Confederates nearest him. "Throw down your rifles and keep moving to the rear." Turning his head he called out to O'Keeth. "Johnny, send a couple of boys back to keep an eye on these Rebels."

With a smile, O'Keeth ordered Danny Cummins and another man to gather the prisoners and take them back. Like a condemned man given a reprieve at the last minute, Cummins and his companion set about performing this task as quickly as possible.

"Settle down, boys," Kevin shouted as Hufty ordered them forward again. "Send up the axmen and pick up the pace."

Hearing the order, Corporal Miller's men pushed their way through the ranks and made their way forward in front of the regiment until they came to the Confederate obstacles. Without pausing, they set about hacking gaps into the line. Crouching, Kevin watched as Amos Flatherly, accompanied by a pair of men from the 40th New Jersey assigned duty as pioneers and determined to do their part despite the reluctance of their regimental comrades, tore madly at the tangle of branches and brush piled high to deny them access to the Confederate line. From the right, the screech of a cannon shell ripped through the night. The first one exploded just beyond where Kevin was, sending him flat to the ground. The boom of other cannons from a Rebel fort just beyond the regiment's flank could be heard.

Picking himself up from the mud, Kevin looked to the front where Miller and his detail were still madly at work, unflinching despite the shell fire. He was about to go forward, in part to judge if their progress was sufficient to allow the advance to continue, and in part to do something rather than lie there and be shot at, when Baldwin Hufty came up next to him and grabbed his arm. "The bastards back there," he shouted, waving his sword in the direction they had just come from, "are shooting at us. Go back there and tell the commander of the Fortieth to get his men to cease fire."

Taking one more glance at the frantic efforts of the pioneers, Kevin then looked at Hufty, gave him a nod, and turned to head back to the rear.

After making his way through the waiting huddles of his own men, Kevin stood upright and slowed down. In the darkness he looked from side to side in an effort to catch sight of the 40th. The flashes of cannon fire and exploding shells both hindered and aided Kevin as they alternated between blinding him and lighting his path. He was looking down at the ground, trying to make his way around a shell hole, when a frightened voice, not ten yards in front of him, yelled, *"They're coming!"*

Glancing up, Kevin was horrified to see half a dozen rifle barrels leveled at him. Raising his hand in protest, he had barely opened his mouth to identify himself when his warning was cut short by the discharge of Union rifles.

Richmond, Virginia, April 2, 1865

VALIANTLY, THE MINISTER ENDEAVORED to continue with his Sunday service despite the appearance of courier after courier. Each one, in his turn, would enter the church at the rear, and reverently remove his hat before scanning the gathered congregation. Only when he had spotted the officer or government official he had been sent to fetch, did he go forward to issue his summons. That something was happening, or had already happened, was obvious. That it was ominous was evident by the grim faces of the couriers and the pained expression of each of the officers and bureaucrats as whispered news from the front was passed to them. It wasn't until after the minister himself was called off to one side by a member of the provost marshal's office that all pretense of normalcy was abandoned. In a voice that quivered as he attempted to keep his own emotions in check, the minister announced that all members of the home guard were to report to the capitol building at three o'clock.

For a moment, Mary Beth considered heeding the minister's plea for those of the congregation who remained to stay with him and continue the service. She had much to pray for, with a brother and a fiancé at the front. However, this was not the time, she concluded, for prayers. Closing her Bible with a snap, she stood up, made her way along the pew, apologizing to her fellow churchmen as she squeezed past them, and hurried out onto the street. Once there, Mary Beth was struck by the number of people hurrying this way and that, most carrying sacks or household items as if they were moving from one house to another. Seeing one well-dressed man walking along at a more leisurely pace than the others, Mary Beth called out to him. "Sir, is the news really that serious?"

Pausing, the man smiled, bowed, and tipped his hat. "I am afraid so, madam. It seems the Yankees have managed to break General Lee's right at Petersburg and there is no hope of undoing the damage."

"Then," Mary Beth responded hopefully, "the war is over."

Grinning at her foolishness, the man shook his head. "No, not at all. It simply means that General Lee will have to move his army away from Richmond until he can find better ground from which to continue the fight."

"But with Richmond gone," Mary Beth countered, "what is the point?"

"My dear lady," the man explained patiently, "you cannot be suggesting that we simply cave in and give up the cause simply because of a few setbacks?"

Seeing no point in pursuing this foolish line of discussion, Mary Beth thanked the man and hurried on her way. There was much to do and not much time. The fair people of Richmond, she reasoned, would not react well to the prospect of Union occupation.

When she reached the front porch of the Westerfield home, she was greeted by the nine-year-old son of Ellen Archer, a poor cousin of Amanda Westerfield. After losing her home and one of her four children to a Union mortar shell in Petersburg, Ellen and her surviving children had taken up residence in the attic with Mary Beth. Though Mary Beth didn't mind the company of the children, lively and cheerful despite the hardships they had endured, Ellen's withdrawal from the world annoyed Mary Beth to no end. Not even the needs of her own children were allowed to interfere with her reading of the Bible, where she sought the peace and comfort she found impossible to find elsewhere.

"Did you hear, Miss Bethy?" the boy shouted as Mary Beth climbed the stairs two at a time. "Did you hear? The Yankees are coming!"

"Yes, Ezrah, I heard," she replied as she passed him and headed into the house. "Where's your mama?"

"Oh," he answered, stopping his bouncing and lowering his voice, "she's upstairs with Aunt Amanda and cousin Catherine, praying."

Feeling the boy's pain at being abandoned at a time like this, Mary Beth stopped, reached out, and wrapped her arm around the boy's shoulder. "Well, then, you'll have to come with me now and help me, won't you?"

The smile returned to Ezrah's face at the invitation to do something. "I'd be glad to, Miss Bethy. What is it we need to do?"

"First things first," she replied. "Where are Missy and the baby?"

"Mother has the baby with her, upstairs. Missy is in the backyard, digging holes with the cook, Prissy, so they can bury the silverware and all."

"How come you're not out helping them?" Mary Beth asked.

Appearing offended at such a foolish notion, the boy stepped back and looked up at Mary Beth. "I'm the lookout, that's why. I'm supposed to warn everyone in the house when the Yankees come, so we can all hide."

Were the situation not as bad as it was, and Ezrah's expression not so serious, Mary Beth would have laughed. But this was no time for such things. "Go out back and fetch Prissy, right away. Tell her to gather whatever sacks or pillowcases she can find. I heard that the commissary department has thrown open its warehouses and are letting anyone who wants to come take whatever they can carry away."

Wide-eyed, the boy blinked, then ran for the rear of the house, shouting as he went. Turning for the stairs, Mary Beth rushed up them two at a time. When she passed Catherine's open bedroom door, she didn't even pause to look in at the three broken women, kneeling on the floor around Catherine's unmade bed, praying and crying for all they were worth. Rushing up to where her mattress was, Mary Beth tossed it and the partially sewn Confederate uniforms that would never be worn aside. Without bothering to find a tool to help her, she pried the floorboard under which she had hidden the money Harriet had given her the previous October.

Only when she saw the white cotton sash, bulging in several places, did she breathe a sigh of relief. Come what may over the next few days, the money sewn into that sash would be a life line between her and a future she still prayed she would be allowed by providence to share with James. Grabbing the sash, she stood up, and looked around the attic just to make sure she was alone. Satisfied that there were no prying eyes, Mary Beth hoisted her skirt and crinolines up over her hips, wrapped the sash around her waist, and tied the loose ends off in several tight knots. Before dropping her skirts and underpinnings back into place, Mary Beth tugged at the sash to make sure her hasty knots would hold and that the sash wouldn't slip down later. Satisfied, she dropped the heaps of material she had been holding up under her arms, smoothed her skirt, then ran her hands over her waist to make sure that the sash or the money wasn't leaving any unnatural bumps or curves in her clothing. Satisfied, she grabbed a bag with a pull string she had used to carry clothes in when she had come here from Winchester, and dumped the contents out onto the mattress, which was still lying in a heap. Rushing back downstairs, she found Prissy, Ezrah, and Ellen's little seven-year-old girl that everyone called Missy waiting for her with sacks in hand.

By the time they reached the commissary dock where soldiers were handing out food that the Army had no way of moving, hundreds were already gathered, pushing and shoving their way toward the front of the line. Halting short of this milling mass, Mary Beth watched in dismay as two women, each holding one end of a bag of flour, tugged in an effort to wrestle it away from each other. In the course of their struggle, a rip developed, causing the bag to split open. As the two female combatants fell over backward, a cloud of white flour dust flew up in the air, covering them and anyone unfortunate enough to be near them when the bag gave way.

Though Mary Beth had expected the crowd, the behavior of the people bewildered her. In three years of repeated occupation and reoccupation of Winchester, nothing like the panic and pandemonium she had seen so far this day had ever occurred. After all, this was going on while the Confederate Army, the home guard, and the provost guard were still in the city. What, she wondered, would become of everyone when they left and before the Union troops were able to make their way into the city to occupy it?

"I don't think we should stay here, Miss McPherson," the cook volunteered as she watched the pushing and shoving and listened to the vile insults and profanity being hurled in the melee before the dock. "Not with these children."

Nodding in assent, Mary Beth and her small detail was about to turn around and leave when they saw two women who were attempting to roll a barrel of dried apples through the crowd. They had almost made it when they lost control of their booty. As Mary Beth watched the barrel wobble and career along the street, the lid fell off, spewing apples in its wake. Breaking free from the ruckus around the commissary dock, children waiting with their mothers ran after the apples, scooping them up by the handful and gathering them in their shirttails. "I'll go get some of them," Ezrah shouted and took off before Mary Beth's hand could stop him.

"Prissy," Mary Beth ordered, "stay here with Missy while I go help Ezrah. When we finish with the apples, you take what we've managed to gather and head back to the house with the girl. Ezrah and I will stay here and gather what we can."

Leery of Mary Beth's judgment, Prissy looked over at the crowd before giving Mary Beth a sideward glance. "You sure you know what you're doing?"

Mary Beth shook her head. "No, I'm not. But I don't see that we have any choice. If we don't take what we can while there's something left, we'll starve. And I'll be damned," Mary Beth shouted above the noise, forgetting that the little girl was between them, "if I'm going to go hungry so long as there's one scrap of food to be had in this city."

Realizing that Mary Beth had far more experience in dealing with this war than she did, Prissy dropped all objections. Holding Missy's hand while Mary Beth ran into the midst of the children with her sack, Prissy watched with a mixture of sadness and disgust as a full-grown woman was reduced to scrambling about the dirt on her knees, scooping up dried apples as they tumbled and rolled about on the ground.

It was getting on into early evening by the time Mary Beth and Ezrah returned. Each of them, weighed down by a bulging sack thrown over one shoulder and held with one hand, clutched to their chest a chunk of meat, Mary Beth's being a ham and Ezrah's a slab of bacon that almost covered his entire front. Running out to help them Prissy and the little girl laughed and giggled. "Oh, praise be the Lord!" Prissy wailed. "I thought the mob had gathered you two up and swept you away with everyone else."

Relieved to be freed from her burden, Mary Beth watched as little Missy, staggering under the weight and size of the bacon her brother had handed her, smiled. "We almost were," Mary Beth said. "It seems like all of Richmond is trying to escape to the south over the James River."

"Can't say that I blame them," Prissy said as she turned with the ham and headed to the kitchen out behind the house. "They say there's looting and all sorts of mischief going on all up and down Main Street."

Too tired and heartsick that things were falling apart like this to say anything, Mary Beth only shook her head.

"Don't you think it would be a good idea to leave now, while we can?" Prissy pushed when she saw that Mary Beth wasn't taking her hint.

Realizing that the cook's comment was more in the way of a recommendation than an idle observation, Mary Beth looked at her. "Where would you have us go? We are two children, a baby, and five women, three of whom are, at best, mental wrecks unable to care for themselves, let alone fight their way through a crowd in the middle of the night."

Casting her eyes up toward the bedroom window where Amanda Westerfield, her daughter, and her cousin continued their prayer vigil, Prissy thought about Mary Beth's observations for a moment. Realizing that Mary Beth was right, the cook let her head drop low between her shoulders without a word.

Anxious to get Prissy's mind off the harsh reality of an uncertain future, Mary Beth asked if there was anything to eat. Perking up, Prissy smiled. "We have apples, and plenty of 'em."

Laughing, the two women went into the small cookhouse in the rear of the main house. As she sat at the table and watched Missy and the cook gather up a bowl overflowing with dried apples, Mary Beth knew that the real reason that she refused to leave the city was James. This was the last place he had seen her. It would not do if, in all this confusion and chaos, she up and left with no way of getting word to him or Daniel where she was going. And with Lee's Army marching off to God knew where and the government itself fleeing, she couldn't imagine how she would find them again. No, she concluded. She had to stay put, here, and deal with whatever came her way until James and Daniel found their way back. Though she could not guess what the odds were of James' surviving this one, last desperate campaign, she knew she had to be there, regardless. That he would survive, that he had, were all that Mary Beth had to hold on to. Anything else, she had concluded a long time before, was unthinkable.

Richmond, Virginia, Dawn, April 3, 1865

IT WAS THE CRYING of the children, clutching her in fearful desperation, that woke Mary Beth. But in an instant, she was wide awake as a new chain of explosions, more violent than any that had rocked the house so far, shook her, the children, and everything about them.

"They've blown up the powder stores," she murmured as she placed a hand on the head of each of the children and drew them in closer to her side. From the stairwell leading down to the floor below, Mary Beth could hear the women gathered in Catherine's bedroom begin to cry and wail. Exhausted by her all-night vigil and random explosions of lesser magnitude, Mary Beth had been able to do little but doze off for a few brief moments. As she rocked back and forth, trying to shush the children and ease their fears, she was beginning to have second thoughts about her decision to stay in Richmond.

"Miss Beth," Prissy called out as she made her way up the stairs, "you'd best come quick."

Looking up from the children, Mary Beth looked over to where the cook's head appeared at the top of the stairs.

"The whole city's on fire and it looks like it's coming our way," Prissy said.

Taking note of the strong odor of smoke filling the room, heavily tinged with the scent of burning tobacco from warehouse fires, Mary Beth felt the hairs on the back of her neck rise. The calamities befalling them, she realized, were starting to reach biblical proportions. Planting a kiss on Ezrah's and Missy's heads, Mary Beth tried to stand. The children, however, hung on to her. "Children," she pleaded, "I must go with Prissy and see what's going on."

"We'll go with you," Ezrah bleated in desperation. Too tired to argue, and understanding their fears all too well, Mary Beth didn't resist. With her two appendages, she made her way down the stairs and out into the street.

Though it was still several hours till dawn, the sky and the street were lit as if it were noon. "We'd best do something," Prissy advised. "I don't think there's anyone left in the city to fight these fires. If we don't go now, we're all going to burn up."

From around the corner, a mounted officer turned his horse and started to head down the street. Pulling away from the children, Mary Beth ran over to the horse's flank, grabbing the stirrup strap as she walked alongside the rider. "Is it true?" she called up at the rider, moving along as if he were asleep.

Shaking his head, he looked over to one side of the horse, away from Mary Beth, then over to the side where she was. "Oh," the rider mumbled glumly. "Didn't see you there." Then, remembering his manners, the rider touched the brim of his droopy hat. "Sorry, ma'am. Had my mind on other things."

"Is it true?" Mary Beth stammered. "Have you given up fighting the fires?"

The cavalryman didn't bother to stop as the two walked slowly down the street. Beth still hung on to the stirrup strap of the rider bent double over his saddle in exhaustion. He chuckled. "Well, I can't say for sure about what the mayor of this fair city is or isn't doing. About all I am sure of is my regiment is finished fighting the Yanks, for now." Lifting an arm, he pointed toward the river. "We're the rear guard, miss. Last out of Richmond. I'm sorry to say, as soon as we're across the bridge, we're going to fire her up and ride off to join Bobby Lee somewhere along the Appomattox."

Twisting her head about, she looked behind the cavalryman's horse, almost as if she expected to see Union cavalry turning the corner. "Are they far behind?"

Despite the concerned look he saw on Mary Beth's face, the rider again chuckled. "To tell you the truth, ma'am, I can't rightly say. You see, I was off busy saying my farewells to a lady friend and, well . . ."

Looking down for a moment to hide her blushing, Mary Beth continued to walk along in silence for several minutes. Then she looked up again. "You said you were going to burn the bridge?"

"Yes, ma'am." Another shattering explosion from the direction of the warehouses along the river lit the already bright night sky with a blinding white light. Stopping for the first time, the cavalryman looked up at the sky, as did Mary Beth. "Well, at least we're going to try to burn it, if it hasn't already been done in." Turning his head, the man looked at Mary Beth as she watched the great, boiling cloud of flame and smoke rise above the conflagration that was consuming the Confederate capital. "Ma'am," he finally said with a sorrowful tone, "I do need to be going. I'd prefer to be on the other side of the bridge when they do get it in their mind to burn it."

Letting go of the stirrup strap and stepping back, Mary Beth clutched her hands at her waist. "Yes, of course. Thank you, and good luck."

Nudging his spurs into his horse's flank to get it moving, the cavalryman watched her as he rode away, bending low and tipping his hat as he did so. "You take care of yourself, ma'am."

Lifting her right hand, she gave him a wave. "You too." When he straightened up in the saddle, she envied him for a moment. He would soon be where James was, away from this awful place. She almost added, "and safe," but quickly dropped that thought. For despite everything that was happening, Mary Beth realized that the war was not yet over.

Returning to where Prissy and the children stood, Mary Beth informed them that they had no choice but to stay put. "They're going to burn the bridge, if they haven't already," she announced, almost relieved that the decision to stay or go was out of her hands. "The best we can do is stay put till the Union soldiers arrive. Perhaps they'll help us put out the fires."

The black cook looked at Mary Beth with great suspicion. "The Yankees? Help us?"

"Yes," Mary Beth responded. "They are not all monsters. I've watched them come and go through Winchester with great regularity and with a few exceptions, they are as decent and as God fearing as any of our soldiers."

Looking down the street, toward flames that billowed out of the windows of homes once occupied by the cream of Richmond society, Prissy shook her head. "Well, if you ask me, Miss Beth, it's not the Yankees I fear most at this moment."

Turning, Mary Beth looked at the menacing scene for a moment. As if to underscore the danger, the facade of a brick home fell forward, into the street, sending a blizzard of sparks high into the night sky where they disappeared into the thick black clouds of smoke that lingered from that fire and hundreds of others. "Mrs. Westerfield's sister lives down that way, doesn't she?"

With a look of suspicion in her eyes, Prissy stared at Mary Beth and nodded. "Yes, she does."

"Do you suppose," Mary Beth ventured, "she was able to spirit away all those stores she was hoarding in her house?"

Almost afraid to answer, for Prissy already knew where Mary Beth was going with this line of thought, the cook shook her head. "There was too many. Samuel, the butler, showed me them one day when I was visiting his sister. They were stacked, floor to ceiling, in the bedroom next to hers so she could hear any of the servants if they tried to sneak in and steal some of her precious hoard. They say not even a church mouse can get in there without the mistress knowing."

Sharing the disdain Prissy's voice betrayed, Mary Beth thought for a moment. It was a risk, she knew, to go about looting, even though no one had seemed to even raise an eye as gangs of displaced refugees and poor folks ransacked every store on Main Street the previous afternoon. And even if she didn't get caught, which was highly likely, it was a sin to steal. For a moment, Mary Beth wondered if she'd be able to justify doing so with the same ease that men did when talking about killing in war. Then she remembered the hungry times back in Winchester, days when she had nothing in the house to eat but a few scraps of moldy bread and considered not sharing that with her own mother. Looking at the children, Mary Beth figured that it would be days, maybe even weeks, before the Union authorities were able to sort things out and get the city in order. Until then, they would be on their own.

"Prissy," Mary Beth snapped, "isn't it written that God looks out for those who help themselves?"

Still suspicious, her eyes narrowing, the cook shook her head. "I don't know about that, Miss Beth. I think that saying was made up by someone who did the same thing you're thinking about doing."

"Well, that may be true," she responded, planting her fists squarely on her hips, "but I think God would forgive us. It would be a greater sin to waste all those precious stores and even worse to watch these children starve."

Hanging her head, as if in shame, Prissy added, "Not to mention us."

"That's right," Mary Beth concluded as she pointed her finger in the air. "Now, take Missy and go fetch the sacks we used yesterday. Ezrah and I will go down to Mrs. Westerfield's sister's home and see if there's anyone there."

"And if there is?"

Hesitating, Mary Beth let her hand fall down to her side. "Well, we'll cross that bridge when we get to it."

Prissy laughed. "That is, Miss Beth, if that cavalryman hasn't already burned it."

There was, to Mary Beth's relief, no one there. Even the front door was ajar. With the approaching fires leaving no need for candles or a lamp, Mary Beth, followed closely by Ezrah, climbed the stairs. Excited by an adventure that was akin to great mischief, Ezrah forgot his fear of the fires and explosion and took to searching the rooms. "Here it is!" he shouted in great excitement as he threw a door open. "And Prissy was right! It looks like a gold mine."

Following the boy in, Mary Beth stood in the doorway for a moment and studied the stacks of food that included a rarity that she had thought had long disappeared from the South, canned goods.

"Where'd all this come from?" Ezrah asked as he began to pick through the trove of food stuffs.

Mary Beth sneered. "It's not hard when your husband works for the Commissary Department."

Too absorbed by his exploration, the boy didn't notice the look of disdain on Mary Beth's face. Then, pushing her disgust from her mind, she set about pulling out those items she deemed most useful and easiest carried, and instructed Ezrah to make a stack out in the hall for Prissy and his sister. "You go with them when they return with the sacks," she instructed the boy.

"Shouldn't I stay here with you?" he asked innocently. "You know, in case you need protection?"

Pausing, Mary Beth looked down at the boy. How noble, and foolish, she thought, such sentiments were. Daniel had harbored such beliefs. How many tens of thousands of other good Southern boys, she wondered, had shared such illusions and paid for them, with their lives? "No," she finally said. "I'll be fine. I grew up on a farm, remember?"

"Well," Ezrah replied, relieved that he would be free to run back and forth with Prissy and his sister, "if you insist."

Mary Beth lost track of how long they worked at scavenging what they could. She would have continued to do so longer, fighting the choking smoke and her own exhaustion, if Prissy hadn't informed her that the house next door to the one they were in had caught fire. "It won't be long, Miss Beth, before this one goes too."

Stopping for a moment, Mary Beth looked at the mass of food still left in the room. "I know what you're thinking, Miss Beth," Prissy challenged as she stuffed her sack with the food Mary Beth had set out. "But it would be an even greater sin if we all burned up and weren't able to enjoy all that food we did get."

Turning, Mary Beth smiled at the black cook and laid her hand on her shoulder, leaning on it a moment for support. "You're right. Go ahead and take this last load. I'll find something I can carry and follow along."

Finished stuffing her sack, Prissy started down the stairs, shouting as she went. "Don't wait too long, child."

Mary Beth didn't. Running into the master bedroom, she pulled a sheet off the bed, and ran back into the room with the food stores. Spreading the sheet on the floor, she threw whatever her hands touched into the center of the sheet, ignoring the fact that a small sack of flour had split and was mixing with a sack of rice and everything else in the pile. Only when she judged that she could add no more to the sheet and still manage to carry it did Mary Beth stop. Pulling the ends over her accumulated treasures, she tied them together, threw the sack over her shoulder with a grunt, and began to make her way out of the house.

When she stepped through the front door, the heat of the burning house next to the one she was leaving hit her. Prissy, Mary Beth concluded, had been right. Thanking providence, she made her way slowly down the steps, into the street, and back to the Westerfield home.

Burdened by her bundle and on the brink of collapse from her efforts, a lack of sleep, and stress, Mary Beth didn't notice the small group of horsemen gathered about a street corner along her way until she was almost on top of them. Only the clicking of a horse's hoof on the brick street caused her to look up. Stopping, she dropped the sack from her shoulder, breaking something that began to run and mix with the loose flour.

One horsemen, hearing her, looked up from under the bill of his blue kepi for a moment. The sight of Union cavalry was not new to Mary Beth. She had seen them many times before. But this time, it was different. This time, she realized, they were saviors. If anyone was to save this city, and what little she had left at the Westerfield house, it would be them. Yet even more important, she realized, their mere presence here, in the capital of the Confederacy, would mean that the war would soon be over. That, she knew, would save James, and Daniel, if they were, in fact, still alive. The killing would end, leaving them free to get on with their lives.

Seeing no danger from her, the Union horseman looked back at the ground, where a companion was picking up a Confederate flag that someone had discarded in the street. The dismounted trooper held the flag up before him, inspected it, then showed it to his companions. A sergeant, without a word, turned his nose up and pulled his horse's head away from the trooper holding the flag. Without taking another look at the flag, the man threw it back onto the ground, where he had found it, and remounted his horse. Slowly, the group rode on, heading up the hill toward the capitol building.

Mary Beth watched them go, then looked at the abandoned flag. Walking over to it, she reached down and picked it up. Unfurling the discarded flag, she took a moment to inspect the symbol of a cause that had, for four years, divided a nation. It was dirty, stained with soot and dirt ground into it from the soles of shoes and wagon wheels that had passed over it throughout the long night that was passing. What, she wondered, had it meant to men like her brother Will, to James, to Daniel? Why had they followed flags, like this one, so blindly, for so long? There was nothing magical about this flag. It was, she concluded as she felt the material, made from rather inferior cloth and poorly sewn.

Still, she knew, it meant something to so many men, men as good and as noble as her brother Will had been. Men, she knew, who were now gone, forever, just like Will. The memory of her dead brother, together with the stress and strain of the past twenty-four hours, brought tears to her eyes. This flag, she concluded, deserved better than this. It would never again fly over a free and independent South, a fact that didn't bother Mary Beth in the least. But it deserved better than to be left in the street, to be trampled underfoot. Rolling the flag into a ball, she carefully tucked it under her arm, went back to where she had left her bundle, and retrieved it. In the early morning light, filtered until it was almost totally obscured by the smoke of fires that continued to eat away at Richmond, Mary Beth went on her way, alone yet confident that all this would soon be over.

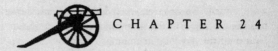

CHAPTER 24

Along the Appomattox, near Appomattox Court House, Virginia, April, 1865

"ONE MORE THROW OF the dice, boys," Josh Major glumly stated as Captain Hamilton D. Lee, their commander, brought the fewer than fifty men still following the flag of the 4th Virginia into line of battle.

Fielding Spencer, standing to the right of James Bannon, gave Josh a vicious look. "It's Palm Sunday. Have a little respect."

"Respect?" Josh replied. "They march us through mud and rain without hardly a rest and one issue of rations they never gave us time to cook properly. We fought to keep the Yanks from snapping at our rear. And then, when they finally let us take the lead, they tell us we have to break through Union cavalry that's blocking the road. Don't talk to me about respect."

Lieutenant Roberts, who had kept to himself during the entire seven-day retreat and spoken only to relay orders, walked up to Josh Major. "I'm tired of listening to your bellyaching. Sometimes I wish you had fallen by the wayside, with the rest of the slackers and cowards."

Drawing himself up straight, Josh Major glared. "I ain't no coward.

I've fought with this regiment for three years and, by God, I'll be with it when we finish."

"Well," Spencer remarked dryly as he looked over at the eastern sky as the red tinges of the morning sun began to show, "I don't think that time will be very long in coming."

"You really think this is it?" a man in the rear ranks asked with an astonished tone in his voice that surprised James. "You don't think we're going to join Joe Johnston?"

Josh Major heaved a great sigh. "Boys," he said, pointing through the early morning mist, "I don't think we're going to make it across this little valley over to where the Yankee cavalry is waiting to greet us."

"Well," Roberts countered as he exerted himself over the tiny command he was charged with, "that may be so. But by God, at least we're going to try. Isn't that so?"

In another time, a rousing bit of bombast such as that would have brought forth at least a half-hearted response from soldiers of the 4th. But no more. They were on their final march, and although most still professed to deny that the end was at hand when such a fate was suggested, every man knew it to be true. Ewell's depleted Second Corps had been gobbled up whole at Saylor's Creek not three days before. Gordon's corps was down to fewer than two thousand after fighting running battles as the Army's rear guard from Petersburg to Farmville. And all of the corps were shedding men, worn out in body and spirit, with every step they took.

Listening to the banter of those who found it necessary to jape in order to mask their fears, James leaned heavily on his rifle and hung his head. He was near the end himself. Fighting dysentery, hunger, and a lack of sleep, only force of habit kept him going during the long march, much as it had during the past four years. Yes, he concluded, this will be the end. It had to be. He was all used up, inside and outside, and nothing, not Lieutenant Roberts' lackluster efforts at stirring, patriotic speeches nor blind faith in General Lee, was going to change that.

"Hey Jimmy," Spencer asked. "You going to be okay?"

Lifting his head from the crook of his arm, where he had been resting it, James looked at Spencer. "Yeah," he replied hoarsely. "Just a little tired."

"You look like death warmed over, Jimmy," Spencer continued and his look of concern grew. "Maybe you ought to sit this one out?"

James didn't answer right away. Instead, he looked into Spencer's eyes. Everyone he really cared about in the regiment was gone. They were either dead, like Will McPherson and Matthew Hazard, missing like Matthew's brother, Marty, or a prisoner, like Daniel. And though Fielding was a friend, and a good fellow to be around, James felt no strong draw to the man. Spencer's loss, James realized, would hardly be felt by a heart that had endured the loss of so many, many friends. So Spencer's suggestion that he "sit this one out" seemed more inviting, more acceptable than James could have imagined.

Then, as the orders that would send them forward, one more time, into battle began to ripple their way down the ranks, James felt himself straighten up automatically, without thought, without regard for his weakened state. After making a quick check to his right to make sure that he was dressed on the regimental colors, James turned back to Spencer. "No, Fielding, I don't think so." Then, as he looked down at his rifle, the symbol of his vocation for these past four years, he added, more to himself, "I've seen this thing this far. Guess I'll see it through, until the end."

When they went forward, with General John Gordon himself at their head, the ragged line of gray infantry gave out the high, throaty screech that had become known to every man on both sides as the Rebel yell. It echoed from their side of the small, tree-lined valley across the shallow creek they were headed for, over to where the dismounted Union horsemen waited behind hasty earthworks to receive them. Not even the crack of rifles and the thunderous report of cannon fire could drown out the warbling noise that seemed to drive the gray ranks on.

Whether it was the yell or the weight of the attack, the Union cavalrymen gave way, faster than anyone had imagined. None waited for the surging lines of attacking infantry to close with them before taking to their heels. For a moment, despite the previous predictions and foreboding, it seemed, to James, just like the old days.

Neither the uphill push nor the now-abandoned earthworks slowed or impeded their advance. All went forward, leaving only a scattering of dead and dying comrades in the wake of their advance. Behind them, the cavalry of General Fitzhugh Lee came up and wheeled to the right, to hold the gap they had blown through the Union encirclement while Gordon faced his men to the left. All of Gordon's men were exuberant, all cheering their dark-haired commander as they went into positions they would be able to hold until the wagons of the Army's trains, followed by Longstreet's First Corps, made it through.

This attack, however, was only the first act of the drama that was to be played out that day. The 4th Virginia had just finished their deployment and was starting to work on hasty breastworks when rifle fire could be heard coming from the right and, even more ominously, from the rear.

Looking back, James didn't need to guess what was happening. He had lived through it at Winchester, and then again at Cedar Creek. Pausing in his work, Fielding Spencer watched as mounted officers and couriers rode this way and that, all looking down the road and off to where Fitz Lee's cavalry was deployed. "What do you think, James?"

Worn out by his sickness and their rush up the hill, James leaned against a tree and looked around. Gray faced, he listened to the growing sound of fighting, now being joined by cannons. Looking back to their front, and catching the glint of many bayonets moving across their front from their right through the trees, James' expression grew grim. "Fielding, I don't think things are going well."

Catching sight of the Union infantry deploying, Spencer didn't respond. Instead, he brought his rifle up to the ready, checked to make sure he had it on half cock with a cap in place, then watched as rank after rank of Union infantry deployed to their front.

The fight was pushed by neither side with much vigor. Knowing full well that he didn't have the strength to force his way through the new force thrown across his path, General Gordon contented himself with keeping the Yankees at bay. Using his cannon and sharpshooters to keep the Union infantry in check, Gordon waited for word from General Lee. The Union commanders, for their part, didn't push the issue. Instead, they contented themselves with pushing more men forward and working around Gordon's flanks.

"What do you think, Jimmy?" Fielding Spencer asked as the two men lay crouched behind their barricade of logs and dirt thrown together with the aid of bayonets, tin plates, and whatever other instruments the men could find to dig with. "Are they going to come at us, or wait?"

James, weakened by that morning's efforts and the bout of diarrhea that he couldn't seem to shake, looked out across the open space between the two armies. Though he couldn't see their faces, he could clearly see that there seemed to be little evidence, other than the presence of the enemy itself, of a pending attack. "They're waiting," he finally replied. As before, Spencer didn't answer. It was, James realized, over. If not for the armies, then at least for himself. He had gone as far as he could. It was that simple, that easy.

Yet it wasn't over. When the order finally came to fall back across the small valley they had crossed earlier that morning, James took Fielding Spencer's hand and allowed himself to be pulled up. On wobbly legs that gave out on him twice in the short march back to their former positions, James made it. There, with a tree to lean against, he watched the fight between the Union infantry on their side of the valley and the dwindling forces of Gordon's corps all around him. Without any emotion, he followed the progress of a mounted colonel from Gordon's staff as he rode out to the enemy lines, returning a short while later with a Union cavalry general with long golden yellow hair, a flowing red scarf, and oversized shoulder boards. Escorted to the rear, the Union general soon returned, passing between the two forces as they continued to exchange shots.

Soon another Union general appeared under a flag of truce. This one was met by General Gordon himself between the lines. "What in the hell," Joshua Major asked as he stood up behind the tree he had been using for cover, to get a better look, "is going on?"

"It's a parley, Josh," James responded.

"I know that," Josh snapped. "I wasn't born yesterday."

"Then why in the hell," Spencer asked, "did you ask such a fool question?"

"What I meant," Josh explained, "was, I wonder what they're talking about."

"Surrender," Lieutenant Roberts, who had been listening to the exchange, announced unceremoniously in a flat voice.

Though many of the men in the 4th Virginia had been thinking just that, Roberts' word hit them like a hammer. Even James felt his heart skip a beat. "They can't be serious?" Josh challenged. "They can't just up and quit, just like that, after all we've been through." Then, as he thought about it for a moment, he added in a softer, more plaintive voice, "Can they?"

No one answered. There was no need to. Up and down the line, as the generals sat on their mounts between the opposing armies, discussing the war, the order to cease fire spread up and down the line. And though there were a few sporadic outbreaks, silence descended upon the Army of Northern Virginia.

Appomattox Court House, April 12, 1865

SLOWLY, CAREFULLY, JAMES LAID out the worn gum blanket that had served to keep him dry many a night. Done with that, he threw his threadbare gray wool blanket, once the property of the United States government, onto the gum blanket. With great care and precision, James squared the two up, making sure that the straggly ends of the wool blanket were folded in so that when he rolled the gum blanket up, none would be hanging out and left to get wet if, during the day, a spring shower blew up. Satisfied that all was in order, he began to roll the two up into a neat, tight blanket roll that would rest comfortably on his left shoulder as he marched off from this bivouac, just as he had done on so many other mornings over the past four years.

But this wasn't like any other morning. Finished with his other labors, and with only his blanket roll to do, James eased himself back onto his haunches and looked around at the other men all about him. This would be their last bivouac. In four years of war, James realized that there had never been anything as certain, anything as final as the events of this day. While the men of the 4th Virginia had greeted many a day or marched into fights too numerous to recall with great confidence, there had always been the fickle element of chance waiting to alter events or make shambles of their officers' carefully laid plans. And, of course, there was always the presence of imminent death lurking behind the cocky smiles, the light-hearted remarks, the casualness that allowed the men in the ranks to face the horror of combat.

Today, however, would be different. There would never be another like this. James and his companions, those who were still with him, would never answer to another roll called out by a gruff sergeant. They would never have to obey another order barked from dry-throated officers too proud to share their own fear. Nor would they be left waiting, in tightly packed ranks, wondering if this day would be the last they would ever see. It was, James knew, the end. It was the end of a struggle, the end of a dream, and the end of a way of life that they had neither asked for or gladly accepted. Yet, as he looked about at his fellow soldiers as they rolled their blankets, donned their accoutrements, or sat, in silence, meditating what the future held for them, he knew he would miss it. As terrible as the ordeal had been, he had been a part of something so grand, so large, that it defied comprehension. And now, it was over.

The gray sky matched the somber mood of the men as they fell in, one more time. There were no drums or bands to keep the time during the march south, across the river that gave its name to the small community that had grown up around the little county court house. Nor was there the chatter in the ranks that had so often amused James during long, tedious marches. Instead, each man was left to deal with this last ordeal in the privacy of his own thoughts.

Partially recovered after three days of rest and rations supplied by the Union Army, James marched along, head hung low, with Fielding Spencer on his left and Joshua Major on his right. Together with Lieutenant Roberts, they were all that remained with the colors that morning of a company that had first marched, 100 strong, out of Lexington, Virginia, four years before. Of the 1,400 men who had served with the 4th Virginia, only 46 answered the rolls that day. All told, 210 men in the five regiments still known as the Stonewall Brigade marched that day.

Whether it was because of their reputation or the name they carried, General Gordon had selected them to lead the Army of Northern Virginia to the site where the formal surrender would be made. It was, James thought, a dubious distinction, made palatable only by the fact that by being first, they would be spared the long wait units farther back would have to endure before going through this humiliation. "We'll be done with it," he told Fielding as he took his time rolling his blanket and ground cloth into a neat roll in preparation for his long trip to Richmond, "and free to go, long before the last of Longstreet's boys are finished."

Though he didn't know all the particulars about James' situation, Spencer had invited him to go with him, back to Lexington. "I doubt if there'll be much back home, Jimmy. My folks wrote last February that things were hard. But it'll be a place to start."

James didn't even hesitate. "Thanks," he responded as he carefully tied the leather straps tight around his bed roll. "But I already have some place in mind."

As the column of downtrodden men approached the ends of the Union lines they would pass through, the Federal division commander drew up his sword, saluted Gordon, and gave the order for his command to present arms. The sound of hundreds of Union rifles shifting from order arms to carry arms, the salute used by marching troops, animated General Gordon. Straightening up in his saddle, he turned his horse to the Union general who had given the order, a Maine man by the name of Joshua Chamberlain. After bringing his own sword down smartly in answer to Chamberlain's salute, Gordon wheeled his horse about to face his own column. In a steady voice, no different than that James had heard a dozen times before, Gordon ordered his men to come to carry arms.

Without needing to be told, the men of the Stonewall Brigade drew themselves upright, dressed their ranks, and brought their rifles up to carry arms. As they passed through the Union ranks, silent except for the steady drumlike beat of hundreds of feet, James glanced from side to side, catching the eye of a Union soldier every now and then. In those brief, fleeting moments in which each held the other's attention, both men realized that this was, indeed, the end. There would be no animosity, no burning hatred. They had met, many times, and on many fields, and fought with all they had. But now it was over.

In silence, he stepped forward when they halted at the spot where their arms were to be stacked and brought his rifle to order arms. Without a word, James planted his rifle firmly on the ground next to his left foot and waited for the man to his right to cross the flat of his bayonet against that of James'. When that was done, the gleaming point of another bayonet was thrust forward from the rank behind James and between the two crossed bayonets. Together, the owners of the three rifles raised them slightly so that the trail weapon could be swung under, locking the three together. When they were ready, the three men lowered their weapons, and accepted a fourth that was passed forward and rested on the others. Done, they stepped away. This simple drill of stacking arms, performed whenever a soldier finished his duty for the day, symbolized the end of the Army of Northern Virginia. The soldiers who had carried those weapons, who had used them to defend their homes, their state, their rights, hung cartridge boxes and belts upon the long, shiny bayonets, and walked away from them, forever.

With the passing of the armies, and the laying down of arms, James Bannon's war with the North came to an end. Yet before he could know peace, there remained but one more battle to be fought.

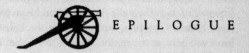

Perth Amboy,
New Jersey, June, 1865

AS THE CONDUCTOR MADE his way through the car, calling out the name of the next stop, he stopped before he reached the last row of seats. James, with his arms folded tightly across his chest and his face turned toward the window, didn't bother to face the conductor's hard, angry stare. Mary Beth, however, slowly turned her head until their eyes met and returned his gaze with one of cold, determined defiance. She had found, since crossing into the North, that this was the best way to deal with such people.

Seeing that the Southern woman wasn't about to flinch, the conductor let the disgust that he felt show before turning his back on her and making his way back to the front. Relaxing, Mary Beth drew in a deep breath and tried to calm herself.

When she was about as composed as the stress of this trip permitted, she turned her attention to James. It seemed that every click of the car's wheels deepened James' despondency. Perhaps, she thought, it had been a bad idea to come here. Perhaps, she lamented, it would have been better had she insisted that they stay in Winchester, or even Richmond. There, at least, they would have been with their own. Yet, Mary Beth sighed, avoiding this ordeal would have done nothing but postpone the pain and agony that they both had endured. Besides, she reminded herself, these people, and not those in Virginia, were, in truth, James' people.

Only when the train slowed, then came to a jerky, jolting halt did

James turn away from the window. Slowly, he faced Mary Beth. With great effort, he forced a smile as he took her hand, which was resting on his arm. Then all hints of the smile disappeared as he prepared to speak. "Are you sure," he asked haltingly, "you want to go through with this? Perhaps I can leave you here, at the station, while I go on ahead and . . ."

The thought of sitting in a train station in the North, to face the scorn and murmured comments, horrified Mary Beth, though she was careful to hide her feelings. Besides, she needed to be with James. Ignoring his suggestion, she leaned her head against James' arm so she wouldn't have to face him as she worked her arm around his and gently squeezed it. "For richer for poorer," she whispered, "in sickness and health, till death us do part."

Though meant to comfort him, Mary Beth's repeating of their marriage vows compounded the gloom that James had been carrying about like a rock. When he had finally found her in Richmond, supervising the affairs of an overcrowded house where she had sought refuge after leaving Winchester, he had nothing to offer her except another mouth to feed. If anything, his acquiescence to her insistence that they marry, right there in Richmond, had made things worse. The marriage provided Amanda Westerfield with a pretext to rid her house of Mary Beth and the resentment she felt for a woman who had come into her home and assumed the role that she, herself, had failed to fill in their hour of greatest need.

Their return to Winchester in May had offered them no sanctuary, either. Daniel was still resentful of James' actions in the closing days of the war and unable to come to terms with Lee's surrender. He did nothing to hide his disgust for the man he had once admired and the sister who had walked away from the land that had been cleared by the first McPherson in America. "You failed Mother when she needed you the most," he had hissed when he could no longer ignore her, "and now you've turned your back on your own kind by marrying a Yankee." Seeing that there was little point in attempting a reconciliation while the bitterness of the South's defeat and Daniel's wound were still fresh, Mary Beth had gladly agreed to go with James when he announced that it was time for him to return to his own home to face his father, and his past.

When the car was empty, James patted her arm. "It's time, Beth," he sighed, preferring to use that part of her name rather than Mary, which had been his mother's. Gathering the half-empty canvas bag that bore a few necessities Mary Beth had brought and the old, worn haversack that contained every worldly possession he claimed, James led Mary Beth out the rear door of the car and down onto the platform. Without lingering, James pushed his way through the crowd, which gave way gladly when they caught sight of his tattered, gray shell jacket. Once on the street, he paused only long enough to get his bearings after so many years' absence. Drawing himself up, he took Mary Beth in hand, turned his face toward home, and started walking.

Slowly, the noisy, crowded narrow streets of the downtown, filled with shops and buildings butting one against another or separated only by narrow alleys, gave way to broad, tree-lined avenues where wealth and power were on display in the quiet, stately homes and well-appointed pedestrians. As they walked, James looked about, saying nothing as images and memories of his youth flashed, in quick succession, through his troubled mind. Mary Beth, her head half bowed, glanced up on occasion and caught a glimpse of the men, in richly appointed frock coats, and women, sporting fashions she was unfamiliar with. Their expressions, however, were no different than that of the train conductor's. Her somber, plain homespun dress, threadbare and patched, and James' odd assortment of worn uniform parts and scrounged civilian attire labeled them as clearly as the mark on Cain had. Feeling more and more depressed, Mary Beth let her head drop lower and lower until she refused to lift her eyes off the pavement, even when James stopped.

"Well," he whispered, more to himself than to her, "this is the moment we've come for." Slowly, almost reluctantly, she lifted her eyes. The house was set back from the street and surrounded by scrubs and flowers, alive and radiant, which accentuated its grandeur with the same grace and elegance that well-crafted jewelry enhances the radiance of a beautiful woman. Had it not been for the black wreath hanging heavily on the front door, Mary Beth would have been relieved. That accursed symbol of death, however, deepened the already oppressive gloom that both she and James harbored.

At the threshold of the house he had once called home, James hesitated, drawing back a step as he gazed at the wreath. "The officer I spoke to at Appomattox said Kevin was wounded. He didn't say anything about . . ."

Mary Beth clutched his arm. She full well knew that James understood how quickly a seemingly slight wound could turn fatal. Both had seen that too many times, over these past few years, to ignore that harsh reality. "Perhaps," she finally offered, "we could come back later, after you've had some time to . . ."

"No," James countered as he stepped forward, his free hand reaching out to open the wrought iron gate. "I came here . . ." Then he corrected himself. "We came here to end this, one way or the other, forever. I will not turn back now." He looked down at his wife. "I've been running from this for five years, Beth. Five years." He looked back at the house, his eyes drawn to the black wreath like a compass needle to the north. "It has to end if we're ever to live in peace."

Together, arm in arm, they walked up the path, never taking their eyes from the door or the wreath. In step, they mounted the stairs, one at a time. With great deliberateness James twisted the knob to ring the door bell, the same one he had heard so many times, so long ago. They were, finally, committed.

When a tall, somberly dressed Negro butler opened the door, James' eyes widened. With everything else so familiar, so much the same as it had been when he had left this place, he half expected to see the Irish maid that had been in his father's employment for as long as he could remember. The butler, after taking in James' appearance in a single glance, was no less shocked. "What," he finally managed to stammer, "can I do for you?"

Clearing his throat, James straightened up. "I am here to see Mr. Bannon."

Puzzled why a Rebel soldier and his whore would be sullying the Bannon doorstep, the butler huffed as he tilted his head back and gazed down his nose at James. "And who, *sir*, should I say is calling?"

Angered by the butler's attitude, but determined to maintain his composure, James drew in a deep breath. "The *other* Mr. Bannon, James Bannon."

Startled, the butler shook his head. While he had been told by other servants of the son who had gone South, he had never expected to see him here, disgracing the fine home of his new master with his presence. Recovering his composure, the servant opened the door, pointed to the study, and walked away after closing the door, but not before glancing over his shoulder at James and Mary Beth until after they had disappeared into Mr. Bannon's den.

Once in that room, the portrait of his mother over the fireplace drew him like a magnet. Placing both hands on the cool white marble of the mantel, he leaned forward and raised his head. Mary Beth, looking over his shoulder, caught sight of the freshly polished brass plate bearing the name "Mary O'Rourk Bannon."

"She was a beautiful woman," Mary Beth finally ventured after watching James for several moments.

"Yes," James uttered without taking his eyes away from the soft, dewy eyes that the painter had somehow managed to bring to life. "And very kind." Drawing back a tear with a sniffle, he turned to tell Mary Beth about her when he caught sight of a woman, dressed in a fine, unadorned black dress with a hooped skirt that filled the double doorway of the study. For a moment, they stared at each other, until a smile lit her face. "You must be James," the woman announced.

Turning her head to see who James was looking at, Mary Beth experienced the first pang of relief that she had felt since beginning this long, desperate odyssey. "Harriet!"

Moving into the room in a rush, the two women threw their arms out and embraced. It was Kevin's wife, James concluded. Mary Beth had told him how they had met. Except for the fact that she was far more beautiful than he had imagined, she was just as Beth had described her. Waiting patiently as the two sobbing women held each other in a warm embrace, James didn't notice the figure pass into the room. Only when he heard "James" whispered in a familiar voice did he turn to face his brother.

The pale, drawn complexion of his brother's face bore no resemblance to the angry face James had last seen at Gettysburg two years before. He was about to step toward him when the flapping of Kevin's empty left coat sleeve caught James' eye. Stopping, he looked at the sleeve, not sure what to do. Mary Beth and Harriet, parting yet still holding each other's hands tightly to lend support to the other at this most trying of moments, watched as the two brothers stood their ground, unsure how to go forward.

It was Kevin, with the hint of a tear in his eye, who took the lead. Stepping forward, he approached James, who slowly raised his right hand to grasp Kevin's. Kevin, however, didn't stop to take it. Rather, he brushed it aside and threw his good arm around his brother's neck and drew him into a hug unlike any they had ever shared before. Without hesitation, and relieved that it was, finally, all over, James threw his arms about Kevin and dropped his head onto his little brother's shoulder.

"Welcome home, James," Kevin choked out through his tears.

Not knowing who the ragged Rebel soldier was walking beside Kevin Bannon, the leading citizens of Perth Amboy stopped in midstride and watched the two as they made their way to Saint Peter's Church. Like most soldiers now returning from the war, the two men walked with great strides, keeping step with each other without thinking about it. Only when the curious onlookers bothered to study their faces did the few who knew the story behind the Bannon family make the connection. When they did, they would shake their head and turn away, unsure how best to react to this strange new development.

Turning and entering the graveyard that had once been their refuge, the Bannon brothers marched slowly up to the foot of a fresh grave. Stopping, the two removed their hats and looked down at the headstone bearing the name Edward O'Bannon. For the longest time, both were silent, lost in thought. James finally broke the silence. "Were you here when he . . . passed on."

"For about a week," Kevin replied without looking over at his brother. "It was a hard week, for both of us. Yet," he continued as he looked up at the sky, "it was a good week. We discussed many things, things I thought we'd never speak of. He told me of the old country, about his father and mother and their trials and tribulations. He told me of Mother and the love he held for her that he never was able to share with another human being. And," Kevin concluded, "he spoke of you."

With a wary look, James glanced at Kevin. "Did he ever know the truth of the matter?"

Kevin smiled and looked back at the headstone. "You know, we never discussed the issue. I think he wanted to, really wanted to, but could never seem to find the words," Kevin stated quietly before looking back at James. "How foolish. So stubborn and foolish, all of us. It's a shame that we were never able to deal with each other in a rational manner that would have spared us all so much pain, so much suffering."

James was not sure if Kevin was talking about the crisis that had shattered their family or the one that had dragged their nations through four years of bloodletting and destruction. That the two events had so much in common had never occurred to him. Dropping his head, he studied each letter in his father's name as he stood beside his brother. Kevin, he decided, was right. The reasons behind the struggle that had led to the terrible, uncompromising impasse that had separated them didn't matter. What was important now, he concluded, was what they did now, from this day forward.

Lifting his left arm, James threw it across his brother's shoulder. Drawing him to his side, James stood with Kevin as they let whatever hatred and sorrow they felt slip away like the late evening sun.

Historical Notes

Leavenworth, Kansas, March 1996

As with my previous book on the Civil War, *Look Away*, this story mixes fact with fiction. The main characters, the Bannons, Harriet Shields, Mary Beth McPherson and their families, as well as their immediate friends and associates, are all fictional. Their actions, however, as well as their thoughts, attitudes, and observations, are based upon first-person accounts of actual participants in the events described in the narrative. In some cases, several historical figures were used as models for a single fictional character. This is particularly true of Harriet Shields. In constructing her character, a woman clearly out of step with her society and culture, I used accounts of Clara Barton, Phoebe Yates Pember, and Louisa May Alcott, all of whom served as nurses.

Events involving the actions of historical characters, such as John Gordon, Robert E. Lee, John Sedgwick, etc., have been recounted in my narrative as accurately as possible. In many cases, there are several accounts of a single action that do not agree with each other. In those cases where there were conflicts, I selected the account that appeared to be the most accurate.

This brief section is designed to help sort out fact from fiction, as well as provide some further background on events depicted.

Chapters 1 & 2

After the bloody battle of Gettysburg, the Army of the Potomac and the Army of Northern Virginia each conducted a series of movements intended to outmaneuver its opponent. Though these efforts resulted in brief and sometimes bloody

confrontations, none evolved into a pitched battle involving more than a portion of each army. This does not mean that the fighting, from the individual soldier's perspective, was any less violent or deadly. For the man in the ranks, fighting was always a vicious and harrowing affair. The events depicted in these chap-
ters are part of the Mine Run Campaign, which was fought from October 9, 1863,
through the end of November. The specific action described is the Battle of
Payne's Farm, fought on November 27 between Major General Edward Johnson's
division of Ewell's Second Corps, Army of Northern Virginia, and Major General
William H. French's Third Corps, Army of the Potomac. Union losses amounted
to 952 and Confederate casualties were 545.

Chapters 3 & 4

By the winter of 1863–64, both nations were in the throes of war weariness. In the
South, true deprivations were making themselves felt. Malnutrition, bordering on
starvation, horrendous losses experienced to date, and lack of even the most basic
of necessities exacerbated the effects of one of the coldest winters on record. The
North, while experiencing a true economic boom, found that the twin victories at
Gettysburg on July 3rd and Vicksburg on July 4th failed to bring the rebellious
Southern states any closer to submission. The growing sentiment that a political
change to bring about a change in the way the war was being conducted was
becoming more and more evident as the nation prepared for the presidential
election of 1864.

Within the camps, soldiers passed the time as best they could. For the Army
of Northern Virginia, survival was of paramount concern. As he had the year
before, Lee was forced to send large portions of his army away to areas where they
could better sustain themselves. Better supplied, the troops of the Army of the
Potomac were able to make their winter camp more enjoyable through special
events such as the Washington's Birthday Ball put on by the Second Corps and
the Army-wide Saint Patrick's Day festival thrown by the Irish Brigade, as
depicted in Chapter 4.

Chapters 5–7

With May came the opening of a new Union offensive by the Army of the
Potomac in Virginia. As it had the year before, the Army of the Potomac crossed
the Rapidan into the dense band of second-growth forest known locally as The

Wilderness. It was Grant's intention to cross this terrain quickly and engage Lee's Army of Northern Virginia to the south of it, in open country where the Army of the Potomac's numerical superiority in men and cannon could be brought to bear. Lee foresaw this maneuver and was prepared to counter it. Rushing forward as soon as the Army of the Potomac started moving, the Army of Northern Virginia collided with the flank of the Union forces in a series of disjointed battles on the same ground that both armies had fought over just one year before. In this battle, fought May 5 through 7, confusion at all levels reigned supreme, both sides barely avoiding total disaster at various times throughout the contest, often by the narrowest of margins. When Grant realized that he would not be able to succeed in destroying Lee's army here, both armies broke off contact. Unlike in past campaigns, Grant did not retreat back north. Instead, he maneuvered to his left, beginning a protracted campaign that would take him from the Rapidan, 50 miles north of Richmond, to Petersburg, south of Richmond, and cost the Army of the Potomac 60,000 casualties in forty days.

Chapters 8 & 9

Grant's first shift to the left ended just north of the sleepy county seat of Spotsylvania County, Virginia. Lee matched Grant's shift and was able to head him off by the barest of margins and dig his army in. Efforts to dislodge the Confederates met with sharp repulses until Emory Upton, commander of Second Brigade, First Division, Sixth Corps, managed to break into the Confederate entrenchments held by Dole's Brigade on May 10. The repulse of this break-in is depicted in Chapter 8 from the Confederate viewpoint.

Sensing that greater results could be achieved if more forces were employed, Grant ordered Major General Winfield Scott Hancock to mass his Second Corps opposite the horseshoe-shaped works held by Ewell's Second Corps. At dawn on May 12, Hancock struck, overwhelming Johnson's division of Ewell's Corps. Only confusion on the part of the successful Union forces and a violent counterattack led by Confederate Major General John Gordon kept the Army of the Potomac from splitting the Army of Northern Virginia in half and destroying it in detail.

The scene depicting Lee's effort to lead the counterattack, and Gordon's refusal to do so till Lee was safely in the rear, occurred as presented.

Many firsthand accounts by participants in the Civil War speak of the "hardest fighting" or "most terrible execution" occurring on this day or that. While I do not doubt that each writer expressed his true sentiments, few would argue that the firefight that took place at the horseshoe, later renamed the Bloody

Angle, degenerated into the most vicious contest of the war. Often fighting on opposite sides of the same breastworks, the soldiers involved engaged in continuous combat from dawn, May 12, until near midnight, when Confederate forces broke off contact and retreated to newly dug earthworks at the base of the horseshoe. The bulk of the 18,000-plus Union casualties and 9,500 Confederate losses occurred during this action, in a space that measured less than one half mile by one half mile. These casualties included more than 2,000 Confederate prisoners and smashed the Stonewall Brigade. The 4th Virginia, alone, lost 139 men out of 175 present for duty.

Chapter 10

The celebrated partisan rangers of John Singleton Mosby were often as much a bane to their own countrymen as they were to the Union forces they were supposedly fighting. The conduct of guerrilla warfare, while not new, was a subject little studied and seldom taken seriously by professional soldiers until well into the twentieth century. The lack of "acceptable" rules of conduct governing guerrilla warfare, combined with war weariness and a dearth of proven counterguerrilla tactics, resulted in cruelties inflicted on civilians and soldiers alike.

While Grant was endeavoring to destroy the Army of Northern Virginia in north central Virginia, the Union forces in the Shenandoah Valley, under the command of Major General Franz Sigel, were ordered to deprive the South of this valuable source of food. Though a small affair (5,150 Union vs. 5,000 Confederate troops), in comparison to Grant's ongoing campaign farther east and Sherman's advance on Atlanta, the Battle of New Market, fought on May 15, resulted in the South retaining the valley and its resources, reopening the traditional Southern avenue of invasion into the North, and creating a legend that is celebrated by the Virginia Military Institute to this day.

Chapters 11–13

Viewed from today's perspective, military medicine as practiced during the Civil War was, at best, crude. This was an era when the relationship between filth and infections was unknown. Not only were antibiotics undreamed of, even the necessity to sterilize medical instruments was yet to be discovered. Hard-pressed battlefield surgeons would operate on patient after patient without washing their hands or cleaning their instruments. Medications used to cure the patient or alleviate his suffering often had results as bad as the illness. These medications included free use of opium and, all too often, "heroic" doses of mercury to cure a number of maladies. One surgeon, in an effort to set a new speed record for amputating a man's limb, did so in a little over forty seconds, at the cost of several of his assistant's fingers. The scenes depicted in the Washington general hospitals, including the death by hemorrhaging and the attitudes of the male surgeons, are all extracted from the accounts of Phoebe Yates Pember and Louisa May Alcott.

After the Battle of Spotsylvania Courthouse, the Stonewall Brigade was reconstituted under the command of a former commander of the 4th Virginia, Brigadier General William Terry. Known as Terry's Brigade, this unit was an amalgamation of fourteen Virginia regiments that had been part of Johnson's division prior to the disaster at Spotsylvania. Though I still refer to the 4th Virginia as a regiment and on occasion, to the Stonewall Brigade, for the rest of the war, these units either ceased to be or were little more than shadows of themselves.

Chapters 14–16

The raid by Jubal Early to the gates of Washington, D.C., in the summer of 1864 was little more than a desperate gamble by Lee to break the siege that was tying down his army at Petersburg. It was also hoped that this maneuver would panic the North and influence the upcoming presidential election. Grant, determined to stay the course he had set himself, was determined to ignore Lee's ploy. Political concerns and pressure, however, forced him to send the Third Division of the Sixth Corps, and then later, the entire Sixth Corps, north to protect Washington.

The Battle of Monocacy, fought on the banks of that river just east of Frederick, Maryland, pitted Lew Wallace (future author of *Ben-Hur*), against Early in an uneven fight. Though a Union defeat, the battle delayed the Confederates just long enough to allow the balance of the Sixth Corps to reach Washington, D.C., just as Early's troops were marching down the Seventh Street Road from Silver Spring. The fighting that took place before Fort Stevens on July 11 and 12 amounted to little more than a skirmish. Though faced, initially, by ad hoc Union forces scraped up in and around the city, Early's forces were too badly winded and spread out after forced marches and the fight at the Monocacy to press an attack on the 11th. By the 12th, the veteran Sixth Corps was in place with sufficient strength to dissuade Early from risking a pitched battle. Disappointed and disheartened, Early's forces returned to the Shenandoah Valley, ending the last invasion of the North in the Eastern Theater of operations.

•

Chapters 17–19

Determined to put an end to threats coming from the Shenandoah Valley, as well as eliminating it as a source of sustenance for the South, Grant sent Major General Philip Sheridan to assume command of all Union forces there, with orders to crush Early and burn the valley. From August through October 1864 Early and Sheridan maneuvered back and forth in the region known as the lower Valley, around Winchester, Virginia.

On September 19, Sheridan, with over 37,000 men available, attacked Early's command of 12,000 northeast of Winchester. Delays and congestion in the deployment of Union forces resulted in a gap between Sheridan's forces that Early's corps commanders, Gordon and Rhodes, took advantage of. From mid-morning until late afternoon, the battle swayed back and forth, with neither side able to achieve a decisive result. Shortly after 5:00 P.M., the Union cavalry conducted a massive charge on the Confederate left, driving it in and routing Early's Army. During this attack, the Stonewall Brigade was routed from the field for the first time. Also, Colonel George S. Patton of the 22nd Virginia, the grandfather to George S. Patton III, was killed.

Defeated, though not broken, Early retreated a short way up the valley. In the predawn darkness of October 19, while the Union Army was in camp around Middletown, Virginia, Early attacked. The surprise was complete and almost fatal. Union reaction, dispersion of Confederate troops bent on looting the rich Union camp, trepidation by Early to press his advantage, and the timely arrival of Sheridan from Winchester reversed the tide in favor of the Union. By late afternoon, Sheridan was able to launch a counterattack that not only swept the Confederates from the field, but shattered Early's small army. With Lee's recall of the remaining Confederate forces in the valley to Petersburg, the last major military operation in the Shenandoah came to an end. True to his orders, Sheridan conducted a campaign of destruction that impoverished the residents of the valley and ended its role as the breadbasket of the South.

Chapters 20–21

As more and more of the South was occupied by Union forces, refugees became an insurmountable problem. Loss of agricultural areas, such as the Shenandoah, exacerbated an already critical situation. Richmond's population swelled to somewhere near four times its prewar size, overwhelming the city and leaving accommodations at a premium. Demands of the war, lack of manpower, and the need to survive after losing everything they had resulted in the entry of women into Richmond's many workshops, mills, and factories.

Yet, despite the reverses on the battlefield, the deprivations suffered by their fellow countrymen, and the coming of defeat that even the most ardent Southerner now admitted, the social elite of Richmond continued to live as high as circumstances would permit. Chroniclers noted that there were many extravagant parties thrown in Richmond during the winter of 1864–65. It reminded one cynical writer of Nero's fiddling as Rome burned.

The Siege of Petersburg, opened in June of 1864, foreshadowed the trench warfare that would dominate the First World War some fifty years later. All that was missing was the barbed wire, (invented in the 1870s), machine guns, poison gas, and bigger and better artillery. The everyday ravages of living in the trenches were compounded by the omnipresent danger of death from a sharpshooter's bullet or dismemberment by an enemy mortar bomb. In an effort to maintain offensive spirit and gather information on their enemy during this stagnant period, both armies undertook trench raids. The one described in Chapter 21, in which the 4th New Jersey responded, occurred as described.

Chapters 22 & 23

With the reelection of Lincoln in the Fall of 1864, the hope of a negotiated peace all but evaporated. With his army dying on its feet and Sherman's army making its way north through the Carolinas, Lee knew that time was finally running out. Yet Lee was a fighter and a gambler. After four years of war and so much bloodshed, he refused to simply up and quit. On March 25, under cover of darkness, he marshaled as much of the Army of Northern Virginia, under John Gordon, as he dared for a bold attack that he hoped would break the siege and send the Army of the Potomac reeling back.

Lee's forces, however, after the bloody fighting of 1864 and a long, hard winter in the trenches, was not up to the task. Though they succeeded in breaking the Union defenses at Fort Stedman, they were unable to widen the gap or exploit their success. The rapid response by local Union commanders doomed this venture to failure. Of the 3,500 Confederates lost, over 1,900 were taken prisoners.

Correctly guessing that Lee had shot his bolt, General George Meade quickly organized a series of hammer blows that, eventually, overextended the Confederate lines and then broke them. The predawn assault on the entrenchments around Petersburg by the New Jersey Brigade described in this book, including the friendly fire incident, occurred as depicted.

The scenes depicting the evacuation of Richmond, the great fire, and the occupation are all taken from actual accounts by women who were there. One of the great Ironies of the war was that, after four years of trying to seize Richmond, Union soldiers found themselves in the position of saving much of the city.

Chapter 24

Though Richmond had fallen and all hope was gone, Lee still found it impossible to admit defeat. It took the Army of the Potomac a week of hard marching, maneuvering, and fighting before the Army of the Northern Virginia was finally cornered at an obscure county seat in southwestern Virginia. Yet even then, when Lee held a council of war on the evening of April 8 to consider the question of surrender, Longstreet advised his commander, "Not yet." One more effort, led by Gordon, to break the Union encirclement, described in this chapter, was undertaken on the morning of April 9.

It is of particular note that, despite the bitterness of the war and the primeval hatred that it had stirred in the breasts of the men who fought it, when it was over, there was very, very little fighting, guerrilla or otherwise. Though the South was to endure a long and bitter period of reconstruction, and the promise of freedom and equality for all Americans was still almost a century away, the war was over.